C000135830

Studies in Europe

ec

Eric D. Weitz and Jack Zipes
University of Minnesota

Since the fall of the Berlin Wall and the collapse of communism, the very meaning of Europe has been opened up and is in the process of being redefined. European states and societies are wrestling with the expansion of NATO and the European Union and with new streams of immigration, while a renewed and reinvigorated cultural engagement has emerged between East and West. But the fast-paced transformations of the last fifteen years also have deeper historical roots. The reconfiguring of contemporary Europe is entwined with the cataclysmic events of the twentieth century, two world wars and the Holocaust, and with the processes of modernity that, since the eighteenth century, have shaped Europe and its engagement with the rest of the world.

Studies in European Culture and History is dedicated to publishing books that explore major issues in Europe's past and present from a wide variety of disciplinary perspectives. The works in the series are interdisciplinary; they focus on culture and society and deal with significant developments in Western and Eastern Europe from the eighteenth century to the present within a social historical context. With its broad span of topics, geography, and chronology, the series aims to publish the most interesting and innovative work on modern Europe.

Published by Palgrave Macmillan:

Fascism and Neofascism: Critical Writings on the Radical Right in Europe
by Eric Weitz

Fictive Theories: Towards a Deconstructive and Utopian Political Imagination
by Susan McManus

German-Jewish Literature in the Wake of the Holocaust: Grete Weil, Ruth Klüger, and the Politics of Address
by Pascale Bos

Turkish Turn in Contemporary German Literature: Toward a New Critical Grammar of Migration
by Leslie Adelson

Terror and the Sublime in Art and Critical Theory: From Auschwitz to Hiroshima to September 11
by Gene Ray

Transformations of the New Germany
edited by Ruth Starkman

Caught by Politics: Hitler Exiles and American Visual Culture
edited by Sabine Eckmann and Lutz Koepnick

Punk Rock and German Crisis

Adaptation and Resistance after 1977

Cyrus Shahan

palgrave
macmillan

PUNK ROCK AND GERMAN CRISIS
Copyright © Cyrus Shahan, 2013.
Softcover reprint of the haardcover 1st edition 2013 978-1-137-34366-6

First published in 2013 by
PALGRAVE MACMILLAN®
in the United States—a division of St. Martin's Press LLC,
175 Fifth Avenue, New York, NY 10010.

Where this book is distributed in the UK, Europe and the rest of the world,
this is by Palgrave Macmillan, a division of Macmillan Publishers Limited,
registered in England, company number 785998, of Houndmills,
Basingstoke, Hampshire RG21 6XS.

Palgrave Macmillan is the global academic imprint of the above companies
and has companies and representatives throughout the world.

Palgrave® and Macmillan® are registered trademarks in the United States,
the United Kingdom, Europe and other countries.

ISBN 978-1-349-46580-4   ISBN 978-1-137-33755-9 (eBook)
DOI 10.1057/9781137337559

Library of Congress Cataloging-in-Publication Data

Shahan, Cyrus.
    Punk rock and German crisis : adaptation and resistance after 1977 /
Cyrus Shahan.
        pages cm.—(Studies in European culture and history)
    Includes bibliographical references.
        1. Punk rock music—Social aspects—Germany (West). 2. Punk
culture—Germany (West). 3. Germany (West)—Social life and customs.
    I. Title.

ML3918.R63S33 2013
781.660943—dc23   2013024477

A catalogue record of the book is available from the British Library.

Design by Newgen Knowledge Works (P) Ltd., Chennai, India.

First edition: December 2013

10 9 8 7 6 5 4 3 2 1

For Alison

Contents

FIGURES

Cover image: Detail from the album *Monarchie und Alltag* by Fehlfarben. Permission from Frank Fenstermacher. Album cover design by Uwe Bauer (a.k.a. Buster Desastser) and Martin Bückner.

ACKNOWLEDGMENTS

Of course I did not do this alone. Without an Anti-Flag concert at the Cat's Cradle in Carborro, North Carolina or a vast network of institutions, groups, colleagues, friends, and family, this project would have been impossible. Over a long period of time and over long distances, they have been invaluable.

My graduate research was funded by a German Academic Exchange Service (DAAD) grant and by a US Fulbright grant. This early funding was crucial and I am immensely grateful for the opportunity to be a researcher and scholar in Germany that the grants made possible. More recently, I have received funding from Colby College's Humanities Division that supported fundamental revisions to my manuscript. The above support made it possible for me to research in Berlin's unique archives, the Archiv für Alternativkultur and Archiv der Jugendkulturen. At the Humboldt University, I was able to work with Thomas Wegmann and Peter Wicke, and I am particularly indebted to my Fulbright advisor, Christian Jäger. Peter Glaser, Thomas Meinecke, and Michaela Melián were all astoundingly generous with their time and personal archives. My interviews and meals with them altered the trajectory of this book.

The number of people who helped me develop professionally, think about writing, and write about West German punk from my days as a graduate student to the present is great. I can only acknowledge them, in fairness, alphabetically: all of my graduate school colleagues who listed to endless presentations of my work—in particular Richard Benson and Alex Fulk, Lisa Arellano, David Freidenreich, David Gramling, Larry Grossberg, Walter Hatch, Jonathan Hess, Seth Howes, Max Kellogg, Arne Koch, Annie Krieg-Kellogg, Alice Kuzniar, Benjamin Lisle, Carleen Mandolfo, Peter McIsaac, Lydia Moland, Sean Nye, Dietmar Post, Ayon Roy, Stephan Schindler, Frank Apunkt Schneider, and Peter Zazzali. Mirko Hall, my first punk rock academic-in-arms, has been and continues to be a great friend, resource, co-panelist, and coeditor. I count myself lucky to have been able to exchange serious and not serious ideas with him.

Without Richard Langston, who mentored me throughout my graduate career, this book would not exist. He guided me through my intellectual training, pushed me to think differently about everything, helped me become a better writer (forcing me to write not merely as a fan but also as a scholar!), and is the catalyst of my successes as a young scholar. Endlessly generous with his time, he was and continues to be a great—and needed—mentor, friend, and colleague.

For their gracious permission to allow me to reproduce their images, songs, and texts in this book, I thank: Blixa Bargeld, Franz Bielmeier, Ralf Dörper, Frank Fenstermacher, Peter Glaser, Carmen Knoebel, Klaus Maeck, Thomas Meinecke, Harry Rag, and Thomas Senff.

Portions of chapters 1, 2, and 3 were presented at the German Studies Association and Northeast Modern Language Association annual conferences. Parts of chapter 1 and 2 were first published in *Popular Music and Society* 34.3 (July 2011), 369–386. I am grateful to Routledge for granting me permission to reprint this work as part of *Punk Rock and German Crisis*. I would also like to thank Palgrave Macmillan, my editors Brigitte Shull and Naomi Tarlow, my copyeditor, and the anonymous readers whose feedback was invaluable.

My well-dispersed family has endured countless conversations about this book in various forms, and they have been supportive and sarcastic, as they deemed necessary. I appreciate and needed both.

Alison, thank you for making me go on walks and more when I didn't think I had the time.

ABBREVIATIONS

AP   Walter Benjamin. *Arcades Project.* Translated by Howard Eiland and Kevin McLaughlin. Cambridge, MA: Belknap, 1999.

AT   Theodor Adorno. 1970. *Ästhetische Theorie.* Volume 7 of *Gesammelte Schriften.* Edited by Rolf Teidemann. Darmstadt: Wissenschaftliche Buchgesellschaft, 1998.

DA   Theodor Adorno. 1970. *Dialektik der Aufklärung.* Volume 3 of *Gesammelte Schriften.* Edited by Rolf Teidemann. Darmstadt: Wissenschaftliche Buchgesellschaft, 1998.

"DC"   Walter Benjamin. "Der destructive Charakter." Volume 4.1 of *Gesammelte Schriften.* Edited by Rolf Tiedemann and Hermann Schweppenhuser. Frankfurt am Main: Suhrkamp, 1972.

MM   Theodor Adorno. 1970. *Minima Moralia.* Volume 4 of *Gesammelte Schriften.* Edited by Rolf Teidemann. Darmstadt: Wissenschaftliche Buchgesellschaft, 1998.

MUP   Jürgen Habermas. "Modernity: An Unfinished Project." In *Habermas and the Unfinished Project of Modernity.* Edited by Maruizio Passerin d'Entrèves and Seyla Benhabib. Cambridge, MA: MIT Press, 1997.

ND   Theodor Adorno. 1970. *Negative Dialektik.* Volume 6 of *Gesammelte Schriften.* Edited by Rolf Teidemann. Darmstadt: Wissenschaftliche Buchgesellschaft, 1998.

PS   Oskar Negt and Alexander Kluge. *Public Sphere and Experience: Toward an Analysis of the Bourgeois and Proletarian Public Sphere.* Translated by Peter Labanyi, Jamie Owen Daniel, and Assenka Oksiloff. Minneapolis: University of Minnesota Press, 1993.

R   Peter Glaser. *Rawums: Texte Zum Thema.* Cologne: Kiepenheuer & Witsch, 1984.

V   Jürgen Teipel. *Verschwende deine Jugend: Ein Doku-Roman über den deutschen Punk und New Wave.* Frankfurt am Main: Suhrkamp, 2001.

Introduction: Representing "No Future"

collapse / sweet collapse
bitter and bitter and bitter
until the collapse[1]

Usually associated with the apex of West German domestic terrorism, the year 1977 witnessed another cultural watershed, namely punk, which went on to influence Germany in the 1980s in profound and significant ways. Assaying punk and its investment in cultural representation—art, literature, and music—details a crucial constellation of contested politics and the complex postwar matrix of occupied political and aesthetic spaces in West Germany.

West German punk, circa 1978, has made some disquieting inroads into the framing of German cultural history—witness punk nostalgia today in recent novels, films, blogs, and musical reissues. This reemergence has (paradoxically) ignored punk or denigrated it to a trivial blip within a canonical continuum of social interventions into the political: the student movements associated with the year 1968, terrorism of the seventies, and the fall of the Berlin wall in 1989.[2] Reading the late 1970s through the Baader-Meinhof gang and the Red Army Faction—and necessarily terrorism vis-à-vis 1968—produces a monochromatic history of social distress seeking to solve a misunderstood dialectic of theory or violence in hopes of progress (toward unification) that obscures the particular historical tensions in which punk found itself. This book asserts, through a reading of punk's aesthetic tête-à-tête with its present, the importance of punk examined as an inventory of crises, an inventory of cultural representation that clearly demonstrates West German punk's adaptation of and uniqueness toward its national and international precursors.

Examining punk's anarchic socio-aesthetic tensions—how it picked up cultural materials to tear down the present and reject the possibility of its own future—complicates and illuminates blind spots of German historical consciousness that have evolved after reunification. Parsing punk's past for the present interrupts the rhetoric of progress and reconciliation, of revolution and social democratic utopia, with a narrative of crises and failures. A poetics of this narrative demonstrates how punk was acutely aware of the failures of previous interventions into the social but that punk—and here is its fundamental distinction—never sought to rectify these to ensure its own duration. On the contrary, and in stark contradistinction to its legacy throughout the eighties, punk was preeminently invested in negation of the future. "No future," thus, is the cipher through which the aesthetics of failure and crisis reveal punk's unwanted future of the Federal Republic. "No future," an under-theorized apocalyptic mantra at whose core lie the coordinates dystopia, an unreconciled past, and failure, holds the vital and distinct narrative of punk's despised present and unintended future. That story began around 1977 in Düsseldorf, West Germany. It is about how the moment of punk died, it failed; yet it nevertheless occupies the subsequent decade that existed in the aftereffects of its aesthetic anarchy. The afterlife of punk's aesthetic chaos provides a hybrid perspective of internal German problems in the eighties, but also an index of transnational conditions—outside a teleology of unification—that are particularly relevant for an occupied, divided German nation. Rather than a history of progress, a history of postwar Germany can be told as a history of discontent. The discontent in a punk history of West Germany is a story imbricated in a shift away from the past, but without fantasies of social rebirth.

Whereas student movements of 1968 and German terrorism both sought to establish (theoretically, violently) their own conceptions of a just, utopian society, punk was decidedly invested in an endless dystopia of the present. Painted broadly, the former were both reactions to the West German "Economic Miracle"—that near two-decade period of breakneck socioeconomic resurgence after 1950 spearheaded by Chancellor Konrad Adenauer—and its dubious ethical, political, and historical foundation.[3] As elsewhere in the world, the 1960s in West Germany saw young radical students at the forefront of social movements challenging political and cultural authority. Markedly different in the case of Germany, students there augmented the typical fusion of Marxist theory and anti-Vietnam paroles with their fight against the legacies of German fascism. To this end, in addition to Marx, Ho Chi Minh, and Che Guevara, students turned to intellectuals from the Institute for Social Research (aka the Frankfurt School) in the persons of Theodor Adorno, Walter Benjamin, Herbert Marcuse, and Jürgen Habermas. Academics and students together theorized that protofascism in a rebuilt Federal Republic of Germany (FRG) could be avoided by continuing with modernist projects that sought to reestablish boundaries that were disappearing between the past and present, between American capitalism and Europe. Yet, due to the intractability of theory (in universities) and "real" change (on the streets), students ultimately turned decisively against their theoretical touchstones. As has often been argued, the students' turn to the streets in the form of extra-parliamentary action (APO) never solved their problem.[4] A misogynist German Socialist Student Union (SDS), the assassination attempt on SDS leader Rudi Dutschke in 1968, and most spectacularly, the murder of protest bystander Benno Ohnesorg by Berlin policeman Karl-Heinz Kurras in 1967, together mark the demise of "1968" and the unmistakable pivot to German domestic terrorism. Transitioning from Molotov cocktails hurled at the building of the conservative-incendiary Springer Press, to bombings of American military bases, to the kidnapping and murder of economic and political leaders, West German domestic terrorism acted where it saw students merely discussing. The RAF and Baader-Meinhof's strategy of "urban guerilla" (in imitation of Fidel Castro and Guevara) meant to create a firewall against what the terrorists saw as a resurgent fascist state personified by those they killed, namely American soldiers and former Nazis reinstalled in positions of power by the US and West German governments. Confirming their fear but simultaneously defeating their strategy, the enduring "Emergency Laws" first enacted by the Federal Republic in 1968 in reaction to an increasingly violent APO ensured that the "German Autumn"—the moniker for the climax of state and terrorist violence in 1977 that found RAF terrorists in prison, murdered, or both— was the solidification of conservative power, not its end.[5]

Specific instances where punk explicitly engaged various facets of either terrorists or students emerge below in discussions of punk's imagined solutions to the quagmire of the West German seventies. What must be understood now is that punk inverted the rhetoric of societal and cultural renewal espoused by its predecessors when it tapped strategies of European avant-gardes. With the everyday detritus, left over from protests in the streets or bombs in department stores, it produced in its own unique ways montages as bulwarks against those governmental *and* resistant forces in contemporary Germany seeking, so punk saw it, to level the present, to erase the past, and to speed a powerful reemergence for West Germany in a seemingly imminent, disquieting future. Bringing punk to the fore redresses the narrative imbalance of the late seventies and eighties and concurrently serves to reevaluate the legacies left behind by the incomplete and failed projects of '68ers and terrorists. In the wake of recurrent failures—of the state to engage in a genuine reckoning with its fascist past, of the institutional black hole of 1968, and of the spectacularly violent demise of the RAF[6]— punk foreclosed the possibility of rescuing the present from the past for the future. Contemporary over-remembrance of November 9 within the paradigm of the Berlin wall, fostered by institutionalized revolutionaries, incarcerated terrorists, and now-affirmative politics of 1968, selectively reinforces a caesura and set historical flow from the past to the present.[7] A punk history is crucial because its infamous "no future"—ultimately a rejection of a unified, utopic present now or in the future—resolutely positioned itself against such delusions of progress. That the story of such rejection has yet to be told demonstrates a lack of interest in the "trivial" by dominant German histories. And while minor histories are rapidly making inroads into and counteracting dominant historical teleology, punk does not offer the same critical purchase as such corrections.[8] Not a story of oppressed, marginalized, or persecuted minorities, a punk narrative reveals instead an unwritten history of the middle. Punk's stand against the usual locus of hegemonic consent binds it to previous youth subcultures, but marks it as unique because of a resolute disinterest in (its own) institutionality. For, while students of 1968 were forced to reconcile their tensions of an anti-institutional fight whose epicenter was in universities, and terrorists were forced to confront internal protofascist tendencies in their fight against a resurgent fascist state, punk's prolific engagement with cultural representation intentionally internalized such dialectical contradictions as springboards for its contestation of the present.

Yet, while enacting a distinct project of social upheaval, punk nevertheless became a home for facets of students' and terrorists' ultimate ideas of social transformation. But punk saw 1968 and German terrorism differently, and its aesthetic products make clear what punk thought was at stake in the eighties. In the student protests framed by the moniker 1968, punk saw a paradox: an oversimplified attempt by intellectuals to reestablish a phantasmagoric past whose academic foundation constrained rather than expanded its strategic intervention. Because students' attempts to theorize more complex positions (vis-à-vis the Black Panthers, Ho Chi Minh, or Marxist philosophers) bound students' actions to the cultural institutions they despised so much, this strategy foreclosed, so punks saw it, the possibility of flexibility. For punks, 1968 had a singular strategy: "No."[9] This "No," however, must not be confused with punk's own rejection of the present. While students of 1968 rejected the contemporary trajectory and catalysts of national politics (i.e., Americanization), they were decidedly invested in resurrecting an idealized Marxist past for their vision of a revamped political future (von Dirke). Similarly, terrorist insurrections of the seventies were, for punk, a violent enactment of the same singular strategy: bombs, not theory, supplanted the monovocal epicenter of change for German terrorism. The lingering presence of fascism in the Federal Republic that was the RAF's singular target was not metaphorical for terrorists in their fight against their fathers' nation. After all, the United States had reinstalled myriad former National Socialists into positions of political and economic power—witness, to name three prominent examples, chancellor Kurt-Georg Kiesinger, attorney general Siegfried Buback, and industrialist Hanns-Martin Schleyer. Though their means were starkly different, German terrorism of the seventies shared many of the students' revolutionary fantasies that interlinked their struggles against capitalist oppression of the "third world" countries and against former National Socialists with those of the Vietcong against American capitalist imperialism, for example. It was, though, precisely the student's theoretical focus (confined within universities) that garnered the most salient critiques of '68 and against which the terrorists positioned their violent interventions. While terrorists had a consciously styled glamour that was admittedly appealing, punk rejected the RAF's delusions of authenticity. For, despite Baader-Meinhof's sensational allure, its violently distilled strategy for creating a steadfast binary between Germany's fascist past and the present still sought out the modern utopia of the '68ers. Though perhaps more practically, punk chose another kind of resistance after the RAF's violence failed to prevent the confinement of terrorists' strategies within another kind of institution—Stammheim prison—that was particularly effective at killing social progress.

Punk's social contexts and aesthetic products show how, rather than correcting the errors of the past and thereby miming '68ers and terrorists, it sought to double the past for chaos in the present. While doubling can function to preserve the self against extinction, punk inverted this: its doubling prolonged that which students and terrorists sought to avoid. The focus of chapter one, dystopia in punk's hands, was put on hold; it created intersections of the present foreclosing the future. Punk reveled in the maelstrom of state/civilian violence of the past, and its apocalyptic specter of the present crystallized the mantra "no future." Manifest sartorially in their use of the swastika and the RAF star, and sonically in songs such as S.Y.P.H.'s "klammheimlich" (clandestine) or DAF's "Kebapträume" (Kebab Dreams), punk's schizophrenic cut ups of cultural representation, as the next chapter argues explicitly, are what bind this revolutionary, counter-discursive, and anti-institutional aesthetic to strategies of the avant-garde. The avant-garde, what Richard Langston defines as the "extreme faction of aesthetic modernity intent on bulldozing affirmative culture," is fundamental for understanding how punk rejected the ritual repetition of those social cycles in the Federal Republic that ultimately helped establish hegemonic stability in the form of collective, accepted, sociopolitical fault lines.[10] Chapter two targets precisely that in punk's fusion of schizophrenia and aesthetics and argues that punk's negative utopia drew its élan from the discontinuities accidentally unveiled by dominant conceptions of progress and violence as fundamental ideals for the future. The opposite of radical for punk, student protests-cum-leftist-environmental Green Party and terrorist violence-cum-emergency laws and state violence demonstrate the affirmative force of programmatic social intervention through their acceptance into and (unintentional) stabilization of mainstream politics.[11] Framing punk as part of the avant-garde makes understandable the internal logic behind punk's unwavering devotion to rupturing representation and to its continuous self-fracturing: punk was never concerned with its own institutionalization, and its apocalyptic visions of the present sought explicitly to avoid steadfast oppositions (of authentic or co-opted) out of the scramble of codes structuring society. To this end, this book assays through dystopia, power and violence, American racism and German fascism, and failure, the ways in which punk's willingness to lay everything on the line achieved what Theodor Adorno—theoretical lightening rod of West Germany—deemed as the precondition for effective philosophical praxis. That strategy, punk's "answer to the traditional surreptitious, absolute surety" of progress, sought to ensure that its own inevitable failure— the debilitating tolerance it came to garner in the mainstream—would be the mainstreaming of a pyrrhic victory (*ND* 30). But punk's willed self-immolation did not avoid the future it never wanted. Against its best intentions, punk's half-life lingered on into the eighties. It nevertheless continued, under the moniker New Wave, to distort channels that typically normalized socially subversive discourse. Despite its anarchic efforts, punk was wrong; it had a future. *Punk Rock and German Crisis* reads that failure—the epic aftershocks of punk's social and aesthetic transformations in music, art, and literature—to lay bare the meaning of its apocalyptic invective.

Sonic Subcultures 1945–1977

Sound mattered for punk's project of corruption. While the prehistory of sound and subcultures indicates a tenuous relationship between music, subcultures, and the mainstream, reading punk's sonic rejection of its present demonstrates how punk music and its representational flotsam were distinct vehicles for critiquing national identity. The possibility of this critique assumes music's active role in the negotiation of national identity, and though such a relationship is not a particularly radical notion, this dynamic becomes more complex within the frame of West German reconstruction after World War II. In a pre- and postwar German cultural context, Adorno's scathing indictments of jazz and popular music as part of the culture industries' fostering of consumption and as part of an insatiable drive to level mainstream society speak to the complex legacy of music when wrestling with West German sociocultural issues. The antithesis of "good" music (i.e., Beethoven) whose sonic details concretely form the totality of its internal musical sense, popular music and putatively improvisational jazz, Adorno claimed, inexorably lead "back to the same familiar experience, [in which] nothing fundamentally novel will be introduced." Thusly understood, popular music functions explicitly to standardize society because it extends the general to the specific and thereby forecloses the possibility of any function other than that of a "cog in a machine."[12] In Adorno's assessment, music has the potential to be wholly antagonistic to individuality because hit songs prescribe what customers listen to, whereby free choice becomes synonymous with "pseudo-individualization" (308). While this unwaveringly pessimistic evaluation of the popular undoubtedly rings true for certain genres and aspects of music, it nevertheless fundamentally underestimates, with its dismissive tag of the "people" as cultural dupes, the ways in which youth cultures have misappropriated outside the reign of capital musical traditions for their own subversive interests. The first three major youth movements after World War II testify to the shortcoming of Adorno's scoio-musical claims. Sonic subcultures preceding punk—the Halbstarken of the fifties, hippies of the sixties, and rockers of the seventies—illustrate the complex interplay between hegemonizing and subversive uses of music that made it possible for punk to conjure its own particular response.[13]

The political vitality of sonic culture after World War II could be heard on the airwaves of the American Forces Network and Radio Luxemburg as occupying forces embraced sonic technology to synchronize the fragmented landscape of West Germany. Transforming the territorializing sound of air raid sirens into music, the Allies deployed music not merely for pleasure but as what Jacques Attali calls "a tool for the creation or consolidation of a community, of a totality." Music is for Attali "essentially political," but in distinction to Adorno's pessimism, along with power from above is born "its opposite: subversion" (6). In the hands of Britain and the United States, the emergent German state was undoubtedly Attali's "monopolizing noise emitter." But the extra-Germanic roots of broadcast music such as American jazz and rock and roll undermined from the first transmission the musical reestablishment and representation of postwar German wholeness by the occupying forces. As various case studies have shown, jazz and rock and roll had unsettling effects that forced the fledgling government to flex its censorship and media muscle to first politicize rock as "degenerate" and then, flipping this strategy, to depoliticize rock as youthful frolicking within (the decidedly political) West German Cold War liberal consumerist identity.[14] For those who chose to listen differently, music enabled a break with oppressive, prescriptive representation. Such was the case with the Halbstarken (hooligans) who emerged in the mid-fifties with the explosion of Hollywood "outsider" films such as *The Wild One, Rebel Without a Cause, Blackboard Jungle,* and *Rock Around the Clock.* Uta Poiger has shown how, concurrent with the sartorial image of the rebel offered by Marlon Brando and James Dean, these films also brought with them rock and roll, particularly Bill Haley and Elvis Presley. While the nascent West German authorities made its "citizens' *cultural* consumption central to [its] *political* reconstruction efforts," Poiger substantiates the threat that unchained rhythms and sex appeal posed to the broader project of reconstruction.[15] Against the malaise of mid-fifties' West Germany typified in Rainer Werner Fassbinder's *Katzelmacher* (1969), the Halbstarken used American rock and roll to mark, as Lawrence Grossberg has argued, "a difference, to inscribe on the surface of social reality a boundary between 'them' and 'us'."[16] Inscribing this difference sonically and sartorially, the Halbstarken of the fifties, particularly young middle-class males, pushed against social segmentation by picking up American styles and labor believed to be restricted to their working-class alternates: Levis jeans, T-shirts, greased hair, and auto repair. Ironically, while the Federal Republic was attempting its own normalization of a society, "West German authorities, if they imagined a society devoid of class hierarchies, certainly did not want to see it symbolized by" the working class, because a contented labor force was the foundation for the "economic miracle" of the fifties (Poiger 82).

Thus, as early as ten years after the end of World War II, young Germans were culling sonic culture from outside their geographic borders in the service of emergent youth subcultures. But, despite the worries incited by mainstream media over Halbstarken's adaptation of American rock's style, sexuality, and violence, by 1959, a scant four years after the arrival of Brando's *The Wild One,* the rebel from America was resignified by the very same forces in the persona of Peter Kraus, the "German Elvis." As such, the magazine devoted to popular music targeted at teens, *Bravo,* became the front line in a battle over aesthetics: the authentic versus co-opted, affirmative aesthetic. Although seemingly putting into play Adorno's lack of faith in popular music, an affective choice of Elvis or Kraus laid in a decidedly political binary of "us" (the German Kraus) or "them" (the American Elvis). While the choices listeners made may have been for them divorced from any explicit political realm, they nevertheless illustrate today how musical pleasures were powerful demarcation lines for identity in postwar Germany. This choice should not be underestimated: Halbstarken's raucous occupation of pubic spaces and their rebel style signified resistance to authoritarian social norms at the heart of the West German state's rhetoric of consensus.[17] Concurrent with the mainstreaming (and softening) of rebel style through Kraus, music-based subcultures of the sixties—hippies—pushed the sartorial destabilization of gender roles into a broader rejection of social conservatism and middle-class aspirations saliently signaled by the "Grand Coalition" of the Christian Democratic Union / Christian Social Union and the Social Democratic Party (CDU/ CSU and SPD) in 1966. In the sixties, the Halbstarken's rejection of fifties' malaise morphed into a battle over the lack of reconciliation with the past, or better, a contestation with the lingering presence of National Socialism in the Federal Republic. Beyond setting the aural fault lines for listeners' affective connections, music subcultures in the sixties exemplify the ways in which music engendered the ability of sonic representation to promote a specific consciousness, or, more problematic in the ears of sixties' youths, foster amnesia. When Jazz, Haley, and Presley ultimately faded from the epicenter of music, they gave way to broadband sociocultural upheaval in the sixties: a combination of lifestyles with cultural, aesthetic, sexual, and explicitly political paradigms. Overtly expanding sartorial gender destabilization of the Halbstarken and indicting the reemergent fascist rhetoric against rock (i.e., when the state cast it as "degenerate"), rock and roll's politics of pleasure in the hippies' sixties became, Langston has argued, "an explicitly political act capable of deconstructing dominant notions of West German identity."[18] This later-sixties' condition was preceded by the dominance of the German Schlager (roughly translatable as "hit"), what Wilfried Berghahn already in 1962 defined as a genre designed to assuage the discontent lurking below the surface of prosperity following the Federal Republic's "economic miracle" (188).

Berghahn's distaste for the blatant sounds of affirmative national identity, 75 percent of which were, ironically, of foreign origin, parallels Adorno's own 1962 revisions to his dismissal of jazz and popular music.[19] Therein Adorno continued to see popular music as a keystone securing the stability of social divisions, simulating "choice" for the popular in an affirmative binary of like/dislike.[20] But in the sixties, bands such as the Rolling Stones, Jimi Hendrix, and the Doors inspired proto-student subcultures in ways that escaped Adorno's bifurcated dead end. Sex, drugs, and rock become tools to push the recreated middle class and its hegemonic establishment into the limelight of contemporary debates, but not explicitly in step with the program of the emergent student movement.[21] While the student protests were organized vis-à-vis politics and not rock (in contradiction to the widespread images of hippies and communes bound up with the moniker "68"), the most apt conjoining of student-era protests and rock was after the fact: the band Ton Steinen Scherben's 1970 hit "Macht kaputt, was euch kaputt macht" (Destroy what is destroying you). Indeed, inciting destruction during their concerts and clearly channeling the destructive ethos of Berlin's streets—most canonically illuminated by the riots in answer to Ohnesorg's murder—Scherben's song could be read as a post-'68 rallying cry for the need to restart violently the political and economic revolution through a cultural revolution.

Concurrently enacting, seemingly, capitalism's hegemony (in which everything could be reintegrated into the existing order) Scherben's call for destruction for renewal simultaneously ushered in the era of "big rock" in bands such as Faust, Amon Düül, and Floh de Cologne.[22] While these "Krautrock" bands fused the students' overt-politicization of subcultures with the fifties' breaking of normative borders, rock as a vehicle of critique faded as the star cult—the demarcation of fan and performer—was steadily reinforced.[23] The above history of sonic subcultures could be read, in the wake of the mainstreaming of the Halbstarken by the 1960s and the commercialization of rock by the early seventies, as the failure of a rock to affect change in the social structures it attacked. More accurate would be to read this history as rock's progressive attempts to "dethrone its rock and roll predecessors who had invoked similar revolutionary decrees only a decade earlier."[24] Rock's transitions, its forward looking logic, sounded out new fault lines in its attempt to engender individuality beyond media-controlled discourse of identity. After repeated installments of rock's progressive venture, punk emerged in West Germany not to dethrone its predecessors in order to improve upon failed interventions into the political, but to resolutely fight its successors.

A Punk Archipelago

Punk's emergence in West Germany is the premier example of how this subcultural moment is a crucial political, cultural, and aesthetic marker in postwar history. Although Iggy Pop had been living and recording in Berlin since 1976—shifting British punk from American rock toward the more sophisticated "Teutonic 'motorik' rhythms of Kraftwerk"—it was Düsseldorf, West Germany that became the unlikely epicenter of German punk.[25] Concurrent with London's Sex Pistols and the Clash and New York City's Ramones, Pop is an early marker for the ways in which German punk's influences and locations represent a resistive geography to the very sociopolitical spaces constructed by occupying forces. Just as in the fifties and sixties, the possibility of a sonic subculture hinged upon that which was meant to be culturally stabilizing: radio broadcasts. Nationwide radio was intended to have an integrating effect on societies both east and west by enhancing common patterns of identity.[26] Unlike the sixties and seventies, which had more ubiquitous musical broadcasts, the geography that can be built from radio broadcasts is not the geography of punk. In the northern British sector John Peel's broadcasts for the BBC's Radio 1 show and British Forces Broadcasting Service fed British punk into Hamburg, while its counterpart in the south, the American Forces Network, brought in country-western and Elvis Presley.[27] The Allies' division of Germany set up clear boundaries of cultural influence and political ideologies; the geography of punk subverted this through technology-fueled underground exchange. Cassette recordings made of broadcasts and mailed to various cities—Düsseldorf, Berlin, Hamburg, Munich—made it possible for young Bavarians to tap into the Clash and Hamburg kids to reinvent American rock.[28] Internalizing the national divisions within the Federal Republic, punk signaled through cut ups of its British origins the drive to push internal German contradictions—foreign constitution of the national, unifying identity in a fractal geography—to their breaking point. In punk's calculus, this breaking point in turn would fabricate an instable stepping-stone into the future. Despite its sonic tie-in to previous subcultures, it must be stressed that German punk was not an attempt, as can be read for the Halbstarken, to pick up virtually unaltered foreign signifiers of dissident youth subcultures. Punk in Germany was not English punk.

English punk emerged in and around London's East End in the wake of Britain's crumbling postwar "economic miracle" as one of a host of postwar youth subcultures such as Teddy Boys, Mods, Skinheads, Hipsters, Beats, and Rastafarians that demonstrated youth's subtle and complex responses to economic and cultural change.[29] Punk kids of the mid-seventies, Jon Savage writes, "were caught in an impossible double-bind: intelligent in a working-class culture which did not value intelligence, yet unable to leave that culture because of lack of opportunity. The result? An appalling frustration" (114). This frustration echoes paradigmatically in songs by the Sex Pistols and the Clash. Sex Pistols' singer John Lydon screamed out his frustration in songs such as "Anarchy in the UK" when he declared himself an "antichrist" and "anarchist" who wanted to "destroy the passerby." This destructive energy continued to tear at the United Kingdom in the Clash's self-titled first album with songs such as "White Riot" and "Hate & War." In their song "London's Burning" the Clash's frustration turned to destruction in a London "burning with boredom." Far from the melodies of the Beatles, "London's Burning" represented, as Savage reads it, a "hymn to the inner city, a trebly sound that nagged like an itch" (220). But even during its high point in 1977, punk did not seek to resolve Britain's postwar miasma. Rather, punk reproduced, says Dick Hebdige, "post-war working-class youth cultures in 'cut-up' form," anachronistically combining elements with their music and style (*Subculture* 26). What, then, did British punk do or want with its "cut-ups?" The Sex Pistols' Steve Jones supplied the answer: "Actually we're not into music, . . . We're into chaos" (qtd. in Savage 152). Despite its British origins and similarly clear investment in chaos, German punk was not about miming the British. For early punks such as Jäcki Eldorado, "it was about finding your own thing, not about imitating some English model" (*V* 65). Indeed, there are parallels between the glimmer of democratic hope in Britain and the USA that were dismantled with the rise of conservative politics culminating in the elections of Margaret Thatcher and Ronald Reagan, and Helmut Kohl's ascension in the FRG as the flip side of sixties' countercultures. Under the hegemonic umbrella of the late seventies, punk on both sides of the English Channel sent out waves of dissident music that was out of synch with the mainstream. But unlike in England, punk in Germany consisted of mostly middle-class kids, some in art colleges, some, such as Peter Hein, already working in a Xerox shop—where he continued to work for years.

There is no smoking gun to show why punk started in Düsseldorf, but most contemporary witnesses to 1977-German punk also locate its origin there without offering any reason for that.[30] While the Stranglers and the Clash played Hamburg's Winterhuder Fährhaus in the fall of 1977, Peter Hein, Germany's "first punk," does not leave any ambiguity about where and when German punk was (*V* 367). The Düsseldorf punk and member of the bands Charley's Girls, Mittagspause, Fehlfarben, and Family 5, locates punk "summer 1977 to summer 1978, in one city, on one street, in one bar."[31] The bar was Düsseldorf's Ratinger Hof, and, along with Berlin's S.O. 36 and Hamburg's Markthalle and Krawall 2000, it built the geographical constellation of West German punk. The brief period Hein brackets for punk did not impinge on the proliferation of bands touring the punk circuit—a few notables: Male, PVC, S.Y.P.H., Charley's Girls, Mittagspause, Din-A-Testbild, Stukka Pilots, Deutsch-Amerikanische Freundschaft (DAF), Weltaufstandsplan, Hans-a-plast, Malaria, Minus Delta t, Buttocks, ZK, Materialschlacht, Kriminalitätsförderungsclub (KFC), and Liaisons Dangereuses. But it was not just the bands that moved about from city to city. Band members continuously changed too, and some, such as Chrislo Haas, Michael Kemner, and Bettina Köster simultaneously played in multiple bands, while padeluun sporadically contributed to Minus Delta t. These various locations, the creation and destruction of countless bands (often during a single performance), and the instability of band members capture perfectly German punk's disruptive scramble, one that was, for Alfred Hilsberg, "the catalyst to do something yourself" (*V* 28). The energy that punk set into motion, according to punk Franz Bielmeier, was in the streets or on the dance floor where "one hopped like a piston in a motor" (102). This energy took advantage of ruptures, "nichtreparierten Stellen," in Düsseldorf that signified what Hilsberg saw as the fractured cultural conditions of the late seventies. "At that time in Germany," he argues, "there was no youth culture, nothing that had anything to do with the reality of youth" (39 and 29). But punk was not the answer. Hein declared in 1979 that he was "already pretty irritated with punk. There is a line on this single ["Adventure & Freedom" by Fehlfarben] 'It is too late for the old movements'—that wasn't just about hippies. That had to do with punks as well. That had to do with all old movements."[32] So in spite of the gap that punk filled for youth in the late seventies, the decade following the "German Autumn" cannot be read as the decade of punk. To no one's surprise, Düsseldorf punk died perhaps as early as 1978. Its followers such as Holger Czukay thought that "punk was great. At the same time I noticed how short-lived the whole thing would be. That was immediately clear. With the 'Kiss my ass' method you can't grow old" (*V* 46). True to its fatalist outlook, punk aesthetic sensibilities after 1978, and even between the years 1977 and 1978, survived in a sometimes antagonistic array of altered forms. If punk destabilized the position of dissident or upstanding citizen, then the artistic remnants of its own chaotic moment pushed this destabilization even further. By 1980, post-punk bands such as Der Plan, Freiwillige Selbstkontrolle (FSK), and Palais Schaumburg sought to create continuously shifting positions from which to critique what they saw as failings in other social moments. FSK critiqued 1968, terrorism, and punk, according to band member Thomas Meinecke, in order "not to arrive with an ideology, but rather cybernetically, take position sometimes here, sometimes there."[33] To this end, punk in Germany starkly differentiated itself from previous subcultures not just sartorially or sonically, but also philosophically. Punk did not want to establish a new order to stave off chaos of the past. Punk wanted chaos. Punk did not want to erect barriers between fascism and the present. It wanted to tear down the present. Punk did not want an antifascist position. It wanted positions that had nothing to do with binaries of fascism. Punk sought a fundamental rethinking of representation that did not efface the past for the future. Understanding West German punk at its apocalyptic core demands assaying it outside established sociological or anthropological understandings. In order to compensate for such incomplete investigations into German punk, those studies are detailed below in order to make them springboards for showing accurately how punk's aesthetic transformation articulated within a distinct project of German dystopia. More than an index of musical and artistic discontent, this book subsequently targets West German punk's uniquely proficient literary quotient—the aspect of its own project that best withstood its destructive imperative. Together, such a poetics of punk testify to a specifically German punk genealogy; they are a key to deciphering the logic behind its willed internalization of contradiction to foreclose the future.

Punk Anthropology

Critical investigations into punk first emerged out of work done in the Center for Contemporary Cultural Studies (CCCS) in Birmingham, England. The work done at the CCCS, Simon Frith writes, "pioneered a theoretical approach to the 'fragmented culture' that marked out social change in Britain at the end of the twentieth century" (175). Ultimately, researchers in Birmingham attempted to define and analyze the space in which British youth culture unfolded. In the theoretical introduction to the groundbreaking study of youth subcultures, *Resistance through Rituals,* youth is understood as a "concealed metaphor for social change" (9). Its authors complicated the category of youth to be defined by the struggle between dominant and subordinate groups, wherein youth subcultures transformed the field of culture, Stuart Hall writes, "Into a battlefield on which there are no once-and-for-all victories, but there are always strategic positions to be won and lost" ("Notes" 233). On the tails of *Resistance through Rituals,* Dick Hebdige published his seminal scholarly work on punk, *Subculture: The Meaning of Style* (1979). Hebdige bridged semiotics, ethnography, and sociology to investigate how punk style used "bricolage" to threaten the visual stability of an image. Subcultures expressed, Hebdige writes, "in the last instance, a fundamental tension between those in power and those condemned to subordinate positions and second-class lives" (132). British punk in the seventies was a conjunctural response by youth to a broader rhetoric of economic and ideological crisis within the failure of social democratic consensus. Beyond demarking itself outside the mainstream with what Hebdige calls "the sartorial equivalent of swearwords" (114), punk subcultures can be understood as a corrective to "non-critical" postmodernism in which modernist categories of ideology and alienation are effaced such that "there is no space to struggle over, to struggle from […] or to struggle toward" (*Hiding* 181–193). While British researchers demonstrated subcultures' sartorial attempts to differentiate themselves from mainstream society, this methodology is not representative of subculture research in West Germany.

German scholarly investigations into punk and subcultures in the seventies were dominated by Rolf Schwendter's 1971 *Theorie der Subkultur* (Theory of subculture) and, later, Dieter Baacke's 1987 *Jugend und Jugendkulturen* (Youth and youth cultures). Schwendter's sociological investigation sought to create structures into which all youth subcultures could be placed, and his top-down analysis stands in stark methodological opposition to CCCS researchers. Schwendter reads subcultures as working in the service of mass culture, whereby he removes the resistance or refusal of youth culture that was central to British subculture theory. Furthermore, his analysis reduces subcultures to a singular response to contradictions in which culture and subcultures are constructed as a whole. In the mind of CCCS researchers, such a unity neglects other multiple contradictions and struggles, which traverse aspects of cultural struggle and mark the face of popular culture.[34] Following Schwendter, Baacke attempts to reduce the tensions and conflicts between youth and mass culture to a singular contradiction between working class and bourgeoisie and he locates youth as simultaneously the victim of, and the trendsetter for, older generations and a new cultural constellation, respectively (6). While Baacke admits that West German scholars largely overlook Birmingham scholars' focus on working-class culture, he claims that if the working class *ever* existed in any sort of confined milieu, then it did not exist in this form in contemporary West Germany (106).[35] Thus Baacke constructs youth not as a metaphor for change, but rather as a unified "disposable-movement" on the cultural level that worked through new dimensions of style, individuality, and identity in the service of mainstream culture (5).[36] Since the work done by Baacke and Schwendter, Peter Ulrich Hein has repeatedly sought to pry apart "aesthetic opposition" in the Federal Republic. Hein's *Protestkultur und Jugend* (Protest culture and youth) uses a sociological base to set up youth cultures as primarily a generational conflict that in the FRG resided specifically between fathers and children. In his analyses, subcultures are destined to be absorbed by culture industries, a pessimistic future Hein buttresses by reading youth as a cultural trendsetter in search of mainstream social identification.[37] Perhaps most important for this analysis, Hein does not read West German subcultures as mere imitation of Anglo subcultures, but rather as youth moments that took advantage of gaps specific to the Federal Republic.

In the nineties, some German scholars began to approach subcultures from a new theoretical model that reflects indebtedness to work done at the CCCS. This less prominent avenue of analysis, demonstrated by Karl Hörning and Rainer Winter's *Widerspenstige Kulturen* (Resistive cultures) translates (at times literally) CCCS cultural studies work into Germany in an effort to get away from the unity-seeking analytical and explanatory Weberian tract of sociology.[38] *Resistive Cultures* reads cultural forms and practices as dynamic, polyphonic, and always controversial; as complex processes about the construction of sociocultural meanings of identity (10). This significant theoretical departure for German social scientific examinations of subcultures was preceded by Thomas Lau's 1992 reproduction of a Hebdige-style appraisal of punk subcultures in West Germany that read how punk held up a "multi-facetted mirror" to challenge canonical values and tradition (137).[39] From the vantage point of these social scientific lines of inquiry, what becomes clear is that a significant disjunction exists between subculture theory as conceived by the scholars in Birmingham and actual West German punk cultures: CCCS subculture theory is not directly applicable to the West German punk subcultures that surfaced around 1977. Punk in Britain was about the historical legacies of British class stratification; punk in the Federal Republic was about historical legacies of German fascism. The materials examined in the following chapters query West German punk as a unique aesthetic moment and as such testify to that difference, to the ways punk's inversion of social intervention played out through its specifically German aesthetic-political strategy. More than an index of its negative strategy, this book unveils through punk's aesthetic remnants the logic of a temporal implosion; between themselves those remnants signal the dialectic of West German punk's "no future," its products, its failures, and its crises.

An Inventory of Crises

Punk's first crisis was the violent moment of its birth: 1977. But this first crisis is also the first marker of punk's devotion to disavowing its present and past. Punks in Düsseldorf such as Harry Rag spoke of textual similarities between what German terrorists and punks criticized, namely expanded police powers under the "state of emergency" declared by Helmut Schmidt's government as a result of resistive violence. But Rag considers punk and terrorism strictly temporal bedmates: "the RAF had in '77 its highpoint—exactly as punk erupted here" (V 74). Though Rag is perhaps disingenuous with his reduction of punk's connection to the RAF or to its British predecessors as mere synchronicity. After all, in spite of their desire to "find their own thing" as Jäki Eldorado claimed, punks ran around Düsseldorf with RAF buttons because Clash frontman Joe Strummer wore them. Similarly, they wore swastikas because Siouxsie from Siouxsie and The Banshees wore a swastika armband. Although this flirtation with terrorism and fascism was imitative, people nevertheless thought that they were synonymous with the RAF. Düsseldorf punk Ralf Dörper remembers a result of wearing the RAF star: "some retirees thought that because of that alone, one was one of the terrorists." Thereby punks themselves ensured that unlike terrorists Andreas Baader, Gudrun Ensslin, and Jan-Carl Raspe, German terrorism survived 1977 as the apparent axis of youth culture. Punk may have been contemporary with terrorism, but crucial for German punk was establishing a strategy from foreign and domestic pieces of cultural representation—here the RAF star from Britain—and subverting them within their own specific contexts. To this end, punk envisioned and tested out different montages of cultural materials in the Federal Republic without becoming the terrorists' violent heir; punk in

West Germany was not about carrying on the banner of terrorism unaltered or miming British punks. For Dörper, member of the punk bands S.Y.P.H. and Krupps, the difference turned on locations and time. "In the middle of the 'German Autumn,'" he claims, "such things had a completely different effect than in England" (51). Just as between British and German punk, there are indeed salient differences between punk and its national predecessors.

Though German terrorism in the seventies, it can be argued, sought through violence to overcome the failings of the various social movements associated with the year 1968 vis-à-vis *Vergangenheitsbewältigung* (coming to terms with the past) that emerged in the mid-fifties, and the elusiveness and (im)possibility of that process, punk cannot be read as simply another link in the chain of cultural processing. For, in stark contrast to the techniques used by punks, German terrorism was disinterested in representation and exclusively used political violence in their attempt to achieve progress away from fascism. Nevertheless, a brief comparison with the RAF makes it clear how West German punk repeatedly appropriated representations of terrorism. Punk, though, simultaneously took up positions antithetical to terrorism because it moved past anarchy via misused images of terrorists; they subverted representations of National Socialism too (figures I.1 and I.2).

The 1981 advertisement for the record stores "Rip Off" and "Eigelstein" mimes the "wanted posters" ubiquitous in the West German seventies (supplanting punks for RAF terrorists) while the 1979 cover of the fanzine *Die Düsseldorfer Leere* showcases a cover image that was ripped from the National Socialist tabloid *Der Stürmer*. The advertisement and manifesto make clear how punk used all available channels in their aesthetic refusal to align themselves with terrorist-sympathizers or their enemies, clandestine fascists. Instead, punks chose both. "Either swastika or RAF machine gun," S.Y.P.H. member Thomas Schwebel recalls, "both were available. Outside on the street they both unleashed the same reaction. Complete disruption" (*V* 51). Punks shuffled these cultural materials and said "the opposite from [...] what one meant" to optimize a chaoticness in their expressions (84).[40] This move away from normative binaries is unmistakable in Dörper's *Die Düsseldorfer Leere* when it asserts that "through the purchase of this consumer good you will become [... an] enemy of the classes, enemy of the system, Vietcong, Nazi, urban guerilla, [...] and a friend of mine." Beyond Dörper's strategy to escape reactionary ideology, there are other, more salient differences between punk and its subcultural predecessors. If the RAF was a violent assault on a segment of German and western politics and society deemed protofascist because of its structural (misogynistic) dynamic,

Figure I.1 Punks chose terrorism. 'Eigelstein' and 'Rip Off' advertisement courtesy of Klaus Maeck.

Figure I.2 Punks chose fascism. *Die Düsseldorfer Leere* courtesy of Ralf Dörper.

anti-Israel politics, and total war operation, then punk must be seen as another assault on this society, one that did not go down the deadly and violent route that the RAF took in its last ditch attempt to assemble a bulwark against fascism after 1945.

By 1977, German terrorism's most violent year, the RAF's modus operandi had come under fire in the manifesto "Buback—ein Nachruf" (Buback—an obituary) penned by a then-unknown Göttinger Mescalero.[41] Therein the author accused the RAF and Baader-Meinhof of miming the state's "strategy of liquidation." Despite equating the RAF's violence with the Final Solution and its contemporary iteration in the Federal Republic's antiterrorist campaign, the Buback obituary did not demand an end to German terrorism. Rather, it demanded a radical social strategy that would completely rethink everything. This hypothetical kinetic social resistance would reject balance, strict argumentation, and dialectics, and instead provide energy: "fast, brutal, calculated." The manifesto wanted a way out of the hermetically sealed mass-media representations of terrorism and a new kind of opposition that was not "simply an imitation of the military, but rather one that they cannot shoot out of our hands." So, by the time punk appeared in 1977 it had become clear that for some subcultural agents not only had German terrorism failed to re-create boundaries and establish progress from a protofascist present, they had also fallen prey to their own protofascist tendencies, simultaneously encouraging and miming the tactics of the state that they despised so much.[42] Internalizing these and other crises circulating in the lingua franca of the Federal Republic, punk tapped into the worst of its subcultural forefathers in its attempt to make real its apocalyptic vision of society. The following chapters demonstrate acute sensitivity to the salient crises afflicting everyday life in the late seventies and eighties, and how, true to punk's apocalyptic "no future," the evidence left in punk's wake rejected the possibility that it could be the solution. Steadfast distancing from such subcultural hubris, punk's longing for a dystopia of the present was resolutely dedicated to its own destruction and failure. The four case studies that follow represent a genealogy of German crises uniquely illuminated through the aesthetics of punk's crises and failures.

Seemingly heeding the "Buback Obituary," punk music, art, and fanzines channeled aesthetic violence of the avant-garde instead of real violence to constitute a negation of the present perhaps able to escape the socio-juridical forces of normalization. Chapter one demonstrates how the foundation for that failure, punk's cut ups, became more than a way to détourn cultural materials; they became a way to enact violence inwardly. But cut ups also signify punk's aesthetic solutions to the delusional utopias of 1968 and 1977. Artists such as Martin Kippenberger, bands such as Mittagspause, DAF, and Male, and fanzines such as *Hamburger Abschaum* and the *Ostrich* used form and content to unleash dystopias in their hegemonic present. Via the band S.Y.P.H. and the punk psychiatrist protagonist Raspe in Rainald Goetz' novel *Irre,* chapter two investigates the immediate crisis of punk's aesthetic strategy. That crisis is of the avant-garde, a Foucauldian crisis of space and power called forth by the violence of 1968 and 1977. Just as the punks in S.Y.P.H. fused the RAF and the student movement, Raspe conjoins distinctly demarcated social positions of doctor/punk, insane/sane, inside/outside. The chapter details the delusional nature of Raspe's self-inflicted violence, how his blurring of social boundaries subverts the asylum's role in Munich and how S.Y.P.H.'s representational crisis of motion versus stasis echoes in Raspe's own apocalyptic incarceration. The next crisis is of an Americanized culture industry in a rebuilt West Germany. Thomas Meinecke's short fiction and his band Freiwillige Selbstkontrolle (FSK) envisioned subversive agency in media by revealing the transnational possibilities of popular culture within the Americanized domain of the Federal Republic. Through Oskar Negt and Alexander Kluge's early eighties' Marxist text *Public Sphere and Experience*—that insists that poaching is relevant for creating a counter-public sphere—chapter three assays a crisis of production and reception in which the specter of American racism threatens to efface the presence of German fascism. Lastly, chapter four zeroes in on punk's willed and necessary failure. A crisis of time and space and a crisis of social corruptibility demark a moment in which the failures of progressive postmodernism made aesthetic contestation of the present a failure. Bookending punk's origins and its demise, the chapter illustrates punk's collapse through the band Fehlfarben's apocalyptic narration and Joachim Lottmann's *Mai, Juni, Juli,* a novel that sought out the center to make it implode. Putting into play philosophical debates over the fate of cultural and social modernity voiced contemporaneously by Jürgen Habermas and Peter Sloterdijk, Lottmann's rejection of German literary and social cultures, of success, and of reactionary postmodernism opposes the isolated cynicism of the jaded activist. Punk's last gasp makes it clear that while recycling failed moments from the past is no means to cure the present, recycling can, paradoxically, engender hate to make one last apocalyptic attempt at harnessing the radical potential in punk's "no future."

While a form of West German punk died in 1978, authors, musicians, and artists used the aesthetic instability incited by punk to push things further. Their aesthetic techniques rejected the rhetoric of progress that made necessary steadfast relations. West German punk rejected that Germans had, after 1977, necessarily exorcised the ghosts of the Nazi past, that subversive media was impossible under the permanent state of exception in the wake of terrorist actions, that there was nothing after the failures of '68, the RAF, or even punk, that the battle over a return to modernism or turn to postmodernism was the necessary battle, that failure and crises were necessarily bad, that just London was burning.

CHAPTER ONE
PUNK POETICS

In the fields with which we are concerned,
knowledge comes only in lightning flashes.
The text is the long roll of thunder that follows.[1]

Theorizing Punk

Punk never foresaw duration: it refused to look forward and the materiality of its primary evidence is particularly unstable. Thus this chapter does not prize any one phenomena or marker as *the* key to unlocking punk for the present. Rather, it shows how songs, paintings, and printed material deliberately fostered a system out of synch with itself, wherein all parts together fought against any unitary, ideal configuration. The ubiquitous fracturing of bands, for example, illustrates punk's drive to vacate itself from the future; performances were dystopic fantasies that in turn crystallized definitively in punk's various textual interventions into its present. Ultimately, I argue below, punk materiality created in its time what philosopher Walter Benjamin, while theorizing dialectical standstill in *The Arcades Project*, called a "constellation saturated with tensions." An apt tool for theorizing punk, Benjamin's oeuvre tests the possibility of solving the present's antinomies. His focus on historical avant-gardes, on the possibility of their aesthetic and material solutions to and impetuses for the effacement of the past in the present, and on the logic of forward-marching progress are in this chapter the means to make legible punk's inexhaustible self-criticism, aggression, and its insistence on de- and recontextualization. The following illustrates how punk's overall anarchic project for the aesthetic contestation of the present was indebted to and simultaneously distinct from such aesthetic legacies: punk's representation of "no future" was more than resignatory stasis. Framing its music, art, and fanzines through Benjamin's cosmic standstill shows how punk's iteration of frozen time was actually a dynamic and vitriolic strategy against the oppressive and oversimplified concept of leftist progress. This chapter thus unveils how punk's aesthetic contestations of its present inverted and entered askew into affirmative circulation of material values to expel itself violently from the normative "continuum of historical process" (N10a,3). Punk music, as DAF singer Gabi Delgado frames it, was one way to avoid fruitlessly choosing a side in the battle in and over culture. Instead, music consisted of "songs, [...] various tracks, that one could turn on and off" as an escape from dead-end binaries of social intervention (*V* 292). In this vein punk created a complex caesura—a differential of the present that could disturb established fault lines—through its alternate distribution networks and its celebration of the mainstream's cast-offs. This willed marginalization of exchange undermined the miasma fostered by West German Cold War liberal consumerist identity when it complicated the leveled middle-class geography of West Germany after the government's crackdown on civil liberties. To frame accurately punk's anarchic textual materials analyzed throughout this book—that are refractory to contradictions and failures and that internalized the means of their own destruction—punk's logic of self-annihilation must first be framed through theories of the avant-garde.

Theorizing German punk and "no future" thusly makes clear how punk saw itself as a strong vaccine against the arrogance of 1968 and 1977 that framed their visions of resurrecting the past as a utopic present. Dictated from above by lifeless spheres of thought (1968) or violent political power (1977) and based on critical reflection and philosophical reason, such advocates of the Enlightenment's achievements continued projects of the past to allow time's forward march away from fascism.[2] Punk did not seek to reestablish modernity's philosophical or temporal boundaries that had been constrained by reason, but it did not turn to indiscriminate postmodern fluidity of decentered subjectivity divorced from purposive action.[3] On the potential logic of a new kind of social movement, specifically circa 1848, Benjamin details an internally destructive social warfare that "no longer advances through the streets; they are left empty. A path is opened within the interior of houses, by breaking through walls [...and] to prevent the return of the adversary, one immediately mines the conquered ground" (*AP* a1a,1). While Benjamin here peers into Hausmann's Paris as a foil for surrealist interventions into sociopolitical life, he provides a foundation for deciphering punk's rejection of 1968 and 1977's spectacularity and its self-immolating gestures. The band Mittagspause turned this violence inward in "Innenstadtfront" (Inner-city front), wherein "no future" was as much about undermining sartorial and sonic boundaries as it was about ensuring the annihilation of the concept of and strategies for progress proffered by students and terrorists. For the latter groups, modernity's telos represented progress, time marching into the future. The converse, postmodern play and its aesthetic pastiche, meant that everything was possible, that progress was over and any barrier between fascism and the present disappeared. Mittagspause's internal battlefield fought both. If the leveling effects of modern and postmodern culture transformed cultural materials into torpid shells of what they once were, then when the band fantasized about quotidian anarchy in the Federal Republic it escaped the trap of postmodernism that Frankfurt School philosopher Jürgen Habermas in 1980 identified as a "pretext for various conservative positions." A battle on the one front against renouncing cultural modernity in favor of a governmentally administered lifeworld of culture, "Innenstadtfront" simultaneously embraced social banality to distance itself from the implicit promise made by projects of aesthetic modernity such as historical avant-gardes that in Habermas' axiom meant to introduce happiness into society.[4]

Concurrent with, but starkly different from Habermas' appraisal of the present and of aesthetic factions of modernity, West German punk sought out a third path upon which it reinvigorated the faded "anarchistic intention of exploding the continuum of history" to foreclose *any* future (*MUP* 41). This apocalyptic overcoming of progress and decline reflects Benjamin's cultural-historical dialectic into which punk entered askew to create, according to (separately) Benjamin and Jäki Eldorado, something different from that which was previously signified (22). Displacing the angle of vision vis-à-vis the past, the present, and the rhetoric of ordered sociopolitical geography, punk unleashed the energy latent within negative components of their environment to create an "apocatastasis," an apocalypse at a standstill (*AP* N1a,3). Truly standing on its head the programmatic goals of affirmative '68er politics (in the Green Party), punk harnessed for its anarchic "no future" of the present precisely what Theodor Adorno—erstwhile theoretical lighthouse and then target of students' discursive spears—called the "zeal directed against the tradition [that] becomes a devouring maelstrom" (*AT* 41). An argument over the possibility of autonomous art and a critical relationship between art and society written with an eye to Germany's past and concurrent with its student revolutions, Adorno's *Aesthetic Theory* envisioned an art that was not reducible to bourgeois society's requirements and that would instead escape the kind of critical rationality (in which alternatives are already established) that framed, in punk's understanding, the projects of 1968 and 1977. Punk absorbed failed revolutions to make them duel one another and itself; its internal and external aesthetic minefield illuminated aporias in contemporary Germany by marking detritus as extraordinary and by seeking to harness apocalypse rather than to usher in a utopia. Punk thereby internalized the catastrophe of the moment to disrupt temporal continuity and to annihilate ideas of progress founded upon vulgar materialism (*AP* N1a,8 and N2,2). More than negating the utopic visions from 1968 or 1977, punk's aesthetic battle with its present resonated in a dystopic celebration of dynamism that inverted the non-place of utopia into an every place. That dystopia, punk's sought-after apocalypse, did not merely revel in the absence of utopic space in anticipation of a biblical apocalypse. In the latter, humans are failures and incapable of creating a blissful, ideal society. The only recourse therein: society must be torn down so that the divine can bring forth an ideal, just society. Plausible fits within a narrative of biblical apocalypse, previous attempts to transform West German society into a just one by students of 1968 and terrorists were failures. In punk's eyes there was scant reason to read the lingering antinuclear and proto-Green movements as anything but affirmative, co-opted agendas.[5] Indeed, the mainstreaming of environmental and equal rights agendas from 1968, paradoxically, became not an overcoming of ideology, but rather the reabsorption of the dynamism of street protests into particular (theological, philosophical, or political) spheres of thought disarticulated from one another.

Punks embraced their visions of failure as a blueprint for tearing down the present, but—and this is key—they refused programmatic goals for or religious faith in a post-apocalypse.[6] While punk comprehended the mystical elements of apocalypse bearing down on its representational strife, it did not confuse these with religious elements. In his appraisal of its ethos, Peter Glaser made punk's aversion to the theological overt: "The methods of protest and resistance / that were developed in the 70s, / have become ineffective / liturgy." Conjoined with such canonized resistance was the punk aversion to the ideology of "authenticity." That misguided loadstone as guiding force of protests from a bygone era, Glaser deemed in 1984, was "merely a speech error / a retainer from the Christian compulsion to confession" (*R* 12 and 19). Reading punk music, art, or fanzines tells part of the dystopic story in which the compulsion to be *the* social movement that would avail West German society of its enduring sociohistorical angst was resolutely rejected.[7] It could never become such a paragon while concurrently sowing Czukay's "'kiss my ass' method" (*V* 46). But against its best intentions, punk did live on. And despite the recent misrepresentation punk has received in the mainstream,[8] there is a missing marker of punk's aesthetic contestation of its sociopolitical present that makes German punk crucial for understanding the eighties: its large number of literary figures.[9] Late seventies' and eighties' literary production—music journalism, novels, and short stories—is so crucial because it culls all facets of punk's aesthetic contestation of politics from that period in West Germany. The apex of punk's anarchic present is in the textual politics of West German punk literature. Therein punk's atomization of representation liberated the enormous energies of history that were trapped within canonical narratives. But this energy, examined in the following three chapters, can only be understood alongside the avant-garde inflections of music, the plastic arts, and fanzines that were punk literature's catalysts.

An Exposé

Punk was about representation, and in the wake of the RAF's bombing campaign in the Federal Republic and the United States' over Vietnam and Cambodia, it used surfaces to create its own "devouring maelstrom" (Adorno) that punks themselves thought were like bombs. There is no better example of this than Peter Glaser's explosive exposé, his introduction to the 1984 literary punk anthology *Rawums,* "On the situation of the detonation: an exposé" (9). But Glaser did not make a bomb, just a text. This difference is crucial. Embracing a vertiginous position by continuously scrambling bits of cultural representation, *Rawums* is a premiere example of how punk injected aesthetic volatility into the theoretical-political projects of students and the exclusively violent political project of German terrorism. Such social movements signified in punk's estimation what Benjamin and Adorno worked out in an epistolary exchange: defunct ciphers. Adorno defined such ciphers as hollowed out moments; these lingered on in the eighties because they had become images that presented themselves as "immemorial and eternal" (*AP* N5,2). Glaser's seminal montage of punks' cultural misappropriation illustrates the breadth of materials punks took advantage of and how these different cultural forms profited from one another, but also how punk's semantic complexity was acutely aware of Benjamin's own angst over technical progress that continually hollowed out things at an ever-increasing rate (N5,2). Anticipating the decreasing half-life of everyday objects, *Rawums* includes verse, essays, short fiction, and invented television dialogues that all fuse image with text. In addition to punk musicians' lyrical and prose contributions, the anthology contains 15 images by Martin Kippenberger and a text-image contribution from Georg Dokoupil, both Cologne artists. With these heterogeneous materials, *Rawums* played with a calculated superficiality of artistic language that manifested itself aesthetically, in a "new period of emergence of avant-gardes, / that of course everyone knows do not exist anymore. / [...] / through the efforts and advancements of a few / and small groups, / 'in the fight against the ruling stupidity'" (17). Here Glaser's new period of emergence (*Vorkriechzeit*) rejects the RAF, '68ers, and affirmative society, but uses the lingering images of these movements to unfold a "stereoscopic and dimensional" representation that refracts the past for the present (*AP* N1,8).

Glaser's fight "against the ruling stupidity" did not pick up these pieces and target bankrupt or worn-out oppositional moments to improve the present or to strengthen a rebuilding FRG. Contrarily, his "explosé" set its sights on unveiling and destroying directionless social criticism and prosaic style. In the slow motion loop of a recycled decade, Glaser's poem savors the energy—flowing through fiber optics or making the author's tie flap in atomic winds—of a concrete urban dystopia. *Rawums* did not simply see a problem in the concrete institutionality of reindustrialized West Germany but rather saw life in the shadows of atomic warfare as a catalyst to move past explicitly political organizations whose members had zero use for cultural representation (11). Punk's use of such montages transformed previous quests for a new non-fascist order into anarchy. Gabi Delgado, member of the bands Mittagspause and DAF, spoke directly to how this aesthetic quest for anarchy was conjured by ghosts of Germany's historical avant-gardes. Specifically, Delgado makes clear the musical connection between Dada and West German punk:

> One of my first texts was "Kebap dreams." That was already basically in the direction of Dada. Pretty soon we were more interested in Dada than punk. And we found interesting analogies. Above all in all the manifestos. That revolutionary element: "We are going to do something really different and blow up society with it. Or at least shock it." We were also influenced by Futurism. (*V* 78–79)

More than an echo of keywords from *Rawums* (avant-gardes, analogies, and explosions), Delgado, like Glaser, does not claim that punks simply picked up the pieces of Dada and Futurism and brought them unaltered into 1977. Rather, punk's tapping into patterns of historical avant-gardes is understood as the unraveling of the latter's DNA and the willful mismatching of genetic code: while the basic aesthetic nucleotides remain, punk specifically sought out a-complementary sequencing. Avatars such as the RAF, students, and historical avant-gardes were used, but punks "made something really different" (*V* 65).

Seemingly in contradiction to its desire for uniqueness, punk was particularly ambivalent about the trouble with the institution of art. Irrespective of their institutional location, punk energy, passion, and motion fed into subcultural montages that turned on what Bettina Clausen and Karsten Singelmann in their essay on avant-garde in contemporary German literature call an "erupting effort."[10] Tangibly, that troika is why punks were not anxious to make stuff that the system might inevitably assimilate. Glaser's *Rawums* demonstrates this ambivalence and energy, for on the one side it explicitly (and paradoxically) attacked mainstream avenues of artistic output and sought to blow up the deadly trinity of 1970s literature: "boredom /

damned lethargic and literature stood / for about the same thing" (9). But *Rawums* was also invested in harnessing academic complicity in this problem, a goal made possible by the internal warfare theorized by Benjamin. Glaser chastised literary critics from within, dismissively asserting that "literary criticism is directionless / and wags with a few remaining / -nesses and -isms this way and that" (15). While there is a clear desire to create punk aftereffects in cultural institutions, the crucial strategy for punk aesthetics was motion; a flow of styles would make unmistakable the need for energy to explore punk's potentially stable institutionality. "It's important now," Glaser claimed, "not to be nailed down, / or to nail yourself down" (16). Echoing the ascendancy of motion for punk's aesthetic contestation of the present, Munich punk and author Rainald Goetz penned his own imperative against programmatic goals. His was to "react quickly and radically; drive thoughts forward radically and quickly; be the avant-garde in your fight. Otherwise you have, and unfortunately this is the dominant status and everyone knows it, the complete opposite: cessation of thought, desolation, muff, and the old trinity: mistakes, laziness, and stupidity" (*Hirn* 94). While Glaser and Goetz's 1984 demands indicate punk's endurance beyond its willed endpoint of 1978, the subsequent chapters on violence, racism, and failure do not pull an original punk moment as a common thread though the eighties. Rather, the materials queried demonstrate the tangible evidence that Goetz's call for aesthetic motion was not an imperative to continue unaltered the telos of dystopia from 1977.

Any attempt at that kind of a punk poetics is a paradoxical task because of the unifying gesture behind establishing a poetics and punk's vacillating use of montage. However, the task at hand does not represent an all-encompassing attempt to bring punk's aesthetic hostility to its present in line with something such as postmodernism, late modernism, or a particular avant-garde. This approach presents, in part, how a poetics of punk cannot adequately function within other reckonings with contemporary aesthetic-political cultures, such as Linda Hutcheon's poetics of postmodernism. Hutcheon reads postmodernism as a complicitous critique of culture; it bought into culture while at the same time critiquing it. Punk did not do this at all; it did not buy into the amazing antidotal powers of the institution of art. Or rather, punk was not afraid of the institution of art. The aesthetic markers examined in the following chapters do not represent examples of an original punk apocalypse put on hold, but how, with punk as its impetus, such motion sought repeatedly to create anew an inescapable vortex. Punk's apocalyptic visions foresaw not just an incited dystopia, but rather the unveiling of the present as such. Its internal logic saw the rhetoric of consent and progress as "grounded in the idea of catastrophe.

That things [were] 'status quo' [*was*] the catastrophe" (*AP* N9a,1). Punk literature such as Goetz's *Irre* (chapter two) used its semantic complexity to flash an image of its own lingering, paradoxical nightmare—a frozen avant-garde moment—in an "oral cavity filled by a scream without a beginning [...] listen[ing] to the timeless silence of the universe" (18). Vital motion creating a black hole that ceased the forward march of space-time disavowed previous failures. Conjoining this inversion of progress with shocking self-mutilation, as the bloody case of Rainald Goetz makes clear, punk aesthetic complexity outlines an effort to destroy, once and for all, every barrier to dystopia. Punk's internal intersection of paths anticipated and railed against its rational assimilation by cultural relations and the aesthetic experiments in which punk poetics become a convergence of failures and crises that demonstrate punk's immanent logic. Contrary to Habermas's 1980 ivory tower contention that the disruption of temporal continuity incited by aesthetic modernism "finds almost no resonance today," punk's own avant-garde implosion of history turned its present into a dystopic event horizon.

Punk's Destructive Character

Investigations into German punk and subcultures outlined in the introduction represent a social and political history of punk. In contradistinction to these social scientific lines of inquiry, this examination queries German punk as a unique aesthetic moment, thus political histories of punk do not tell the whole story. Previously Greil Marcus unfolded in *Lipstick Traces* an avant-garde labyrinth uncoiling from British punk in the narrative starting point of Malcom McLaren, member of the Situationist International and manager of the Sex Pistols. Because McLaren made flyers for the Sex Pistols that mimed Situationist International flyers, Marcus correlates punk style with Guy Debord's "détournement," the theft of aesthetic artifacts from their contexts and their diversion into contexts of one's own devise. In McLaren's hands, punk détournement produced a "politics of subversive quotations, [...] misappropriated words, and pictures diverted into familiar scripts" and then blown up (168 and 179). Like Marcus, Neil Nehring's *Flowers in the Dustbin* details punk's investment in the uses of "high" and "low" cultural forms to illustrate punk's indebtedness to the avant-garde as it worked through and against culture. For Nehring, punk's adaptation of the vanguard of modernism was crucial for its intentions of "overthrowing the fragmentation of cultural experience, among institutions like academia and mass media, [that itself] is essential to a more widespread, lucid rejection of the authoritarian plutocracy that dominates the globe" (2). Similar to the position developed in this book,

Nehring locates British punk and avant-gardes outside elitist modernist or pessimistic postmodernist arguments, whereby punk becomes a salient example of "the possibilities of refusal and resistance in advanced capitalist society" (327).

Punk music aided in this refusal, David Laing writes in *One Chord Wonders,* because it had the "ability to lay bare the operations of power in the leisure apparatus as it was thrown into confusion" by punk's do-it-yourself method of production.[11] Brought to bear on the legacy of the West German "economic miracle" in the eighties, West German punk's Teutonic détournement represents a critical counter discourse that exposed the ideological content of mass-produced music by revealing the extent to which the power bloc constructed and supported ideology (recall Peter Krauss, the "German Elvis"). In the following sections of this chapter, music, art, and fanzines demonstrate how West German punk violated its own boundaries of high and low culture through astute use of chaotic montage to create uniquely German moments of "irruption" (Nehring). In latter chapters, these moments of "irruption" become specific intersections of punk music and punk literature that sought to prolong the bouts of sociopolitical crisis in the West German eighties.

To that end, West German punk embraced a decidedly apocalyptic avant-garde whose willed fleetingness came together "in a flash with the now to form a constellation," evident in Glaser's "explosé" for example, in which the rhetoric of progress from past to present was brought to a standstill (*AP* N2a,3). The figural relation to the past that punk created with its fractured images, songs, and texts sought out an apocalyptic atomization of the present, the kind of sudden eruption previously seen in German Expressionism, through which the shock to the system would come from interior application. Internalizing such destruction to cultivate madness à la F. T. Marinetti's psychotic murderers of the moon's light, punk's anarchic constellation was a stimulant against narcotic sedation of the present fixed upon a singular past. That many early punks in Düsseldorf were art-school students trained in aesthetic theories made this avant-garde inspiration possible. But as the persons Martin Kippenberger, Moritz Reichelt, Georg Dokoupil, and Jörg Immendorf demonstrate, such training became, in proto-punk's discontented hands, something discordantly wedded to its alternate sociopolitical constellation. While there is an overt avant-garde lineage around Düsseldorf, this is not the case for Hamburg, Berlin, or Munich.[12] For those other coordinates of a punk constellation, Blixa Bargeld of Einstürzende Neubauten in Berlin for example, desolate cultural contexts of the phantasmagoric past—scarred land ("Narben im Gelände")—became the concrete inspiration for a working-class variant of Düsseldorf's art-school punk (*V* 239). But this use of the material past must not be misunderstood as the reification of historical continuity, particularly in Bargeld's harnessing of Berlin's industrial apocalypse. Inversely, punk's look back was, as Einstürzende Neubauten's use of scrap-metal instruments demonstrates, an aesthetic intersection of ruins littered with the shrapnel from its explosion of its hegemonic present. As such, that which punk emitted in its present created a battlefield on which a Benjaminian contestation between "fore-history and after-history" played out (*AP* N7a,1). This constellation of dangers illuminated the phantasmal presence of the past to make its fractal nature fundamental for deploying the ruins of the present against the future.

"No future" and punk apocalyptic anarchy finds its Benjaminian predecessor overtly in what he calls "the destructive character." The destructive character, the domain of passionate youth, knows only one activity, the erasure of all traces of our times. Punk's anarchistic and apocalyptic "no future," to take Benjamin's words, "only avoids the creationary" ("DC" 397). In effect, Benjamin's essay provides a traditional definition of the avant-garde, namely an aesthetic moment bulldozing the present that literally stood "in front of the traditionalists." Benjamin's destructive character, aware of the past in the present and the looming specter of failure, does not waste time fretting. Exactly because it acknowledges its own fleetingness, Benjamin argues that the destructive character is reliable and flexible (398). His assessment of the destructive character helps to grasp the importance of Holger Czukay's prophecy of a quick death for the social moment of punk and simultaneously the Clash's "London's burning with boredom." Such boredom is dialectical for Benjamin because "all human activity is shown to be a vain attempt to escape from boredom, but in which, at the same time, everything that was, is, and will be appears as the inexhaustible nourishment of that feeling" (*AP* D1,5). Punk internalized such an affective paradox in its unwavering quest for an aestheticization of its "schizo-look" for something that mattered (*V* 101). It envisioned that it could escape this dead-end trap by harnessing what Bargeld sensed was a "violent implosion" into and out of which something new was emerging (155). Harnessing the mechanical energy surging through its own constellation, punk did not seek communicative rationality—that would only further impoverish society. Oppositely, punk used chains, ball bearings, and tape to channel Marcel Duchamp's complete transformation of the everyday (124). Thus boredom as affect operated not as passive resignation, but rather "the threshold to great deeds" within a world of lingering, but untapped, catastrophes (*AP* D2,7). Punk's strategy of fragmentation and apocalypse were thereby similarly in step with Benjamin's concern about assimilation by the "institution of art."

Crucial for punk and its apex in literature, Benjamin argues for a do-it-yourself aesthetic to counteract the power of "the bourgeois production- and publication-apparatus [and its] assimilation of astounding amount of revolutionary themes, [that] can even propagate, without seriously questioning its own status or the status of the class ruling over itself" (II.2 692).

The problem with production occupied students around 1968 too, but its institutionality, in the end, ensured their self-deception; that "they were in control of an apparatus, that in reality control[ed] them, that [was] no longer, as they continu[ed] to believe, means for producers, but rather means against the producers" (697). Seemingly reaching an accord with Habermas, punk understood the political/violent "no" of 1968 and 1977 much as he did, namely as the "rigidity of cultural impoverishment by violently forcing open *one* cultural domain, [...] and establishing some connection with *one* of the specialized complexes of knowledge." Through dilettantic play with representation, punk explicitly avoided such specialization that substituted "one form of one-sidedness and abstraction with another" (*MUP* 49). When the Clash sang of a London set ablaze by boredom, or when Einstürzende Neubauten deployed industrial objet trouvés as instruments underneath highway overpasses, they not only "drove the incommensurable to a crisis point," but also mimed the task of the destructive character (II.2 443). Indeed Bargeld defined punk's own destructive character by citing Benjamin's. "When someone tells us that we are destructive" Bargeld stated in 1982, "then that is something positive for me: 'The destructive character [...] does not know what it wants, but rather only, that everything that is, it does not want.'"[13] Punk, as previously Benjamin, envisioned a destructive force that was the "enemy of the bored-person [...] who did not foresee duration." There was no path forward for punk's destructive character, just intersections of ruins ("DC" 397–398).

But whereas Benjamin saw the nightmarish chaos of modernity as something to wake up from, the band Felhfarben sought to prolong the apocalyptic dream of "scorched earth [...as] status quo." Fehlfarben's desire to freeze the Sex Pistols' "I wanna be anarchy," echoes the stasis that Benjamin read in Nietzsche's appraisal of eternal recurrence "as a Medusa head: all features of the world becoming motionless, a frozen death throe" (qtd. in *AP* D8,6). Despite the frozen death throe, this does not constitute a condition of passivity, for even at zero degree Kelvin, as Alexander Kluge points out and the band S.Y.P.H. sings in "klammheimlich," there is obstinate motion.[14] Punk's paradoxical position, antithetical to modernism and postmodernism and only calling for destruction, including its own, was its solution to the Federal Republic's quagmire of rehashing modernism or slipping into postmodernism. Its implosive time binds it to historical avant-garde moments such as Futurism that Richard Langston has argued signaled not merely a "movement that began in 1909 but rather the inner logic of all avant-gardes, [futurism] describes the avant-garde's self-designated position outside and ahead of present time."[15] Punk's avant-garde became, as such, a "harbinger of an immanent revolution," in an always only imminent, masked apocalyptic landscape of mainstream West Germany in the eighties (26). The inventory below illustrates how punk montages astutely and antithetically combined time, image, and space to test out and freeze a chaotic avant-garde. Within this halted continuum, punk conjured the phantasmagoria of avant-gardes past against the miseries of the eighties to allow "primal history [to enter] the scene in ultramodern get-up" (*AP* Da,2).

This "no future" moment separates punk from Peter Bürger's classification of institutionalized Neo-Dada, a Dada imitation that merely "negates genuinely avant-gardiste intentions" (58). Bürger argues that while montage and Neo-Dada represents the destruction of "the representational system that had prevailed since the Renaissance," it ultimately replaces this system with a contradictory albeit stable "relationship of heterogeneous elements" (73 and 82). Montage's shock is for Bürger that which ushers in a "change in the recipient's life praxis" (80). Early German punk songs, "Innenstadtfront," "Apoklaypse" and "Verschwende deine Jugend" (Waste your youth), oppositely, used shock for destruction, not improved life.[16] Although Bürger continues to claim that montage's total meaning is part of contradiction integrated within itself, this cannot hold for punk if one considers that the constant shifting of bands and members, their constant misuse of representation, their anarchic aesthetics, and their dystopic proclamations ripped up the "syntax of social life" to prolong dystopia, not to recuperate the present (Marcus 164). Chaotic montages of RAF star, swastika, anarchy, and "no future" explicitly turned representation into a surface irritant or a chaotic jumble in which a banal television test screen became a classic punk rallying cry in Mittagspause's "Testbild" (Test screen).[17] The montage of television image, the compression of days into minutes, and the acoustic cacophony of guitar, heavy drums, scratches, and squeaks in "Testbild" give way to a distorted three-chord chorus and agonized refrain. Volker Hage provides an alternate conception of montage useful to pry apart Mittagspause's sonic instance of collage when he argues that montage binds different stands together "without giving an obvious connection between them."[18] "Testbild" broadcasts this logic when television image and sound inexplicably merge not in a living room with a television, but on an echoing chaotic wasteland. Mittagspause's agonized guitar produced an atmosphere with an overriding sense of destruction, frustration, boredom, and anarchy inside a middle-class living room to unveil seventies' sociocultural malaise as the eternal return of nothing: a television test screen broadcast daily. A parable for aesthetic and intellectual defeat by 1977, Mittagspause's television test screen recalls a kind of emergency takeover of broadcast media by the government, further underscoring the necessity of punk's underground networks of communication.

Just as the dust and rain dulls life in Benjamin's reading of boredom, the eternal repetition of "the phantasmagoria of modernity" within the misery of the eighties echoing in the final cry "Testbild" suggests an empty wasteland across which Mittagspause's montage continues endlessly (*AP* D9,2).

This space did not allow for recuperation or aversion of hegemonically controlled transmissions, but rather sought out sonic means to annihilate the polarizing and homogenizing force of uncritical acceptance of historical process that made visual and sonic elements lifeless. Beyond immediately contemporaneous parallels, the following chapters uncover, through literary and musical production, the aesthetic preservation of the chaotic montage in "Testbild" whose epic rallying cry first sounded in 1979—a year *after* band member Hein declared punk dead—to draw a more complete picture of how the aesthetic chaos emitted by the year 1977–1978 sought desperately to supplant real violence with aesthetic violence and put theory into action. But before that, the form and context of punk's initial aesthetic chaos must be accurately framed.

An Inventory of Effects

Music

Punk's sonic misrepresentation, demonstrated above by Einstürzende Neubauten and Mittagspause, culled from mass culture and from everyday life the profane materials necessary for its montages. Through the bands S.Y.P.H., FSK, and the Fehlfarben, chapters two, three, and four (respectively) demonstrate a tight bind between acoustic and literary punk moments, how music and text are autonomous in an Adornian sense (not reducible to a harmonious and meaningful whole), and how they seek to represent themselves in contradiction to hegemonic social beliefs. Music is paramount not merely because it was a fundamental catalyst, but also because one can hear today the manifold ways it chose to internalize and unchain contradictions; how punk's aesthetic warfare in music turned capitalist society's antagonistic nature against itself. Infolding antagonisms that normally ensured aesthetic failure of social critique, punk music inflected progress/decline or terrorist/upstanding citizen against its predecessors and into itself. As discussed in chapter two, S.Y.P.H.'s "Zurück zum Beton" (Back to concrete), for example, embraced the concrete jungle as an escape from the same metropolitan prison that made possible the experience of social contradictions as such. An attempt to reveal the phantasmagoria that was West Germany after the "German Autumn," S.Y.P.H.'s song stands as a non-redemptive intervention into the social whereby music played a vital role in punk's avoidance of established "use" by disobeying existing social norms such as those solidified through Krautrock and the *Schlager*. Jacques Attali argues that the stabilization of sound in recordings "interpret[s] and control[s] history" (7–8), a power that American and British radio signals in the Federal Republic used to monopolize myriad channels available and to ensure the durability of reestablished state power, thus engendering Adorno's "pseudo-individualization." Despite such pessimistic outlooks for resistive music from the late seventies, "Zurück zum Beton" engineered a different calculus of sound in which music became a dialectical confrontation with time, politics, and representation.

That punk sought to unleash the strictly channeled potential immanent in mainstream music can be understood as an escape from the banality ushered in by the Schalger, itself a powerful factor in consumer integration and cultural homogenization.[19] Similarly, punk's dissolution of boundaries between producer and musician and particularly between musician and non-musician rejected divisions of labor that relegated sixties' and seventies' rock and roll to the buttressing of social hierarchy, not social transformation (figure 1.1). The sonically induced melee below is a visual marker of DAF's dissolution of social boundaries, a different kind of performance than punk's sartorial destabilization, and the materiality and sonic construction of

Figure 1.1   No Boundaries, by Carmen Knoebel.

punk music makes audible in the present such anarchic montages of the past.[20] Einstürzende Neubauten and Palais Schaumburg demonstrate this attempted revision of sonic criterion superbly. They used found materials, debris pilfered from construction sites, as instruments or a recording of a noisy group of school kids passing by to unveil eighties' West Germany as an entropy-rich system through which flowed dissonant currents of history and culture. Reading the eighties as an "archipelago of chaos" (Hayles) instead of a leveled terrain of contented middle-class citizens, Blixa Bargeld recorded songs for Einstürzende Neubauten underneath highway overpasses to create a volatile aesthetic and affective flexibility. Penning his own paradoxical manifesto for "modes of construction for collapse" (*Bauweise des Zerfalls*), Bargeld set his sights on hegemonic blockage: "evidence against stasis / tactics against stasis / [...] anti-stasis / injection of intensity into the tactic."[21] Crucially, Bargeld did not merely oppose stasis with motion—that would have merely resurrected a failed strategy from the sixties and seventies—but brought this dialectic to an anti-stasis standstill, precisely the intersection of ruins that Bargeld culled from Benjamin. Einstürzende Neubauten's instruments and recording locations demonstrate how this tactical intensity challenged individuals' naïve, reified engagement with objects (and society more broadly) and thereby the possibility of anarchistic subjectivity. For Neubauten guitarist Alex Hacke this chaos created "a measurable energy in the city. Everyone was searching. Everyone was doing something new" (*V* 155).

While Einstürzende Neubauten celebrated debris, Palais Schaumburg transformed the energy of which Hake speaks and the mainstream desire for rehabilitated postwar cityscapes into a rallying call for punks in the song "Wir bauen eine neue Stadt" (We're building a new city). A chaotic, dialectical city in which the band synthesized opposites—stones and sand, water and mortar—while using a minimalist yet unending array of sounds. Palais Schaumburg's paradoxical city was far from the image of a contemporary, ordered West German metropolis. Punks did not just found a new city upon the fluidity of concrete, they constantly reused materials for their city, particularly their own. Because band members shifted freely, they began to transform their own songs, demonstrated classically in 1980 by Fehlfarben's "militürk" (militant turk) a détournement of DAFs "Kebabträume" (Kebap dreams). Aside from transforming the electronic original into ska-punk, Fehlfarben changed the line "hürriyet für die sowjetunion" (freedom for the soviet union) into "milliyet für die sowjetunion" (nationality for the soviet union). This is not merely a play between freedom and nationality for the Soviet Union; when the bands sing the Turkish words "hürriyet" and "milliyet," they do not just mime the language of a marginalized ethnicity in West Germany. *Hürriyet* and

Milliyet are both Turkish national newspapers, akin to *Bild* in the Federal Republic. Thus the songs create a West German battle cry for transforming the Soviet Union by injecting Turkey and sensational yellow journalism into the equation. Pushing paranoid discourses of nuclear annihilation orbiting the front line of the Cold War to their end point, these bands posited a different kind of social revolution by unchaining marginalized and mainstream cultural representation. Furthermore, DAF and Fehlfarben's song(s) are a scathing indictment of Cold War capitalist ideology—the kind fostered by the Springer Press and *Bild*—that dehumanized communist Soviets and migrant Turkish laborers into an Other. "Kebabträume" and "militürk" were the soundtrack to a rhetorical and aesthetic disavowal of punk's own middle-class positions—themselves made possible by Cold War economic forces and the labor of West German reconstruction—that demonstrates sonically their pursuit of "no future." Such energetic and rapid transformation challenged stable consumption of punk music and mainstream monovocal narratives told by the American nuclear warheads peppering the German landscape and xenophobic media.[22] That DAF and Fehlfarben remixed elements of their own songs made it possible for them to enact punk's invective and question the stasis of their own positions. Such aesthetic motion was their unmistakable means to reengineer previous failures, but it was not the only tool.

Punk music turned toward failure linguistically by singing in German. For punks, singing in German was not about nationality, but rather about destructively and energetically working with the broken.[23] Much like the expressionist scream from Goetz's *Irre* above, Bargeld "came to singing from screaming." The apocalyptic narrative of a cold star collapsing into an even more powerful black hole, Einstürzende Neubauten's "Kalte Sterne" (1981) envisioned energizing through contemporary Berlin's metamorphosing sociocultural-historical landscape "a final implosion."[24] Turning the drive for rebirth on its head, the song literally created through debris Benjamin's "trigonometric sign," the aspect of the destructive character that does not deny or mask the destructiveness latent in the reemergent state ("DC" 397). While Bargeld's admitted yearning for chaos pushed punk anarchy to an extreme, what remains important for the broader project of punk dystopia is how punk took advantage of certain highly charged concepts—terrorism, violence, German culture, and fascism—and let them appear in various combinations throughout its constellation. Punk thereby subverted authorized versions of these markers that had crystallized (in) the mainstream. Interspersing acoustic and lyrical noise created a space with unarticulated possibilities whereby punk's "semiotic guerrilla warfare" (Hebdige), in contradistinction to the RAF's "urban guerrilla," used aesthetic violence to reject splits between past and present.

Halting Benjamin's dialectic within its interconnected aesthetic network, punk's iteration of historical avant-gardes in the band Male's 1979 song "Risikofaktor 1:X" (Risk factor 1:X), for example, recathected violence in an industrialized West Germany with fascist rhetoric of "blood and soil." Instead of forging a political stance, Male made into a rallying cry its "immanent dynamic in opposition to society" (*AT* 336). The variable risk factor embraced by Male, according to band member Bernward Malaka, was inspired by the macabre mutilation of a body. He recalls that "once there was a woman who slipped and got trapped by her hair in the escalator. That was a horrific scene, a real shocker, but for us also emblematic of the technology that is rolled out for us."[25] Such punk sentiment voices what Adorno argued on kitsch and vulgarity, namely that the vulgar had become the darling of capital's advertising program and that this fusion was in fact the means-ends rationality of utility, a splicing of progress and violence (*AT* 356).

Placing an unknown variable at the heart of their equation, Male clearly sought not to offer programmatic solutions to the quotidian, state-induced or state-enacted violence that encouraged a polarization of art into ideology and protest. Oppositely, Male's song created a kind of differential calculus along sonic, political, historical, and aesthetic coordinates that refused to commit to a solution. Punk lyrics were a new kind of social critique that only offered destruction, and, Christian Jäger argues, they demonstrate what mainstream literature lacked. Jäger locates in punk lyrics a voice "on the one side against the hippies of the '68er-generation who had become comfortable and on the other side against the North Rhein-Westphalia variant of Social Democracy, whose Christian lack of rationality and their consensus-orientation was seen as a resignation of left-radical societal-analysis and tolerance-terror."[26] Mittagspause thematized precisely that miasma in their 1979 song "Innenstadtfront" ("Inner-city front"). Therein the band narrated how mainstream idolization of the "new Babylon" that a then-reassertive and supposedly contented West Germany projected outwardly was in fact ruled inwardly by ignored "panic and chaos." Positioning themselves as a unique avant-garde attacking the (dis)quiet of this fascist front, Mittagspause's song did not communicate a directive or some kind of supplicative and corrective discourse. Instead, the band reproduced social development in sonic terms without directly imitating it. "Innenstadtfront" let German society into its narrative but only as the nightmare it refused to acknowledge. Miming voluntary self-censorship—what punk saw as the nightmarish modus operandi of the late seventies and early eighties—was the overt focus of Male's 1979 song "Zensur, Zensur" (Censorship, censorship). Directly challenging petty bourgeois fantasies and delusional totalizing narratives of the present that positioned themselves outside any hermeneutic imperative, "Zensur, Zensur" mocked the absence of critical bite in resistive-cum-affirmative politics of the past that now articulated themselves in formal structures of power. The "blindness" and resignation of terrorists and students that Mittagspause embraced in the song, in effect reveling in their passivity, stands on the one side in direct opposition to the frenetic guitar and snare drum, on the other it voices perfectly punk's "indomitable mistrust in the flow of things" ("DC" 398). Fittingly for sounds that eschewed duration, punk music never reached mainstream ears as its sonic precursors had. Though its politics of sound were certainly front and center, it remained an internal catalyst whose logic remained dilettantic noise to outsiders. Conversely, a practice of punk aesthetics that on occasion made dramatic inroads into establishment discourses was punk art.

Art

Geographic, economic, and aesthetic sutures bound plastic arts and punk, a union demonstrated splendidly in the persona of Martin Kippenberger. Active in Cologne/Düsseldorf, Hamburg, and Berlin, the bidirectional influence between Kippenberger and punk is perfectly evident in his management of and programming for Berlin's S.O. 36 and in his 1981 untitled painting of two men standing in front of the Rattinger Hof (from the series *Dear Painter, Paint for Me*).[27] In addition to such economic-aesthetic markers, Kippenberger's literary production, such as *No Problem—No problème* (cowritten with fellow punk artist Albert Oehlen), laid out a programmatic connection with dystopia and anarchy. Echoing Benjamin's contestation of resistance, consent, and modernity's telos, the two authors declared therein: "We don't have problems with visual effects, because that's what we all are."[28] Detailing the socio-aesthetic realignments in Kippenberger's works illuminates a punk aesthetic grounded in visual arts, one where crisis and catastrophe reign and one that drew upon failure as a generative strategy. In his hands, failure produced aesthetic-textual themes articulated within formal consumerist-political structures of late capital, witness *Capri by Night* (1982) or his sketches on hotel stationary. Confrontation and exchange with other and its own aesthetic positions, a dialectic of (feigned) commercialism, semantic subversiveness, the impossibility of the avant-garde, the power of psychoses, conceptual flexibility, cynicism, and negativity as a riposte to mainstream delusions of contentedness are the many currents in which Kippenberger's works avoided "selling out to a myopic praxis to which they [would] contribute nothing but their own blindness" (*AT* 338). To express his laundry list of discontent with present and past artistic production and their mishandling of history—to make real the experience of social contradictions—Kippenberger explored, Ann Goldstein argues, "the banal, the degraded and the distasteful" to create a paradoxical "parasitic" aesthetic that rejected dependence on a host.[29] An example host in this instance would be the Documenta exhibition of contemporary art in Kassel, against which Doris Krystof positions the "blatant Do-It-Yourself aesthetic [... that] raised a whole range of questions concerning the nature of artistic existence" of Kippenberger's 1987 *Peter—The Russian Position*.[30] The *Peter* pieces enact a punk poetics of negation that sought to escape the sanitized revolt of the past. To this end "Peter," or better, the "petering" process—for "Peter" became in Kippenberger's hands a verb connoting dilettantic play with the everyday in general and with refuse in particular—invented a unique critical distance to shine light on the duplicitous and affirmative tendencies of social and historical functions of art. The afterlife of such aesthetic insurrection will remerge below when the following chapters engage state violence, the tension between American racism and German fascism, and the crisis of aesthetic production.

Kippenberger's embrace of punk's aesthetic warfare demonstrates, Diedrich Diederichsen argues, a "position of skepticism not only regarding the classical genres and institutions of the visual arts, but also their critique and the institutionalization of that critique." Just as the sonic moment of punk, Kippenberger, Oehlen, and artist-in-arms Werner Büttner accused, Diederichsen continues, "the conceptual and media-based approaches of the 1970s with tautological neatness and narrow-mindedness, they turned to painting as an ostensible zero medium, one that—on analogy with the reduction of the punk song—promised something like the complete preeminence of content."[31] Refusing oppositional binaries, Kippenberger repeatedly engaged both the specter of German fascism past and present and the fundamental legal-social complexity called forth by the "Emergency Laws" to counteract domestic terrorism. In paintings such as *With the Best Will in the World, I Can't See a Swastika*, a tangle of rectangles in which a viewer from a German-historical context can only anticipate a swastika that never emerges, he has exploded the swastika—that marker of the German present-past par excellence—and visually brought to an apocalyptic standstill the rhetoric of progress away from the chaotic past into an organized present. The 1985 triptych *Three Houses with Slits (Betty Ford Clinic, Stammheim, Jewish Elementary School)* makes the rehabilitation from a destructive past contingent upon juxtaposition of the extra-juridical "non-space" (Agamben) of Stammheim prison and the possibility of a new generation of Jewish children after Germans' failed liquidation of their parents and grandparents. *Vergangenheitsbewältigung* becomes in Kippenberger's triptych dialectical since the criterion for such a process—solving the violence of the past via an isolated American rehabilitation clinic—is generated by its own internal violence of the present. *Three Houses with Slits* ultimately denies any adequate transformation of consciousness and forecloses the possibility of any satisfactory, new standard of objectivity.

Martin Kippenberger charts geographic, economic, and aesthetic points in the West German punk constellation. Mortiz ® (Moritz Reichelt) is a sterling example of the sonic and plastic crosspollination of punk aesthetic experiences. Member of the band Der Plan, whose bizarre stage costumes pushed against too much "deadly seriousness" but still sought out a subversive irony with the antireform parole "The world is bad, life is beautiful," Reichelt brought avant-garde antagonism to bear on his drawing of Der Plan's album covers and the band's backdrops (*V* 175 and 178). Wry silliness, Reichelt's album cover "There is a light in front of us" is a scathing indictment of vacuous daily life and a lack of thinking on the part of the German public. The three figures marching across the cross walk refuse that paradigmatic ordered behavior of West German society: crossing the street *only* once the streetlight turns green. Crossing on red, the figures in Reichelt's critique makes clear the ease of such a radical inversion of German behavior with the leader's "Snap!" However, the cover does not simply posit crossing against pedestrian traffic signals as the solution to contemporary social restrictions on freewill. The three rebels, despite crossing on red, are nevertheless crossing within the prescribed crosswalk and in lockstep with one another. Recalling Kippenberger's painting *With the Best Will in the World, I Can't See a Swastika*, Reichelt's street is a series of hasty linear strokes, out of which one expects to find a swastika pattern. No fear, for the stability of the present has been assured by the "zebra stripes" that provide safe passage across the abyss of the German present-past. Rejecting any kind of programmatic solution to either crossing against the light or the specter of German fascism, Der Plan continued this trend sonically when it picked up what punk rejected as worthless: "airport music—elevator music" (*V* 181). Miming the dead-end trap of leftover political resistance, Reichelt's background canvas for Der Plan's 1980 tour did not push off eternally the constitution of a swastika: it was up front for all to see.

A chaotic jumble of signifiers from eighties' sociopolitical life in West Germany, the stage background has not just a fully assembled swastika, but also an atom (dually signifying atomic power/destruction), fish skeletons, human skulls and bones, hand grenades, a hammer and sickle, scissors, and wrenches, all of which build the foundation for the nightmarish cityscape in the background. Above this jumble, the interloping autobahn leads nowhere and three ominous triangular-roofed buildings are, when compared with the dunce hats worn by the rebels crossing on red, anthropomorphized and thereby suggestive of another dead end, namely state surveillance of the everyday and the rebels' concrete indoctrination into this system. Détourning the fantastical creatures floating in the skies of Marc Chagall's expressionist paintings, Reichelt has a shark riding a bicycle, a mouse with a dagger, a cooked turkey, and an open copy of *Capital*. The playfulness in the band's background signifies a core element of Der Plan's innovative punk philosophy. Reichelt explicitly contrived ways to avoid punk seriousness with what he saw as punk's original humor by adapting the American notion of "to jerry reeg [*sic*]." More than humor and the desire to play, Reichelt's carnivalesque aestheticization of Der Plan was intended "also to address people without theoretical backgrounds" (*V* 180–181). Seemingly channeling Mikhail Bakhtin, Der Plan certainly turned clowns into kings—often positioning themselves on stage as such clowns—whereby sonic experimentation fused with artistic alternatives to authority and normative social resistance. Songs and canvasses provided the means to test continuously sociocultural logic, unleashing polyphony ideas and truths.[32] The band's endless testing and contesting of cultural-political life acted out a demand for equal dialogic status for alternative voices, but also insisted upon an intentional ambiguity that prevented the band from assuming an authoritarian position vis-à-vis its audience.

In addition to Kippenberger, Oehlen, and Reichelt, other punk artists emerging from Düsseldorf's Art Academy and/or circulating in punk's geographical constellation were Gottfried Distl, Blixa Bargeld, Wolfgang Müller, ar-gee Gleim, Mike Hentz, Isi, Muscha, and Harry Rag. Part of Peter Glaser's *Rawums*, text-print montages from Kippenberger and Dokoupil (guitarist of the bands Wirtschaftswunder and Silhouettes 61) critiqued previous youth moments through their aesthetic rejection programmatic and explanatory theories in favor of a changing, fluid style. Two Kippenberger prints in particular, "Arafat" and "Peurto Escondido," play with locations of previous youth identification, namely Palestinian and Central American revolutionaries and an exotic affection for Central America. A plain sheet of paper with felt-tip lettering and a lacquer square off-center, "Arafat" dresses down the Palestinian sartorial and revolutionary trendsetter with its only indicative "is tired of shaving" (190). This print equates would-be radical beards (of hippies) with laziness and ridicules the unchained affection of young Germans for Arafat's scarf while mocking the laziness for which members of Baader-Meinhof were kicked out of their terrorist training camp in Palestine. "Puerto Escondido" chastises the would-be Latin American ex-patriot romantic revolutionary (approximating Mexico for Cuba or Bolivia) who mimes a wanted poster by taping a photo booth portrait onto a shred of newspaper, but who has diarrhea because of the food and really desires the bourgeois comforts of home (192). While Kippenberger's collages reject balance of individual elements through chaotic application of aesthetic and real elements, it simultaneously calls into question the representation of such "radical" moments. The collages undermine, as Richard Murphy has read for German Expressionism's avant-garde innovations, "the inherent conservatism and the sense of reassurance [...] from the familiar, [...] to destroy the audience's comforting illusion of having a conceptually mastered or 'fixed' reality" (71). This is evident in *Rawums* in Dokoupil's montages that combine seemingly unrelated text and image. Images from a museum catalog of sculptures amended with thick black marker and his own verse, Dokoupil's aesthetic products created new, dystopic human forms out of presumably hard-cast classical shapes. These augmented human shapes question the rigidity of form and difference, as Dokoupil calls out in his verse line "Curtains that have irregular folds, have a similar function as curtains, that have regular folds" (82). The abstracted figures complicate representational stability of the familiar, while the text mocks putative variance in bourgeois commodities that reassure consumers of their individuality. Because Dokoupil withholds any markers directly connecting image and text, he presents aesthetic anarchy that revels in its own artificial construction and juxtaposition. With his marker he distorts the organic form of the sculptures—ambiguous forms that destabilize "realistic" representation—and his verse reconstitutes discourses of representation because it abstains from providing meanings and connections between image and text. Though both Kippenberger and Dokoupil's contributions to *Rawums* critique the institution of art—their prints strive for a certain degree of incoherence that questioned assumptions about representation—including Kippenberger alongside Dokoupil in *Rawums* was an internally provocative move on Glaser's part for it harnessed the oppositional tendencies in the two artists' works.

Dokoupil's exoticism in *The Africa Pictures* (1984)—that themselves echo in *Rawums* in artist Gottfried Distl's prose contribution "Europe for the Africans"—was the target of Kippenberger's *The Is-Not-Embarrassing Paintings* of the mid-eighties in which the latter took up what he saw as clichés and banalities of oversimplified "wildness" to inflect them onto fantasies of German culture.[33] Such oppositional tendencies within punk speak to its willed fractal nature, and its instance here in the plastic arts resonates in other internal tensions for German punk such as those between "art-school" and aggressive punk bands demonstrated by Palais Schaumburg and Kriminialitätsförderungsklub (criminality advancement club). Punk used this self-inflicted animosity as a merciless working though of avant-garde strategies (literally in the rift between Kippenberger and Dokoupil) that ridiculed failures while expressing solidarity with historical avant-gardes. Intently invested in fraying putative division between aesthetic institutions such as art and literature, *Rawums* makes clear that for punk, plastic arts were no longer possible within an individualistic framework by secondarily including artist Jörg Immendorf via a text by Hubert Winkels. In "Patriot Kills the Federal Eagle," Winkels dances on an apocalyptic volcano through the artist, and in a typical punk response to the specter of postatomic-consciousness can only whisper in a literary shout: "BUT IT WAS AWESOME" (53). Despite being born ten years too early to be generationally punk, Immendorf nevertheless drew inspiration for his *Café Deutschland* series from the Rattinger Hof. *Café Deutschland* maps the field of contested politics in the eighties—domestic spying, terrorism, persecution of the left via §88, nuclear politics of the state, antinuclear protests, cooling off of East-West relations, and so on—and, as such, metaphorically locates the negotiation of all of these crises as internalized in the Rattinger Hof, and thereby in punk.[34] Reconstituting his paintings much like the fracturing and reassembling of bands, Immendorf's 16 installments of *Café Deutschland* (1980–1982) discredit notions of originality that granted art's supposed aesthetic autonomy. In effect illustrating Adorno's contention that art was ideological in its presumption of autonomy and intrinsically superior expressions, Immendorf's entropic détournement of his own work constantly remarked critical spaces along myriad sociopolitical fault lines (*AT* 337). Immendorf thereby reimagined an aesthetic social praxis that could bring into play truth and ideology, but in dialectically destructive images breaking out of preexisting forms of the rational. That logic runs to the core of punk fanzines.

Fanzines

What is particularly interesting about punk fanzines is their chaos. Punk fanzines created chaotic relations of word and image and rhythm, not in the service of what N. Katherine Hayles calls a "void signifying absence," but rather as an entropy-rich media system that expanded connections between music, art, and literature to counteract the pseudo-stability of the cultural matrix (8). Punk's underground investment in print media simultaneously demonstrates their aversion to mainstream newspapers and a desire to have their own effects resonate via printed material. Punks produced fanzines—independent, low-budget, irregular magazines—that were not information for fans by fans. With fanzines, punk attained a kind of technical progress in their semantic complexity—moving beyond sartorial style, sonic disturbance, and plastic inversion—that made militant literary production into the unforeseeable. Fanzines revealed the political and ideological content of journalism that had been contested in the past. Of course, punk fanzines were as fleeting and internally fractured as the bands on which they reported, and indeed the number of fanzines was as prolific as the number of bands. They inspired Peter Glaser, retroactively, to make a poem out of their titles. An excerpt from his poem: "Ostrich / Unwanted / Everything dead / Deep impact / Junk / Boredom / Smear / Ass-kick / Stupidity / Scum / Deal / No fun."[35] Unsurprisingly, punk's interest in detritus is unmistakable in its fanzines. Encased in old McDonalds's packaging, garbage bags, or tin foil, fanzine's anarchic materiality deconstructed commercial aspirations of clean, aesthetic appeal required by mainstream journalism. Inverting the technical style that constituted dominant social discourses in media, the Dadaist tradition of such punk fanzines manifested itself as collage (figure 1.2).[36]

Hamburger Abschaum's dissonant surface, with its front and center, paradoxical self-indictment of its literary infraction against noise ordinances, embraced the environmentally destructive industrialization of Germany with its own aesthetic variant of "industry punk." Mocking commercial viability and the Hansa city-state, the left side of the fanzine's first issue retooled the city seal to read "With punk in your ear embrace the world" while the right side affirms adherence to this message:

Figure 1.2 *Hamburger Abschaum* #1, by Thomas Senff.

"[that is] how I listen." *Hamburger Abschaum* was not interested in masking itself as non-mediated image. Forcibly conjoining the pages with a safety pin and showing their "most reliable co-worker"—a Swiss-style army knife—the fanzine gives voice to unacknowledged relationalities in the everyday, but also uses its tin-foil wrapping as a dysfunctional magnet that estranges elements of real life "from their extra-aesthetic existence" (*AT* 336). Despite the clear interest in detritus, punk took advantage of emergent new technologies "cassette-copiers, photocopiers, Polaroids [...] fast media" to accelerate their skewed entrance into journalism (*V* 307). Refusing to become luddites of the eighties, punks used technology and cities, not communes and nature, to free subjectivity and representation from myopic battles with the culture industries. Punk Frieder Butzmann speaks directly to what pyrolator calls the political "subculture of records" in do-it-yourself publishing. "That was the political dimension," Butzmann realized, "that one could make and distribute records oneself. That above all one could make things quickly. Record today, publish tomorrow. [...] That everyone could do this" (157). Fanzines' semantic complexity did not build upon the linguistic possibilities of their context and the materiality of their objects to mediate their proper place within society—such a fit could only demonstrate fanzines' ideological functions. Instead fanzines' dedication to contradiction challenged passive consumption. Any aspirations to resistive consumption had to be founded on subversive production after the well-documented, epic battles between students and terrorists and mainstream journalism. Their rapid production binds punk fanzines to the kind of transformative production that Benjamin felt was lacking in so much leftist literature. While fanzines' materiality and publication aesthetic made possible a rupturing of mainstream literary apparatuses, this cannot, Benjamin argues, "linger." When they refunctionalized journalism, fanzines worked epically "not to represent conditions, but to discover them," and they were quite in touch with their necessarily brief half-life (II.2 698). This awareness ensured that they did not present themselves with the kind of authoritative voice that for Benjamin smacked of fascism (701).

Pushing anarchic juxtaposition even further, the fanzine *The Ostrich* completely turned away from any claim to "authenticity" in its content, instead publishing stories that were "simply [...] pulled out of the nose" (*V* 32). *The Ostrich* fragmented reality and created what Murphy, while theorizing avant-garde construction of subjectivity, calls "a constellation of personae, a series of mutually conflicting and contradictory roles" (18). Franz Bielmeier's collage for *The Ostrich* #3 prolonged exactly such contradictions alongside punk's nightmarish chaos of modernity (figure. 1.3). The cover again shows the aesthetic tool, this time a straight razor, with which Bielmeier violently created ruptures to misappropriate image

Figure 1.3 *The Ostrich* #3, by Franz Bielmeier.

and text. Again front and center is the swastika accompanied by ransom-note lettering (announcing not those wanted for their violent insurrection but those bands circulating in West Germany). The images demonstrate perfectly punk's chaotic misuse of representation: the names of bands and images of musicians Johnny Rotten, Blondie, and Lou Reed surround an image of Adolf Hitler and the fascist rallying cry "Deutschland erwache" (Germany awake). Revealing the fusion of fascist signifiers and radical left violence, *The Ostrich*'s semiotic complexity demonstrates a "noise of channels" (Bolz) that refused a common denominator. This knack for aesthetic irritation was an imitation and transformation of mainstream journalism such as *Die Welt, Bild, Sounds,* and *Spex,* in which punk authors such as Joachim Lottmann and Diedrich Diederichsen would later undermine "authorial fetishism" by penning stories under the other's name.[37] Such antagonistic inroads into dominant culture were crucial for punk fan-zines' ability to express its discontent with print media in nonprescriptive ways. Expanding punk's sartorial cut up's into mainstream journalism, the influence of fanzines' montages in *Sounds,* Alfred Hilsberg argues, demon-strated "the pessimistic turn away from the world of concrete-silos, beard-wearers, and pigs in order to create our own determination of content and form in music and language."[38] *The Ostrich* used literary noise to create disparate and contradictory experiences of the text that were not interested in organizing boundaries. The cut-up images highlight the artificially stable representations of mainstream discourses, even "oppositional" ones that *The Ostrich* sought to take up. While there was no unifying code of interpretation for that collage, Rainer Rabowski's first edition of the fanzine *brauchbar/unbrauchbar* (Usable/Unusable) demonstrates fanzines' flexibility perhaps best of all.

Volume number one of *brauchbar/unbrauchbar* delivered almost 100 pages of text in a plastic freezer bag. The individual reader completely determined the order, use, and significance of these pages. Rabowski abstained from any organizational markers and put the final product in the hands of the readers.[39] Texts such Rabowski's, following Bürger's anal-ysis of Dadaist poems, "should be read as guides to individual production. But such production is not to be understood as artistic production, but as part of a liberating life praxis" (53). However, Rabowski's fanzine was not interested in making one live a better life; his fanzine cared about its anarchic potential. *Brauchbar/unbrauchbar* demonstrated punk's compli-cation of binaries because it contained good and bad as well as truth and ideology. *Brauchbar/unbrauchbar*'s feigned dualism seeks to escape "the utopia of self-sameness in art works" in a move away from "ever greater totalization that assigned art its specific function and completely polar-izes art into ideology and protest" (*AT* 348). The RAF, as the students before them, worked hard to create a sense of "us" versus "them." The title of Rabowski's fanzine, alternately, challenges binary construction of use, whereby the irony stems from the putative choice of "A" or "B" for the read-ers. Presenting the reader with a bag of material ultimately unleashed a host of choices, not just usable/unusable, but order, orientation, connection, and so on. Thus *brauchbar/unbrauchbar* refused to dictate practice and encouraged unforeseen uses of the bits of cultural representation; it made transportable the multitudinous affinities between subjects and objects—normally suppressed by rationality—that the bag contains. *Brauchbar/unbrauchbar* transformed printed material from something static into something dynamic: the organization of the materials was continuous and shifting whereby each user spontaneously brought the anarchistic papers into motion again and again.

Punk fanzines make unmistakably clear how their own instance of aesthetic violence was meant, not as something invented or unique, but much more radical within the eighties, that this was a mirror-image of the kind of violence meted out by mainstream journalism. *Der Spiegel* and *Bild,* fanzines unveiled, vociferously sought to hide their own aesthetic violence by disavowing their aesthetic tools. *The Ostrich* and *Hamburger Abschaum* pushed even further the ideological juxtaposition of everyday narratives and their visual signification available from news kiosks nationwide. Thus the aesthetic anarchy was not an invention of punk, but rather another example of punk forcing their readers to discover its present's sanitized journalistic aesthetic as such. The self-annihilation promised and represented by fanzines materiality came to fruition. But the experimentation in journalism is crucial for understanding broader representational anarchy in the eighties because of marginal-cum-mainstream punk authors. The literary case studies below look precisely at the antagonistic intersection of mainstream publishing and at the lingering corpse of punk's aesthetic contestation of the present. The next three chapters analyze that, as Glaser argues, while fanzines brought "new styles, new tones, and new positions into literature, [they] truly unfolded themselves for the first time a few years later. Affirmation, radical subjectivity, identification with pop culture, computer experiments, etc."[40] *Rawums* is a perfect example because it was published by Kiepenheuer & Witsch, a mainstream publishing house, and as such did not seek to avoid commercial reproduction or financial gain. Nevertheless, *Rawums* was invested in making literature and literary criticism into something different, into something not nailed down. The shifting positions in the text vis-à-vis media and punk—such as Rolf Lobeck's "blablatext," whose title appears to dismiss literature but a 12-page narrative follows nevertheless—refused any once-and-for-all victory between high and low culture (62–77). After the rise and fall of these fanzines, the aesthetic circuit was turned into a feedback loop whereby some punks entered explicitly into the publishing world to subvert further the phantasmagoric normalcy and normalizing force of literature. Ultimately brought to bear on novels, fanzine style that seeped into and transformed more mainstream 1980s literature, Hubert Winkels argues, into stories "of the beginning and the end [...] and of the apocalypse" (12).

The next three chapters assert the prominence of punk in German literary and cultural history not merely because it has gone lost between the bookmarks of 1968 and 1989, but also because of the epic crises detailed therein. West German literary and cultural histories of the eighties still reside in what Paul Michael Lützler declared an "interstage," recalling Glaser's directionlessness of literary criticism (40).[41] This interstage survives on insufficient theoretical analyses of eighties' literature stuck in a quagmire attempting to negotiate a literary divide between postmodern-ism and modernism.[42] It is exactly toward scholars attempting to divide high and low and postmodernism and modernism whom Glaser himself made an obscene gesture seven years earlier in his "Explosé": "he waves at the guardians / who control the border between high and trivial / literature in Europe" (R 16).[43] Punk's contemporary renaissance represents a turn back to a moment of cultural and political opposition to the politics of '68—a politics that has moved from protest to mainstream and that affirmatively haunts contemporary life. Although the resurfacing of punk represents the resurgence of an oppositional moment to sold-out '68er politics, this renaissance creates nostalgia for punk that lacks a historical conception of the crises that drove the aesthetic and political project of the 1980s. In addition to blurring what punk was, it also collapses German punk with its British predecessors. That the aftereffects, the afterglow of destruction, was all that could be transmitted into the future that punk did not want for itself makes such misunderstandings the norm. Confirming the temporal evidence of punk's paradoxical futurity lies exactly in those texts that exhibit and that emerged from punk's crises and failures. The following indexes that past in a future that did not exist for punk, for it is only after the chaotic moment of punk had given way to the scramblings of post-punk, that the appropriately spectral constellation of punk can be read.

CHAPTER TWO

PSYCHO PUNK AND THE
LEGACIES OF STATE EMERGENCY

The coincidental conversation with the man in the train, the one that, in order to avoid a conflict, is reduced to a few agreeable sentences that you know can only lead to murder.[1]

Straining against the strictures of the durable emergency laws and the solidification of conservative power with election of Helmut Kohl in 1982, punk sought to reconstitute the present from its misunderstood ruins. Evidence of this struggle against the parasitic effects of and symbiotic relation between the Federal Republic's self-defensive and offensive reconstruction—that effected compulsory citizenship via a corporate, legal, medical, and cultural constellation buttressed by the United States' fears of Soviet encroachment—churns in the flotsam and jetsam left in punks' wake. This chapter analyzes distinct musical and literary instances of punk's response to that crisis of hegemonic stabilization: the band S.Y.P.H's riposte to state and media violence circa 1977 and author Rainald Goetz's literary retaliation to the subjective event horizon of the Federal Republic's state of emergency. In what follows, I show how at the core of this aesthetic resistance lies a strategy of upheaval dependent on destabilized positions of social disturbance and on the anarchic scrambling of social codes. In its turn to the past that it did not want, punk fractured the failed catalysts of social revolution in its attempt to stave off normalization of the status quo. Punk's dystopic fantasies of success against a crisis of cultural stagnation are, in S.Y.P.H. and Goetz's hands, a performance of terrorist violence that represented an indictment, a critical edge, against the insanity of the real. Their transformation of the seventies' real violence into aesthetic violence illustrates their contemporary crisis, namely that emergency laws truncated a posteriori the possibilities of subjectivity— founded by logic and Enlightenment philosophy—permitted in the public sphere. They thereby voice punk's distaste for leftist discourse that had become in its eyes affirmative: hollowed out, lifeless, and affectless. Via

S.Y.P.H.'s sonic misuse of media-terrorism and Goetz's literary misuse of federal laws after Kohl's election, each section of this chapter examines a different iteration of simultaneous, discordant locations. This strategy against a stable subjective position of terrorist or student (a binary that fostered social torpor) was punk's attempt at the evasion, subversion, and misuse of state power. To that end, punk obliquely channeled the students' theoretical fiend Theodor Adorno and overtly brought the RAF's crosshairs to bear on itself. Adorno's writings on the potential of aesthetics for social transformation are an apt tool here precisely because of his lack of faith in such processes "from below," a position held by the producers under investigation here. Additionally, Adorno, working with Max Horkheimer, sought in 1944 to theorize a way to rescue the project of the Enlightenment in the wake of its epic failures. Along with his writing on time's forward march, Adorno's work on aesthetic interventions into the present finds unmistakable parallels in punk's representation of "no future"; they echo below in Goetz's contradictory aesthetic ripostes to the mechanical transformation of society and subjectivity. Punks' sonic and literary misuses of the status quo as catastrophe are the heritage of its violent past, they also testify that punk's anarchic hope for a dystopic future, however tantalizingly close to fruition it came, was always destined to succumb to its destructive present.

Solingen—Berlin—Düsseldorf: S.Y.P.H.

In 1978, the West German punk band S.Y.P.H. engaged in a dialogue with West Germany's Red Army Faction. Or was it a dialogue about terrorism? On their EP *Viel Feind, viel Ehr* (Lots of enemies, lots of honor) they sang a song entitled "klammheimlich" (clandestine). It was, to use Peter Glaser's term again, an "explosé," an explosion and exposé all at once (*R* 9). Their song destroyed the veil surrounding the truth, the truth surrounding West Germany in the age of homegrown terrorism. However, S.Y.P.H. became afraid of their bomb. Ultimately, they had to change the title to "Pure Joy." The original's intertextual reference to the infamous "Buback Obituary"—wherein the Göttinger Mescalero declared his clandestine pleasure ["klammheimliche Freude"] at the news of the RAF's murder of attorney general Siegfried Buback in April 1977—was too hot, too controversial, too dangerous. The visual of German punk and German terrorism merging into one for a second, S.Y.P.H.'s strategy and dilemma, illustrates the conjecture of a broader crisis after 1977: a crisis of ever-omnipotent culture industries, but also of Foucauldian power and space, of knowledge, and subjectivity.

S.Y.P.H. came from the Düsseldorf suburb of Solingen, and Solingen punks Thomas Schwebel, Uwe Jahnke, and Harry Rag founded Syph in 1977. Shortly thereafter, Ulli Putsch joined the trio, and in 1978 the band changed its name to S.Y.P.H. "I came to Syph," Schwebel recalls, "because it was dirty. Harry Rag then just put the points behind the letters, so that it would always be capitalized. That way everyone always asked himself what it meant" (*V* 47). S.Y.P.H. consisted of a steadily shifting constellation of local punks but Schwebel, Jahnke, and Rag remained the stable points of the combo as S.Y.P.H. played Berlin's S.O. 36 and Düsseldorf's Ratinger Hof, opened in 1980 for British avant-garde punks Gang of Four, and ultimately became more splintered after their 1985 album *Wieleicht* (howeasy). In 1978, S.Y.P.H. took its album *Viel Feind, viel Ehr* and the song "klammheimlich" on the road to the first punk festival in the S.O. 36 and then back to the Rattinger Hof.[2] Rag recalls that "Germany was quite hysterical" during the time S.Y.P.H. moved from Solingen to Berlin to Düsseldorf.[3] The catalysts for this hysteria were the actions of second-generation RAF terrorist Christian Klar and the sensational accounts of the bombings accredited to him by mainstream media outlets. In this hysteria, S.Y.P.H. unleashed *Viel Feind, viel Ehr*, with a cover comprised of two seemingly banal images: a baby carriage and a young man wearing sunglasses carrying a camera. Harry Rag recounts that "because of the pictures on the cover we had immediate trouble" (figures 2.1 and 2.2).

Though the trouble reaped by the band was surely anticipated, for the pictures were of the baby carriage used in the kidnapping of Hanns-Martin Schleyer and the young man was Christian Klar.[4] A year after Schleyer's kidnapping and murder and concurrent with Klar's actions, S.Y.P.H. made an album with pictures they had ripped from the mainstream weekly *Stern*. Later accompanied by the tagline "For Rudi Dutschke," the student leader who had died while the band recorded their EP, this graphic fusion of punk with terrorism and with the student movement mined new frontiers for the production of shock. But S.Y.P.H.'s album should not have been really shocking—S.Y.P.H. should not have really had any trouble—given that for years such images had flooded the imagination of the Federal Republic. Perhaps the disquiet incited was not the effect of the images themselves but the band's aesthetic deployment of violence, the astute use of which came to misrepresent a decade of divergent factions of social resistance for their album cover. Their dissident aesthetics sutured students with terrorists to produce a semantic opaqueness capable of overcoming clear delineations of "us" versus "them," of upstanding citizen versus terrorist, of terrorist versus student, incited by media such as *Stern*.[5] Indeed, reshuffling the album's

Figure 2.1   Front cover of S.Y.P.H.'s *Viel Feind, viel Ehr*, by Harry Rag.

dialectical title broadcasts its internal logic: there was much more than enemies and/or honor. S.Y.P.H.'s heteroglot aesthetic strategy signals on the one hand punk's immunity to the vortex of mainstream media's uniform message condoning terrorism and praising the Federal Republic's lockdown on citizens' movements, but also, on the other, to the solidified barriers able to interrupt its synaptic transmissions. Unsurprisingly, Rag remembers, printing presses refused to help S.Y.P.H. produce its album cover montage of pirated images. That they "therefore had to make the cover with photocopiers"—in the end altering Klar's face with a black

Figure 2.2 Back cover of S.Y.P.H.'s *Viel Feind, viel Ehr*, by Harry Rag.

marker—proved to be the band's initial aesthetic escape from the control society's impingement on social flexibility. Walter Benjamin, in a citation of Paul Valéry, addresses precisely the kind of metropolitan malaise that made the album cover so effective. What in S.Y.P.H.'s context could be called "leaden times," Benjamin describes the "frictionless cycle of the social mechanism that abrogates certain modes of acting and feeling" (I.2 630). Benjamin's concern was how technological developments and the acceleration of his present effectively numbed the pedestrians to the shock of negotiating the nascent electric energy surging through the public sphere. S.Y.P.H.'s was that "back then everything was thrown in one pot" in the mainstreaming of self-policing citizens and atrophying possibilities for sociopolitical insurrection in the interminable half-life of Germany's emergency laws. If in the West German seventies the flood of images of terrorism pre-programmed and thereby decathected responses, then S.Y.P.H.'s trouble from *Viel Feind, viel Ehr* demonstrates their clear success in shocking the viewer out of always already formulated responses to such images.

The two images on *Viel Feind, viel Ehr* neither provided a map with which to orient one's self nor told who the enemy was or to whom the honor belonged. The misused images and text did not instruct how to avoid the one or gain the other; they distanced themselves from slavish respect for steadfast positions of RAF sympathizer or law-abiding citizen. The album cover was as such a continuation and simultaneously "a different quality of publicity than with the *Ostrich*," because the absurdity of the album was real, not invented. This breaking out of fixed positions that was not programmatic but rather "should be a provocation. Typical punk. Directly with the cover say: 'If you buy this record, then you are going to get it. There's something dangerous inside'" (*V* 190). It remains to be seen, though, just how dangerous this escape from the continuity of signification was. S.Y.P.H.'s punk semantics opposed the jargon of the "German Autumn" whose military-industrial control of daily life had, as Adorno read in the previous (yet lingering) successes of National Socialism, gained its traction through the "blind and rapidly expanding repetition of designated phrases." Such compulsory language (Stammheim, terrorist, victim, emergency, etc.) blights any potential autonomy of an image and ensures social torpor (*DA* 189). Obliquely engaging Adorno's "canon of prohibitions" that produces social sediment of collective reaction, S.Y.P.H.'s images and the song lyrics themselves (discussed below) reject the hypostatization of enemies and heroes, of the general for the specific. Indeed, the band could have been heeding the philosopher's dictate on aesthetic experimentation that demanded a certain amount of risk-taking to avoid being swept up and neutralized by the culture industries. For against such repressive tolerance stands the capacity for art to "contain certain traits that are not foreseeable in the production process, that, subjectively, the artist can be surprised by his work" (*AT* 60–63). Band members suspected *Viel Feind, viel Ehr* contained precisely such unforeseen effects, evidenced most clearly by Uwe Jahnke, who was scared enough of what damage this "exposé" might do that he ultimately deleted his last name on the back of the EP.[6] As detailed below, S.Y.P.H.'s own fear was justified: they themselves experienced the destructive failure of their aesthetic bomb.

The song "klammheimlich," a chaotic acoustical montage of sound bites from reports of RAF actions overlaid with S.Y.P.H.'s musical and lyrical additions, reshuffled acoustically the reorganized images on the cover.[7] The track consists of reports on the Schleyer kidnapping, RAF demands for the release of RAF terrorists jailed in Stuttgart's Stammheim prison, accounts from the hijacking of Lufthansa's "Landshut," and the deaths of Baader, Ensslin, and Raspe in Stammheim, all sampled from evening newscasts. An unending array of electronic distortions and synthesizer noise, "klammheimlich" accompanies these news reports with cycles between loud and silent. The sonic chaos of the synthesizer and electronic guitar feedback crests and falls only to rise again, as if echoing across a wasteland of technology, the familiar television voice an anchor for the listener to hang on to. Laid on top of this dystopic soundtrack drifts Ralf Dörper's lyrical montage "heroism / possessions / home / Stammheim." The words erupt out of the track at irregular intervals; S.Y.P.H. withholds any explanatory key, rhythmic sense, or intention. Instead, the words that could be easily used to create binaries of one's home (*Eigenheim*) versus the terrorists' home (*Stammheim*) are set into motion across an apocalyptic soundscape. The song vacillates its acoustic distortions to destabilize the media-driven keywords, a vacillation that simultaneously alludes to the slipperiness between its bookends "heroism" and "Stammheim." In an age of idealized social intervention, the genuine sense of heroism for RAF terrorists—heroes purging the Federal Republic of lingering fascist structures of power—speeded its members not just to Stammheim prison, but also toward a confrontation with a network of emergency state powers anchored by a host of incarceration sites in West Germany. As such, the pseudo-defined keywords in "klammheimlich's" sound collage produced S.Y.P.H.'s punk sense of "no future": an avant-garde dystopia put on hold. The song uses lyrics and an atonal array as a scalpel in a punk vivisection of the media broadcast. But the operation was not interested in dictating other uses for mass media. S.Y.P.H.'s sonic and plastic montages positioned themselves ambiguously vis-à-vis terrorism when they misused Christian Klar and news broadcasts to destabilize the culture industries' absolute respect for empirical details (of law, of place) and the terrorists' oversimplifications of Marxist-revolutionary theory. In sum, S.Y.P.H. tested the possibility of adapting and morphing Klar into a better terrorist via punk's subversive aesthetics. Their sought-after escape from oppressive means-end rationality of use vis-à-vis mainstream media's conscription of German citizens into oppressive rhetoric of citizenship and revolutionaries' fetishization of foreign icons, following Adorno, was encrypted into the album as a work of art, whereby the cover and the songs were the fuse for its "social warhead" (*AT* 338).

Viel Feind, viel Ehr's own "explosé" had no interest in what would remain in its aftermath. It merely sought to escape the binary of static or dynamic form, an aesthetic short-circuit that the album and song unmasked as an eternal return of the same. Moving beyond stasis and dynamism, S.Y.P.H.'s album pointed to the ignored chaoticness of ordered late seventies' West Germany in a decidedly non-programmatic revelation of antagonistic yet nevertheless affirmative moments. They thus effectively sought solutions to the simplification of anti-discourse that cultural theoretician Klaus Theweleit criticized as a crucial problem between 1968 and 1978. Theweleit reads the decade following "1968" as a gigantic "reductional movement." What was once radical was no longer so: "That which I previously described as a liberating language-explosion of the 60s was taken back by the start of the 70s, bound-up, smelted down to two or three prescribed, almost institutional languages, bony and evaluative language from Left-institutions" (34). The faux-dialectic of adaptation or resistance, of enemies or heroism, S.Y.P.H. revealed, was in fact a dead end. Klar did not become a better terrorist in their hands. In the end, mining terrorism for a more radical form of punk music failed. Both options, terrorism and punk, created a punk "explosé" that was too hot to handle. The explosion backfired on S.Y.P.H. They got too close to the Göttinger Mescalero. Fusing punk and Klar began to glorify terrorist violence. Spoofing media by reusing mass-media images and broadcasts trapped them. S.Y.P.H. found itself too close to terrorism, too close to its sympathizers, too close to state surveillance. In spite of producing music that made punk Chrislo Hass feel for "the first time that music, because of its power and position, could crash a regime," S.Y.P.H. seems to have decided that fusing terrorism and punk in "klammheimlich" did not have the agency they envisioned or wanted (*V* 48).

S.Y.P.H. mistakenly discovered that both options were a trap. The acoustic motion in "klammheimlich" became stasis. It was mired in concrete, a cessation of motion that would eventually dominate their 1980 song "Zurück zum Beton" (Back to concrete). In that song, S.Y.P.H. sang of a dream where they see trees and open spaces, only quickly to return to their strictly organized concrete cities. Rag sang "disgust, disgust, nature, nature / I want concrete pure / blue heaven, blue sea / long live the concrete-fairy / no birds, fish, plants / I want to dance in concrete." Uninterested in lamentations of social decline, "Zurück zum Beton" embraced the concrete world of urban guerilla warfare. They denounced the natural world and the escape it represented by returning to the artificiality of concrete cities that caused pain and weakness (*V* 89). Having failed at unmooring society, and likely sensing the inevitable march of conservative politics, S.Y.P.H. poured concrete over their community to create a bulwark against the hegemonic nightmare of traversing the present. To stave off any resolution of the useless binary of opposition or assimilation, to make unmistakably permanent the catastrophic eclipse of the present, "Zurück zum Beton" remained refractory to Benjamin's avant-garde by bringing affirmative dialectics to a standstill. S.Y.P.H. did not seek to restore natural processes but rather lamented society's oppressive bonds that withstood their joining of terrorism and punk. To decipher why S.Y.P.H.'s fusion of punk and terrorism was doomed to failure and why punk and terrorism were each a dead-end trap, this chapter now turns to punk's emergence into the literary mainstream. About the time S.Y.P.H. was recording the album *Wieleicht,* a member of the contemporary punk scene in Munich published his fledgling novel *Irre* in 1983. Punk life in *Irre* is located in the concrete environment of the Munich metropolis. Terrorists still exist. In *Irre* they find themselves legally empowered in Munich's institutional spaces. There are still punks in the local punk scene. Years after S.Y.P.H.'s and the RAF's failures, this punk novel sought to evade the pitfalls of state-sponsored hysteria and constitutional treason in its search for a third path. The remainder of this chapter asks whether *Irre* enacts a distinct and effective iteration of punk's anarchic aesthetic in its solution to violence and surveillance, or if it just makes another punk return to the quagmire of concrete.

Paris—Munich—Klagenfurt: Rainald (Maria) Goetz

In 1978, a young medicine and history student published the essay "He's Making His Way. Privileges, Adaptation, Resistance" in the leftist organ *Kursbuch* under the name Rainald Maria Goetz. In 1981, an aspiring author published a review of Botho Strauß's novel *Paare, Passanten* in the magazine *Der Spiegel* under the name Rainald Goetz. The man who appears to have been modeling himself after modernist Austrian poet Rainer Maria Rilke spent the intervening years studying in Paris and Munich, and he commuted frequently between Munich and Berlin. The early text in *Kursbuch* laments the "ideological conformity of both sides" in the fight between the Schmidt government, RAF terrorists and leftover '68ers (32–33). As the student recounts his shifting locations—Paris, Munich, and Berlin—he recognizes his privileged position as student and author, but simultaneously he seeks to get away from "the static of his own positions" (42). To escape stasis he constantly shifted "from the medical studies [...] to history studies [...] from there into literature." But he returns to his previous loci. He creates new disruptions. He chastises his colleagues "in front of the psychiatric institute: you idiots, do you have any idea what I am really doing" (34). To reconcile the apparent intractability between the classical privacy of literary expression and contemporary publicity of political action, the student gave up fetishsizing resolute conviction in a position. Instead he chose a subversive slipperiness "to question *everything*," whereby he founded a fickle strategy through which he was no longer destined "to have to arrive at a specific point." The self-inflicted destabilization of his own arguments, he makes clear, proved to be his "salvation from adaptation, [and] his isolation" (41). Such a position, that taps into social action though isolation, that demands dilettantism and theoretical precision, that gains traction through "powerless rage" (38), is rife with contradictions that avoid the "absolute correctness" Adorno argues inevitably leads to tautology (*MM* 79). Above all, the young student's horror on the one side of his "readiness for adaptation" (32) and on the other at the impotence of contemporaneous resistance is grounded, as is Benjamin's theory of aesthetically engendered progress, "in the idea of catastrophe" (*AP* N9a,1). The lack of any viable solution to the quagmire of late seventies' Germany, that the emergency became the status quo, was the catastrophe that Goetz could not help but see as "a constellation of dangers" threatening to trap him in their gravitational fields (N7,2).

The student's uprootedness took him to Berlin where Rainald Goetz published his critical-affirmative review of *Paare, Passanten,* "Im Dichtigkeit des Lebendigen." The review mimed Strauß's novel insofar as it also finally turned away from "the long-since trusted critical paths" (234). Echoing disdain from the *Kursbuch* essay, the review laments the early eighties' cementation of what Benjamin calls an "*instinct* culture, which continually takes up more and more of the elements of civilization, thus making them a lifeless possession, and withdrawing them from the sphere of that conscious activity by the efforts of which they were at first obtained" (N14a,3). In the book review, such deadening of progress is made possible by the "orientationlessness" of those positions that functioned within an oversimplified, contemporary version of the Marxist dialectic, "a rakish method, with whose help one can take care of topics without fear of revisions" (234–235). *Paare, Passanten,* the review claims, smacks of nostalgia for the past, of echoes of faded triumphs, and shied away from hard labor of reviving Adorno's *Minima Moralia.* Not content with merely lamenting Strauß's failure, Goetz lifts the gauntlet he himself threw down with his own channeling and radicialization of Adorno's dense and unflinching dialectic. The review, in tune with the "constellation of dangers" lurking in its own specific sociohistorical context, catalyzes the thickness of (a nostalgic, better) life that Strauß queries with a riposte—one that echoes S.Y.P.H.—"for television, for neon, plastic, and concrete" (232). Goetz's budding campaign to lay everything on the line in the name of ending once and forever a return to a phantasmagoric past was willingly and psychotically careening towards S.Y.P.H.'s concrete dystopia. What became of Goetz's attempt to fuse terrorism and subversive aesthetics—the strategy of taking up all available positions in the good fight against the "pull of assimilation" laid out in these two pieces—is the story below. Most biographies of Goetz neglect or underemphasize these two early pieces, and thus neglect how he moved about and bridged various locations and professions.[8] Most biographies begin with the year 1983, when Goetz unleashed "Subito" as his first installment of a theory of collage in fiction. At the Ingeborg Bachmann Prize competition in Klagenfurt, Austria, Goetz sliced open his forehead with a straight razor. He did this while reading "Subito," an excerpt from his forthcoming novel *Irre*. This self-inflicted wound mimed the excerpt from which he read: "With my straight razor I unmask the lie. With a clam hand I set the straight razor on a particularly choice part of pristine skin and make a good, visible cut into the epidermis. [...] The fresh bright blood, obeying gravity, seeks its way down and creates such unique ornaments on the skin" (*Hirn* 16). The cut and the gushing blood were the author's own textual performance of insanity. The razor, an artistic tool with which Goetz unleashed the interiority of his text on his audience. The liars were his judges, audience members, and German literary figures. With his wound, Goetz created a rupture in the divisions of a literary world he dismissed as having the mental capacities of drunken Germans at Carnival.[9] The problem, Goetz screamed at his audience in Klagenfurt, was that contemporary German literature, because it was dominated by the cemented styles of the "Peinsäcke" (bastards) Heinrich Böll and Günter Grass, canonical authors later juxtaposed with spina bifida–ridden infants and atrophied brains, only exasperated the mainstream cultural conservatism of the 1980s (*Irre* 250–278). However, as Goetz's blood began to cover the pages from which he read, he ceased to just read. Rather, he transported the text into the lived presence of the Klagenfurt Prize. The cutting questioned borders; it ensured that the text was not simply inside the text. The insane performance from within the text used the body as a conduit for a textual instability to take place: Goetz's performance unleashed insanity as radical. With this combination Goetz sought to escape the ossified canon of German literature, the idiots and their trusted paths, worn-out and safe methods, and the pull of assimilation.

Unsurprisingly, there was no shortage of reactions to the "enfant terrible" of Klagenfurt (Waschescio and Noetzel 35). In 2002 Eckhard Schumacher published "Klagenfurt, Schnitte", a text consisting entirely of citations about Goetz's performance. The reactions are truly fantastic insofar as they dismiss the action as a publicity stunt, place the cutting on par with Van Gogh slicing off his ear, read the action as a reprise of

Christian myths such as Christ offering his blood at the Last Supper, or claim that Goetz just tried to irk literature critic and jury member Marcel Reich-Ranicki (281–286). Although these responses are quite off the mark because they read Klagenfurt unto itself, even more analytical reactions to Klagenfurt miss the point too.[10] The cut, the blood, the tirade, the performance of insanity, do not represent "a contempt of reason" or the search "for fascinating horror" as Strasser reads it (16–17). Waschescio and Noetzel correctly identify Klagenfurt as some sort of punk action, but they paradoxically use Klagenfurt to read in *Irre* a "*stabilization* in a world of splintered production of reality and reason" (31, emphasis added). Peter Gendolla looks beyond the sensation of Klagenfurt and reads the cutting and the blood as significant because of the self-infliction. Because Goetz cut himself, he formulated "a dimension of meaning-production, that lies before or aside from established social mechanisms, an originally aesthetic idea of the breaking-up or breaking-in of meaning into the naïve, up to that point unconscious body, with which he then enters into a social function" (163–164). But just like S.Y.P.H. and others who tapped into punk's chaotic montages, Goetz did not seek to offer therapy for psychosomatic degeneration. Rather he unleashed that which had been systematically confined to a non-space in society. Klagenfurt belongs to the aesthetic-juridical conflict between movement and the cessation of critical thought, and the violent act of cutting seeks to rupture indisputably the leveling continuum of the present. As Goetz dripped blood and read of blood dripping, he prolonged and doubled an aesthetic moment, violently creating a montage of text and reality. This is what Klagenfurt was all about: a montage that combined the performance of madness with the intellectual-artist. Klagenfurt is a crucial springboard for understanding *Irre*.

Sickness–Confinement–Convalescence: The Asylum and Punk Scene

Irre is a mess of a text. It is at times unreadable. *Irre* tells the story of Dr. Wilhelm Raspe, a young doctor seeking to heal the sick citizens of the Federal Republic, who shares his first name with Germany's last emperor and his surname with terrorist Jan-Carl Raspe. The novel has a triptych structure, the first of which is a series of aphoristic passages, an assemblage of dialogues, monologues, and citations that surround Raspe, the budding psychiatrist who "will revolutionize German psychiatry" (116). The second part, itself divided into five sections of starkly varying lengths, is a stream of transcribed conversations between Raspe and a vast array of doctors, schizophrenics, punks, hippies, professors, students, and himself that are at times a reimagination of the stream-of-consciousness monologues from the first third. The final third fuses, indeed unabashedly recycles yet again, the previous two narrative strands in a chaotic—and psychotic—montage of fragments, sketches, and images. Throughout, the novel consistently destabilizes subjectivity. The indecipherability of "schizophrenic" from "normative" voices points on the one side to narrators' unreliability but also to Raspe's desperate campaign against the ghastly "pull of reality" (176). That fight, he is certain, demands he "turns against himself" (328).

Irre is a story about that turn: about what Raspe does as both a doctor and a punk, about what the patients and doctors in the asylum do, and about what his punk friends do. The narrative follows him as he spends time in the hospital and the local Munich punk scene, during which he is often in such an intoxicated state that the two milieus begin to blur. He elevates this nightmarish vertigo to the "vital principle with progressive dynamism of waxing excesses of upheaval and reality [...] into the realm of world- and self-destruction and ultimately to catastrophe" (328). Despite Raspe's willed bipolar condition it is nevertheless crucial to understand these distinct narrative spaces and exactly what people do in each of them.

The asylum is a series of hallways, lecture halls, meeting rooms, dining halls, common rooms, treatment rooms, and patients' cells. Patients are brought into the asylum if they are deemed psychotic by the *Law on the Internment of and Care for the Psychically Sick* cited early in the novel (Bavarian internment law). This legal paragraph clarifies that the state's actions concerning the interment of psychotics are intended to create security and order: "Whoever is psychically sick, or is psychically disturbed as a result of mental weakness or mania and thereby endangers public security and order, can, against or without his will, be brought into a psychiatric hospital or other such institution" (*Irre* 17). Once patients enter the asylum, they are "instantaneously trapped in the control of this law," a law that encodes the myth of utopia promised by the Enlightenment and founded on the strict Cartesian binary of subject and object (37). Such laws operate dialectically, insofar as their existence makes their existence unnecessary, and *Irre* makes clear that their specter is sufficient. While law certainly makes possible that the asylum and doctors' actions are "legally justified," law's specificity is moot. "Since few patients know their legal position, [the threat of the law] almost always functions" (85). Much like the language of the law, the language of psychiatry in *Irre* is based on abstract reason of physical and moral inhibitions that have been deemed fundamental for civilization, a condition that binds the novel's polemic with the self-destructive disaster of the Enlightenment as Adorno outlined. Though the punk scene is the more spectacular site of intoxication in the novel, the asylum and its laws' efforts to constrain subjectivity for order, as Adorno has argued on the totalitarianism of the Enlightenment, supplies "the narcotic inebriation [...] in which the self is suspended, in its death-like torpor [...] of its blind determination to remain unified" (*DA* 50–51). Clearly experiencing both physical and cognitive implications of the emergency laws that Rainald Maria Goetz (as others) felt on his very person circa 1977, Raspe begins to mime the strategy he sees in schizophrenia, specifically when his patients struggle and have violent outbursts. In those fights against the repression—by (emergency) internment laws—of manifold affinities between subjects and objects, Raspe sees potential escapes from discourse-fueled torpor in the public sphere.

In the asylum, the patients smear themselves with feces and tear open old wounds and doctors attempt to control the patients with drugs, straps, and straightjackets.[11] To prevent discordant traversing of institutional barriers—to enact stasis—wards violently restrain Schneemann, one of the interred who resists being placed in a straightjacket, with "an obviously painful grip on his jaw." Another ward "pressed with his freed hand onto the patient's larynx" (191). No mere passive witnesses to all of this during his time in the asylum, Raspe talks extensively with his patients and he learns from them: "through them he wanted to learn how to understand, how we could, without psychology, learn to speak of ourselves anew" (261). This overt turn to Futurist Filippio Marinetti's "Let's Murder the Moonshine," that itself wanted to instill the interred as the spearhead of an avant-garde revolt, does not seek to create a unified front against a similarly unified political opponent, but rather is an inventory of potential for a revolution. A source of information that "in the estimation of order represents itself as sick, devious, paranoid—as 'insane,'" is precisely what Adorno zeroed in on as a "cell of convalescence" for the dialectic (*MM* 81). Rejecting vulgar dialectics in the rhetoric of confinement for freedom, of progress over decline, and by embracing stereoscopic vision of the excluded that tap him as an anarchist in the asylum, Raspe makes unmistakably clear the asylum's disinterest in healing—or even punishing. Its violent intensity provides the foundation for a functional norm, a homology for the enduring crackdown on civil liberties under the guise of fighting terrorism. Precisely the asylum's violent intensity that Raspe sees embodied in the patients themselves—who slam their bodies against walls in rage, a dynamism signifying an untapped and misunderstood potential that Raspe comes to mime on the dance floor—is what he hopes to read as a blueprint for unleashing madness' destructive character. To this end, he talks for hours with the patient Kiener about "the burning of ashes" (the patient's fantasies of self-abolition), but the conversation never comes to an end. Forestalling a unified answer, their talks constantly take unexpected directions because of Kiener's random and interruptive questions (216–217). As *Irre* progresses, Raspe internalizes a similar self-fracturing strategy, precisely the kind of methodological proposal Benjamin reads for the avant-garde, wherein the "previously excluded, negative components [...] displace the angle of vision [such that] something different from that previously signified emerges" (*AP* N1a,3). Raspe also learns from his experiences with his friends while in the punk scene. The punk scene consists of bars, concert halls, Munich's streets, apartments, and subway cars and is dominated by violence, drugs, and alcohol. The names of the two punk pubs in *Irre*, "Damage" and "Größenwahn" (megalomania), are keywords for what happens inside them. While in "Größenwahn," Raspe's punk friend Nine-Finger-Joe approaches him looking rather worse for wear: "the left eye is bloodshot, the lids swollen shut, shoulders and arms are scratched, the undershirt is dirty, he must have fallen down." This was not the result of some personal vendetta, but rather an attempt for Joe and another punk to find out "who's tougher." In the wake of the RAF's failed (and failing) violent insurrection, punks such as Joe tested the possibility of adapting radical terrorist violence by turning it inward. Repulsed by the long-trusted strategies of violence against the oppressive state inspired by romanticized images of revolutionaries such as Che Gueverra, Joe's answer to his sociohistorical tar pit is "the beautiful senselessness of the question," a violent protest that demands nothing. Picking up on Joe's model, Raspe receives his own damage at an XTC concert: "A punch from a fist in my face [... I] only felt pain and rage, indescribable rage, [...] a deep wound and [I] hope that blood is not running out of my mouth" (92–94). Punk violence—metonymic for the escape from "logical" binaries—surpasses a mere yoking of divergent affective subjectivities because they conjoin insanity in the guise of megalomania (*Größenwahn*) with the lack of any ego ("senseless") and ecstasy (XTC) with rage. Thus, the punk scene becomes a testing ground for a counterstrategy "that does not let itself be integrated in the province of heteronomy" (*MM* 143). Misusing the laws to which it was subjected, punk music in *Irre* creates another such province. After drinking hash-laced tea, Raspe goes to a concert with his friends. In his intoxicated state and unable to cope with the sonic impact of the bass that he had so enjoyed just moments earlier, Raspe cowers in the corner of the concert hall:

> I pull myself into a corner in the back of the hall, cower in a corner, and while I try to control my thoughts they turn against my fear to go crazy no fear that will pass you know that no fear just passing just pharmacologically induced psychotic condition, I fall into a deep, thought- and picture-less sleep. (64–65)

In his semiconscious stream-of-consciousness condition, Raspe works through his own psychotic moment induced by drugs and the destabilizing effects of punk music. But whereas Schneemann was violently restrained, here the would-be schizophrenic—Raspe—is the doctor whom the state approves to stem the damage the schizophrenic can do to society. Raspe does to himself for pleasure what the doctors in the asylum do to the patients, reaping the flexibility of madness, as Michel Foucault reads in the dialectic of madness and civilization, namely that "madness is the false punishment of a false solution, but by its own virtue it brings to light the real problem."[12]

In *Irre*, madness unmasks a lie, the lie that Goetz's cut unmasked at Klagenfurt, the logic behind the social effects of which Adorno provides in *Minima Moralia*. Therein Adorno writes that "the immorality of the lie is not in its infraction of the sacrosanct truth. [...] Whoever lies, shames himself, because with each lie he must experience the ignobility of the social, that forces him to lie, if he wants to survive" (32). The lie of Raspe's present is the legality of emergency laws that founded their afterlife in the eighties by vampiristically draining semantic freedom to enlist the citizenry in a fight against an enemy supposedly vanquished. To unmask the lie of a constitutional, democratic society, Raspe misappropriates the order of the asylum and the streets of Munich through drugs and language. Because he misuses language, medical knowledge, and drugs throughout the novel, it is difficult to pin the punk doctor down. The psychiatrist Raspe interacts with doctors and patients. The punk Raspe sways from intoxication to sobriety so often that already with the first line of the novel he wonders where he momentarily finds himself: "I didn't recognize anything" (11). In effect, his perception of the world is a jumbled montage of physical violence, drugs, locations, and knowledge. As he subverts for pleasure the very techniques the state and mechanisms of discipline would have him use to subdue himself and others, his double and contradictory locations makes him seem as schizophrenic as his patients. He argues with his personalities. "I do my work and I do it well.—That sounds so cynical.—I forbid that!— What?, what do you mean now? Someone spoke in Raspe's head, they were remarkable arguments. Raspe listened to the idealist, a disillusioned one, a drinker, a cynic, a desperate one" (176). Raspe listens to myriad voices in his head, but he resists harmonizing them. He wants chaotic discourse. By listening to the noises in his head, he avoids what Norbert Bolz has called the "civilizing force" of chaos. Chaos can become progressive if one allows a "selection in chaos, i.e. differentiation of media in a background of noise—literally the difference between the letters and the Between the letters." By listening to the schizophrenic noise in the asylum and in his head, Raspe explicitly avoids "the introduction of oppositions whatsoever" (*Chaos* 12). The absence of any common denominator in *Irre's* mental-montage is reflected in Raspe's searches for "amnesia" (222), a search that makes it difficult to tell "who I am, where, and why" (212). By tapping into schizophrenia, Raspe makes his presence in any location seem fleeting and forecloses the possibility of having to obey a singular manifesto or concept for insurrection.

Ultimately, Raspe desires the deorganization of his mind and body such that "the sum becomes random" (Bolz, *Chaos* 78). He tells explicitly of his desired self-deorganization: "Raspe wanted the most brutal, ordinary, abrasive face. He didn't want to know any language any more, just bits of dialects. He wanted to have a fist that attacked unconditionally" (222). Raspe uses his damaged body to create an anarchistic wasteland, an "ätzender Irrtum" (acidic mistake or acidic state of insanity), that freezes an avantgarde moment in an "oral cavity filled by a scream without a beginning, listening to the timeless still of the universe" (331 and 18). The inverse of students' endless belaboring of their theoretical arsenal against entrenched government forces, Raspe embraces the liberating force of error and failure. His chaotic scrambling of spaces, discourses, images, and sounds creates in the narrative "a racing rhythm [...] that crashed" (223). *Irre's* chaotic narrative, that in the third part of the novel fuses not only schizophrenia and punk, but also image and text, is the literary manifestation of Raspe's "theory of self-infliction" that he first demonstrated at a Carnival party. There he turns up wearing red shorts and shirt, "decorated on arms, legs and on the throat with countless cuts, adorned by fresh lines of blood [...] the straight razor attached to the throat with a leather strap." Whenever another party guest asks how he made his costume, Raspe responds by cutting himself anew. "If someone gestured laughingly at his thigh and said, perfectly fooling imitation super realistic plastic say where did you get that, he, without comment, but friendly enough [...] slowly, in plain view, cut very deeply into the skin." Although Raspe talks of his wounds as ornaments, other guests, as a result of this ornamentation, "reacted with alienation, they spoke of tastelessness." In the novel the distinction between real violence and fake violence vanishes. The violence enacted by the asylum—a metonym for Federal Republic—as a means of control, becomes, just as the guest remarks to seeing Raspe's wounds, "perfectly fooling." According to his theory of self-infliction, Raspe's wounds become "ornaments" that transport ideas and actions, insane ones normally contained within the asylum, outside into the streets of Munich (19–20). Thus, the violence of the asylum uses the body as a vehicle, a means with which to break out of ordered boundaries. As such, *Irre* presents an avant-garde theory of montage through Raspe's body—an instance of body modification that the text represents as radical—that tweaks out the hopelessness and negative utopia voiced four years earlier by S.Y.P.H.. The novel tests how Raspe interfaces uncontrolled psychotic behavior with psychiatry to create a subversive use of knowledge. An insane act such as slicing open one's body, after all, is crucial for Raspe's montage because the "stylization and aestheticization of insanity [...] is the real pre-figuration of artistic production, [...] that the psychotic attains effortlessly and beyond calculation, while the artist, often enough, has to struggle to no avail" (78). If the cut can be understood as what Adorno called a "self-created symbolic rupture" from compulsory adaptation, then it also signals what Raspe fears most of all: that he may himself be insane (*MM* 257). Any potential difference between Raspe's fate and the effects of his resistive gestures from the punks of Munich or the patients is the subject of the next section.

Fottner—Hippius—Raspe: Between Adaptation and Resistance

Irre repeatedly juxtaposes Raspe with schizophrenics and doctors—in particular Fottner, one of the interred—and Dr. Andreas Hippius. Through this juxtaposition of characters, *Irre* explores Raspe's medical knowledge as a form of control, and how he scrambles and misappropriates this knowledge as power. The prominent role that the asylum and medicine play in *Irre* necessitates a brief turn to Foucault's investigations into the interrelatedness of capitalism and confinement of the "sick." In *Discipline and Punish* and *The Birth of the Clinic*, Foucault locates the creation, the criminalization, and the fear of psychotics in the eighteenth century. His archaeology of the prison examines the effects of a field of mechanisms, generally operating under the guise of modernization and control, as elements to be developed for the successful production of capital. He examines further how these effects have become intertwined with "mainstream" functions of state apparatuses of democratic societies. The intertwinement and entrenchment of the asylum and the state, of medical knowledge and power, makes institutionalization superfluous. *Irre* marks its entrance into the problem and limits of discourse (i.e., the problem of how cultural and linguistic practices have effects beyond producing meaning) with the citation of the German internment law. In the novel, the asylum's modus operandi is to drug patients who then cower in some sort of fetal-like position, muttering incomprehensible fragments: "There they babble like crazies" (139). The patient Kiener, for example, "says all day just one, pretty much confused sentence." However, these schizo-mutterings are deceptive. If one actually listens, as Raspe does, then "an amazing complexity, at the same time logical and insane, appears" (217). Raspe embraces this mode of psycho-discourse. He begins to mime the speech of the asylum, forcing "the patients and himself to an even more reduced dialogue" (140). Such language, what could be called the jargon of schizophrenia, creates one line of flight outside disciplined modes of communication laid down by the culture industry's positive representation of its juridical syntax and vocabulary (*DA* 149). But the schizophrenics need not even speak to enact their unique capacity for subversion. Their internalization of anti-language encrypts into their bodies an indifference to modernity's demarcation of stasis and dynamism vis-à-vis progress; they become as such bodies of resistance. The patient Fottner is one such body. During a presentation meant to teach students about healing by Dr. Schlüsser (senior doctor in the asylum), the junior doctor Raspe realizes how Fottner's sheer existence, his unwillingness to yield to modernity's postulates, unmasks the lies of the clinic. Because of this, Raspe himself experiences a shock to his habitual point of view that is normally reserved for patients in therapy. While in the lecture hall, he is dumbfounded that the schizophrenic's "apathetic silence was a bedrock against the hobbling, abstruse babble, a motionless knowledge of distress." Fottner doesn't appear to pose a particularly grand threat because he is "bewegungslos" (motionless): he cannot move or traverse any boundaries. But while the patient stands in the static state the asylum desires, he still "made each correct word concerning the character of depression and Fottner's condition instantaneously into a lie" (207). The interred can be immobilized, but their existence lays bare the operations of the asylum and the lie of medicine. Visually, Fottner is Adorno's "compulsory citizen" par excellence, but *Irre* leaves no doubt of the normalcy of his conscription (*MM* 31). In this demonstration it also becomes evident that it is impossible to read the repressed, as postmodern theorists of anti-psychiatry Gilles Deleuze and Felix Guattari argue, "through and in the repression, since the latter is constantly inducing a false image of the thing it represses."[13] The patient Fottner does not present his schizophrenia or manic-depressiveness for analysis. Rather, he only exhibits what the repressive apparatus, the asylum, gives him to represent. Exceeding its own dictate to create social harmony by means of a subjective homogeneity between general and specific, the asylum drugs Fottner into a catatonic state, thus destroying the organism on which it bases its power. Here *Irre* uses Fottner to unmask how disciplinary institutions such as the Munich asylum in which Raspe works do not misdiagnose the cause of their patients' psychoses. But their task in the asylum was never about healing; internment of citizens does not result from misunderstanding or faulty analysis. Organized by violence lurking below the surface, the state inters schizophrenics, otherwise known as those who ignore "the standardized behavior for an individual as natural, decent, rational" (*DA* 45). In *Irre* schizophrenics such as Fottner lay bare these operations for stability and stagnation and the psychiatrists recognize the schizophrenics' clairvoyance. In an echo of Foucault, the novel makes unmistakable how doctors recognize that "through psychoses our societies' fundamental contradictions appear to us unaltered." Thus, despite the potential of that position to transform society, both those legally allowed to keep citizens interred and the interred who see through the rhetoric of national security are unable to use medicinal knowledge or its inverse to fight "the truth of our reality that is recognized in psychoses" (38). Fottner clearly fails, for he remains bound in the asylum. However, excessive attempts to bind and limit Fottner have, unintentionally, created new breaks that can be potentially manipulated.

Whereas Fottner remains constrained, Raspe entangles his unorganized body with medical power to create frictions for which the normative modes of constraint (prisons, schools, work) cannot account. When Raspe struggles, in either the asylum or the city, he creates entropy in the space he occupies. Rupturing the asylum's enclosure, Raspe's disturbance emerges on the streets of Munich. His erratic behavior in Munich disrupts and disturbs "all of the highly valued honest citizens [who] later complained to the newspapers, that the big bad punks, on what should be a long Saturday of shopping, were allowed to screw around without the police getting involved, identifying them, so that the serious disturbance of the honest citizens could be prevented." The "rioting, fun, and ruckusness" that takes places in the pedestrian zone disturbs the organized and controlled society of Munich in *Irre* (62). Targeting more than the citizens, this disruption uses psychotic behavior to impede the functioning of capital: the shoppers cannot shop because of the punks' disorderly behavior. The policing of such behavior makes possible mainstream functions of the state. Raspe's "Aktionen" (actions) prevent smooth consumption, but also subvert mainstream societies conception of riots, revolution, and resistance. As Slavoj Žižek writes on contemporary violence, the punks in Munich "were neither offering a solution nor constituting a movement for providing a solution. Their aim was to create a problem, to signal that they were a problem that could no longer be ignored" (77). For instance, Raspe infuses the simplest of outings with chaos. Riding in the subway to a Freiwillige Selbstkontrolle concert results in stoppage of all subway traffic. Cops appear everywhere and ultimately eject him from the train.[14] These actions represent Raspe's affective and physical performance of an individual straining against the straightjacket placed on him as a citizen. He mimes Fottner's silent rage and catatonic state as he recounts how "a manic bellows in me. He roars so loudly [...] I hold his mouth closed, with all my power" (238). In his interstitial position of doctor-punk-patient, he refuses to give in to his desire to rage for fear that would make his project too unified. "That is why I have to constantly interrupt myself," he explains (269). Raspe thereby brings the "object of his aggression"—the pull of assimilation and stasis—to bear on his person and thus chooses to represent "the repressed principle of society" (*MM* 50). In public, this strategy is evidenced by the actions and inaction carried out by Raspe and his punk cohorts, which contain multiple indecipherable and unpredictable meanings. Analogous to the doctors' misunderstanding of Fottner's stasis, the most dangerous aspect of Raspe and the punks' actions in the streets and subways of Munich, for the state, is their unpredictability. Echoing the medical failures inside the asylum, the state is not in the capacity to understand the logic therein and thereby to predict where the punks will go next. Even if they luck out, they are never prepared for what will happen. Contrarily, the punks' rampaging through the streets and voluntary self-control, according to Raspe, "runs according to plan" (60–62). The disjunction between the clarity of the confusion for the punks and the pure confusion of the police highlights the successfulness of these affective riots and the politics of anti-civilizing chaos.

Raspe's aesthetic, medical, and political foil inside the asylum is Dr. Andreas Hippius. While his surname Hippius references hippies, the sworn enemy of punk, his first name alludes to Jan-Carl Raspe's partner in crime, Andreas Baader. The third allusion to the Hippocratic oath makes clear the novel's appraisal of '68er revolutionaries and terrorists as instutionalized practicioners failing in their oath of helping those in need, though in markedly different ways. The novel dismisses these early seventies' oppositional groups that still try to resist the state's dogmatic dictates "in spite of so many disillusioning experiences" (40). More than keeping in line with traditional punk hatred of "hippie-granola-freaks," Raspe hates "the embarrassment of aging '68ers" (167 and 290). This hate is reserved for those who retain worn-out inflexible methods—dialectics, for example—that help one resolve issues "without fear of revision."[15] Here, distancing oneself from a previous movement provides a means of not pigeonholing oneself. Wedding oneself to any singular position makes it possible for "punk-hippies and professor-hippies to stand next to one another." Once punks and hippies stand, they solidify their position and institutionalize themselves, thereby ceasing to represent any potential hero because "the hero is the constantly moving person" (320–321). The derogatory comment about hippie-professors explicitly targets the student movements circa 1968 and the university system that was in many respects their springboard. But it also holds punk accountable "to questions *everything*," including the "static of [its] own positions" in any strategy of adaptation and resistance (*Kursbuch*). Much like Peter Hein did for punk in 1978, Raspe dismisses elder subcultures as narrow and contained moments. Because of their emphasis on theoretical discourse and the isolation inside institutions, students are for him the kind of intellectuals that "have all arguments against bourgeois ideology down pat, [yet still] succumb to a process of standardization" (*MM* 235). What Raspe casts as students' inability to put theory to work echoes Adorno's entreaty for theoretical praxis that too often becomes trapped in the dialectic of "the fear of the powerlessness of theory [...] that itself concedes to the powerlessness of theory" (*MM* 49). Raspe makes explicit why Hippius is one of those intellectuals whose behavior is a dead end. Within *Irre*, Hippius is another "whose critical idealism will be ground up without fail in the institutions" (42). For punk, the past had proven the impossibility of altering the effects of discourse within any institution, be it prison, an asylum, or a university.

Hippius illustrates the limitations of '68 because he does not traverse the boundary between inside and outside, asylum and city. His fixed location limits his ability to protect patients; the change he can enact is bound within the asylum's borders. Within these borders Hippius's "unconventionality, [...] has gotten some things moving, yes, here he has a not entirely unimportant function, it doesn't have to be immediately called political, a humanizing function, a destabilization of all of the super-adjusted colleagues, [...] a destabilization, that, in the last instance, serves the patients." Andreas incites this destabilization in the asylum by changing the comfortable conditions of sartorial discipline: he has a ponytail. A system that Hippius disturbs "already through his hair," the asylum reads this ponytail as "a diversion from the narrow-minded conception of normalcy." Hippius's disturbance challenges the doctors' sartorial narrow-mindedness, a stylistic tradition homologous of the ossification of medical practice such as electroshock therapy. Although Hippius's is a moment of change, his behavior becomes normal to the doctors in the asylum. Hippius's actions become nonthreatening because doctors stabilize it once these subtle changes are inscribed in the history of the asylum in the minutes from doctors' meetings.[16] Furthermore, Hippius's spontaneity, his putative radical position within the institution, is nothing like that of the punks' rampaging in Munich. His potentially subversive diversions from the norm are quite literally a joke. Raspe recounts how the hippie "greeted those around him with one of the spontaneous jokes that are expected from him. Then he was quiet and ate" (40–42). Worse than his comedic role in the asylum, Hippius's behavior is predictable. Bögel, one of Raspe's colleagues, drives the last nail in the coffin of '68 when he talks about the "the subcutaneous modification of the codes [...] in the wake of the student movements." What was this great modification of the codes of behavior? "Through a fine strategy of subversion," the doctors in the asylum could choose not to wear a necktie in the asylum. Bögel lays out the potential (resurrected) future of 1968, namely that if Raspe tries hard, he may be able to make it such that doctors can wear their jackets open (123). It would seem that anti-institutional discourse cannot change the effects of discourse in the domain of the asylum.

Here Raspe speaks explicitly to the ineffectiveness of anti-discourse without action for anything other than sustaining civilizing boundaries. He concludes that those who try to use medical discourse in the asylum in a new way "all say the same thing, one already knows the sentences, that then promptly come out." The students and hippies of '68 recognize that "this whole thing is just one giant patient, that goes nuts, gets medication, gets disturbed and goes berserk again, it's the same with all of them, and in that regard, as time passes, it becomes just a singular member, who always tells the same sorry family- and partner-stories, always the same" (40–41). Tellingly, *Irre* echoes punk's appraisal of and logic for differentiation from its subcultural forefathers. The hippies, students, and terrorists culled into the person of Hippius personify the singular strategy— "No"—against which punk resolutely positioned its "no future." The hippie in the asylum represents a potentially radical moment in *Irre* because he recognizes that medical discourse is the power exercised on the whole population. But this is a normalizing discourse of power, because the medical oppression of the population and the discourse of power are mutually reinforcing.[17] Hippius does not get outside of the institution and enact the change that the punk and doctor Raspe can, he operates exclusively within the discourse of medicine. He does not, as Raspe does, chaotically blur discourse, motion, noise, violence, inside, and outside. Hippius does not establish spaces where (medical) discourse can be turned on itself and made into a starting point for an oppositional strategy. This is what Raspe does. He subverts anti-institutional discourse into action, the possibility of which is provided by his own medical knowledge. If trapped inside the asylum, however, it can only be revised into something affirmative. Raspe, the punk psychiatrist, speaks directly to this when he thinks of his program versus that of the hippie-stand-in. "I wonder why Andreas was obviously so concerned with only saying definitively revision-proof statements as if any speculative sentence could be instantly used against him" (44). The other potentially radical doctor in the asylum is clearly constrained by adherence to the ideology of "absolute correctness" that could never lead to social transformation (*MM* 79). Hippius remains ineffective because what he says is destined for revision, destruction, or just becoming a sartorial bagatelle. Raspe knows "that in the clinic he as an individual can't change a thing, just as every other individual" (*Irre* 210). But he does not stay inside.

Raspe's schizophrenic movements take medical discourse outside the asylum and bring punk chaos inside the asylum, and he speaks of this back and forth. Absolutely committed to motion, he recounts how "once I was inside. Since then I run in a panic away from it. That's why I always have to go back inside" (240). Raspe does not allow himself to be limited or terminated by external boundaries between sanity and insanity; the punk in the asylum has more liberty because other doctors never understand what he is doing, but also because he harnesses what the patients know. He learns from them, "Through them he wanted to learn how to understand, how we could, without psychology, learn to speak of ourselves anew" (261). Raspe moves from location to location, and within each arena, he is twitching, muttering, running, and rioting like a madman. Raspe must harness schizophrenia because then the text has to deal with his actions: "The world has to deal with my mania" (282). Additionally, insanity inspires unpredictability and indecipherability in his motion. "Going, Standing, Going, its all the same, keep going. If I were to lay down, I couldn't go. Because I have to go, I don't lie down. Because I don't lie down, I go" (12). The "Going, Standing, Going" represents a moment of physical resistance to the narrative strictures (borders) placed upon Raspe and his body.[18] These metaphorical strictures have become, through the civilizing processes of modernity, metaphorical and naturalized as a part of citizens' identity. The schizophrenics are interred because their identity doesn't conform to the norm, they do not recognize these natural disciplinary codes. This lack of recognition creates innumerable—and unpredictable—points of confrontation and instability.[19] Raspe magnifies these moments in both milieus. Each moment, taken outside its strategic and state-organized border into a third space, creates an in-between that produces at least temporary inversions of power relations. In the novel, the doctors seem to control the patients and Raspe is denied a clear victory. Raspe even questions his own project in the last line of the novel: "Is it ultimately unified, my work?" (331).[20] However, this conception of "control" and the apparent pessimistic conclusion of the novel diminish the importance of Raspe's moments of resistance. Indeed, the impact of these localized moments are inscribed in *Irre* itself by the effects that they induce on the entire network in which they are caught up. The history of these moments, the novel itself, is in the history of the asylum, the written narratives that Raspe creates after his fleeting bed-visits, and the chaos of Raspe's "Aktionen" in Munich (60). Whereas Hippius represents institutional discourse, Raspe uses the technique of montage to expose the insidious nature of discourse by exploring the fluidity of inside and outside. Both Fottner and Hippius are ineffective in *Irre* because they do not cull medically powerful discourse and a liminal position between the asylum and the outside. *Irre* tests how Raspe interfaces psychotic behavior with psychiatry to create subversive use of knowledge through motion. This is what makes Raspe so special. He uses his motion to create a third space between the asylum and the punk scene.

Cells—Pubs—Studios: Motion and Stasis

Irre juxtaposes Raspe's movements and performances with a list of postwar agent provocateurs (various authorities, artists, punks, and other schizophrenics) who remain either inside or outside. The latter three figures—K., Wolfgang, and Bernd—are foils for Raspe's anarchistic use of knowledge. Raspe drinks a lot of beer with his friend K., a psychiatrist turned artist, who "considers [...] the so-called crazies the normal ones." K. does not seek to change the operations of the asylum, and "comes well-enough to terms with the insanity of normalcy" (38). After a schizoid monolog between Raspe and himself on how one can sedate patients, the desired effects of such sedations, and the ultimate uselessness of these "treatments," the following discussion takes place between Raspe and K.:

- – Insanity Insanity Insanity, Insanity I say, that is revolt.
- – Bullshit.
- – Logically, insanity is revolt, it's art, man!
- – Uh-huh.
- – O.k., I am exaggerating, but if you had just read the things I did, from Laing and from Cooper.
- – It's all crap.
- – That is where the vague romantization of insanity ends, and what lets loose, is its necessary politicization, and on the edges even the opening of the artistic dimension of insanity. (31)

Having decided to make insanity his strategy to resist modern divisions of life, Raspe's iteration manifests itself through the aesthetic fusion—*Irre's* use of montage—of insanity, violence, and the logic of interminable emergency law. The necessary politicization and the inevitable eruption of the artistic dimension of insanity both outside the clinic and inside the city is the kind of immanent social critique that could break the duality of art as autonomous entity or social phenomenon. Against a mere "critical oscillation" wherein autonomous art founds reactionism and social art founds self-negation (*AT* 368), Raspe's attempt to radicalize the clinic, what he calls the "courage to face the CONSEQUENCE OF PATHOS," is not scared of mistakes and, as been shown, explicitly channels self-destruction because he has to work out something much more difficult, "namely the truth about everything" (330). As an artist, K. holds a similar privileged position, one that can harness psychosis for productivity. Although he seeks to mine this relation, K. maintains a position outside the asylum and his artistic attempt to expose the unchecked power of medical discourse fails. Raspe's punk friend Wolfgang recognizes, as K. does, the psychoses-inducing project of society. Wolfgang notes that West Germany is a "society that consistently makes its members sick, above all psychotically sick, and helps psychiatry to survive. You [Raspe] heal the people, who because of their sickness react correctly to the inverted conditions of their lives, for no other reason, than so that they can once again function in the conditions that made them sick." Society makes its members' psyches sick; those who recognize this operation are destined for the asylum. Wolfgang understands the role medical discourse plays in society, but he is not a doctor, he is merely an intelligent member of the Marxist student group at the university. Though he accurately spells out the Marxist dialectic of sanity in society, Wolfgang does not negotiate the inside/outside divide between the mechanisms of control and those subjected to this control. Wolfgang's isolated and permanent position, his dialectics ("rakish method") represent only part of his limitation.[21] The more fundamental lack is that he has no access to medicine. Thus, though he recognizes the asylum's function, Wolfgang's "formulating lips briefly effect the situation, they freeze everything, but nothing else" (154–155). Wolfgang recognizes the bankrupt nature of the asylum, but all he does is obscure the individual with the general while numbing his audience into a catatonic state with his endless discourse, a problem with radical theory and social transformation that reemerges in the next chapter.[22] Wolfgang's inability to do anything with this knowledge underscores the importance of Raspe and K.'s medical knowledge, and the uniqueness of Raspe's dual role as doctor and punk. Against the choking immanence of mechanically operating theory, montage opens up *Irre*'s aesthetic dimension of insanity. While in and out does not exist for the asylum—the laws of insanity and internment govern daily life—Raspe exposes and subverts the insidious nature of this differentiating discourse by creating a chaotic space of violence and anti-discourse. In *Irre*, this aesthetic dimension is opposed by the law governing and determining illness, a "law of sickness, a law of medication." Despite being "trapped in the control of this law" the patients try to resist: "fighting forwards, wake up, wanting to wake up out of this nightmare, but already knowing with the first scream, that this is not a dream, but rather a reality following a foreign, insane law" (37).

The asylum constructs a system of strategic positions, a condition whose effects, Foucault argues, are "manifested and sometimes extended by the position of those who are dominated."[23] Fottner, for example, must be constantly kept in a catatonic state to prevent him from becoming a *moving* danger. A perfect location for the "misunderstanding of concentrated power and diffuse powerlessness," the asylum is a dialectical space wherein the dominated can exert power over their ruler by forcing the doctors to take bizarre actions (*MM* 233). That the conditions of possibility of the public sphere rest indeed upon such a masochistic contract fulfilled in secrecy—yet demanded by the polis—is what *Irre* posits as the heritage of the sixties and seventies, violently inflected in the eighties. This is particularly evident in the "torture chamber," wherein doctors still subject patients to electroshock therapy that, in *Irre*, has long been debunked as medically sound (97). Doctors grasp at electroshocks and lithium in an attempt to decode the scrambled and seemingly meaningless systems of the insane. Raspe's brief exposure to the medical director of the asylum Meien "the Shocker" was "horror from this violent therapy" (187–189). Surpassing the horrifying images that remain in Raspe's mind—"terrifying images of the faces, subjected to the electric stream, that cramped into revolting grimaces"—is the doctor's acceptance of the electroshock as a means to impede motion by destroying cognition (189).[24] The most crucial aspect of the shock, Meien tells Raspe, is amnesia. "If we shock below the seizure threshold or not long enough and we do not trigger a bout," Meien details, "then we don't get the retrograde amnesia, you understand, then the patient remembers the entire procedure, he remembers fear and pain" (95–96). Nowhere else in *Irre* is there a more clear parallel to what Adorno and Horkheimer called "Le prix du progrès." Their price of progress is the codified use and misunderstood effects of chloroform—that, rather than numbing, merely induces amnesia of the excruciating pain experienced during an operation; a parable for the transcendental conditions of science and totalitarian system of Enlightenment philosophy (262–263). In *Irre* this tragic dialectic of pain and forgetting that objectivizes subjects has become just like Raspe's Carnival self-mutilation "perfectly fooling" for the mainstream and is precisely what Raspe wants to ask the Federal Republic if it is willing to accept.

The conflict for both Raspe's willed amnesia and patients' forced amnesia remains one of the schizophrenic motion "fighting forwards" and psychiatric ossification "trapped in control." The medications and electroshocks are the doctors' only recourse to prevent the effectiveness of schizophrenics' breaking of borders. In the end, the doctors succeed in preventing the kind of "compelling awakening" that Benjamin theorized would be the drastic refutation of "everything 'gradual' about becoming." Although the "Copernican turn of remembrance" is forestalled, because those interred in the asylum do not recognize the systems of codes that would normally lead to a state of control over their bodies, the asylum's task becomes much more difficult (*AP* K1,3).[25] The interred of the asylum in *Irre* have the potential to subvert the asylums strategy for domination over the insane patient's body; the insane create a network of relations that the doctors in the asylum cannot decipher. Because of this, the relations between the control mechanisms and the schizoid are constantly those of tension, active, rather than stable ones of discipline and control for mainstream society. This is why miming insanity is so crucial for Raspe if he hopes to successfully wrest himself from the clutches of internment laws. Raspe gets outside of the confines of schizophrenic anti-discourse located within the asylum through revolutionary psychiatry. Specifically, he parlays his brand of punk psychiatry with R. D. Laing's reading of schizophrenia. The doctors in the asylum dismiss Raspe's uptake of Laing's anti-psychiatry as "All-seeing stupidities" (200). Laing is an uncontrollable freak in their eyes and Raspe is chastised by Dr. Beyerer for trying to bring Laing into the asylum's lecture hall:

> Your mental masturbations, you can spout that off on someone else. You can babble at someone else with your mother fucking Laing [...] and if you want, then you can come into the clinic for once. Then I'll show you a psychotic. [...] Then you can see. The crazies are just crazy. Laing and his mental-jerk-off has nothing there. The insane are just crazy. You can see for yourself. (32)

Ironically, the doctor seeking to debunk Laing works within the dyadic structure against which Laing explicitly argues.[26] The opposites and thresholds Raspe seeks to fuse and transverse are prominent in the above quote ("come into the clinic"). The quote features an outside and inside, a city diametrically opposed to the clinic, a boundary that one does not *normally* cross ("come into the clinic *for once*"). Thus, the doctor calling Laing a fraud embodies one of those psychiatrists, to summarize Laing, who is not prepared to get to know what goes on outside the clinic, an ivory tower academic who faces the same criticism as former '68ers.[27]

Raspe taps into anti-psychiatry in the vein of Laing, but he harnesses motion to push beyond the familial structures lurking in Laing's own analyses. To put theory into action, Raspe must get out of the clinic. "On one side the good narcotics, the music-actions and the anarchy-scene," Raspe thinks, "on the other side work in the clinic" (60). This does not set up a dyad of inside and outside because Raspe continuously traverses and confuses the divide between asylum and pub. It is clear that this is not something abnormal for him, as he recounts "I go around in the scene since then as an outsider, and I am, logically, more of an insider than ever" (235–236). Raspe must move back and forth between the asylum and the punk scene because "to stand nicely on the correct side, anyone can do that." His breaking borders and movements would be nothing if they did not return to reshuffle the asylum and develop "the next subversive strategy" (330–331).[28] Deleuze and Guattari's writings on anti-psychiatry are crucial here because they argue on behalf of new, dynamic representations and theorize the creation of a new social order that counters juridicio-medico discourse and its modern boundaries. *Irre* uses avant-garde motion that does not seek unity, balance, or progress; it prolongs punk's "no future" with the apocalyptic chaos of Munich, medicine, violence, motion, text, and image. Whereas for patients such cognitive blind spots engendered their internment, amnesia, the result of barbaric medicine, is exactly what Raspe seeks out. He willingly submits himself to the social pathogenesis of schizophrenia, but at its inverse. The Cartesian heritage of the Enlightenment, Adorno argues, ultimately transformed the subject into "empty, excitable shells"; in other words, into objects. Through Raspe's remapping of space and misuse of laws, he deconstructs objects and language in his arsenal to create an indecipherable fragment of dialects for his "unconditional attack" (222).[29] Deleuze and Guattari argue that schizophrenics experience their bodies as a random jumble of fragmented parts as well as a solidified, unindividuated mass; the schizoid body becomes, for them, a "body without organs." Raspe uses chaotic motion and medical knowledge and as such represents the possibility of that deterritorialization of the self and the public sphere. His performance of schizophrenia and the possibility of making real Deleuze and Guattari's body without organs culminate in the chaotic montage of *Irre's* third section. The novel retells, deconstructs, and misuses its own stories; it never gives the same explanation or reads the same event in the same way.[30] Following his schizophrenic patients, Raspe invents his own frenetic movements that produce unforeseen breaches. Movement provides Raspe with the way out of the dead end, out "of the question [of hell or salvation . . .] go and speak. Break out of the narrow-mindedness" (12–13). The asylum—for *Irre* the institution of literature—seeks to assign a causal process that produces anomalies and threats. Raspe disrupts this as a self-medicating, self-inflicting doctor to scramble through aesthetic violence inside and outside into an anarchistic third space.

Asylum—Munich—Klagenfurt:
Herr S. versus Raspe versus Goetz

Raspe declares that "the world has to deal with my mania" (282). If the world—*Irre*—deals with his mania, then the novel indicts itself as part of the problem it seeks to resist. Texts in the novel are immediately dismissed as unbearable, lumped together with the rest of the garbage, stinking, rotting, piled up all over the narrator's room. On the first page of the narrative the unnamed "I" asks "Had I ever opened a book and heard something other than this droning, unbearable droning in the ears, louder with each sentence?" (11). *Irre's* opening literary salvo against literature (as previously seen with Rolf Lobeck's "blablatext" and Glaser's "explosé") represents a turn to anarchistic hate in order to harness the potential of schizophrenia in the aesthetic realm of literary production. Juxtaposing asylum and punk violence, *Irre* ignores divisions and sets its protagonist in chaotic motion. The asylum's patients in *Irre* are decentered schizophrenics, capable of infusing chaos into Munich, capable of becoming instable bodies and subjectivities. Within the novel, however, these new bodies and subjectivities fail; the patients stay in the asylum. Raspe's is the lone moment of escape, and the "anarchistic-creative potential" of Raspe's chaotic-psychotic movements becomes the novel's own anarchistic montage. Tracing Raspe's progress, his experimentation with ornamentation, with breaking borders, and with performing insanity represents the aesthetic output, the culmination and combination of Raspe's actions as "observer and collector" (260). Raspe rips at his organs of communication, in effect ripping at the novel's literary constraints, to prevent *Irre* from introducing meaning, order, or binaries. He demonstrates the constraints exerted by (medical) discourse upon his body—here a metonym for *Irre*—while simultaneously using his medical knowledge to achieve damage. Raspe "immediately wanted to poke out both his eyes with sewing needles and then immediately stab again in thalamic regions, [...] and then kill the memory in the back lobe" (328–329). Raspe attacks parts of his brain that are vital for deorganization: vision, the thalamic region (which ensures coordinated functioning of the brain), and memory. This produces fissures and gaps in cognition and thoughts, damage that creates chaos, an unorganized head. *Irre* uses Raspe's violence to his own body—his performance of insanity and his desire to damage his brain—to misappropriate images and texts. *Irre* thereby tests out the spectrum of shock and the effect of an anarchic breaking of borders within a body of literature, the novel. Ruptures in the neat divisions of this literary world create gaps, thresholds, and conditions for movement. Movement is a sign of affect and affect is a body in motion. "In thinking there is something energetic that comes out of affect: goals, content, tempo, fluidity, and the manner of thinking orient themselves to the momentary interests, needs, and goals" (255). *Irre* does not use Raspe's motion for programmatic proclamations, but rather ignores divisions between the asylum and Munich and the punk scene in order to create a dynamic and entropic text, an avant-garde montage that prolongs a schizophrenic release from stasis.

Punk in *Irre* set in motion the world that punk forefathers S.Y.P.H. experienced in their moment of defeat as pure concrete. *Irre* is the recipe for making real the impossible dream in S.Y.P.H.'s "Zurück zum Beton."

If S.Y.P.H. failed to make a better terrorist out of Klar by fusing him with punk's subversive aesthetics, then *Irre*'s absolute unhinging of empirical details of law, place, and subjectivity, seems to be the triptych necessary for any escape from the culture industries' oppressive rhetoric of citizenship and revolutionaries' fetishization of foreign icons. *Irre*, Goetz's early writing, and his bloody performance seem to have detonated a kind of aesthetic "social warhead," for the punk Raspe is not bound by binaries, such as state surveillance, mass media, terrorists, and sympathizers as the punk Klar was.[31] *Irre* undoes the concrete dystopia, the place where terrorists and hippies were institutionalized and ineffective. It all goes back to Klagenfurt: performing insanity, bridging this with medically powerful discourse, wielding this aesthetically, making the text more than a text, making the text a weapon, like a razor blade. The self-inflicted damage, Raspe's ornamentation, is precisely the conscious investment in something that *Irre* acknowledges as corrupt, without purporting to be outside this corruption, that creates the potential for subversive moments. This is what happened at Klagenfurt. The split personality of the narrative in *Irre* makes it possible for the text to have effects outside of itself. *Irre* matches the schizophrenic confusion of location with damage inflicted to organs of communication and literary production; the final parts of the text to be consumed are not just texts, but images as well: the novel cuts the splintering story to insert images of Goetz and Goetz's artistically altered body, bringing the outside in (297–298). But a more literal assault on communication and borders is underway in *Irre*. Ears, eyes, mouths, and fingers are bleeding and under attack in this novel. The first inmate presented in the novel is Herr S., whose "fingertips are deeply jagged, scarred, bloody. Herr S. rips at the remains of his fingernail, rips a piece out of the nail bed. It bleeds." This self-destruction is not a random act. Quite oppositely, Herr S.'s is an attempt to uncover everything, "freilegen" (15). For *Irre*, the self-inflicted violence exerted by Herr S. to his body does not constrain the state's capacity to negotiate this damage for control because any static resistant gesture is co-optable. That condition becomes evident after stacking up Herr S.'s self-infliction against Raspe's self-infliction.

The logic of self-infliction—that it misuses the power-knowledge of medicine—emerges through Raspe's damage to his body. In his own effort to free everything ("freigeben"), his damage removes Raspe from normative modes of constraint through its use of destruction to reach a state of "self-abolition" (19 and 35). The story of this process, the novel *Irre*, represents Raspe's resulting aesthetic production, which he uses to "spit, […] snot, and vomit in the lying face of all that clinic shit" (35–36). Here the clinic must be expanded to include the literary audience Goetz attacked in Klagenfurt. Herr S.'s "freilegen" and Raspe's "freigeben" are both acts that seek to annihilate their unified existence. However, Herr S. is a failure. He "returns into his time- and nameless world" (15). Raspe's "Blutrinnsalen," the sinuous flows of blood subject only to laws of gravity, move him, like "Subito," from sphere to sphere. Raspe's self-abolition is the dream of the creation of a desubjectified nomadic body. Raspe turns to punks and schizophrenics to make clear that "the only one, who can hold together this insane project, is logically a brightly insane and simultaneously insanely bright I" (279). Raspe is clearly in a bind. He clearly suffers form the same slipperiness of space and of heroism as thematized in "klammheimlich." While the insane in the asylum represent a blueprint for his performance—ultimately his quest for a body without organs— his performance is not insanity, he isn't interned in the asylum. His self-mutilation is not heroic, it is mimetic of the violence in discourse that Foucault outlines. Raspe is not Deleuze and Guattari's organless body. He is an "ICH"—an I—who seeks self-abolition but knows that his complete success will permanently leave him in the asylum (279). Thus by cutting himself, the sign of the body without organs threatens to become a sign of his own immanent internment in the asylum, it threatens to make "it all unified, [his] work" (331). This is the reason why, or better, the internal logic why Goetz did not win at Klagenfurt. It is not the body, but *Irre*, that stands proxy, vial self-mutilation, performance of insanity, and motion, for a true heroism. It is just a performance in the end.

CHAPTER THREE

POST-PUNK POACHING, SUBVERSIVE CONSUMERISM, AND READING FOR ANTI-RACISM

By the end of 1980 the musicians had become the better writers.
The book of the year was an LP:
                    "Monarchy and Daily Life" by Fehlfarben.[1]

After 1979, the spectacularly anarchic and antagonistic moment of punk and "no future" was no more. Although for Peter Hein and Fehlfarben it was well past its prime, the case of the punk-psychiatrist Raspe demonstrates that disappearing by means of subversive adaptation and destabilized positions continued to be the 1983-logic behind a punk escape from affirmative social intervention. In light of *Irre's* project, Fehlfarben's dismissal of punk—that it was "too late"—would seem wrong. To square the band's dismissal with punk's chaotic afterlife in *Irre,* Fehlfarben's invective must be understood as an avant-garde imperative à la "no future": it was attuned to a radical futurity for punk to become something else. If focused on the performance of insanity as with Raspe, then *Irre's* internalization of its present's juridico-medico malaise is one example of how punk's "no future" did not die insofar as it continuously took on other lives. Drawing on literary and sonic markers, this chapter examines the realization of both imperatives—"no future" and "too late"—in the form of a subversively affirmative post-punk existing prior to, concurrent with, and after *Irre* and S.Y.P.H.'s chaotic fusion of knowledge, power, and motion. True to the unique musical-literary quotient of West German punk, when post-punk picked up strikingly different materials to counter hegemonic stabilization in West Germany's eighties, the resulting transformation created within youth subcultures musicians, witness Peter Glaser's assertion in the epigraph above, as arbiters of critical discourse. Punk's sonic and visual insurrection depended precisely on the replacement of ivory tower voices because daily life for punk bore out the unmistakable legacy and ineffective critique of the Frankfurt School in the practically and theoretically inescapable economic miracle-cum–state of emergency. That reality, as the banality of Fehlfarben's album artwork for "Monarchy and Daily Life" that this book's cover illustrates, offered nothing but a flat landscape of tenements and the chimera of contentedness. Indicative of the dialectical tensions between factions of punk and between punk and the mainstream, the year 1983 highlights the continuing relevance and realization of Fehlfarben's demand for a new form of subversive punk élan: Goetz's Klagenfurt performance and *Irre's* publication alongside the ascension of an affirmative form of punk in bands such as Nena and Die toten Hosen. While the trap of *Irre* was made clear above, bands that came to represent punk in the mainstream neither represented an original punk ethos nor had they perfected S.Y.P.H.'s apocalyptic wasteland from "klammheimlich." Quite the contrary—Nena, for example, reestablished stable divisions between performer and audience, consumer and commodity, and producer and distributor. Straightforwardly miming mainstream angst vis-à-vis the Cold War and thereby confirming Adorno's lack of faith in popular music, punk in Nena's hands broadcast an affirmative syntax and vocabulary. This negation of punk style—a domestication of dilettantism—makes unmistakable the fact that despite the chaos, anarchy, and self-destruction of its schizophrenic uses of representation, punk was subsumed by the culture industry. But this was only the fruition of its willed failure.

The unlamented loss of any original punk moment is the enactment of punk's resolute opposition to any sacred, timeless position. Bands in the eighties such as Palais Schaumburg, Der Plan, Andreas Dorau und die Marinas, and Freiwillige Selbstkontrolle (FSK) unfolded a dialectical relationship with Mittagspause's apocalypse to give rise to a form of punk discordant with this original nomenclature; they show how rather than one of progress, post-punk's relation to its punk past is one of actualization and emergence out of a destructive verve. Instead of mourning the demise of its 1977 iteration, post-punk was absolutely contingent on and "determined by the images that [were] synchronic with it" (*AP* N3,1). Not a seamless sequence from failed anarchy into an unwanted future, post-punk bands' interest in shifting and transforming constellations of cultural representation induced a series of historical forms, an extension and transformation of punk in reaction to a different historical context. The rise of conservative politics with Helmut Kohl and Ronald Reagan, the "Bitburg Incident" (Reagan's wreath laying at a cemetery with Waffen-SS graves), new tensions between the American military presence and West Germany's pacifist citizenry, the emergence of the Green Party in 1983, and the demise of the first generation of German terrorists and the ascension of the second and third forced punk in the eighties to shift. It could not be solely interested in scrambling space to highlight the insanity of sanity or in S.Y.P.H.'s dialectical trap. Through its investment in representation and consumption as a strategy against stabilized or affirmative instances of punk, post-punk must be understood as what Lawrence Grossberg has defined as a mattering machine able to contradict the "consumer economy's attempt to regulate the structures and rhythms of daily life."[2] To this end, post-punk used the same media—fanzines, art, and music—but massaged them to unleash products able to subvert the integrating effects of standardized political arguments against bourgeois ideology always already subsumed, Adorno argues, under a "process of standardization" (MM 235). The secret history of this transformation and of punk's subversive consumption can be read exceptionally through the band FSK and its member Thomas Meinecke's short fiction. Together they demonstrate a productive aftershock of Fehlfarben's demand and a synchronous engagement with literature and music for punk's project of "no future." Within the hegemonic context of a version of punk produced by the culture industry, FSK and Meinecke shifted from chaotic insanity to voluntary and pleasure-oriented consumerism to attack the thing that had attacked, and consumed, punk. This chapter poses FSK and Meinecke as representative of a post-punk allegiance to counter-hegemonic media consumption, a form of agency able to escape the vortex of unreconciled violence, fascism, and racism. Understanding their tactics requires assaying the problems and sources of media in West Germany; in the eighties no other media conglomerate affected the Federal Republic more than America's. To illustrate their unique post-punk fight against the effects of nonindigenous culture, the importation of which threatened to obscure the historical precedence and contemporary persistence of German fascism with American racism, the following shows how the band and Meinecke's musical-literary production constitutes stereoscopic counterproducts. The nuances of those songs and texts attained the innocuous subtleness of the culture industries' products, yet at their core they aspired to rupture the latter's stable classification and organization of agency and identity.

Affirmation as Resistance

In 1980, Freiwillige Selbstkontrolle (voluntary self-censorship), the name for Germany's equivalent to North America's parental advisory system for cinematic releases, performed its first concert in Hamburg's Markthalle.[3] The band's self-titled first release followed the same year. Thomas Meinecke, one of the four founding members of the band, recalled that during FSK's second performance in the Prunksall of the Munich Art Academy "the audience erupted immediately into a massive fight.

Because of what we were representing there. They didn't know: Is that a sect? Are they being paid by the GDR? Are they fascists?"⁴ This anecdote highlights a strategic and aesthetic adaptation of punk into post-punk: whereas S.Y.P.H. were surprised by their aesthetic bomb, FSK surprised the punks, they overcame their audience's vulgar expectation of punk. Via its indecipherable fusion of fascists, socialists, and punks, FSK split an apocalyptic atom to harvest residual energy from the culture industries and subcultures' "hollowing out" of punk. By blasting punk out of the historical continuum of the early eighties, FSK prevented punk's "no future" from attaining the fixity of the status quo. Their second concert is an example of that strategy, of how they complicated the index of participation in subversive aesthetics to complicate general understandings of the consuming life in late capitalism. The logic behind the band's melee-inducing escape from the media black hole of representation and consumption—a crisis that threatened to normalize punk—can be read through the song that caused the fight. "Moderne Welt" (Modern world), in which FSK affirms a West Germany consumed by Americanized popular culture, was a moment in which the chorus "We say Yes! to the modern world" represented for FSK the greatest means for political dissidence.⁵ Sung by Michaela Melián and Wilfried Petzi with a vocal style miming the Velvet Underground's Nico, "Moderne Welt" is a call for passion and feeling in a world where people could really be "totally in love with this world" even though "it breaks some hearts." Through their song about the affirmation of capital, FSK avoided falling into what Adorno reads as the trap of the culture industries—wherein music "degenerates to ideology"—because they refused to hide the contradiction and intractability of market forces and aesthetic autonomy (*DA* 181). Instead, FSK assimilated contradictions into their own productions: they transformed folk song rhythms by using a violin to simulate a speaker screaming with feedback, an itchy background noise in stark contrast to the deadpan and listless, cyclical repetition of lyrics. They thereby mocked the affirmative syntax of the new and recathected youthful passion with cultural stagnation. Thus, despite the flatly affirmative refrain—FSK sings "It doesn't get any better than right here" and "We are o.k.!"—this song does not envision as complicitously dreary a situation as it must have sounded to the punks fighting in the audience.

FSK's complex, multinational, and multimedial praxis took advantage of the detritus in an increasingly Americanized pop culture of consumption to confuse what punk was. "Moderne Welt" demonstrates perfectly how the band's intricate instance of post-punk contradicted fatalistic visions of a mindless consumer devoid of agency; it unmasks Germany's huge offering of available identities and West Germans' fantasies of being

Superman, mandolin players, of looking like military officers, or of isolating themselves in a nice book. The opposite of delusional, these dreams are targeted as representative of an everyday, contingent wealth of social identities, meanings, and pleasures available. Such identities, crucially, are not prescriptive, but rather available to Germans in "Moderne Welt" for transformation—for misuse—as they see fit. The possibility of such identity production through media consumption, as Alexander Kluge writes on the dialectic of cinematic experience and authenticity, hinges on the audience's attentiveness vis-à-vis inter- and extra-medial orientation. The principle of authenticity—a retainer from bygone eras for punk—can thereby escape mainstream media's dominance over individuality when listeners "test and decide" the personal relevance of "reality and appearance [*Schein*] at a given point."[6] Thomas Meinecke's cybernetic manifesto "New tips: Twilight in Western-Europe 1981" relatedly argues that by affirming the conditions of consuming life in late capitalism, by saying yes to the modern world, FSK differentiated itself starkly from "the dumbest and nevertheless most noteworthy generational-comrades [who] quickly reached their final conception of the world, [while] we cyberneticians reexamine our methods of thought and action through their adaptability for the modern world, which is constantly transforming."[7] Punk's insanity produced stasis, seen above all in S.Y.P.H.'s problem with concrete or the immanent internment of *Irre's* Raspe. Meinecke's manifesto in FSK's fanzine *Mode & Verzweiflung* concludes that if the culture industry was subsuming, confining, and transmitting its own commercially viable versions of punk, if punk was mired in concrete, then punk's apocalyptic chaos had to transform.

Assaulting the mainstreaming of successfully marketable versions of punk, FSK escaped the threat of commercial, legal, and aesthetic internment by poaching media. They constructed a constantly shifting constellation of television news reports, voices, sounds, and images by consuming and using these materials in unintended ways. The paradoxical reaction to FSK's show was a reaction to their complex and contradictory mix of punk, electronica, and American and German country, musical genres they combined with political, revolutionary, violent, and banal lyrics. Through that complex matrix, this chapter unveils how, despite the hegemonic context of 1980s' West Germany, this condition did not, as Grossberg argues for rock music, "incorporate resistance but construct[ed] positions of subordination which enabl[ed] active, real and effective resistance."[8] In what follows, FSK and Meinecke's subversive consumerism and their misappropriation of and unanticipated participation in West German popular culture testify to a specifically Teutonic post-punk moment of resistance. And one cannot put too fine a point on their counter-hegemonic media consumption: FSK and Meinecke's fight against that which ate punk also targeted what Oskar Negt and Alexander Kluge together call the public sphere of production. Despite their assessment of the "decaying forms of the bourgeois public sphere" under capitalism, Negt and Kluge theorize in *Public Sphere and Experience* the possibility of subversive products.[9] Crucial for reading FSK and Meinecke's iteration of post-punk, this early eighties' Marxist text insists that poaching is relevant for creating a counter-public sphere. Producers in precisely such a domain, FSK and Meinecke mis-used what Negt and Kluge called "traditional media [...] (for instance, press, publishing, cinema, adult education, radio, television, etc.) [...to create] **counter-products of a proletarian public sphere: idea against idea, product against product, production sector against production sector**" (149 and 79–80).[10] But there is a tension between what FSK and Meinecke did to media and what forms of media Negt and Kluge insist aid the creation of a counter-public sphere. The latter argue that most tele-vision does not provide the raw material that viewers can use to create a counter-public sphere. Whereas network television is antithetical to the creation of a counter-public sphere, "classical media," such as radio, news-papers, and movies, are exactly what should be mined.[11] Despite their use of popular media such as "Dallas," FSK and Meinecke's post-punk poach-ing of television separates itself from Negt and Kluge's critique of the fate of the bourgeois public sphere under late capitalism through an investment in the subversive agency of reading.

In this respect, FSK and Meinecke follow John Fiske, who argues that any television show, any media broadcast, represents something that the viewer can subvert for his or her own oppositional sphere. Negt and Kluge argue explicitly for a counter-public sphere, which is exactly wherein FSK and Meinecke operated. They did this, though, by using what Fiske calls "excorporation," in which elements of dominant culture are stolen and used for private, "often oppositional or subversive interests" (315). While there is a discrepancy between Negt and Kluge and Fiske about the dif-ferent location of agency, in the medium or in its reception, the impor-tance lies in the broad agreement that media—television, photographs, radio, and film—presented FSK with opportunities to subvert hegemony and deterritorialize the public sphere.[12] Before and after Raspe's failure to do this on his person, FSK's music and Meinecke's short fiction unveils what the person qua producer can potentially achieve. While a necessary lack of cohesiveness dominates these musical and literary texts—a failure to congeal that multiplies the fields of analysis—diachronically reading FSK's songs and Meinecke's fanzine fiction characterizes and preserves the manifold ways in which post-punk resignified media to subvert hegemony. The praxis of FSK and Meinecke's media poaching, specifically of media that migrated in a loop between the United States and West Germany, and simultaneously the evidence of media poaching and of German problems with Americanism, is demonstrated perfectly by the song "I wish I could 'Sprechen Sie Deutsch?'"

Poaching the American Sector

For FSK, it was impossible to reflect on being West German in the eighties without talking about America, American consumerism, and American pop culture. Such nonindigenous culture was crucial for understanding the sonic and political space of the Federal Republic because differences between America and a Germany occupied by American soldiers since 1945 were anything but clear. Front and center on its album titles between 1984 and 1989—*Goes Underground, American Sector, In Dixieland,* and *Original Gasman Band*—this German-American matrix, if only by virtue of the English language, demonstrates how for FSK the foundation of popular culture in 1980s West Germany had its historical counterpart in the United States. More than narrating the transformation by American GIs of the American Sector of Germany into Dixieland, or a Dixieland inhabited by Gasmen, what FSK did was blur dominant divisions between, and stable representations of, America and Germany, of foreign culture in Germany.[13] This blurring mattered, for one, because in the eighties, and really since the student protests of the sixties, many Germans despised the United States and the ubiquitous presence of US military personnel in the Federal Republic (Willet 1–15). But FSK did not simply regurgitate terrorists or students' anti-American ethos in "the blind, rapidly expansive repetition of designated words" that Adorno argues commercializes and trivializes political speech and acts (*DA* 189).[14] FSK's blurring of putatively rigid boundaries, poaching from both America and Germany for their own means, created antagonisms that challenged not just failures in previous social moments, but the larger transnational public sphere as well. This blurring turned on its head the moment of "no future" and its celebration of Walter Benjamin's "destructive character" to seek out new coordinates for new constellations. While punk endeavored to prolong chaos in order to revel in Benjamin's intersections of ruins, post-punk sought to awaken from this nightmarish moment. Working through past and contemporaneous failures and misunderstandings without embarrassment, FSK interlinked what Kluge calls "horizons of perception" when they actively processed forms and conditions—normally ignored in daily life—constitutive of mainstream media.[15] Taking up a flexible position in the dialectic of producer and receiver, of media and medium, FSK's deceptively playful hit "I Wish I could 'Sprechen Sie Deutsch,'" from their

1987 album *American Sector,* simultaneously demonstrates this awakening, blurring, and media poaching.

Sung by Michaela Melián in fake English-accented German against polka-country sounds, "I Wish I could 'Sprechen Sie Deutsch?'" tells the story of an American GI in Frankfurt hanging out in bars. The agent provocateur "must have said something that meant something else," because the GI winds up in jail (orig. in English). Alas, the poor American never finds out the cause of the incarceration, whatever he has been told as a reason remains a mystery: "I nix verstehen" (I not understand). The remaining lyrics, guidebook phrases such as "another beer [...] a big one," suggest a vacuous exchange of stereotypes between Americans and Germans. Yet the line "I must have said something that meant something else," conversely, gestures to the cross-cultural misunderstandings in what could mistakenly be ignored as banal in the German-American lyrics. FSK's poaching created deliberate misunderstandings of the German-American fusion that became productive precisely in its adaptation of the boring. Hacking into an American soldier's quotidian discourse, FSK made no attempt to escape West German sociocultural malaise experienced by bored GIs or the stereotypical encounters between German pub owners and American patrons. Instead they used the boring, overlooked arrest of a rowdy drunk as the threshold to, and rhythmics for, transforming subversive sonics after 1977. The infusion of GI discourse into the Federal Republic—a transnationalization of its lingua franca—allowed for unpredictable results and productive misunderstandings of which Melián sings ("I not understand"). In addition to the lyrics' toying with the musical medium, the song's undulating guitar produces distorted tones, suggesting that the track is playing off speed. The temporality of the sound expands and lengthens into an irregular sonic moment as FSK's soundscape—obliquely channeling S.Y.P.H.'s—moves forward as it is constantly halted and slowed. Melián's throaty vocals match the other instruments as the lyrics become momentarily trapped by her vocal cords; voice and mechanical instruments combine to abstain from linear rhythmic sense and narrative flow, hinting that the song is disinterested in itself.

Such remixing of tempo and language makes possible a counter-reading of the GI-German linguistic combination. FSK's song demonstrates the presence of cultural flows, not dominance, and the bilateral nature of American–West German culture's transnational fusion in its misuse of the linguistic and acoustic hegemony brought by American GIs. Indicative of their deftness at heeding their manifesto's call for flexible identities, FSK used fantasies of Americans in Germany to yoke authenticity from the affirmative. But here authenticity in media, as Kluge posited in 1983, "is not just that a circumstance or form is correct. Authentic is the direct confrontation of collective surroundings and individuality." Correspondingly, FSK's fantasy of American agency in the Federal Republic does not obliterate Germans' own. America's installment of German political and economic leaders, the encroachment of capitalist American social norms, or Germany's population as proxy for the Cold War instigated the political exasperation and violent desperation of the students circa 1968 and the RAF, respectively. Inversely, FSK's song creates a "productive moment of individuality," wherein the fight over the constitution of identity in the Federal Republic shifted from the angst of the sixties and seventies to pleasure.[16] Recognizing what Benjamin calls the "bundle of instincts which society has a strong interest in repressing" (*AP* D4a,2), FSK's transnational fusion exhibits a theory of power that integrated into their products the phantasmagoria of German identity signaled by the mainstream's mythic refuge of tolerance and liberalism, of sociability and nostalgia, delusionally attached to the Enlightenment (*MV* 34). The band mimed this affirmative posture, but their musical and lyrical a-complimentary representation stands opposed to the "shallow rationalism" of faith in progress (*AP* D10a,5). The song's eerie closing—the sounds of boots marching in unison—is an unmistakable reference to the present-past, whereby Hitler's beer hall putsch threatens to resurface and become resignified in the march of bored and confused American soldiers across the Federal Republic. By highlighting the very real specter of the past in Germany's contemporary occupation by the United States, FSK brought to bear their "more radical modes of thinking and acting" against oversimplifications of consumption and agency in the increasingly leveled mainstream of the FRG (*MV* 35). Ultimate proof of FSK's theory of representation, though, remains in another cultural vector to "Sprechen Sie Deutsch?"

FSK pirated the song from an American country music single, "Danke Schön-Bitte Schön-Widersehen," recorded in Nashville, Tennessee by Saturday Records in 1961. The singer, Eddie Wilson, had big dreams of becoming a country music star. But instead of releasing the single in the United States, Saturday Records released it in West Germany to test its appeal to the GIs. Wilson's single topped out at number 17 on the German radio hit parade. Once the B-side only made it to number 25, it seemed as if his career was over. While FSK was not on a quest to resurrect Wilson's career, a failed country music singer nevertheless plays a central role in FSK's commitment to post-punk in 1987. Eddie Wilson was the American country music name of Stuttgart native and German emigrant Armin Edgar Schaible. Schaible's dream, inspired by GIs and Swiss folk music, was indeed to become a country music star in the United States.[17] This information in hand, mapping FSK's song becomes a difficult task. A

German native, inspired by the music American GIs listened to, dreamed of making this music himself under the guise of an American-sounding moniker. He immigrated to Tennessee, assumed an American name, and sang a song rife with stereotypes of American behavior in Germany. On the one hand, these could be German (i.e., Schaible's) stereotypes of GI behavior he saw in Stuttgart, on the other, American (i.e., Wilson's) stereotypes of what Americans saw as typical German behavior. A more complex appraisal would read them as a German's Americanized stereotypes of the sounds and images he consumed in the American Sector of Germany, transported across the Atlantic into America for consumption there only to be brought back.[18] The complex, bidirectional, and dynamic network of consumption and misrepresentation muddies the waters when discerning the impact of the GI-linguistic infusion into the song. Blatantly and ineloquently mashing American and German together, FSK's subversive praxis does not generate a seamless product. Instead it hints at the excess in cultural flows circulating in contemporary Germany; the historically ominous conclusion of that montage underwrites the band's logic for the acute need for such medial-political reorganization. Through its ever-layered and ostentatious linguistic articulation the song borders, but does not become, what Kluge calls a medial **"Babylonian speech-confusion."** As a result of its technological capabilities, mainstream media had the potential to present bureaucratized images that were of no use to the viewer because of their total assimilation and simplification of a better world. Acoustically and lyrically disavowing such simplification and facilitation of leveling, FSK's song springs the trans-Atlantic gaps—in Schaible/Wilson's song and in daily life with American GIs in West Germany—from the prison of "symbolic gravitations" that would annihilate the multiple possibilities of interactions between producers and materials as well as producers and receivers.[19]

To that end, tone and vocals become in this sonic montage shares of cultural capital resistant to any idée fixe of German or American identity. Notions of static GI language—schematically bound up and preorganized by the culture industries and political/military forces—are debunked once it is consumed and then regurgitated by a German trying to mime GIs. If other Germans consume the German's consumption, this song reveals, the effects of and participation in the bogeyman of American consumerism and the culture industry in the Federal Republic did not have to be passive. Through its subversive consumption of American products, FSK's participation in the cultural loop of Wilson's song and Schaible's description of GI behavior in Stuttgart testifies to multiple instances wherein a "stranger's position is taken up" and, as Kluge argues, "tested."[20] FSK thereby unmasks what Gerd Gemünden argues is a misconception of

Americanization or "American cultural imperialism." Far from a unified or unifying process, Gemünden unveils this process as one that "triggered a wide variety of responses." Not the outright, often simplified rejection of Americanization enacted by students or terrorists, FSK used American consumerism to remix Wilson's song and make public what Gemünden calls "the creativity of reception [that] deflects monolithic accounts of one culture imposing on another" (17). In FSK's hands, American consumerism is resignified into "a playground for the imagination and a site where the subject comes to understand itself through constant play and identifications with reflections of itself as an other" (19). As such, although sonically strikingly different, FSK's song must be understood within the avant-garde futurity of Fehlfarben's "too late" lyrics: through FSK's disavowal of national and temporal organization the second-order referent becomes self-reflexive, through migrating media the referent became the referent again. Thus the specter of a hegemonic American culture industry, FSK reveals, actually presented a complex network of appropriated representations—normally encouraging users to adopt false conceptions of their environment and their place therein—that could be tested and (re) combined in what Negt and Kluge call a "lengthy dispute" between social interests and media (*PS*1 49).[21]

FSK's collage rejected mainstream attempts to obscure as homogenous linguistically and culturally heterogeneous communicative possibilities. With the album name and the song FSK made a double move of indictment and appropriation, they created discord for clear delineations of the problem and solution, location and context, and message and media. FSK took punk and America and West Germany into their own hands; they remade and envisioned different modes of consumption as part of what Meinecke deemed "the tactically affirmative strategies of the early eighties" (*MV* 8). This strategy exposed gaps in representation—that in hands of culture industries "classify, organize and compile [...] so that no one can escape"—with which FSK could test a third path away from West Germany and Americanism (*DA* 144). As earlier the examples of S.Y.P.H. and *Die Düsseldorfer Leere* made clear, an escape from the hegemonic magnetic field compelling aesthetic normativity was not really possible. Thus instead of escape, the song "Sprechen Sie Deutsch?" turned inward as a means of getting out; in the band's hands, the latent aesthetic volatility tapped catalyzed the shifting manipulation of media poached from discourses in West German popular culture originally from the United States. This and other songs were about German fantasies of American consumerism transformed into a commodity for Germans; they reveal, ultimately, how these fantasies about the United States were always about Germans' own projections and fears. When they resignified to test what could be done with this material for subversive pleasures, when they demanded pleasure instead of fear and loathing, FSK ostentatiously displayed their poaching in unexpected ways to show how the consumer was completely administered and proscribed autonomy by the culture industries' aesthetic products (*AT* 33). The album *American Sector* makes clear that the revolution of which they sang three years earlier[22] or wrote six years' prior in their manifesto was anything but one-dimensional. Their revolution never became more concrete; FSK did not succumb to S.Y.P.H.'s failure because post-punk was about the possibility of a subversive space in media that could combat a salient crises of Americanization wherein the specter of racism threatened to efface the lingering presence of German fascism.

FSK's songs transformed the representation of culture in media into something else. They did not attack imaginary identities as a problem in contemporary West Germany, but rather saw the ability to bring Superman out of the cinema and onto the streets as crucial prerequisite for imagining new kinds of affective identification for West Germans. FSK stole objects from their context and gave them other uses but did not seek a unified work of art. Instead, FSK's cut ups sought what Hage calls literary montage's "divestiture of the construction principle," a revelation at the heart of Freiwillige Selbstkontrolle (66). Band members spelled out exactly such a modus operandi in their cybernetic manifesto "Neue Hinweise" when they demanded that they and others together "adapt our vigilance to the games and revolutions of the constantly changing situation: today disco, tomorrow revolution, the day after tomorrow an outing to the country. This is what we call voluntary self-censorship" (*MV* 36). Voluntary self-censorship—a mix of dancing, revolution, feigned-fascism, Americanism, and German nationalism—was a call for a kind of flexibility, an ability to transform media in the right way at the right moment. Clearly not a turn to punk chaos but rather to disquieting compliance, FSK's move relates them to Benjamin's flâneur. The quintessential observer of Paris's arcades, the flâneur principled in dialectical flexibility saw exterior as interior, landscapes as cityscapes, and past as present. This unsettling made him the phantasmagoric target of the police and counterpart to "revolutionary philosophemes of the period" (*AP* M2,7). The "double ground" upon which the flâneur walked, the simultaneous yoking of disparate banalities, is FSK's voluntary self-censorship: a carefully complicated consumption and misappropriation that destabilized stable relations between performer and audience as well as producer and consumer (M1,2). This complication of consumption used information management to bring punk's ethos back into motion through astute exploitation of ignored gaps in mainstream media.[23]

Media-Poaching for Literature

FSK's song "Sprechen Sie Deutsch?" constructed something new out of a transnational information exchange by delinking national representation from mainstream binaries. Their unruly consumption and transformation of punk under the specter of mass-media outlets in the eighties is further evidenced by FSK's Munich-based underground magazine *Mode & Verzweiflung* (Fashion & Despair) in which Thomas Meinecke published short fiction that poached news from mainstream presses. As was the case with FSK's treatment of Schaible's song, Meinecke's prose was intensely interested in remixing foreign material: his literary tracks examine the transmission and reassemblage of American culture in West Germany as a foil for the reassemblage of German culture via the United States. However, if FSK and Meinecke were interested in anything indigenous, then it was German history. To refunction these source materials, Meinecke's fanzine essays used radio and newspaper reports as raw materials for *Mode & Verzweiflung's* dispute with social interests and media through which they created the possibility of escape from what Kluge calls the "colonialization of consciousness."[24] Creating literary intersections of the unexpected, the stories draw upon a matrix of German and American history, information from fundamentally different spheres, such that questions arise, connections emerge or disappear, the important becomes banal, and the banal becomes informative. Meinecke pushed the confusion and manipulation of the medium further with his remixing of his already resignified stories in his collection *Mit der Kirche ums Dorf.*[25] More than a reshuffling, the literary maturation of the *Mode & Verzweiflung* project—*Mit der Kirche ums Dorf*—forecloses the complete understanding of singular media that for Kluge would be in lockstep with hegemony. Reading these two disjointed texts in tandem indexes the complex matrix of resignification in both and makes clear how *Mit der Kirche ums Dorf* put into action the cybernetic manifesto "New tips" from *Mode & Verzweiflung.*

Meinecke's essays in *Mode & Verzweiflung* represent counterproducts because they do not tell history but produce histories based upon poaching. A literary battleground on the field of West Germany's American popcultural hegemony, the fanzine created a cybernetic montage of subversive consumption to inspect German-American cultural transfer as a never-ending, vertiginous feedback loop that imagined new kinds of transitory identities. Narratives about Germans and Americans moving between America and Germany, about Germans moving around Germany, about pictures and postcards imported into Germany, and about American television shows that occupy Germans' time, *Mit der Kirche ums Dorf* enacted what Meinecke called in his 1986 obituary to the eighties, the "passionate praxis" necessary for post-punk to avoid any self-heroism or self-eternalization (*MV* 117). Focused on migrants and their use of media, Meinecke's case studies reveal how these instances of transient populations could escape the methodological regression that ideology imparts through mainstream media (TV, radio, and press). Against the impoverishment of subjectivity that culminates in social discourse presenting itself as immemorial and eternal, FSK and Meinecke's corollary to punk's "no future" was decidedly not as spectacularly destructive as Einstürzende Neubauten's or S.Y.P.H.'s, yet it continued in an altered form to reject the future bearing down on the Federal Republic. A radical strategic inversion devoid of blind allegiance to punk but still opposed to punk nemeses, FSK decided through "cybernetic points of view and from the principle of permanent revolution for the clear Yes to the modern world, and thus we will always lay everything on the line to stay awake, while the Nay-sayer becomes ever blinder to the world and thus degenerates his No into a farce" (*MV* 33). A necessary inversion after the politics of Kohl and lingering emergency laws made an eighties' quagmire wherein "no future" was unmistakably commercial and reflective of the sociopolitical status quo, FSK's affirmative resistance was resolutely invested in continuing Walter Benjamin's strategy of social movements by entering the mainstream in order to mine the interior.

Mode & Verzweiflung does not create a clear teleology—in fact just the opposite—as individual texts seem at times completely out of synch with one another. However, this confused collection reorganizes history at an individual level of experience and as such channels Negt and Kluge's call for historical awareness of the decomposition of the bourgeois public sphere and demonstrates the ability to be a "sensual" user of media. Sensualness in classical media, Negt and Kluge argue, "incorporated [people] as autonomous beings," which stands opposed to new mass media that "dispense with pluralism" (*PS* 151–155). A subcultural instance of this theory in action, *Mode & Verzweiflung's* "passionate praxis" reshuffled history and media to create a "dangerous liaison between intuition and intellect," a synthesis that brought, Meinecke continues, "a completely new answer to the question of heads or tails, namely head and tail" (117). As such, the tactically stylized stories in *Mode & Verzweiflung* push against what Adorno calls the "withering of experience" to engender a pluralism capable of escaping the binary oscillation between unproductive hegemonic positions (*MM* 61). Just as the young medical student from the previous chapter fought against the pull of codified adaptation or resistance, Meinecke's post-punk vignettes give voice to a new kind of circulation able to link subversively the gaps, what Negt and Kluge envision as neural synapses, that make the transmission of information into the future infinitely variable

(*GE* 67 and 239). By stealing from both sides of the left/right, affirmative/subversive binaries and resignifying them, *Mit der Kirche ums Dorf* signals the mainstream's continued failure in its present to take advantage of those valenced moments in media that could have been used differently. A crucial facet of this reexamination and adaptation in *Mit der Kirche* is the insertion of photographs. Specific pictures and their effects will be discussed later. For now, it is important to understand that the images incite spatial disjunction in the narrative, interrupt consumption of the text, and make the fanzine stories into montages; a triptych questioning the organization, teleology, content, and history of such narratives.

Attentiveness to ignored spheres of experience—peace during the Cold War, West Germany through America, racism instead of fascism—interlinked German history with the creation of counter-publicities through media poaching to make public and pleasurable what Negt and Kluge call "a hidden relationship within daily life" (*GE* 97). For Negt and Kluge, the link between history and counter-publicities is about the necessity of historical awareness for the public sphere. Negt and Kluge specifically speak of awareness as mourning that they claim is necessary because the public sphere has become:

> **The organizational form of the "dictatorship of the bourgeoisie"** [...] that network of norms, legitimations, delimitations, procedural rules, and separation of powers that prevents the political public sphere [...] from making decisions that disturb or nullify the order of bourgeois production. It is the organized obstacle to the material public sphere and politics—**the opposite of the constitutive public sphere**. (*PS*5 5)[26]

There are, they simultaneously argue, "**contradictions emerging within advanced capitalist societies [that possess] potential for a counterpublic sphere**" (xliii). Drawing on another affective impulse, FSK's penned call for pleasure in their manifesto—a map for post-punk affect vis-à-vis organization, relationality, and harnessing of contradictions—sought out what Adorno tapped as a the category of freedom in *Negative Dialectics,* namely "a critique and transformation of a situation, not its confirmation through decisions made under its fixed structure" (n225). The creation of emancipatory and new relations from historical production processes made possible sites of counter-publicities, a category that can negate existing conditions of abstraction (Hansen 202). By taking control of the signs of American cultural hegemony in West Germany, FSK demonstrated that Negt and Kluge's theoretical counterproducts of a proletarian public sphere were indeed possible in the eighties, even if the band used television as a means to an end (*PS* 79–80). The point becomes treating history as fiction, because history is as fragmentary as it is self-perpetuating.[27] Meinecke's literary poaching of media for history builds off FSK's interests in acquiring materials necessary to change the forms of social power and to make public both the structuring role of racism and the subversively active role possible for mass-media consumers of West German identity.

These montages wrest control from mainstream media with ostentatiously pirated pictures and narratives to present what Kluge calls a "formworld" that lays out the ignored connectivity in the public sphere. The thereby emergent "endless chain of processing" between viewers, users, and nonusers mints media and produces reception.[28] Because Meinecke abstains from prescribing use for the photos or for the narratives (recall *brauchbar/unbrauchbar*), the hijacked images engender a multiplicity of reading practices. If representation, as Fiske argues, is a means of exercising power through which one can act upon the world in a way that serves one's own interests and "the construction of subjectivity is political," then these texts demonstrated "the power of the subordinate to exert some control over representation" (317–318). While *Mit der Kirche* poached mainstream media and thus subverted attempts to use television, film, and newspapers as agents of homogenization, this is not the case for everyone in its stories. Some West Germans in these texts have failed social strategies built upon fraudulent images and discourses. As a potential solution in the age of television (what Negt and Kluge call the age of "new media"), Meinecke also picked up the pieces of "old," classical media. This is crucial because "new media," Negt and Kluge write, "are in a position to dispense with pluralism and to deliver their output directly to individuals." Such programs "**do not merely comprise an abstract all-purpose package ('to whom it may concern') [but represent] a focused opportunity for exploitation**" (*PS* 154–155). Television, the source of some of the images, represents a potential site of exploitation because it can be produced with the individual's position in mind, rather than fragmenting reality as they argue on behalf of classical media.[29] However, these images in Meinecke's vignettes, as Miriam Hansen argues for Negt and Kluge's footnotes, "respond to the text from various speaking positions, multiplying perspectives on the argument at hand" (xxvi). Here, Hansen reads how Negt and Kluge's use of montage inscribes in the text the maximum potential for readerly imagination. Similarly, *Mit der Kirche* exposes an "openness" of supposedly hermetically sealed narratives from films, magazines, and postcards. Becoming thereby what Fiske calls "producerly," Meinecke's texts provide a "'menu' from which the viewers chose," that is, a diversification that could be audience produced (319–321). The stories in *Mit der Kirche* move beyond the reflexive taking of sides, past self-protective neutrality, to consider the internal inconsistencies of all available positions. A narrative strategy built upon poaching, particularly self-poaching, the subversive praxis of self-censorship makes it possible to escape a culture, "New tips" declares, that had degenerated to stupidity spawned by its dialectical trap of "communists or fascists" (*MV* 36). Conversely, the stories' constantly changing environments (disco, revolution, and parties into the countryside) reject the idea that anything could be presented as an unbiased description of the situation. The "truth" of these stories is in a verisimilitude that indicted their own construction while celebrating the possibility of their reconstruction. Ultimately, Meinecke's collages must be understood as an "explosé" that challenged the persistence of German racism in West German identity politics, a form of structural hate and violence limiting the possibilities of agency in the FRG precisely because it lived off the projection of racism as a US problem. Turning inward and outward, his deployment of cybernetic textual practices, the following demonstrates, tested how resignification made possible the creation of antiracist politics from mainstream racist content.

Subversive Consumerism and Antiracism

Mainstream media representations of skin and nationality constructed images of Germans in popular discourse that obscured the histories of fascism in Germany with racism in the United States. Meinecke's stories engage West German discourses on skin, color, and identity by exposing their potential for deceit, a potential that, *Mode & Verzweiflung* asserts, was part of the "modern dream of subversion." On the one hand, the "tactical study of style" outlined in the fanzine, once brought to bear on the stories in *Mit der Kirche ums Dorf*, sought to disrupt the processes through which representation was habitually achieved (117). On the other, the latter collection made clear how mainstream narratives and affect in West German media that were poached for *Mit der Kirche* were intrinsically tied to questions of blackness and its ideological representation. Several stories in *Mit der Kirche*, "Three death anecdotes," "A ruined day," and "Pilot dies in cockpit: passenger safely lands plane," exemplify the legacies of racist words and images, notions of primitive and civilized, and racially motivated violence within the culture industries' project of constructing a stable, consuming West German identity as a barrier to communism. Because West German identity was simultaneously being constructed as a bulwark to the fascist past but under the umbrella of Americanization, the discourses and idealized images of subjectivity smuggled racist scaffolding into Germany, precisely the racially structured discourses that generate subject positions, as Paul Gilroy argues in *The Black Atlantic*, that "give way to the dislocating dazzle of 'whiteness'" (9). In the case of Meinecke's poached stories, the "dazzle" of whiteness that Gilroy argues hinders political organization and cultural criticism supports the naturalization in West Germany of violence against blacks (19). Recreated narratively, linguistically, and pictorially, this violence in the Federal Republic's mainstream media was dislocated from racist origins to be rearticulated into popular discourse. Such dislocation, Meinecke's stories demonstrate, had deadly repercussions in praxis and foretold of an "evolutionary dead end" as a result of its supplanting fascism with racism.[30]

Pirated stories from the mainstream press, Meinecke's vignettes mimic mainstream jargon when they refer to pastries as "Negerküsse" (nigger kisses) and expound on the historical visit of an "African" statesman, a "laughing nigger regent [...] the king of the moors" to West Germany (*MdK* 108 and 14–15). The racist names for baked goods and the reduction of nations to mere representatives of an amorphous "Africa" are juxtaposed with a woman reenacting Josephine Baker's banana dance and blues guitarist Blind Willie Johnson (figures 3.1 and 3.2).

Figure 3.1   Blackface, from *Mit der Kirche ums Dorf,* by Thomas Meinecke (13).

Figure 3.2 Blackness, from *Mit der Kirche ums Dorf,* by Thomas Meinecke (103).

That Josephine Baker's "banana dance" is not Baker herself but rather a white woman playing a blackface role of Baker is all the more problematic given that the television image was taken from the cover of the magazine *Quick*, an illustrated weekly that in its heyday had a circulation of over 1.5 million.[31] The wide circulation of the *Quick* image represents pictorially the racist lingua franca in West Germany (signifying pastries as "nigger-kisses"), a discourse that taught and normalized blackface. Blind Willie Johnson—an image imported into West Germany from unknown sources[32]—signals another problem in West German identity politics in the eighties, specifically with the presence and circulation of images of blackness in West Germany. The images, linguistic signification, and narratives detailed below make unmistakable the texts' collective thesis that while Germans had vocabulary to describe blackness, they did not have the ability to distinguish that which they signified as blackness from that which was actually black. *Mit der Kirche's* texts thereby reveal a "forgotten," perhaps even "reconciled," racist element circulating in West German discourse wherein Germans play their own kind of blackface role, one that simulates social content and a reconciled past. Specifically, US racism—the blackface role of Josephine Baker—gets confused with blackness from the United States—Blind Willie Johnson—and circulates in the Federal Republic as a force of identity formation when it differentiates Germans from an Other. When these images appear in the context of the racialized story "A ruined day," and in stories that have superficially little to do with race, such as "Pilot dies in cockpit: passenger safely lands plane," they highlight the normalization of racist discourse and the timeliness of FSK and Meinecke's demand that consumers of mainstream media adapt critical reading practices as a tactical requisite for any counter-agency.

Thus when they transfigure media representations through dynamic appropriation and reappropriation, Meinecke's texts make clear how mainstream images cited African Americans as fantasies for German racism, a move that concurrently displaced historical and contemporaneous problems of racism onto a foreign culture either abroad or internally (in the persons of American GIs). Meinecke's vignettes consumed and refunctioned media to demonstrate how the "dazzle" of whiteness used African Americans to project any and all German problems with racism and identity as an effect of American cultural flows. In the story "Three death anecdotes," when a German in this story plays black, other Germans take what they see as real. In one anecdote, black is something "shit-colored," something to shoot and kill, like a wild boar. A young German sleeping in a "shit-colored sleeping bag" is shot by a farmer, a death, the slain boy's mother testifies, attributable to skin color. "If anyone had pointed out the fatal implication of the so-called shit-color," the mother is certain, "then she could have easily enough changed its color, to flesh color, for example" (88–89). At its most extreme, when this story echoes the mainstream naturalization of white as "skin-colored," its characters in turn naturalize shooting something brown in West Germany. This undercurrent of racial violence built upon white-black binaries ripped from print media and retold in Meinecke's stories reveals, when read in tandem with the *Quick* image, that West German popular media circulated what Gilroy calls "conceptions of culture which present[ed] immutable, ethnic differences as an absolute break in the histories and experiences of 'black' and 'white' people" (2). This anecdote warns of deadly repercussions of inadequate racial consciousness and of blackface because other Germans misconceive the young boy's resignified skin color. The boy resignifies his skin, but the German farmer does not realize this is the case because he is not a poacher, because he views color via the "immutable" differences of which Gilroy writes. The farmer takes everything at face value, or better, at the value of skin. Conversely, even if she does so under the same structure of absolute racial difference, the boy's mother realizes the power of resignification because she knows that had she transformed the color of the sleeping bag from its commercial color, she would have prevented her son's blackface role and ensured his survival.

Another tale in "Three death anecdotes" criticizes West German fetishization of black affect. The Germans in this story lament how "again and again we Central-Europeans were forced into comparison with niggers."[33] In this equation of blackness with nationality—recall the visit of the regent from "Africa" above—the blacks come out better because of an essentialist disposition: "at nigger-funerals they dance, at Central-European funerals however, an oppressed atmosphere rules" (83). Beyond essentializing affect as black, Germans in this story try to seek out justifications for their inability to mourn the past. As detailed below, such murderous and oppressed atmospheres are not just about funerals, but about mourning the tragedies of mass murder, specifically German *Vergangenheitsbewältigung* (reckoning with the past). Here the replacement of non-reconciled fascism with "foreign" racism—a doubling meant to preserve the West German self against extinction—is precisely what inhibits Germans' ability to mourn their past. As the example of the slain boy demonstrates, misunderstanding blackness leads to Germans affectively or physically playing blackface, a strategy with a deadly outcome because it supports the immutable break between blackness and whiteness but also because it deflects the guilt of insufficient national mourning and reconciliation with the past onto an Other. This dazzle of whiteness blinds the consumers of national culture in "A ruined day." A story that reveals how racism as popular discourse and race as national identity mask a fascist present, "A ruined day" is about the state visit of a regent "from the so-called third world" (12). Deconstructing binary oppositions of race in the Federal Republic by stacking up racism and the arbitrary constructions of West German whiteness, this story based on historical fact tells about a day ruined by the regent's inattentiveness to the "Tarzan pictures" drawn by German children and the fright his companions "massive plate-lips" gave to the same children (15).

In preparation for the visit of the "moors from the Orient," the Bonn government decides to hold a contest seeking the perfect West German family. Once chosen, this was the family "that was to be presented to the chocolate-brown king." The chosen family, the Renzels, is meant to present how (well) a West German family lives in the social market economy. That the paradigmatic West German family has to be "sent the appropriate brochures" on its existence speaks to the ideological fantasy that this family represents. These brochures unmask the construction of content in the morass of 1980s West Germany, an illusion that turned on "affluence for all, dissolution of class-based constraints, the social question completely resolved, general contentedness in the country paired with a sensible portion of problem-consciousness" (12). But it is not just the Renzels who are media projections of ideology. While the use of "so-called" calls out the twofold constructedness of the racist discourses, clearly showing how the idea of the West German is as constructed as the racial identity of the visiting dignitary, it also reveals the commercial designing of an "ideal" German identity and the prevalence of a violent and racist sociopolitical lingua franca vis-à-vis an imaginary black identity. "A ruined day" thereby examines the legacies of American racist discourse in West Germany— witness the blackface Josephine Baker—as a foil for the fanatical and ideological construction of mainstream cultural content as part of the "Economic Miracle" ("affluence for all"). Though the Renzels present and allow a phantasmagoric and unified image to be constructed of them when they passively take up the elements offered, it is not just the Renzels who do not poach what they are given. Constructing the Renzels as a paradigmatic West German family surrounded by hegemonic popular culture in the wake of West Germany's Economic Miracle, this vignette demonstrates the continuation of such discourses that were encouraged by the rhetoric of conservative politics and a head-on drive toward a market economy in the Federal Republic. But more problematically, the story exposes the slippage between the mainstream language that constructs an image of Germany or the African statesmen and fascist war-syntax.

The final decision in the contest to be the West German family par excellence is spoken of as an "Endausscheidung" (final elimination or final shitting) (12–14). Here the "final decision" (*die Endlösung*) is resignified and made into a "final shitting." But "A ruined day" does not poach the Holocaust. Rather it poaches the feigned reconciliation with German history and the Renzels' misunderstanding of the monumental tragedy of German history.[34] The linguistic displacement of racism onto America to create a national identity allows these figures to use fascist language; constructing national identity in this manner ignores the racism of nationality latent in confections or weekly magazines and allows the resurfacing of fascist affect for the present. This is precisely the political and social malaise of a fascist present that inspired punk's apocalyptic dreams. To this end, here the "final decision" does not signify the elimination of Jews in concentration camps, but rather the elimination of shit, the abject, waste. The abject in *Mit der Kirche* signifies the elimination of those in whom the fascist fantasies of the German race live on. This story reveals the truth of the "final decision," namely that Germans should consider themselves the abject because national popular identity is constructed vis-à-vis a blackness that becomes, for Germans with this constructed nationality, the abject. Thus that which should have "no future" is the national identity and affirmative agency dependent on displacing the abject onto an Other in the service of sustaining essentialist dispositions and fascist affect.[35] In "Three death anecdotes" Germans as abject manifest in the death of the German boy in the "shit-colored sleeping bag"; in "A ruined day" the Renzels make other Germans the abject: they unwittingly enact punk's apocalyptic dream, for they only won once this abject had been dealt with, once the other would-be examples had been annihilated ("vernichtend geschlagen"). But the Renzels are not alone. Once caught up in the contest to be the family presented before the "nigger regent," the citizens of the Federal Republic feel "an old fighting spirit coming alive [...] one that was thought to have been dead for forty years" (12). Post-punk's counter-hegemonic media consumption reveals that while its enemies were engaged in their own self-destructive media practice—passive consumption—time passing only painted over the legacies of fascism with racism—swapping one deadly identity for another—and offered zero hope for any nonviolent agency.

In part, such agency resulted from the highest levels of government that contributed to the cultural capital buttressing such media projections of West German identity. This is reinforced by the mass-media distribution via *Quick* of the Josephine Baker image, and racism as an American export (Johnson) rather than an aspect of German identity. Indeed, *Quick* and the Renzels—who "soon conquered, virtually in a triumphal victory pro-cession, a secure place in the final selection"—demonstrate the widespread and contemporaneous specter of German racism. The family thereby sig-nifies their uncritical uptake of media that encouraged fantasies of a recon-ciled past and primed an "old fighting spirit" of fascism under the guise of a present of content (12). "Pilot dies in cockpit"—a story about American Fred Gant's miraculous survival and landing after the pilot of a small plane in which he was flying has a heart attack—is the next story in the collec-tion continuing to pry apart and misuse these racist and violent discourses. There are two reasons why Fred's tale of survival is in West Germany: one, because he survived, but more interestingly, because Fred carried the newspaper account as a clipping in his wallet. In the story, Fred's friends bemoan how he constantly retells his survival of this catastrophe. The problem for the friends is not that Fred retells his story inasmuch as Fred always tells the story the exact same way. The nameless narrator-friends bemoan how "because Fred Grant really only tells this one story, and tells this one story always in exactly the same words, we know this story inside and out" (18). Fred is a terrible user of media because he destroys the pos-sibility of suspense when his narrative technique vacates the possibility of "sensual experience."[36] Fred's friends ultimately wish that because of this uncreative repetition, it would have been better had Fred been the one who had died in the plane. While the migration of this narrative from Davenport, Iowa (where the story originated) to Germany seems interesting, Fred's friends reveal that this is not the most important part. The most important part of Fred's story, that he ignores, is that it is a narrative at all. Narrative is the useful part of the story because it is poachable, which is precisely what *Mit der Kirche* does. The poached version has an image of a black man being lynched by the Klu Klux Klan (figure 3.3).

The image, appropriated from D. W. Griffith's *Birth of a Nation* (1915), is not an image of white men lynching a black man, but rather of white men lynching a white man in blackface. This fantasy of racism is white men lynching a white man. This is an image of white people performing their own fears and of the ways such fantasies lead to nation building. Just as with the Renzels and in "Three death anecdotes," the discourses that led to the lynching of this man have not been examined, but they have found their way into the vocabulary of the figures through the United States' rebuilding of Germany. The German equivalent of blackface was in part the racist-fascist language in the Renzel's

Figure 3.3 Lynching as cultural transfer, from *Mit der Kirche ums Dorf,* by Thomas Meinecke (19).

story above. But more importantly, it is the son covering himself with a "shit-colored sleeping bag," the "nigger-kisses," the "nigger-reagent," and a fake Josephine Baker. The deadly repercussions of blackface roles such as those in *Birth of a Nation* surface when the Germans think that the son covered in brown is brown and when the Renzels act out their fascist fantasies and annihilate other Germans. But there were more fundamental implications for German popular culture and American consumerism. The lynching scene from *Birth of a Nation,* a movie about the foundation of America resting upon violent, racist origins, is not a solution to Nazism. The "oppressive atmosphere" stagnating over West Germany and inhibiting *Vergangenheitsbewältigung,* these stories propose, is in part caused by attempts to tag any presence of racism in the Federal Republic after the Holocaust as an American problem (83). Because the Germans in "Pilot dies in cockpit" create an unbridgeable divide between West Germany and America, they do not consider anything about the newspaper clipping that has migrated across the Atlantic with Fred (bringing racial violence back across the Atlantic along with it) for that violence would be American. This demonstrates how Germans miss the point: the endless repetition of this narrative—as the cyclical stories Raspe lamented in chapter two—creates the problem of recurrent violent histories built upon fascism and racism. Though repetition is not limited to Fred's story. It is, rather, indicative of the sociohistorical feedback loop between the United States and West Germany. The effects thereof emerge narratively when the image of the lynching gets into the text and transforms the narrative and Fred's history, but practically in the daily life of those punks who refused to ignore the repeating specter of fascism in the persons such as Hanns-Martin Schleyer and Chancellor Kiesinger or companies such as Bayer and BASF whose reparations attempted a sociocultural effacing of Germany's present-past. Subversive consumption of Fred Grant's story, conversely, makes a violent, oppressed past audible in the present. By creating strategies to uncover the "hidden" racism lurking on the surface of this story, Meinecke's texts envision and constitute counter-public production against German racism that would otherwise provide a stabilizing force to secure a precarious position (Gilroy 163). Thus the texts from mainstream media outlets that Meinecke reworks are choice, for the racist ideologies imported into West Germany alongside colportage reveal what Gilroy analyzes as "the importance of ritual brutality in structuring modern, civilised life" (119).[37] Though *Mit der Kirche* makes clear the need for antiracist positions made possible through critical discourse and critical uptake of narratives circulating in media, the means to create antiracist and antifascist counterproducts as solutions to the psychological problem of the abject or affect is nevertheless not unbridled media poaching.

History, "Dallas," and the Limits of Poaching

The feedback loop between the United States and Germany that *Mit der Kirche* uncovered and poached contains circuits of US popular culture that were saturated with racialized discourse. The media distillate of this mixture demonstrates the belated effects of Germany's own "forgotten" history of race problems, as the phrase "Endausscheidung" (final elimination) and an "old fighting spirit" make clear. These effects of German racism are intrinsically tied to the history of suffering, thus understanding the possibility of forming counter-publicities in the eighties, and thereby of strategies to counter the repercussions of persistent racism, necessitates a turn from the present to the history of Germany, to how German history was remembered. In the Federal Republic, the history of capitalism—the system of modernity that made Nazi killing factories and their Taylorian-efficiency possible—and that history's boundedness to suffering were present in contemporary media. For *Mit der Kirche ums Dorf* there was no better example of the age of late capitalism and suffering in media than the television show "Dallas." More than the need for an ethical position vis-à-vis history, the stories dealing with "Dallas" in *Mit der Kirche* testify to the limits of poaching.

"Boston Tea Party" is the first instance of "Dallas" in the collection and it makes public two opposing uses of migrating media and migrating narratives. Reports on letters sent from America by Werner Feldhagen to a group of friends in Germany, the domestic Germans in "Boston Tea Party" are skeptical of the trans-Atlantic "information about discoveries that are apparently only able to be made in the USA" (22). The German emigrant Feldhagen, after months in America, sends a postcard detailing relevant events from the television show "Dallas." Feldhagen decides that, in light of the tragedy surrounding the potentially irreversible death of Bobby Ewing, "television-reality is, when compared with social reality, the higher of the two." Feldhagen's friends do not buy into his example post-punk poaching. They respond in another postcard that this sociocultural evaluation is "nicely settled." However, they reject his "segmenting of the socio-media field into multiple realities" and instead declare this theory a dead end, "particularly with emigration" (25). Feldhagen's friends in West Germany thus argue for a unified individual and singular reality in spite of the inter- and transnational opportunities demonstrated by Feldhagen. The dialogue initially about the modern phenomena of "ideological stagnation" due to infatuation with "Dallas" ultimately demonstrates divergent uses of the television drama when the poacher Feldhagen inverts their claims of "Kulturversumpfung" into *Kulturverpflanzung* or *-vermehrung* (cultural transplantation or multiplication). Feldhagen's misuse of media

thereby critiques his West Germans friends' inability to successfully incorporate the socially subversive possibilities offered by history, migration,
and media (22). This is so crucial because in stark contradistinction to
his friends' interest in universal media consumption, watching "Dallas"
in Germany and in the United States did not mean the same thing. Fiske
has examined how "Dallas" specifically has been misused by audiences in
North America. For him, negotiating the meaning of "Dallas" allowed "the
socially situated viewer an active, semi-controlling role" in the production
of meaning, both dominant and oppositional (82). Demonstrating such
flexible agency, Feldhagen, the German academic watching "Dallas," sees
the actor playing Bobby Ewing as expendable. Were Bobby Ewing to die,
however, that is "irreversible" (*MdK* 25). Whether the actor playing Ewing
dies is irrelevant because it is specifically the use to which audiences can
put the role of Ewing that holds subversive potential. In other words, it is
not the trajectory of the narrative, but its status as a narrative at all that
can be used. Thus Feldhagen, like Fiske, sees in the narrative of "Dallas"
consequent and diverse identities standing at the ready for social change.
Feldhagen demonstrates how, if one is on top of his or her television watching, he or she can outdo the culture industry. Here the ideological stagnation ("Kulturversumpfung") is caused by the potential reduction of the
"menu" (Fiske) from which viewers can choose. This stagnation cannot be
turned into cultural multiplication ("Kulturvermehrung") by Feldhagen's
friends because they passively upload or completely ignore the usability of
the images they have before them.

In "Boston tea party," the characters in West Germany do not reexamine problems of nationality and identity. That the observations vis-à-
vis media realities can apparently ("angeblich") only be made in America
signals a resignation on the part of Feldhagen's friends to what they
erroneously perceive to be American cultural hegemonic domination.
Contrary to this myth of American cultural imperialism bemoaned by
Feldhagen's friends and signified by "Dallas," Feldhagen, like Ien Ang,
shows how the television drama actually contains "mutual relations [that]
are extremely complicated" (7). Though Feldhagen's phenomenological
migration brings national discourses on media and culture into motion,
the ability to misuse media was already in West Germany, evidenced in
the story by the last postcard from West Germany featuring an etching
of the Boston Tea Party. Alas, Feldhagen's friends fail to consider why
Germans have a postcard with an etching of the Boston Tea Party to
send. Instead, they argue whether this really was the image on the reverse
of their epistolary dismissal of perspectives and positions made possible
by migration. Edgar, one of Feldhagen's friends back in Germany, is the
only figure who thinks the image on the postcard was indeed an etching

of the Boston Tea Party. The other two friends, Ludger and Arno, claim the image was of cats in front of Brussels' "Atomium."[38] Edgar suggests, however, that the Boston Tea Party image was chosen "purposefully" (25). In other words, images have consequences. But whether the purpose was only that Feldhagen lives in Boston, or whether it was that the rejection of trans-Atlantic material is revolutionary (a position embodied by Feldhagen's friends' rejection of "Dallas") remains unanswered and in the user's hands. The latter is a final moment of failure for Feldhagen's friends in the complex network of image and text and history. If carefully read (what Feldhagen's friends do not do), this story lays the foundation for caring about the transnational multiplicity of meanings opened up by migration. There are multiple, contingent symbolic possibilities in the appropriation of media to which some of the Germans in the text remain oblivious. *Mit der Kirche* makes clear its critique of this obliviousness with a picture of a man standing by a piano that makes the text into a collage (figure 3.4).

Figure 3.4   Blackface or Drag?: A German playing an Italian impersonator of a Romanian-born Hungarian composer: from *Mit der Kirche ums Dorf,* by Thomas Meinecke (23).

The image, a still from the film *Der Italiener* (Ferry Radax, 1971), based on a fragment and screenplay by Austrian author Thomas Bernhard, holds exactly the manifold meanings that Feldhagen, Fiske, and Ang cull from "Dallas." The cryptic-experimental film, written by Bernhard and filmed by Radax, is about a young Italian man who listens incessantly to Béla Bártok records while the residents of the house in which he is lodging mourn the death (possibly suicide) of the family patriarch. The Italian begins to play Bártok's music, poaching the Romanian-born Hungarian composer's music for himself. Furthermore, Bernhard's literary text changed its nomenclature with the subtitle "A Film." Thus the still image from Radax's movie, poached once by Bernhard and then by Meinecke, represents an attempt by *Mit der Kirche* to expand its own literarym oniker.[39]

The film and the still appear to have, superficially, little to do with this narrative. However, the point here is to demonstrate how Fiske's "menu" multiplies representation; Bernhard summarized the project of his film-fragment similarly, namely as a textual instance of "work as experiment" (163). Feldhagen's friends ignore the diverse meanings possible because they do not experiment, a monumental failure because their praxis ignores the destabilization to monovocality that lies at the core of collages' rejection of synthesizing a unified meaning. Thus the actual image is subservient to what it signifies; what Edgar's "Boston Tea Party" threw overboard was what the "Atomium" signaled: the complex, transnational network (via capitalism and tea trade or a World's Fair) for the multiplication of meaning. Fragments such as *Der Italiener* fundamentally transform the text, but the friends miss the subversive moment because they neither read nor connect them. Oblivious to what has accompanied his postcards from the United States—they ignore the potential for transforming German-American cultural exchange into a gateway to pluralism—Feldhagen's friends do not demonstrate proof of an individual's inability to create their own uses for media, only their failure to do so.[40] His friends are the idiots that *Mode & Verzweiflung* bemoans serve as inspiration for mainstream German citizens (38). Such social self-regulation—Negt and Kluge define it as "the principled indifference, the conservatism of elementary forces"— produces progress as an apathetic, conservative forward momentum into a singular future through lingering, ruined paths (*GE* 49). Meinecke's texts seek to undermine dialectical self-regulation, an organizational condition whereby parts of the same social organism have antagonistic rationales for change but rather than facilitating emancipatory processes, "normal" social impulses cement the status quo. His vignettes assay that alienated orientation to theorize an alternative self-regulation as "the complete recognition of the varied laws of motion that regulate the forces colliding in humans"

(55). While Feldhagen can poach "Dallas," characters who poach do not always have appropriate materials at their disposal; they sometimes come up against the limits of poaching.

American pop culture ("Dallas") and German history (the Holocaust) meet up in "A waste of an evening." In this story, the evening is a waste because "Dallas, as we all know, was canceled because of Holocaust" (*MdK* 41). "Holocaust," an American TV series, followed the Weiss family as they tried to survive their deportation to various concentration camps. Produced for a US audience, "Holocaust" had, as Andreas Hyussen argues, "a totally unanticipated and unintended impact in West Germany."[41] As Huyssen explains, many critics spoke of a "national or collective catharsis" that unfolded in Germany because of the American television series "Holocaust," which enhanced "identification with the Weiss family," a Jewish family trying to survive the Holocaust (113). "'Holocaust' was condemned by critics," he also explains, "as a cheap popularization of complex historical processes which could not help the Germans come to terms with their recent past" (94). But not all Germans embraced this American-imported *Vergangenheitsbewältigung*. While Huyssen is interested in the compatibility of emotional representations of history for Germans reconciling the "Final Solution," Meinecke's two stories about "Dallas" lay out why the psychosocial relevance of "Holocaust" misses the point. Dismissing "Dallas" or "Holocaust" as trivial, dangerous, or ahistorical assumes that these programs had but only one use. Conversely, as Feldhagen shows above, there are multiple interpretations possible for audiences. That "Dallas" was canceled does not please the German viewers in the story because "Holocaust," after all, "we saw that three years ago" (*MdK* 41). The intrusion to "Dallas" means that the ongoing tragedies of capitalism lose out over the historical tragedies of genocide. This may at first appear as a reduction of the Holocaust to just another media event, but one much less popular and current than "Dallas." However, the juxtaposition of this story with Feldhagen's poaching of "Dallas" creates an intertextual dialog between pessimistic and positive views toward the value of television. The parallel between "Dallas" and "Holocaust" cannot be reduced to popularity in America, as was the case with the former, and Germany, as was the case with both.

The debate around "Holocaust" is crucial in this argument because, as Huyssen points out, "'Holocaust' betrays very clearly" the elements of the culture industry that, as Meinecke's oeuvre argues, prescribed identity and impinged upon agency (96). The crucial role of "Holocaust" here is, as the nameless narrative "we" in the story "A waste of an evening" points out, the Holocaust is not poachable. The evening is a waste because "Holocaust" rightly addresses a moment of German history as fixed history. Just as

Fred Grant retells his story of survival over and over with the exact same words, the "we" in "A waste of an evening" know exactly what will happen to the various members of the Weiss family (*MdK* 41). Rather than suggesting that "Dallas" is better than "Holocaust" simply because it is newer (although that plays a role), it rather demonstrates how some things could not be resignified. This story is not Holocaust denial or one that posits *Vergangenheitsbewältigung* was somehow complete, but rather a quest for programming suitable for poaching. The agency *Mit der Kirche* envisions through its vignettes was about poaching German history, about determining the historical conditions of images, and how these images and histories could be resignified at what Negt and Kluge call "a higher historical level of individuality" such that experience could be disorganized from above or below in the service of dismembering media (*PS* 154). This play made the dominant media—*Birth of a Nation, Quick,* "Dallas"—look incoherent and arbitrary and thereby unmasked the politics of uncertainty. "Dallas" was better for talking about the Holocaust precisely because it is about capitalism and suffering (of the Ewing family); the Holocaust and the elimination of Jews are not to be poached—that would imply equivalency in these tragedies and the affective reaction to "Dallas" and "Holocaust" shows this is not the case. After all, the potential death of Bobby Ewing, Feldhagen reports, unleashes "clear turmoil" in America (25). As illustrated above through the example of German's racist self-defense of their shortcomings vis-à-vis affect and mourning, Germans have significant psychological blockage to such an affective release. In contradistinction to the newness of death in "Dallas," the fate of the Weiss family in the Warsaw ghetto and in concentration camps is well known: "How does that interest us today?" (41). The shocking death in "Dallas" engendered a new moment of mourning in the United States, and while the death of Weiss family members cannot do this anew for West Germans, they must nevertheless not forget the barbarism of capitalism and modernity. Thus the need to watch "Dallas" is the need for the possibilities of affective agency outside binaries of repressed or enacted racism and violence. Horkheimer and Adorno's condemnation of mass culture as something that primarily manipulates the masses thereby fits here dialectically because the friends seek out an active participation in television while their rejection of passive and false sense of pleasure from television confirms the philosophers' critique. The problem was not that the Germans in Meinecke's text tired of "Holocaust," but rather that the show itself did not offer the diverse possibilities for transforming social reality that "Dallas" had.

So here it seems that the Germans in "A waste of an evening" are somewhere between Feldhagen's friends and Feldhagen. While they know they cannot resignify some history, to what use they put the Ewing family remains a mystery. This hopeful moment stands nevertheless in opposition to the West Germans in these texts who fail to develop successful strategies for tapping into the hybrid geographical and historical positions that media and travel create. This suggests that there were radical possibilities in being an unorthodox West German consumer of popular culture able to push at the limits of what American popular culture constructed in the Federal Republic as the space for politics and history. This was, after all, what the manifesto in *Mode & Verzweiflung* really called for. The inability to consider these possibilities makes characters such as Feldhagen's friends those whom the manifesto declares the "embodiment of turned-around and muddled thinking par excellence" (34). The audiences of transnational media exchange have at their disposal the means of becoming a creative, participating force. Meinecke's stories in *Mit der Kirche* show that readers, like texts, can take advantage of media by resignifying the culture industry's ideological intentions. Replaying information onto and into itself, the feedback loop in *Mit der Kirche* is what *Mode & Verzweiflung's* manifesto declares a "Handlungsanweisung" (strategy) for cyberneticians (33). Feldhagen, like the stories in *Mit der Kirche*, considers not only the content, but also the medium and the geographical-cultural matrix. Within this matrix, the fragmented messages and hybrid content represent a moment in the eighties, Meinecke writes, of "the modern dream of subversion with passionately driven praxis cybernetically derived, and above all tactical exercise in style" (117). Docile and oblivious acceptance of this information imposes the foreign onto conceptions of the national whereby West German identity ignores its partial constitution by the United States. Feldhagen's friends and the collective "we" passively take up the information in these images and texts: West German society does not consider the change that this reading and signifying strategy injects into the possibility of agency and for subverting violence. As the last section of this chapter makes explicit, democratizing subversive consumption occurred though precisely the musical-literary fusion as a means to reject academic monopoly on critical discourse voiced by Peter Glaser—Meinecke's praxis of the theory laid out in *Mode & Verzweiflung* was itself thematized to critique "higher" forms of cultural consumption.

Counter-Publics and Production

A self-indicting story about the "concentration weakness" of literati and the sinking value of "so-called literature," "A glimpse under the shoes" takes place in an academic reading circle where authors present their latest cultural criticisms and literary forays (*MdK* 70). The pivotal figure is Ulli, a new member who seems to have some trouble being accepted by the more seasoned members. More than recounting Ulli's attempts at adapting to academic standards, "A glimpse under the shoes" juxtaposes the derangement (Umnachtung) of hippie literary reading circles with a picture of what appears at first glance as a 1970s sex-bomb (figure 3.5).

The woman in the image stares with a frozen, detached gaze off camera. This blank stare suggests an image of the circle's participants, unable to concentrate and fazed by Ulli's cultural criticism that links soccer, love affairs, and pop music's inheritance of Marxism. Alternatively, she could represent the narrative "we," the "non-literati," who, after hearing the participant Ulli's cultural criticism, are followed by a "curious feeling: We lift the foot, first the left, then the right, and carefully look at the soles of our shoes" (72). The use of "us" and "we" makes the non-literati narrative voice a collective. On the one hand, that collective enacted punk's anti-'68er turn away from sheltered intellectual engagement in the Federal Republic; on the other, it is a turn away from the mainstream rhetoric of consent and progress, away from the kind of viewer—critiqued in Meinecke's vignettes—who knows but a singular narrative of the past and

Figure 3.5 Drag: A Question of Reading, from *Mit der Kirche ums Dorf,* by Thomas Meinecke (73).

its clear, singular trajectory to the present. Celebrating the fusion of avant-garde aesthetics, music, and literature that underwrote punk's project of dystopia, the text reveals that it was precisely the non-literati who in the last six years (since 1978) had regained "the lost concentration through the means of mobile adaptation" (70). This mobile adaptation—adapting to divergent and unexpected uses of media, images, and texts famously voiced by Leslie Fiedler in his 1969 "Close the Gap" lecture but also in FSK's manifesto—makes the non-literati far more intellectual and critical than intellectuals. The literary circle in Meinecke's story, conversely, is a collection of those in the literary establishment who rejected Fiedler's call such as Marcel Reich-Ranicki, previously Rainald Goetz's target. Indeed, one can hear echoes of Goetz's dismissal of the canon, of the "bastards Böll and Grass," when Meinecke's story locates those canonical voices as that "what we soon began to call New Primitivism."⁴² Clearly less bloody than Goetz's Klagenfurt performance, the narrative voice nevertheless chastises the reading circle participants, isolated from society, as misdirected students who do not personify the postmodern theories they espouse. Rather, the circle's participants reproduce the same errors as 1968: they "find themselves [...] on the same level as the student, who, we remember, wanted to take the television away from the proletariat." Thus the circle represents an attempt to isolate and control what is considered worthy for intellectual discussion but also who was allowed to participate in (intellectual) consumption of culture. From their sequestered position, the literary circle simply mimes the conservative literary group "Gruppe '47" that sought to create a clear delineation—a "zero hour"—from the past for cultural renewal. In an echo of punk's dismissal of established critiques, the literary establishment and their self-celebration in this story is again in the person of Günter Grass: "It's Gunter's turn, the thirty-two-year-old printer. His stirring report of a quotidian workers-struggle, [...] is immediately and enthusiastically taken up" (*MdK* 70–71). This is exactly the type of mistaken affective investment that the manifesto "New tips" in *Mode & Verzweiflung* rails against, namely a discussion of "deep whiney-ness that degenerates into sentimental social criticism" (34). "A glimpse under the shoes" blew open such hermetically sealed space, the rightful ownership of "critical reading," and democratized participation in such criticism.

Recognizable as part of the bourgeois public sphere, the space of the reading circle mimes the isolation of eighteenth-century salons. *Mit der Kirche* makes clear its aspirations for a solution to such antiquated critical forums that Hansen argues stand in opposition to the space of Negt and Kluge's counter-public and "absolved leftist intellectuals from having to engage in forms of organization that amounted to self-denial and nostalgic misreadings of contemporary social and cultural realities."⁴³ Because it is devoid of discursive contestation or potentially unpredictable processes, a condition responsible for the "almost complete derangement of the literati," the reading circle in "A glimpse under the shoes" cannot be any sort of oppositional public sphere. Correspondingly, the concrete problem with literature in the text is exactly concrete: the circle's members, with the sole exception of Ulli, rely on literature alone; they are disciplinarians.

But even though the interdisciplinarian Ulli draws together sport, music, and Marxism, and as such represents a potentially anti-discursive moment in the circle, he does so in a predictable manner with a cemented style. Just as with the hippie-psychiatrist in *Irre* who told spontaneous jokes that everyone expected, "the circle had become used to Ulli" (71–72). Again, the isolation of the circle is its most tragic moment because what was at stake with Ulli's text was, to continue with Hansen, the "very possibility of making connections—between traditionally segregated domains of public and private, politics and everyday life." This is a pivotal moment because a collage of image and text is for Hansen a crucial "morphology of relations" that encouraged the reader to "draw his or her own connections across generic divisions of fiction and documentary of disparate realms and registers of experience" (xxxiv). The subject in the inserted picture, a transvestite competing for the Miss All'America contest in the film *The Queen* (Frank Simon, 1968), clarifies the text as an alternative to orthodox literary production, reception, and use.

Fittingly for *Mit der Kirche's* project of linking putatively disparate elements, the still coincidently also appears in Parker Tyler's essay contribution to Rolf Dieter Brinkmann and Ralf-Rainer Rygulla's Beat-inspired collection *Acid,* and Tyler's essay provides serendipitous analytical insight to Meinecke's story. Tyler's essay exposes limitless gender and sexual possibilities: hetero-, homo-, and bisexualities must be expanded (264). Not expansive sexuality ties Tyler and Meinecke's story together, but rather an explosion of social constructions wherein everything is a question of reading. Ulli's project is potentially subversive because, like Tyler's, it seeks to constantly blow up the limits of discourse when it draws lines between points and practices (sports, sex, and music). What nonacademics find offensive and cause for checking their shoes for feces is the literati's lukewarm take on engaged cultural criticism. The academics grant "literary-status" (71) to Ulli's texts in spite of skepticism to the value of his ideas, a noncritical uptake that places the literary group's members in the circle of "boundless affirming humanists" lamented in *Mode & Verzweiflung's* manifesto (32). Rather than passionately engaging Ulli's work, the circle has become accustomed to him. More disparaging is that the critical text has been subsumed into a canon of literature that is isolated from a sphere where it could have real effects. "A glimpse under the shoes" fused media and text to create a feedback loop between various levels and thereby becomes a kind of hyper-media that debunks the academic lingua franca of stable representation and knowledge. The integration of heterogeneous materials—detritus—encourages problematic, parallel processes that represented a series of overlapped analyses and potential alliances. Forms of organization become, in effect, forms of disorganization, and thereby create lines of flight outside isolated pockets of intellectual consumption of culture. A metaphor for all of Meinecke's texts, "A glimpse under the shoes" calls for an explosion of literature's ossified social uses. His stories, because they contain various bits of other texts and because they reshuffle their own materials and positions, dissolve what Hansen calls the "mutually paralyzing cohabitation of bourgeois and industrial forms of publicity" (xxii).

An intervention into the sociopolitical history of West Germany, *Mit der Kirche ums Dorf* creates antiracist, historically aware politics in which nothing is original, or better, in which everything is original. Rereading German popular culture and history for antiracism imagined another kind of German history and identity that was not structured by violence. For Meineck and FSK, the politics of poaching transformed the hopeless condition of mass culture under late capitalism into a dynamic site. When they made representation dynamic and experimental, when they reconceptualized the public from the perspective of unpredictability, conflict, contradiction, and difference, FSK and Meinecke manipulated discontinuity into a catalyst for escape from what the band called a "evolutionary dead-end." And in that strategy lies the corollary to punk's "no future" and Fehlfarben's "too late"—for the band and author thereby displaced affective identities, including punk, onto other areas. When they interrogated the specter of a supplanted American history for West Germany they sought to envision postwar German modernity free of fascism and made clear the vital role an alternative mode of media consumption for any escape from the centripetal forces of American racism and "forgotten" West German racism. However, it cannot be stressed enough: this was not some libertarian push to solve the problems of American-German modernity. A political project and not one that encouraged the endless proliferation of identities, the cultural anthropology and subversive semiotics in *Mit der Kirche ums Dorf* and *Mode & Verzweiflung* resignified mass-media images to unmask the destructive nature of the unproblematic uptake of discourses and their historical legacies. Rather than offering a clear answer, the images in Meinecke's stories represented an "an intelligent play with styles, that constantly tries to determine their historical context" (*MV* 118). This cybernetic iteration of "no future" was all about semiotics and meaning and poaching and context. However, blackface and drag ensured that things—either in the mainstream and passively accepted or in alternative media—were never what they seemed; Meinecke's texts signal through montage a feedback loop that mutated relations and encouraged subversive consumption. An example of and catalyst for an oppositional public sphere, the band and fanzine vignettes make clear the political implications of a post-punk mode of media consumption, namely that such counterproduction could create products, practices, and agency able to escape the deadly consequences of feigned reconciliation with racism, fascism, and history. The legacy of that counter production is the story of the next chapter.

CHAPTER FOUR
AFTER PUNK: CYNICISM AND SOCIAL CORRUPTIBILITY

those are stories read in books. stories from daily life.
[...] stories and i stole them. it occurred to me later
that it can be better said. [...] there is so much
and nothing that i want to tell you.[1]

According to Thomas Meinecke's last essay for *Mode & Verzweiflung,* his and FSK's attempt to subvert the sociopolitical mainstream via post-punk reading practices ended in 1987. "Last Contribution: Quarantine" concludes that the "dark belief in the good in politics will have to be, sooner or later, replaced with the shining belief in its corruptibility" (123). Such sentiment is unsurprising. For if the meltdown at Chernobyl a year prior was not enough to deter the political and social appetite for nuclear Cold War, then the dynamism of a subculturally spawned apocalypse—punk's good politics—stood slim chance of altering the trajectory of the public sphere. Attuned to that reality, certain factions of eighties' punk changed course; they disavowed adherence to chaos and dystopia and instead willingly took up mainstream positions. Thus, while punk fanzines such as *Ostrich, brauchbar/unbrauchbar,* and *Hamburger Abschaum* were never meant to last, Meinecke's pessimism at the demise of *Mode & Verzweiflung*'s resistive politics should not be taken at face value.[2] In light of the culture industries' ability to level the most apocalyptic moments, his exaltation of corruption and failure must be understood through a different logic, one that underwrites punk's perhaps most cunning move: selling out by means of adapting affirmative mainstream aesthetics. This chapter details that move, how punk feigned the death of shock, chaos, and subversive consumption to engender the social torpor it despised so much. Precisely the sounds and narratives of affirmative culture that for years were celebrated in the mainstream became, through adaptation and reproduction, no longer anathema to punk's apocalyptic fantasies but rather the means to lull its enemies to sleep. A strategy synchronic with the nuclear winds and violent politics of

its present, punk's move left untapped the chaotic energy initially fundamental for its dystopia to redirect the apocalyptic fantasies-cum-realities
that resided in the core of West German sociopolitical culture. When it
channeled the aesthetic processes in music and literature through which
the values of the status quo erected rigid dichotomies, punk disavowed the
apotheosis of aesthetic rationalization of cultural values that ensued the per-
ilous circular movement of adversarial cultures. A radical departure from
ushering in apocalypse, punk thereby began to harvest subordination; it
began to celebrate cultural impoverishment resulting from failed sociopolitical self-determination as it erased itself from its present.

Punk materiality—fanzines, music, and literature—clearly lent itself to
this disappearance: fanzines sought not only to alter radically the form and
thereby the content of literature but also to ensure that this rupture had
no future, the instable composition of bands intended to dethrone any star
cult, and Raspe ensured the reestablishment of the barriers torn asunder by
his psychotic performance. This chapter shows how that troika made easy
punk's ostensible self-erasure from the eighties, and also how it represents a
secret means of infiltration. Testament to how punk excelled at foretelling
its demise while concurrently insinuating itself on the mainstream, before
its corpse could grow stiff the music magazines *Spex* and *Sounds* had sucked
up its aesthetic. Monthly publications that envisioned themselves as venues for the intersection of music and pop-culture journalism, of emergent
German authors and Marxist theory, *Spex* and *Sounds* were mainstream
iterations of punk journalism. When they paired articles on the work of
Kippenberger and stories about the suicide of Joy Division's Ian Curtis
with fiction by Goetz and cultural theory by Diederich Diederichsen,
their pages make unmistakable how both deployed subversive collages
of choice material in an attempt to resignify, to determine the popular
from a liminal position located outside and inside. In effect the magazines culled S.Y.P.H. and Goetz's quest for agency under emergency laws
alongside FSK and Meinecke's subversive consumerism. And though both
magazines clearly devoured punk and post-punk, neither represents some
journalistic Moloch whose power formed a constellation of imitative writers in a punk-esque attempt to contest the margins and center of society.
Punks themselves passionately and willingly engaged this testing ground
as a new post-punk space that could perhaps still be subversive despite its
mainstream location. *Spex* and *Sounds* failed. Punk's venture to recycle
a punk past in the middle stood no chance of resolving the subculture's
impending confinement or decaying agency. Quite oppositely, though
Sounds completely destabilized its own sociopolitical intervention with
regular corrections to its previous claims and positions—moves testifying

to the magazine's attempts to establish itself as a critical-theoretical rather than a consensus-seeking organ—Frank Apunkt Schneider points out that its valorization of a destabilized and theoretically informed position found zero resonance. Whereas British pop songs orchestrated "cultural battles" (*Kulturkampf*), the reality of *Sound's* musical-critical project paled in comparison. The readers' letters bear out how "no one discussed its ramshackle theses [...] no one applied them or resolved them."[3] Though evidence supports Schneider's argument, the logic behind *Spex* and *Sounds* was never really about bringing down upon themselves the vehement disapproval sought out by punk in the form of S.Y.P.H. Rather, with their projects of centered destabilization, specialized experiences, and modes of knowledge, they ultimately (if unintentionally) buttressed the stagnation and codified continuation of punk's critical invective. *Sounds* editor Diedrich Diederichsen is unambiguous on the failed project of a mainstream approximation of punk aesthetic practices or theory. In 1983, he contrasted the vitality of pop theory in the United Kingdom with the "dumb Germans who wanted music and had their fill of it. May they choke on it!"[4] In light of punk's inability to alter the trajectory of the FRG by adapting violence or subversive media production, it would seem, then, that its turn to the avant-garde was successful only in confirming that modernity had exhausted the possibility of aesthetic resistance. Evidence of this hopeless condition are the pages of *Sounds* and *Spex*. Clearly reaffirming capital's deep penetration into countercultural production, what becomes clear by reading punk alongside *Sounds* and *Spex* is how at either the subcultural or at mainstreamed level, punk's frenetic aesthetic praxis failed to halt the onslaught and future march of social conservatism and normalization; its anarchic materiality failed to stave off the effacing of Germany's pockmarked present. This chapter examines that ultimate crisis of time, space, and aesthetic production, a crisis of social corruptibility demarking a moment in which the failures of progressive postmodernism made punk, *Spex,* or *Sound's* aesthetic contestation of the present a failure. Rather than its end, punk's demise put into play philosophical debates over the fate of cultural and social modernity in ways adapted from the confinement of aesthetic production to the culture industries' means-end rationality. Because it channeled a mode of negative resistance dependent on that repressive logic, punk's end makes clear how recycling failed moments from the past was no means to cure the present. Paradoxically, though, its end also shows how recycling could engender punk's affective élan—hate—to make one last apocalyptic attempt at realizing the radical potential in "no future."

An Unfinished Project

Because he walked in the nuclear winds theorized four years earlier by Glaser in *Rawums* and made real by Chernobyl, when Joachim Lottmann published articles in *Spex* he did so in an environment that had normalized punk's apocalyptic fantasies of "no future." Framed between Diederichsen's assessment of punk's journalistic failure and Meinecke's quarantine for subversive consumerism, the emergent writer and member of the punk, literary, and art scene in Hamburg and Cologne bemoaned in 1985 the end of politics whatsoever, "because nothing works through politics anymore, with this 'fake'-politics—and the other, the real, has gently slipped away, it seems."[5] The binary of real versus fake politics or boring talk opposing violent action created a social stalemate, a condition wherein the Federal Republic had become the contemporary instance of Carthage. When Lottmann declared in his title "Ceterum censeo Catharginem delendam esse," he instrumentalized the recycled city of the ancient world—Carthage—to justify the destruction of Germany, the recycled land of modern Europe. But this was not some esoteric reprisal of punk's apocalyptic fantasies destined for the same fate as Diederichsen's musical-theoretical theses on cultural struggle. The forefathers of European modernity positioned rational thought as the cure for the classical violence that made Carthage's destruction logical; Lottmann's pathology of the West German eighties heralds precisely such philosophical discourses of modernity as a cure. There was no ideal to be found in the present, just a nexus of destruction fueled by the transition from the old to the new, devoid of a parallel improvement of social and moral norms. Two decades of social unrest, the heightened reality of nuclear (self-)annihilation, and the Federal Republic's economic sinkhole speak to the facile fantasy of mere teleological progress. Thus, Lottmann diagnosed faith in a redeemed modernity as quaint if it lacked the powerful union of rational standards and the market economy, coordinates Frankfurt School philosopher Jürgen Habermas contemporaneously linked to neoconservative cultural and political trends. Yet if framed with his unmarked punk dilettantism in mind, the author's unwavering endorsement of societal and cultural modernization as the logical and just backlash to failed insurrections unveils the text's dedication to the subversive affirmation embodied by Der Plan's play with Chagall, *Capital*, and conformism in their album covers and stage backdrops. The Latin title is a particular form of Cato the Elder's dictate that does not take shape until well into the Roman Empire, is absent from any extant fragments of Cato's speeches, and is a restructuring of Cicero's quite different paraphrasing of Cato.[6] Overtly yet erroneously channeling the ancient world that constituted Enlightenment philosophy's Other, the title sets the stage for an intelligent play with calculated style, for feigning intellectualism, in the text's furtive mission to cast an affirmative foundation on shaky, violent ground.

All of the classical-cum-modern gymnastics that the title encourages are but a preview for the article's real target, the contemporary instance of philosophical-political discourse. Lottmann pleads with his television—the vector of politics and philosophy—to show him something that matters, but he rejects what it offers: "That is supposed to be politics? This blather? Is there nothing else? A street-fight for all I care, a bush war, mutinying soldiers, a car bomb." The television tries again and again to show the narrator subcultural politics that matter or that could change society, but nothing works. At last, "he finally admitted to me, my little television. Politics—that's over" (27). In light of the union of actors and conservative politics under the sign of Reagan, Lottmann concludes that subversive attempts to misuse the media had reached a nadir, nostalgically begging for a modern age of innocence and progress. Television's omnipotence in Lottmann's essay "The Political Television" promises to fulfill this desire. Another instance of Benjamin's "constellation saturated with tensions," emerges in the 1986 article wherein Lottmann appears at odds with Meinecke and FSK's faith in subversive reading and in step with Negt and Kluge's assessment that new media indeed "dispensed with pluralism" (*PS* 154–155). "The organizing factor Nr. 1 of our society, television," the article argues, structured society with complete autonomy (55). Postpunk in Meinecke's hands can be understood as what Hal Foster dubbed a "postmodernism of resistance," as something that changed the object and its social context to resist the status quo. In Lottmann's calculus, television's capacity to (re)organize completely post-punk or any subculture's counterproducts made clear that broadcast media was what mattered, not people's use of it or their action independent of it. The latter is unambiguous in his conclusions on the unsuitability of media for alternative social transformation. "Throw away your guns RAF-people!" he declares, "As long as my little 'National Color TV' sets the order of things every night you guys have no chance."[7] Lottmann's position is eminently pragmatic, for terrorists' spectacular actions or those who imitated the RAF for political gains withered under the speed and normalizing power of network television. Concurrent with the successes witnessed in FSK and Meinecke's counterproducts and Goetz's bloody assault, punk's flight to the fringes—its attempt to define itself through aesthetic violence, fanzines, and subversive consumerism—was becoming the location of everything. Punk's turn to aesthetic violence in its attempts to escape the defeated logic of protest and adversarial culture was no cure for the flattening of contrast between the given and the possible. As such, what Lottmann unveils about the productivity and efficiency of the West German public sphere is what Herbert Marcuse in the 1960s called the "rational character of its irrationality." Dictated from above, a public sphere, the likes of what Lottmann saw in 1986, enacted unmistakably a transformation of destruction into consumption, a mutation that ensured the defeat of countercultural aesthetics by the perpetuation of forms of struggle within a static system of "oppressive productivity."[8] What was once an attempt to destabilize the grip of ideology in everyday life, punk's contestation of the margins became the new mainstream.

In the wake of such failure the only space left for any attempt at another punk or post-punk ethos would, then, have been in the space vacated in the center. If it was affective politics that Lottmann sought after punk, then he had to go back inside the institution that everyone had once tried to escape or blow up. Enacting his clandestine invective, Lottmann began to write for the national newspaper *Die Zeit* in 1986. Holding high the banner of his journalistic institutionalization, Lottmann celebrated his corruption in a series of neoconservative rants that dismissed the possibility of effective aesthetic resistance. However, it was only from this affirmative location, this chapter argues, that Lottmann, bolstered by his mainstream creditability, secretly set his sights on inciting a self-erasure of the culture industries by forcing the inside to attack its own space in media and in the popular. The author leapt at the chance to over-affirm rational standards, especially moral ones, and to heighten neoconservative arguments to the point of self-oblivion. In April of 1986, he dismissed pop and punk because both had been co-opted by mainstream French cinema. "The sought-after adaptation of British pop-coolness," Lottmann writes, "only leads to fact that with every actor one thinks: As nice as the punk-outfit is, this guy would rather sit in a bistro, drink red wine, eat cheese, and babble while gesticulating wildly."[9] Miming conservative sociological thought, Lottmann unveiled the adaptive potential of pop culture as a mere façade for people who would rather be doing something else, as an instance of subcultures working in the "service of culture," as the sociologist Dieter Baacke contemporaneously argued (5). But for Lottmann, while mainstream readers of *Die Zeit*—just as those of *Sounds* and *Spex*— only simulated interest in the popular's potential for political dissidence, they nevertheless now had ample ammunition to dismiss its supposedly radical intervention once versed in its co-opted instances. Arming the mainstream thusly, Lottmann's August 1986 review of *The Karate Kid II* ostentatiously ignores FSK's subversive consumerism.[10] His review echoes the boilerplate hopelessness under American pop-cultural hegemony that seemed destined to dominate the globe and make nothing matter, not even Hiroshima. Ostensibly ignoring the Ukrainian meltdown four months prior, the review instead picked up World War II in its prosaic anti-American argument against the FRG as a nesting ground for an American nuclear arsenal. One-upping his own pedestrian lamentations, Lottmann segues awkwardly to absent generational discontent in the United States. "93 percent of US-youths want to be like their parents," he complains.[11] While certainly the popular, media, and the margin had failed, I argue below that Lottmann's method for besting the culture industry's denigration of contemporary resistance to a "postmodernism of reaction"—that repudiated modernism and celebrated the status quo—was in effect to trick the status quo into defeating itself.

Instead of chaos and detritus, Lottmann unleashed completely the flow of conservative talking points to unbridle cultural modernization. Through the optic of FSK and Meinecke's unruly transnational consumption, the hidden logic behind Lottmann's embrace of the overdetermined relation in the Federal Republic par excellence (American cultural hegemony) becomes clear. That youth no longer felt any contradiction between their generation and their parents', that youth culture was present but defunct, mattered not. Lottmann encouraged this conjecture with his own obliteration of any difference between the mainstream and the margin. Attempts to willingly take up a position in the center, his articles signify a double position adapted from the failure to make an outside and the failure of resignified popular media. A steady diet of newspaper articles may lead one to tap Lottmann with a modicum of success in the mid-eighties. But Lottmann did not study the failures of punk and post-punk to achieve success. Lottmann was not interested in success. He wanted failure. His contributions demonstrate a unique legacy of punk's dialectical dedication to "no future" precisely because of the manifold failures and crises he experienced and declared. After all, the aesthetic and thematic correlation between this late punk and his 1977 forefathers are unmistakable. He harnessed 1987 televisual malaise through its late seventies' iteration in Mittagspause's "Testbild," the politeness of German rebels under the guise of contented American youth witnessed in Der Plan's album "There's a light in front of us," and with feigned affirmation of the phantasmagoric social opportunities in the eighties he echoes perfectly the song "Angriff aufs Schlaraffenland" (Attack on the land of plenty) by the early eighties' punk band Die Radierer (The Erasers). With that early triptych as scaffolding, this chapter unfolds Lottmann's covert continuation of "no future" under the banner of an unwavering hatred for cultural decline à la social conservatives. Lottmann's use of punk ten years after its death anticipated and demanded social conservatives take up his cynical fatalism. His work, clearly the least spectacular of any instance of punk discussed in this book, is a crucial coda, for it denotes an aesthetic counterargument to Habermas's contemporaneous plea for a completion of the project of modernity.[12] The conditions of possibility of Lottmann's work are the failures of punk that engendered the author's ultimate dedication to "no future": the astute and radical manipulation in the center of punk's crises.

Lottmann's empty resoluteness to surrender must be understood as an authentically punk posture ontologically rooted through its modality of "no future" and resolutely wedded to the avant-garde's discourse on modernity that stands opposed to Habermas's solutions for cultural modernity's aporias. While Habermas redeemed the promise of emancipation and enlightenment, Lottmann's texts caused their mainstream venues to trip over themselves in hasty and anticipatable affirmation of the author's dismissal of subversive cultures. In his last-ditch attempt to prove his thesis—that freedom and autonomy could only come through an acknowledgement of their complete impossibility—Lottmann refused to encourage subversive consumerism, to hope for the mainstream to murder the moonlight, or to sustain modernity's rationality. Instead, his narratives cloaked themselves in the culture industries' robes, not to enter the sphere of social modernization and mine its interior in the vein of Benjamin's assessment of the avant-garde, but to let it unwittingly take over the fight of social unrest. Whereas Habermas distinguished between societal and cultural modernization to show that the latter ills society in his attempts to delink capitalist modernization from culture, Lottmann escaped the "church of Habermas"—signaled by his turn to "healthy arrogance" against communicative settling—when he used his prose to heighten the neoconservative disdain for art in favor of rational morality to the point where, if taken up by readers, it would reach self-oblivion.[13] This affirmative punk strategy ultimately directed against the false normativity of a West Germany under course correction from the turmoil of the sixties and seventies seemingly affirms, as Habermas asserted in 1980, that "the anarchistic intention of exploding the continuum of history [...], an aesthetic consciousness which rebels against the norm-giving achievement of tradition [...] finds almost no resonance today."[14] But Habermas's proclaimed death of the avant-garde underestimates what this chapter argues Lottmann's oeuvre channels, namely the avant-garde's interest in miming norms that would "restrain libertinism, restore discipline and the work ethic, and promote the virtues of individual competiveness" in the interest of erasing those ethics and virtues forever (42). Producing from within stories that were thematically fatalistic and aesthetically bad, Lottmann's narratives were about cynical acceptance, not about FSK's disquieting compliance. When they forced the reader to hate them and affirm a romantic past, the stories unflinchingly pinned social malaise onto subversive cultures, inspired hate of insurrection, and recathected social integration. The ultimate attempt at an apocalyptic event horizon, punk in Lottmann's physics refused to offer an alternative, it sought to use the dark energy latent in the culture industries—its "oppressive productivity" honoring the status quo—as the catalyst for a violent implosion. The articles discussed thus far were but Lottmann's entry pass into the culture industries. From within he could finally inspire a full frontal, self-annihilating assault.

The Aesthetics of Hate

The few articles above pale in comparison to Lottmann's literary production of the period. By 1987, Lottmann had written between 40 and 50 novels, thousands of pages, bound by the author himself.[15] But this massive literary oeuvre was neither a contemporary contribution nor subcultural correction to the West German canon; 98 percent of it remained on Lottmann's bookshelf. However, his bookshelf is more than a private archive of withheld novels. The hyper-productive author was a literary factory who personified the aesthetic failure of which he wrote in his articles, and the bookshelf frames and anticipates his project's negative trajectory. Though the collection could be understood as an archive of failure if success is based on commercial proliferation, or as an archive of history that has never been told, it is best understood as a cynical archive dedicated to late eighties' cultural failure. Whereas the pessimist invested in punk's original "no future" would write not expecting to publish, the cynic who channels the legacy of "no future" would only publish if publishing could be a gesture of contempt, a gesture of hatred. Lottmann's monumental literary failures signify not a punk project of destruction, for there is clearly production here, but rather a project of negation, whereby he reclaims for himself punk's "no future" in light of punk and post-punk's corruptibility. An archive to the end of the line, the bookshelf foreclosed the possibility of any kind of relationship with the affirmative "ritual elements" (Marcuse) that, Lottmann's articles argue, permeated aesthetic production in the eighties. There was no public future for these texts.

Revealing the logic behind the epigraph at the start of this chapter, the author's cynical project of failure—one that affirmed the remoteness of art from life, withdrew social unrest into the specialized complexes of production, and reified morality and law—illuminates a punk genealogy from Peter Hein and the Ratinger Hof to Lottmann's articles in *Die Zeit*. Bookending the origins and erasure of punk, Lottmann and the band Fehlfarben present historical products contingent on the results of struggles that could have come out differently, products not founded on the idea of progress but on an actualization of aesthetics that annihilated the idea of progress. Because he unchained rehashed conservative discourse,

Lottmann disclosed the role it can play in overcoming its own rigid cultural dictates. Thus the author's subcutaneous instrumentalization of a punk past for his present, for example, was not an instance of this same recycling in *Spex* or *Sounds*. On Fehlfarben's 1980 album "Monarchy and Daily Life," the band enacted a sonic precursor to Lottmann's strategy, and the discursive tension for those staking out a political position through aesthetic production in the West German eighties is unmistakable on the album. The band's assessment that on the streets a "ban on speaking ruled" ("angst") evinces the sonic-narrative dead end in their song "das sind geschichten" wherein Hein sings "there is so much and nothing that i want to tell you." The album, as Peter Glaser asserts in the CD-booklet for its rerelease, was predicated on "a new, provocative position: compliance and affirmation."[16] Precisely the band's strategy of supplanting shock and protest with unbridled celebration of the "crystal clear beauty of modern life" in the eighties subsidizes Lottmann's rejection of punk: his refusal to publish was a scorched earth strategy à la Fehlfarben's "apocalypse" that also celebrated the lowbrow sensationalism and literary leveling in their song "militürk."[17] Additionally, his texts obliquely enacted the fatalism of "those are stories," for Lottmann's breakneck rate of aesthetic production—when framed through his published work—signals a literary attempt to flood the market with enough noise to foreclose the possibility of attending to any one message. In his latter-day praxis of Fehlfarben's plight, Lottmann's 1987 novel *Mai, Juni, Juli* incited the ire of the mainstream feuilleton precisely because its narrative was an unreadable mess. Not only did it have nothing to say, but its resurfaced old material—a poorly enacted literary montage—denigrated as merely a period of decline the aesthetic progress celebrated by the press in the persons of contemporary authors and the "Group '47." Overtly and clandestinely, Fehlfarben and Lottmann disclose the aesthetic malaise that the mainstream clung to so dearly—with its high praise for Hanns-Josef Ortheil, Christoph Ransmayr, Patrick Süskind, and Günter Grass—as nothing more than the "inexhaustible nourishment" of boredom (*AP* D1,5). Judging *Mai, Juni, Juli* narratively, critics blasted Lottmann for sampling Knut Hamsun's *Hunger* and for reprinting part of his *Spex* article on Münster in the novel. But that he reaped the neoconservative disdain he inflicted on other aspects of youth culture was nothing more than the mainstream press falling for the trick played on them: they mistook as its own choice the novel's justification for "its violent expulsion from the continuum of historical process" and the ensuing genesis of an aesthetic caesura (*AP* N10a,3). The strategy of ostentatious sampling, in step with Fehlfarben's own admission that its songs told "stories from daily life [...] and they are stolen," walked the double ground of affirmation and resistance witnessed in more spectacular interventions against the self-validating processes of the West German eighties.[18] *Mai, Juni, Juli's* unoriginality forced the feuilleton to dismiss the novel as "crude babble sold as parody," but the novel's secret goal was to unveil all literature as ineffective.[19] Enacted through its intervention into aesthetic production as a neo-bulwark to qualitative social change, the novel ultimately brands literature as complicit in neoconservative girding of capitalist modernization, the partner to cultural modernity. Recycling in popular culture—Reagan as the final instance of media poaching, French cinema as the final instance of punk's scrambling of signs, kids miming their parents instead of changing the future—makes unmistakable Lottmann's acknowledgement of the impossibility of freedom and autonomy. Adversarial factions only succeeded in hardening the aspirations of the "rational organization of social relations" and in engendering the continuation of violence from Carthage to the Federal Republic's emergency powers (*MUP* 45). However, *Mai, Juni, Juli* lays out a strategy through which freedom and autonomy can nevertheless spring forth from an impossible situation, one whose coordinates were hate, rage, and cynicism.

An unlikely theoretical ally in this analysis because of his disdain for the Frankfurt School and popular culture is Peter Sloterdijk and his 1983 analysis of dynamic cynicism. Kynicism, an affective position that Sloterdijk argues can release a "moral scandal of criticism; after which the conditions of possibility of the scandalous unroll," echoes in Lottmann's rejection of German literary and social cultures, notions of success, and postmodernism of resistance, and also in the feuilleton's vitriolic reaction to his novel.[20] If modernity was based on subjectivity and the power of critical reflection, and hopes for overcoming the contradictions of modern subjectivity were pegged to philosophical reason, Lottmann's resolute fight to drive the social via dynamic cynicism (Sloterdijk's example is a man urinating into the wind) strove to unveil rationality as vacuous. Hate—the kind that Lottmann's articles encouraged and experienced—was an apt tool for the author, to continue Sloterdijk's appraisal thereof, because it carries out "the annihilation [...] up to the very end. Only if the old could be completely erased could the reconstruction of the correct relations begin on an empty swept construction site."[21] However, the philosopher's vision of a return to premodernity is precisely what the internal logic of Lottmann's texts facetiously mimes; Sloterdijk's philosophical-social goals resonate in the very neoconservative ideals that Lottmann sought to push to the point of absurdity and self-erasure. Indeed, *Mai, Juni, Juli* dismantles the former's claim that critical theory had become stagnant and the avant-garde stale, for if there is anything unifying behind Lottmann's misanthropic texts, it is an unwavering dedication to the flexibility and bulldozing of the present embodied by Benjamin's "destructive character."

The crucial philosophical, aesthetic, and cultural conjuncture that *Mai, Juni, Juli* represents through cynicism and hate squares the novel with part of a reconstructed modernity that cannot return to or reuse the past in celebration of the present, but that must rather stew in its own ruins. An antipode to a postmodernism of reaction and a postmodernism of resistance, Lottmann's cynicism represents "an unwelcome revelation [...] that rips down the veil of conventions, lies, abstractions and discretions, in order to get to the point."[22] In stark contradistinction to its surface, this instance of hate put into action does not signal an affective position that resigned to the neoconservative ideals it valorized. An astute rewiring of punk shock after its normalization, hate, Lottmann's strategy unveils, had merely become the only affect whose energy could cut through the haze of an affirmative postmodernism that vacillated between the poles of reaction and resistance. Benjamin's intersections of ruins had become intersections of content; Lottmann's texts celebrate this condition wherein the rhetoric of consent and progress ultimately signaled an inescapable catastrophe, namely the status quo (*AP* N9a,1).

Setting up a very different kind of "Inner-city front" than Mittagspause's in 1979, Lottmann allowed neoconservative verve to turn against itself. When he declared the death of subversive youth cultures by celebrating the resolution of generational strife in the United States or the FRG, he negated the ability of "adversary culture" to support the legacy of social interventions that had run their course (Marcuse). When his stories foreground the artificiality of any attitude and turn to failure, they fuse themselves with authenticity to signal, as Lawrence Grossberg argues on rock and music, "a new cynical relationship to the ideological."[23] Because at their core they insisted on the ostensibly debunked moniker "no future," Lottmann's articles and archive harnessed a "structure of feeling" against ideology in an attempt to make something matter in the wake of so many failures in mattering, they made failure matter.[24] Failures mattered because "nothing but the sheer spectacle of a negative affect remain[ed]" after Lottmann attacked "the last vestiges of meaning and pleasure."[25] Although the narrator of Lottmann's novel knows that it is a "great crime to be misanthropic," he uses his centered position to reject everything in the mainstream and the margins; he declares free time, pop culture and literature failures, and thus advocates universal consensus in his rearticulation of punk within pure negativity.[26] Lottmann's neoconservative horror at social decline, at the crisis of social corruptibility, is the most important moment in his reengineered "no future" because it made possible what Grossberg calls "grotesque inauthenticity," a strategy defined by a "logic of 'ironic nihilism.'" The desperate need to make something matter "outside the social systems of difference through an affective indifference," punk nihilism in Lottmann's hands took "no future" to turn hate into feeling, harness rage for negation, and mobilize these in an attempt to differentiate the very ideological boundaries of everyday life that limit social practices and agency.[27] By decentering punk's apocalypse in the equation, Lottmann's socio-aesthetic praxis theorized and enacted a noninstrumental relation to transformative practice—one invested in a form of subversive agency attuned to its impossibility. If there was no hope of an affective relation to mediated existence and recycled history after all attempts to stave off mainstream culture's frantic "dogmatism and moral rigorism," then perhaps instead of mourning, failure could found a new relation to the ideological and eke out a new relationship to history, society, and the public sphere (*MUP* 50). Hating the indifference of failed relationships, Lottmann's texts represent an instance after the failures of punk and post-punk that seeks to fulfill punk's ultimate apocalyptic prophecy: End it all by stopping the endless recycling of narratives and strategies. End it all by embracing the crises and failures in critical deconstruction of tradition and a pastiche of pop-historical forms. To stop the endless postmodern recycling by seeking out failure, Lottmann's entire project turned to one novel, a novel that failed.

The Logic of Crisis and Failure

Mai, Juni, Juli: Ein Roman (May, June, July: A Novel), Lottmann's lone published manuscript from the eighties, is on its surface an unlikely heir to punk's apocalyptic fantasies. But when it uses "grotesque inauthenticity" masked as productive recycling to end neoconservative backlash, it deploys a logic whose ultimate success would lead to its own cessation. Infolding failure into itself while cloaked in the trappings of affirmative moral criticism, the novel's cynicism transformed "no future" from a failed mantra into an articulation of feeling based on failure. Because it was predicated on failure, it was neither an attempt to open a gap between the past and present nor was it an argument for continued faith in alternative production that could transform consumers into producers. Rather, by disingenuously disavowing its subcultural foundation, it attempted to get outside ideological abstractions and unmask self-failure as the necessary energy for historical progress. Though it mimed narratively en vogue literary aesthetics ostensibly to harvest literary success, in effect *Mai, Juni, Juli* recounted the crises brought forth by the mainstream ratification of pluralizing dynamics of violent and theoretical insurrection, subversive mass media, punk, post-punk, and postmodern pastiche. As such, Lottmann's novel refused the fateful dialectic of social liberation and cultural modernization and instead flaunted its dilettantism in the face of its ivory tower counterpart Habermas, for the novel is the aesthetic consciousness that demarks all cultural modernization as "a great seductive force [...]

quite incompatible with the discipline required by professional life" (*MUP* 42). Attending to the links between *Mai, Juni, Juli* and punk's "no future" unveils the conditions that, for Habermas, ensured the inefficiency of radical aesthetics but simultaneously the possibility for the novel to enter into a social function. The philosopher's devaluation of aesthetic intervention is in *Mai, Juni, Juli* the condition of possibility for literature qua aesthetic product to pass itself off as ineffective. As argued below, the literary trends the novelist mimes (at the intertextual and extratextual level) are the embodiment of the intractability of professional life and radical aesthetics that Habermas argued foreclosed the completion of modernity. Nevertheless, *Mai, Juni, Juli* unveils literary praxis as affirmative-cum-destructive when it highlights its own internal impossibility, such as the concurrently incompatible logic of resistive youth cultures with the novelist's romanticized profession. In his framing of Fehlfarben's album, Glaser argues for the band what the novel seeks out, namely a narrative "hymn for new realism that did not evade artificiality and contradiction."[28] Specifically, Lottmann's production, as Hubert Winkels inventories, celebrates its literary artificiality when it mimes to reveal as inept "the social-critical novel, the romance novel, the political and pornographic novel, the novel with Dadaist verve, the committed and autobiographical novel, the popular and intellectual novel, the historical novel and the novel of our times."[29] Obliquely channeling both Adorno's lack of faith in cultural criticism and Nietzsche's subversive cosmology of eternal return, *Mai, Juni, Juli* thereby used negation to drive those lingering conditions of modernity that enabled barbarism to the point of their own internment and annihilation.

Mai, Juni, Juli's cynicism vis-à-vis previous aesthetic demands for the products of authentic self-experience that are able to rebel against sociohistorical normalization is quite overt. Disarming explosive elements of cultural modernity, the "novel that changed everything," the narrator asserts early on, required a theme that was "fashionable" (7 and 27). *Mai, Juni, Juli* manipulates the contradictions between aesthetic production and market forces, of social transformation and historical trauma to cloak its aesthetic fantasy of unchaining those social-aesthetic forces that engender failure as a private crisis. Putting theory into praxis, the novel's 1987 publication with Kiepenheuer & Witsch made possible the novel's first crisis of reception, form, and content. Lottmann wrote *Mai, Juni, Juli* after he received an advance and three months housing from Helge Malchow, editor at Kiepenheuer & Witsch publishing house, and the fledgling writer spent May, June, and July of 1986 in Cologne, Germany. After its publication, the press panned *Mai, Juni, Juli* as the "most trivial phenomena that the 80s have ever produced."[30] Some critics used their disdain to rebut Glaser's *Rawums* and its 1984-heralding of social transformation spurred by cultural invectives drawn from music and the aesthetics of the "New Wilds."[31] Of course, those who made broadly dismissive gestures of both texts were exactly the targets of Glaser's collection and of Lottmann's novel. The former dismissed literary criticism that once again bemoaned the death of literature[32]; the latter preemptively called forth this crisis by directly attacking the ivory tower's "Autorenfetischmus" (authorial fetishism).[33] More to the core of Lottmann's cynical cessation of punk, the disdain emanating from the feuilleton smacks of the intellectual elitism of those dedicated to Enlightenment rationality (and its aesthetic unity of form and content); such critical assessments—just as sociological appraisals of punk—clearly have ready-made responses to deviant and divergent style. After all, Glaser's anthology is open ended, his explosive exposé introducing the collection has, in stark contrast to Lottmann's novel, a narrative intensity that sees speed and energy as solutions to the redundant "Lahmarschigkeit" (lethargy) of aesthetic production that characterizes *Mai, Juni, Juli* (*R* 9). Lottmann's novel, conversely, lazily recycles literature in order to arm the critical press with the axe needed to smash *Mai, Juni, Juli* to bits. As discussed below, it even gave the press the narrative proof to link aesthetically and thereby to debunk Glaser's claim for speed when Lottmann's author-narrator cranks out a newspaper report—an insignificant piece on popular culture—in "record time" (108). If *Mai, Juni, Juli* was the legacy of Glaser's literary punk verve, then both were indeed worth dismissal. As discussed at the end of this chapter, that Lottmann's text had effects on past production, reveals the effectiveness of his cynical nihilism and the success of failure for "no future." Though he experienced its wrath après la lettre, Glaser had no use for the feuilleton. In stark contradistinction to *Rawums, Mai, Juni, Juli* depended on its dismissal as "crude babble." Correspondingly, nowhere was the latter's failure more successful than in Lottmann's poaching of Hamsun, an intertextuality that purposively sought to incite the ire of the feuilleton. The hate unleashed thereby testifies to the effective logic of failure for *Mai, Juni, Juli*: through the uncontrollable release of negative affect, let the mainstream unwittingly unmask all literature as guilty of the same crime, let that unchained feeling cause an aesthetic meltdown. For, if the critical press hated *Mai, Juni, Juli* for poaching Hamsun, then it would de facto indict the novel's poaching of Johann Wolfgang Goethe, Heinrich Mann, Karl May, Friedrich Hegel, Wolfgang Borchert, Friedrich Schiller, Karl Marx, Theodor Adorno, Klaus Theweleit, Rainald Goetz, Rolf Dieter Brinkmann, Günter Grass, J. D. Salinger, William Shakespeare, J. R. R. Tolkien, and Tony Parson. The novel mimed those authors as failed literary "Simulanten" (simulators) to create a pastiche that made unavoidable Lottmann's chastisement for intertextual references (15).

The trap he set for the feuilleton was to make it unwittingly reveal its own lethargic and affirmative intertextuality. To that end successful, the reviews follow what seems to be an obligatory script in rejecting the novel: Lottmann was published because he was an insider, he sampled Hamsun, and he reprinted a *Spex* article. We have seen this before, the feuilleton argues, and therefore *Mai, Juni, Juli* did not need to be read. As a result, *Mai, Juni, Juli* soon went out of print. But with its ready-made rejection, Lottmann's ostentatious sampling encouraged the feuilleton's delusions of grandeur, forcing it to unmask the "internal conceptual weakness of neo-conservative thought" embodied by journalism's investment in buttressing "master" thought and narratives (*MUP* 43). Because of his borrowing, Lottmann's entrance into the literary center did not simply take up a central position, but took a canonical one. By claiming itself as paragon, the novel's crisis and failure—forcing the feuilleton to bring recycling, if for only one text, to an end—signals a moment of victory, a pyrrhic one wherein the culture industries enacted punk's invective. This unwelcome moment of divestiture of mainstream literature cannot be understated. After all, contemporary novels that recycled the texts of antiquity—Ransmayr's *Die letzte Welt*, Süskind's *Das Parfum*, and Ortheil's *Fermer*—were held up by the literary establishment at home and abroad as literary masterpieces.[34] *Mai, Juni, Juli* earned the ire of the critical press because the novel's celebration of sampling the canon debunked antiquity as worthy of recycling and simultaneously forced the feuilleton to reveal its hypocrisy. Its redone aesthetic modernity replaces the clearly cyclical flow of narrative aesthetics with a blatant mirage of progress constituted purely by sheer repetition. Operating within a subtle avant-garde temporality, when it anticipated and narrated the feuilleton's rejection of *Mai, Juni, Juli*, the novel simultaneously broadcast the feuilleton's own crises. More than ending a novel, when the feuilleton called for *Mai, Juni, Juli* to go out of print, it enacted the novel's critique by rejecting a Habermasian attempt at a jump-started modernity; viewed through the optic of *Mai, Juni, Juli*, the mainstream ended precisely what it meant to encourage. The novel's mainstream logic for its material worth—it was legitimate because of the aesthetic value of the things it contained—was rejected.

That Lottmann's novelist embodies an anti-Habermasian position is evidenced by the former's monomaniacal yearning to start anew the project of modernity through literary refurbishment, witness how the young writer begins and abruptly cuts off his many novels that mime the ideal of perfection and moral improvement contained in and enacted through the canon. On the one side, these reanimated novels narrate petty bourgeois yearning for a canonical narrative to obey, on the other side they divulge a crisis of affect, a crisis of mattering. For more than unveiling aesthetic fashion as eternal return, what the novelist does is channel Benjamin's schematic for social movements whereby the narrative failure resolves "to gather again, in revolutionary action and in revolutionary thinking, precisely the elements of the 'too early' and 'too late,' of the first beginning and the final decay" (*AP* a1,1). *Mai, Juni, Juli* is such a sterling example of late punk aesthetics because it is the defunct thing that stands "in as images of subjective intentions, these latter present themselves as immemorial and eternal" (*AP* N5,2). Despite channeling past literary masterpieces whose reprisal should have been a typeset for success, the narrator abandons the hope of changing the world with literature. The novel ends without a completed novel, and the nameless protagonist signs up as a mate on the same boat as in *Hunger*: "On top of the obviously new name an older, previous ship's name was decipherable because the covering paint was flaking off, 'Copégoro.'" The feuilleton's identification of this intertextual reference and ensuing dismissal of the book's value merely echoed what Lottmann's novel had already done, for it was the narrator who bashed the literary pastiche as something "completely dated, but [...] being newly repainted" (248). Because Lottmann indicted his own retooling of *Hunger* as a bad knock-off—one clearly masquerading as new but ostentatiously and poorly redone—he preemptively robbed himself of the authorial legitimacy of which the feuilleton divested him. The novel demonstrates a misuse of aesthetic materials in its attempt to annihilate the idea of progress in favor of actualization, a break with vulgar aesthetic naturalism that would posit truth in the connection of art and the practice of life (*AP* N). Lottmann's brazen remaking of *Hunger*, with its "abandonment of an aesthetics based on 'appearances,' which [in an age of simulation], are so easily falsified," is clearly kitsch.[35] Thus, though the critical press misunderstood the novel's "specifically aesthetic form of lying," it thereby unwittingly supported the novel's unmasking of a historical and social conjuncture, namely the presence of kitsch on one side and academe on the other (Cálinescu 229). This is how the novel creates a moment of punk's "no future." Through a context in which the feuilleton's reaction to *Mai, Juni, Juli*, but also through the novel itself, aesthetic experience and affect are revealed to have solidified into a recycled mass of automatisms. A literary instance of Kippenberger's refusal to "sell out to a myopic praxis" that contributed nothing, the only strategy left for aesthetics at a time when difference had ceased to matter was *Mai, Juni, Juli*'s nihilistic indifference (*AT* 338). Lottmann's stop/start narration and bad borrowing from the canon uses kitsch to perfect its aesthetic deception and self-deception. As the narrator starts and stops the 23-plus narratives afoot in *Mai, Juni, Juli*, he reveals the absence of any social relevance of contemporary literature, he reclaims literature for life by examining its death.[36] Kitsch, but also punk's recurrent failures, made it possible for the novel to consciously promote "an aesthetic modernity that was [...] radically opposed to the other, bourgeois modernity" and solidifies the novel as the aesthetic heir of punk's apocalyptic fantasies (Cálinescu 162). For the misanthropy that the narrator knows he must avoid for success and the misanthropy that Sloterdijk argues is necessary to "rip through the veil of conventions" is exactly the protest that the punk iteration of kitsch engenders. "In the face of the false and complacent humanism of the day's demagogues," punk's resolute investment in bringing the forward march of time to a standstill is the aesthetic surprise that *Mai, Juni, Juli* contains (Cálinescu 162). The mainstream feuilleton was not outraged by *Mai, Juni, Juli*'s violence or aggression (Goetz) or by its feigned fascism (Meinecke), but by its feigned normalcy. Though the book claims, following its subtitle, to be *Ein Roman* (a novel), it is predicated on the impossibility of the conditions of being just that.

In the novel's first paragraph, the nameless protagonist describes the impossibility of his existence as a novelist. "Mornings I couldn't get out of bed and evenings I had depressions. In between my head exploded. I often sat for half a day in front of a wall of nothing, a draped window, in front of my desk and thought: I am an author" (7). Despite his best efforts "to persevere at his desk and to think, [...] in front of the widow naturally," he flees his apartment in Hamburg for a stay in Cologne (12). He travels from Hamburg to Cologne and back, makes an excursion into the countryside, spends hours in cafés and bars, and actually writes a bit. The narrator's transcription of this "astreine Wirklichkeit" (genuine reality) reveals social stagnation and an overwhelming lack of creativity and inspiration (88). He wants to manipulate popular culture in literature, to get outside of the contradictions of optimism and pessimism—the keystones of adversary culture—but his attempt to use popular culture subversively meets defeat at the hands of uninspiring pedestrian life in the Federal Republic. He observes from a window in a café as people "strolled across the pedestrian crossing zones when it was green, and got in line and waited when it was red" (41). Impossible to overcome here, this crisis of the public sphere—the failure to find inspiration in daily life or to think outside the parameters dictated by societal modernization—is exactly the one enacted years prior by Der Plan. The slavish valorization of modernist tropes in literature echoes in pop-cultural pedestrians who obey crossing signals, both of which demark the masochistic social contract that Sloterdijk argues has out-flanked the creative-critical (22). Dismissing the potential in subversive cultures as did Der Plan in 1980, the narrator cannot find anything that matters. After all, writing about "genuine reality" flies in the face of his dictate that "it couldn't be the writers task to confirm that which was already in the world" (152). Thus, the novelist targets solitary melancholy, the last remaining promise of reviving the radical potential of the Enlightenment (Sloterdijk 24). Such feigned aspirations to the literary institution sought to break into the hegemonic structures of everyday life that punk once sought to expose, a paradoxical turn to "no future" that promises, briefly and weakly as the narrator boards the freighter, that there could be something beyond these crises. Begging the mainstream to end it as a literary instance of recycled French cinema, *Mai, Juni, Juli*'s inimical potential to negate the possibility of its own existence enumerates crises to enact the lost potential of punk's apocalypse.

Against Return

While clearly trapped in the postmodern dilemma of endless simulation and recycling, Lottmann's narrator does not himself burn down the house that literature built. That such destruction was necessary is unambiguous in the wake of systematic imperatives of a revamped economy and the FRG as the democratic firewall that had set back the literary-aesthetic clock to the age of German Classicism—witness the narrator's loft "in which nothing has changed since 1795" (9). Enlightenment tactics to encourage authentic self-experience had been banished to such original, isolated lofts, as Christian Jäger writes on eighties' literature, after "the previous generation, through purveyors such as Peter Handke or Botho Strauß, had clogged the prevailing literary channels."[37] Uninterested in merely reinforcing the blockade to the aesthetics of the past enacted by those authors, *Mai, Juni, Juli* did not move on from or against such proponents of the "New Subjectivity" of the 1970s.[38] Instead, by miming the past for the future, the novel exposed resignatory relativism as an aesthetic red thread in West German cultural production, one that ensured the continuation of but one feeling, boredom. In that *Mai, Juni, Juli* reflected the reality in media, it did not argue to end literary traditions or seek to mutate cultural contents, but rather manipulated for its nihilistic fantasies the spaces opened up on the inside. Effectively détourning the spaces accessible through the author's unabashed affirmation of cultural decline, the novel compelled the culture industries to turn vehemently on literary narratives previously praised. To achieve this, Lottmann's author "had to steal from the oblivious world, [...] never give an advance hint about what he had cooking [and live] without concern amongst people, apathetically almost, then, at home and behind the curtain, to let lose" (8). Concurrent with his turn to the praiseworthy canon for inspiration, he nevertheless echoes precisely the neoconservative indictment of artistic production for its separation from daily life. On the one hand the writer has internalized the resignation to "melancholic realism" of being ruled that Sloterdijk sketches as the fate of resistive cultures (169). On the other, he echoes perfectly Habermas' schematic for societal modernization—wherein there was no room for cultural modernization—because a lack of social identification and withdrawn narcissism rendered affective aesthetic experience in *Mai, Juni, Juli* torpid: "Dissidents don't exist anymore, just simulators" (15). The narrator's romantic desire for effects, his insistence that "it was only important that it was done!" is his rationale for valuing action over the specifics of production (79). A testing ground and inspiration for failure, the budding author's conclusions about aesthetic production spell out the hidden logic behind the novel's fantasy of commercial success and canonical relevance, namely to incite (its own) failure. "Why was a book there," he speaks aloud, "if after the first half-page, you didn't have the urge to run outside and imitate the book? If you didn't have the idea after the first good sentence that you wanted to carry out? When a book inspired me, it always inspired my life" (244). Playing the role of his own target, the novelist's ruse was that he was willing to lay everything on the line in his attempt to inspire his colleagues to do the same.

To that end, the narrator differentiates himself from the West German citizens he encounters because while the larger population picks up culture to continue it, he turns to the popular to end it. He feigns a search for sartorial inspiration on the streets of Cologne—both at a café and at the scene of local pop culture—only to find the anticipatable boring citizens of Cologne. "They came over, dressed boringly, with five-year old fashion hanging on an un-charming body." The poorly dressed people have uninspiring lives with uninteresting stories, they talk of "a job, a boyfriend, the bed-conversations, the conflicts 'more freedom for her/him,' [. . .] both lay naked in bed, both are quiet between the pathetic standard-sentences." These bad narratives and style function doubly. They buttress the status quo, but also, as Sloterdijk culls from Nietzsche, they show how "new values have short legs. Dismay, nearness to fellow citizens, security of freedom, quality of life" are the curtain behind which cynicism lurks (10). The failure of communication that matters is in *Mai, Juni, Juli* not just a catalyst to failed literary aesthetics, but the condition of possibility of cynical nihilism. The narrator reaches such a state of indifference after spending time in popular culture, recognizing how the popular indeed unleashed something, but rather than renewal, it "unleashed the old obsession of ANOTHER, of a BORING life" (42). Despite sartorial stagnation in which fashion is the ever-new return of the same, the narrator makes an attempt to go along with the mainstream demands that would constitute boring life. He tries to narrate slowly and in typical fashion "thoughtfully, in order to do justice to the many residents. When nothing came of that, I just started writing and hacked my report into the squeaking machine in the record-time of thirty minutes" (107–108). In the end, he resorts to writing with a vehemence that pushes his typewriter to its limits, an attack on the means of production not as a strategy to reprise what Glaser claimed was the unique energy in punk aesthetic unpredictability, but rather to harness and turn inward the energy from a crucial contradiction between aesthetic production and reception. His speed channels the velocity with which the mainstream devours subversive politics (echoing Habermas's estimation), while calling out the financial trump card that foretells the intractability of "thoughtful" production and effective aesthetics. Here, literary production is the legacy of something that had run its course. The novelist's writing inverts passion into a hateful rage to make reading literature awful; it uses itself as a prime example of why "a rationalized everyday life could not possibly be redeemed from the rigidity of cultural impoverishment by violently forcing open *one* cultural domain, in this case art, and establishing some connection with *one* of the specialized complexes of knowledge" (*MUP* 49). In an act reminiscent of the problem with isolated ivory tower academics and critical theory witnessed in the previous chapter's end, Lottmann's narrator also indicts the isolation of "specialized complexes of knowledge" from purposive action when he arms his longed-for detractors by gleefully and poorly fetishizing Marxist theory. Branding his own reaction to critical theory the way mainstream media and academics framed both '68ers and the RAFs while simultaneously resurfacing the student dedicated to what Rainald Goetz called the "rakish method" of dialectics, the narrator admits his absolute disinterest in what Hegel, Freud, Marx, or Adorno mean. Celebrating in himself the theoretical dilettantism of which students and terrorists were accused, he speaks of how he wants to enjoy the Frankfurt School's tête-à-tête with capitalist modernization as vapid teenage poetry:

> It's all poetry, after all, good and bad, whereby good poetry contributes to the good of the world for a long time. Luckily I read that stuff back then as poetry, I never wanted to re-translate, just enjoy the vehemence of the syntax, and preferably not know what expropriation of the expropriature meant, not what it REALLY means. (157)

Unable to write "thoughtfully" ("nachdenklich") because of his intellectual adolescence and his atrophied dialectic of good and bad, the narrator tries to write energetically to inspire energetic consumption, but instead his boring stories create within the literary establishment a release of negativity so forceful that it could finally bring it all to an end. Four years earlier Glaser saw frenetic energy as quintessential to punk literature, as the quality that made it "adrenaline infusing / disruptive and aggressive. /

Cutting, / offbeat, / funny. / Appropriate." With its catalytic inversion, *Mai, Juni, Juli* détourns from within precisely what Glaser claims punk literature enacted, namely the testing of "strategies between violent dismissal and offensive affirmation" (*R* 15–16). Though the novel purports to recycle literature just like popular literature of the eighties, his position as insider is radically different from Raspe's and indeed more akin to Raspe's nemesis Andreas Hippius. Thus, though the untrustworthy narrator laments his inability to draw any energy from this style, what he really does is turn that energy inward—he seeks to send its effects uncontrollably against one another to create a literary event horizon.

To this end, he dives into pop culture, punk music, and the *Bild* newspaper to fuse the canon with the margins. But his move is not an illumination of the power of the popular or a journalistic corrective. Rather, it is a catalyst for public hate of it all. The narrator wants to relish the vehement syntax of daily life as the aesthetic inadequacy fundamental for the imposition of hierarchal relationships that would favor postmodernist reconstruction. Eminently punk at his core, he wants to transform the culture industries into a singularity of aesthetic negativity able to unleash the destructive violence of literature and leave behind a macabre wasteland. Contributing to the creation of such a force, the author arms the mainstream with further evidence of the social ills spread by the "location of the local pop-culture [where people] transformed their life into deed." Affirming that pop culture is a farce, the young writer finds no difference there. "Here everybody was friends," he concludes, "everyone had the bloodshot gaze from constant beer consumption. And even though I probably looked like Count Bobby amongst the Papa-Indians, they gazed good-naturedly at me" (48). All the author gets from his time in pop culture is a headache because the truth is that the subversive potential in the popular is merely teenage angst, adolescent alcoholism, or the leveling effect of social niceties. When the young writer tries to find "the CORRECT theme [. . .] he had to go onto the square and grab people by their collars and scream at them: What interests you? [. . .] Speak, you zero!" (34). If this is the site of aesthetic experience, occupied by the readers of *Sounds* who Diederichsen hated, if this is where art is put into action and spurs cultural modernization, then the pessimism resulting from these anthropological findings is the "radical nakedness and revelation" of the constitutive element of culture that Sloterdijk claims can rip down the "veil of conventions and lies" (28). However, whereas Sloterdijk envisions this unveiling as the means to make sane the eighties' "schizoid culture," his desire to set the clock back two hundred years and remedy cultural criticism of the affective stagnation he claims Adorno propagated is precisely the neo-Nietzschean postmodernism that would plunge the Federal Republic into a technocratic abyss

(172). While he laments its absence, the young author never really desired contact with the popular, and contrary to Sloterdijk's misinterpretation of culture as schizoid, the narrator shows his proponents are merely dumb. Though unconcerned whether readers understood "anything more—why should I care? Was I my reader's keeper?" the narrator is unable to stick to his guns on this matter. Instead, he constantly tells his reader when a bit of a story begins or ends: "I started [...] I interrupted my report [...] I stopped" (88, 112, and 137). In light of his desire to end aesthetic contestation of the present, his megalomaniacal realization, that there "are no REAL writers anymore, that I was the last, or if you will, the first," borders on Raspe's desire for self-abolition. But whereas Raspe's dilemma hinged on his imminent internment, Lottmann's narrator is already inside, whence he can convince his fellow culture industry inmates that quitting is what a real author would do. Aspiring to incite literary failure in others, he fantasizes that after his "huge success hundreds and thousands would imitate me" (9–10). Perhaps afraid that mainstream literary avenues would catch onto his ruse, the novelist foretells the actual reaction journalists would have to *Mai, Juni, Juli*'s project of negation. His claim that "the feuilletonists would never recognize such things" is almost correct (13). The feuilleton did hate his text and ended its existence, but it did not follow this example.

Such partial success of negation and failure is crucial for two specific instances of canonical poaching in *Mai, Juni, Juli*, of Struwwelpeter and Thomas Mann, both of which show how the canon had lost its cultural relevance. The first intra-novel with a title, *Quellkopf* (Swollen-head), is recycled from Edward Verrall Lucas's "Swollen-Headed-William" (1914), a World War I-era anti-German parody of a Struwwelpeter story.[39] Struwwelpeter stories are highly didactic and generally designed to illustrate to children the consequences of misbehaving, and in the anti-German version that *Mai, Juni, Juli* poached, "Swollen-Headed-William"—Emperor Wilhelm II—kills innocent doves. Lucas's political satire was relevant in its time because of the contemporary popularity of Struwwelpeter stories and the Kaiser's military aggression. The novelist's text is irreverent vis-à-vis this forerunner not just because the context is completely irrelevant, but also because of the feigned importance of kids' stories for mainstream novels. While it harks back to the valorization of destruction evident in the Carthage article, this revamped story is not about criticizing the saber rattling of the German Emperor or of the FRG-United States saber rattling during the Cold War. Oppositely, *Quellkopf* narrates the failure of the popular's inheritance of such tradition when it follows a young protagonist as he spends a night in bars and whose head swells to explosive dimensions as the result of too much drink. Only a leather belt, cold water, and six aspirin prevent his head from blowing up. The second intra-novel with a title, *Pixie*, is the narrator's "porno novel," an adaptation of Heinrich Mann's *Professor Unrat*. Here a 17-year-old punk girl replaces Mann's dancer and an unlucky 42-year-old radio-editor "Daddy" replaces the professor. Throughout the fragment, Pixie has plenty of sex with Daddy, her punk friends, an artist, and a New York musician. At the end Pixie is gone, and Daddy winds up broke, divorced, and remarried to a Japanese woman, presumably in California. These texts were, on the one side, entertainment; on the other, textual fragments that celebrated as vacuous the very same intertextuality that won so much critical acclaim in the eighties. But the novelist never gets to that point because the intra-novels also celebrate abrupt cessation. When both of these novels remain incomplete, the novelist fails to complete his contributions to a new canon and instead denigrates contemporary critical literature as a pornographic bagatelle. Popular culture—city bars, cafés, clubs, and the ostensibly scenic West German countryside—meet the same fate. These spheres collide in the national *Bild* newspaper that "the people loved and 'understood'" (149). Crucially, the narrator does not rehash highbrow disdain for *Bild*; he is not fazed by *Bild*'s reputation as a gigantic "lie- and repression-machine." The *Bild*-aesthetic contains subversive potential, "in that it mixed news elements, graphic elements, feelings and other affects, such that something OTHER than reality arose, a SECOND reality, so to say, or even an oppositional reality" (148).

Yet, seven years after Fehlfarben's détournement of DAF's "kebab-träume" sought to reimagine social revolution via the "second reality" of yellow journalism, whether the pulp news *Bild* produces contains material constitutive of an oppositional public sphere is moot. It does not matter if the author is not in the repressive publishing machine because—as Diederichsen lamented about absent engagement with pop-cultural theory—Germans make poor use of this potentially subversive material (227). Indicting *Bild*—but also the critical press—as a gigantic lie- and repression-machine likewise recalls clearly Adorno's indictment of such projects of societal modernization. Years earlier he wrote that "when critics on their romping place, art, ultimately do not understand what they are judging, and with gusto allow themselves to be demeaned to propagandists or censors, then the old dishonesty of the business fulfills itself through them."[40] The narrator is clearly versed in the quagmire of academic criticism of *Bild* and popular culture as well as in popular indictment of academic elitism and esoteric aesthetics. His joy when the editors at *Bild* ask the young novelist to create an "opinion piece" testifies to this. The writer hates producing opinions "because as a writer I wanted to narrate, instead of reasoning. In my view a description was far superior to an opinion. Opinions are something for insecure people with a minority- or educational-complex. It's obvious" (29). That the masses are unable to form their own opinions recalls Germans' inability to think or act individually, as evidenced above the scene of frozen pedestrians at crossing lights who are the consumers of the feuilleton and *Bild*. Though these are the citizens of Cologne who "understand" *Bild*, they cannot take advantage of the "oppositional reality" produced by its manipulation of disparate elements. Buttressing societal modernization, *Bild*'s montage uses its "oppositional reality" to forge opinions, a pedantic and historical process unavailable for transformation. In contradistinction to the products of poaching, mass-distribution of *Bild*'s opinions in *Mai, Juni, Juli* transforms the German countryside into "the inexhaustible reservoir" that breeds ("brütet") German fascism (226). *Bild*'s boulevard propaganda, its opinion pieces, helped create a West German mass-psychology "sleeping in the body of the German folk since the times of the 'Stürmer,' and that was not pretty" (31). Rather than calling for the end of such mainstream journalism the way students of 1968 demanded an end to the Springer Press, the narrator runs amok with cultural taboos, writes whatever he wants, tells of his interruptions, pirates the canon, and drones on about those points he knows they do not want to hear. Though he announces that no one "would be interested in my old friends," he ignores this moment of clairvoyance, and proceeds to recount the story of his time with old friends (28). Above all, the novel's repeated failures armed the critical press with the rationale for thinking itself safe by maintaining, as Cálinescu describes reactionary modernism, the canonical standards of "old masters against the intrusion of commercialism and corrupt market criteria." Those very intentions of protecting that which the mainstream deems cultural treasures ensured that they are the corrupt market criteria shrouding the Federal Republic in the quagmire of social liberation and cultural modernization. While the reactionary nature of the mainstream to radical aesthetics could be undermined by the affirmative, *Mai, Juni, Juli* feigned its desire for reestablished "aesthetic standards" in order to unveil and unleash the "overriding and innermost logic of Modernism." Understood through that reactionary logic, the past that rational standards defended would be unveiled as a chimera (Cálinescu 290).

Leisure and Fascism: The Matrix for Hate

In a reenactment of German romanticism, the narrator makes a day trip to the countryside with his school friend Stephen T. Ohrt so that the two of them can recuperate from the degeneracy of the cities and be inspired to artistic production. Instead of peaceful nature, the countryside circulates "picture perfect fascists," such as a family that harassed the two for parking their car on the side of the road. Thus the nature that the novelist seeks is highly problematic: instead of a site of unmediated aesthetic experience it is an impetus to nationalism, for the floral landscapes outside Cologne is the bucolic scenery that gave the crypto-fascist Hamsun cause to write in the 1920s and signaled the fertile soil wherein German fascism "breeds" (222–226). Far from the idyllic landscapes of Casper David Friedrich, the novelist discovers "the homeland of Germany, [...] where the horror grows, that we carry in the world, there was no love here" (228). The only strip of life the narrator claims he discovers in the countryside that is not clearly fascist is a trail of ants. After this sarcastic remark the author studies the ant's organization, their well-ordered discipline, and marching in step, as he previously studied the pedestrians waiting for the crossing signal. The friends flee the countryside. Juxtaposing their sojourn into nature with its transformation into a contemporary place of leisure, the narrator and Ohrt sneak onto a tennis court of "The Club on the Alster." The two are not members for many reasons, most importantly because "since 1945 a block on the admittance of new members is in effect." This does not stop the determined friends from persevering and playing a few sets of tennis. Fittingly, the two cause confusion when real members are perplexed to find their court occupied. Unaware that the friends are interlopers, real members are exasperated, exclaiming "this is...our hour...we've been playing here at this time for twenty years...we don't understand...?" (233). The narrator and Ohrt elude detection time and again until they encounter a 55-year-old "grand lady" (237). While Ohrt weaseled out from the previous three encounters with members whose hour of play had been appropriated, he is no match for the lady, particularly after her kind demeanor makes an about-face upon finding out that the boys are not members. Speeding away in a car, the narrator recalls how the lady's "transition from 'charming' to 'chillingly brutal' was too fast and yet, smooth, fitting, real." The lady's unflinching reaction to their illegal presence in the cultural bastion "was SS-mentality" (239). His artistic energy at an ebb, Ohrt returns home with the narrator in tow.

Although in Ohrt's house "the walls lived, like pictures, from millions of paint-splats and obscure structures," the artist himself hates "wild painting." While his paintings indeed reflect the opposite—"controlled form"—this painter uses maximum flexibility "with twenty-thousand different brushes" (217–218). As such, the artist's style broadcasts a certain kind of distrustful stability, just as *Mai, Juni, Juli*'s title made a disingenuous gesture by calling itself "a novel." Inverting the threat of aesthetic unification in *Irre, Mai, Juni, Juli* feigns the faithful miming of a modernist novel, but it is "completely instable, all of it" (226). Ohrt's dismissal of the "wild" painting typical of the eighties and the dubious title "novel" of Lottmann's book represents its nihilistic indifference, whereby the novel badly reconstructs forms in order to make a difference when nothing made a difference anymore. And hereby *Mai, Juni, Juli* squares itself explicitly with punk. For just as Dick Hebdige argued for punk style, the novel sought with "grim determination [. . .] to detach itself from the taken-for-granted landscape of normalized forms, [and] to bring down upon itself such vehement disapproval."[41] This aggressive narrative inauthenticity also binds Lottmann's novel to punk's anarchic invective, as Diederichsen has argued for music, because its hope for failure "only comes from aesthetic advances that are made in connection with political or aesthetic or criminal anarchism. The program of micro-politics only has effects that differentiate themselves from the pyrrhic-victories of previous cultural revolutions."[42] The copious intertextual moments in *Mai, Juni, Juli*, like the millions of paint flecks on Ohrt's walls, question why the novel's myriad text fragments can be put together in the first place. The "Formstrenge" (controlled form) that the novelist reads in Ohrt's art is actually a devotion to dilettantism that Ohrt and the novelist both exhibit. Such play emerges in a provocative form able to release a shock, an attack on so-called progress that in its basic idea had become nothing more than what Marcuse called a "peaceful instrument of domination" (7). In *Mai, Juni, Juli*, the narrator's play with failure demonstrates, to continue with Diederichsen, "that in making mistakes one can play more exactly and transgress mechanics" (19). Through failure and transgression *Mai, Juni, Juli* made mainstream literature the matrix for and self-reflective of hate. But this was not the hate evidenced by the novel's reception. That was hate because of facile claims of its deficient intertextuality, this new matrix emerged because social modernization had made cultural modernization stagnant.

Mai, Juni, Juli differentiated itself from previous literary moments because it did not want to change the object of critique. Instead, *Mai, Juni, Juli* wanted to end all critique. Canonical literature could be recycled and celebrated, but there was no genuine social relevance for such remade narratives, just as "Quellkopf" and "Pixie" were not worthy of publication. But the novelist also critiques canonized punk authors such as Goetz and Rolf Dieter Brinkmann by rehashing the verve that heralded punk's entrance into the cultural production. By 1987, Goetz's performance at Klagenfurt had rocketed him to a high perch in the Suhrkamp publishing house and amongst the very literary opinion-makers of the feuilleton that *Mai, Juni, Juli* bashes. Misspelling Goetz's name as Götz, the novelist makes Goetz into the last of his kind, an intertextual reference to Goethe's anachronous title hero in *Götz von Berlichingen* (50). Lottmann's rejecting a repetition of punk's literary forefather—Brinkmann—is a similar attempt at selling the death of punk by miming popular disgust. The narrator plays dumb as to who Brinkmann is, remarking laconically "there was one German author, who once wrote a book in Italy that was supposedly powerful, 'Rom, Blicke'" (30). An early proponent of new realism and eventually beat and avant-garde literary trends from the United States, Brinkmann did not write *Rom, Blicke*. It was, rather, published four years after his death from the bound version of some of his collected materials, letters, notes, pictures, and newspaper clippings. Beyond this, though, Rome and Italy are paradigmatic locations for traveling to and writing in for German authors since Goethe, a paradigm that—witness the narrator's despair, or inversely, Ortheil and Ransmayr's successes—continued to dominate literature in the late eighties.

Conjoining the place of inspiration for canonical literature (Goethe) and a representative of avant-garde literature of the seventies (Brinkmann), the novelist rejects the possibility of continuing Brinkmann's scathing attack on German literature. An attack *Mai, Juni, Juli* assesses as "angeblich kraftvoll" (apparently powerful) but obviously unsuccessful, Brinkmann's prose, verse, and collages of the seventies represent an earlier attempt to break the very same cultural monopoly of feuilleton and canonical literature that Lottmann's novelist rails against. Prefiguring *Mai, Juni, Juli*'s fusion of modernist literature with the boulevard press tactics by almost 20 years, Brinkmann lashed out at the German fear of Leslie Fiedler's call for a new affective literature founded upon connections between the canon and pornography, between sci-fi and non-fiction.[43] For Brinkmann, German writers were lazy sluts ("Schlampen") who rejected Fiedler's argument "because it is difficult and demands concrete effort, to give up treasured positions and to dare the attempt, to begin anew with one's own writing."[44] The novelist in *Mai, Juni, Juli*'s meets these Germans in the countryside and the city. One Cologne native tells Lottmann's protagonist that "Brinckmann . . . I pleaded, that he never, never, never came back . . . that he went far, far away" (201). In a sense, Brinkmann's disgust with the German literary establishment is the driving logic behind *Mai, Juni, Juli*, for beginning anew is exactly what the novelist does, and his disgust with German literature and the reading public recalls Brinkmann's rhetorical question "Should I involve myself in this sad and boring litany?"[45] Brinkmann's attempt to find a solution in language and literature ultimately leads him to give up literature for image-text collages, eventually commanding "Deutschland verrecke" (die a miserable death, Germany).[46] The novelist in *Mai, Juni, Juli* lives in the aftermath of Brinkmann's wished-for miserable death of Germany, the Germany that was for Fehlfarben nothing more than a "daily dying-off" ("das sind geschichten"). Ultimately rejecting its own continuation of Brinkmann's project as a delusional, *Mai, Juni,*

Juli must negate Brinkmann in order to ensure "no future" for literature because so much of Brinkmann's work was published after his death, but also because it was transformed from avant-garde formlessness into mainstream literature. If an author dying, this attack reveals, is not sufficient to negate literary production, then inspiring the feuilleton to enact an end and the novelist's departure signal his last-ditch attempt at a destructive gesture that he hopes will inspire others.

The author's trip to Madagascar aboard Hamsun's ship points not toward resignation, but rather a last, subtly scathing gesture toward mainstream West Germany. His inscription as a mate leaving behind the hell of eighties' West Germany represents a disingenuous gesture calling out his own crime. Though he knows it was "the gravest of crimes to be misanthropic," the novel is predicated on misanthropy (24). While his departure putatively signals failure, in light of the fascism breeding in the countryside and preserved in the cities, the apparently pessimistic end to the text offers a what Eric Santner, while considering ways for a reconciliation of Germany's fascist past, calls a "radical rethinking and reformation of the very notions of boundaries and borderlines, of that 'protective shield' regulating exchange between the inside and the outside of individual and groups."[47] The novelist ends literature because he discovers during the course of trying to write a novel that literature itself was such a "protective shield." This shield is literature that "described, once more, that which there already was" (Santner) precisely what the narrator claims cannot be the task of literature ("it couldn't be the writers task to confirm that which was already in the world" [*MJJ* 152]). The dissidents-cum-simulators whom the narrator deems failures are those who construct this shield, those who ensure the recycling of narratives that, because they do not deal with fascism, insinuate that fascism is no longer a problem (148). This stunted narrative circularity haunts everyday life in the novel, a specter residing in the tennis club where the members do the exact same thing for 40 years. But the novelist compresses time. While the fascists in the tennis club have been doing the same thing for 40 years, by refusing to rehash Goetz's impact in German literature, the novelist rejects what authors have been doing for four years (since *Irre*). As a structure of feeling, hate to end these cycles is crucial, the narrator argues in synch with Meinecke's assessment, because fascism has continued as the foundation of all German affect. The novelist observes that "with Germans there are certain feelings, that have always existed, [...] that National Socialism took advantage of: and these feelings could also be taken advantage of by a new National Socialism in new dressing. One had to see this, in soccer for example. When a goal is scored and so on" (91). This unwelcome narrative moment highlights *Mai, Juni, Juli*'s clandestine investment in punk's "no future" because its neoconservative verve displaces the "burdensome and unwelcome consequences of [...] capitalist modernization [...] on to cultural modernity" (*MUP* 43). The novel is thereby simultaneously in step with what Schneider has argued was at the core of punk's use of fascism for shock. Whereas "the FRG-left explained the possibility of mass-murderous anti-Semitism via capitalist interests in exploitation," Schneider argues, "FRG punks unashamedly voiced, that [such gestures] were mere lies, nothing more than guilt deflection." By forcing itself to act out a Nazi past, punk differentiated itself "from the revision-safe working-though of German history" that later became the standard narrative for the Berlin republic.[48] Thus it is here that the novelist states the importance of cessation most clearly: recycling modernist narratives reifies the "consequences of dogmatism and moral rigorism" because the praxis of everyday life is oriented vis-à-vis aesthetic production that recycles the very conditions that engendered and prolonged fascist structures of feeling (*MUP* 50).

The young author sees the effects of these conditions in an omnipresent fascist specter when "the passing century in its most ghastly form plods by in front of my eyes." This utter disgust at contemporary West German society—that he "couldn't see anything else anymore"—provides a clue as to why the author refuses any sort of hippie novel ("An eco-novel, no thanks") (22). Hippies wanted to save the world, punks mockingly wanted to see it paved over, as S.Y.P.H. member Thomas Schwebel makes clear in his comments on the song "Back to concrete." The song, for Schwebel, "was the answer to the 'Back to Nature' of the Greens-movement, that was founded at the same time. These land-communes and flowing towels were for us the absolute worse thing [...] Kiss my ass with your stupid nature! We live here in cities."[49] Paving over the world, ensuring "no future" free from, Schneider argues, "any kind of catharsis," was the only solution the novelist finds to prevent the recycling of the markers of the National Socialist past.[50] The novelist declares "no future" for West German narratives because of the simulation of reconciliation and refusal to mourn traumatic pasts was the simulation of wholeness and the effacing of the insanity of sanity. Years earlier, Fehlfarben mimed the romantic yearning of the FGR when they indicted and celebrated their own "silencing of the truth" ("gottseidank nicht in england"). There is no love left, so the thumbing of the nose—*Mai, Juni, Juli*'s narrative kynicism that debunks simulated intactness and consent by continuously running amok with all cultural taboos—creates the conditions of possibility for hate. Hate is the solution because the crises of politics, the public sphere, and literature ensure failure, but failure in the mainstream only ensures a return, a recycling of the same events in new dressings. Lottmann's novelist narrates German history "in an irreconcilable manner," one wherein a Nazi past became something other than the "ritualized forms of a too easily reconciled past."[51] In such a morass, politics becomes defunct and fascist desires work not only through the rhetoric of consent, security, and normalization, they haunt even putatively socially progressive political parties such as the SPD. The narrator, when asked about his favorite fascist, insists that "'it is fundamentally impossible for a clandestine SPD-member to have a 'favorite fascist.' I would rather die than answer such a question." However this refusal is short-lived. Pressed once more, he contradicts and indicts himself as paradigmatic of SPD-members, declaring his admiration of "Adolf himself, clearly" (174–175).

Because he rejects the ostensible inward turn of 1970s literature— that at its core represented an effort to differentiate and distance one's own moral and political dispositions but inadvertently served societal modernization—the novelist comes into difficulties with his publisher. Though the publisher insists "no more problem-literature in the 80s!" this is exactly what the author "wanted so badly" (31). His publishing house's wish for a simpler literature recall Fredric Jameson's assessment of pastiche, the celebrated literary form of eighties' German literature, as a mode to recall a time far less problematic than the present.[52] But effacing cultural crises is precisely what this punk illumination refused. As such, the novelist pushes *Mai, Juni, Juli* to Adorno's endpoint: cultural modernization is barbaric after Auschwitz. Just as Fehlfarben in this chapter's epigraph, Lottmann's narrator steals stories and tries to find a better way to tell them. He realizes, however, that as much as he seeks a meaningful (his)story, he has nothing to say. He wants to end the possibility of narration, but he can only end his own. *Mai, Juni, Juli*'s motley narrative seeks to create conditions for opening up new discursive spaces and subject positions outside what Hebdige, while reflecting on punk subcultures, calls a "petrified hegemony of an earlier corpus of 'radical aesthetics.'"[53] This search fails. Bad style and lack of passion calls forth the need for Sloterdijk's kynicism because "the mechanisms, whose relative brutal openness characterized fascist style, have sunken into the subliminal and atmospheric masks of adaptation, good will, and forced convictions" (242). Lottmann's version of punk was a last gasp attempt to create a constellation of cultural materials that mattered and could be used to shape identity before difference ceased to matter. If postmodernity collapsed the specific with the general and effaced difference, then *Mai, Juni, Juli* envisioned itself as an apocalyptic time bomb festering in its core. If everything had been leveled, and differences disintegrated, then Lottmann's debunking the recyclable as worthy of recycling is a "strategy of undoing" the simulation of intactness.[54] The author targets radical and critical introspection, an indictment of oneself as a foil for indicting society. He engages through the course of the novel the disillusionment of his generation, the end of Enlightenment thought, and the collapse and failure of progressive thought. Clearly channeling Adorno's argument that "cultural criticism finds itself positioned in the last stages of the dialectic of culture and barbarism," the novelist tries to stop as many arbiters of cultural and societal modernization as he can.[55] Fascism endured, Adorno posited, because "the objective conditions of society that engendered fascism continue to exist" in the very monuments of German literature that *Mai, Juni, Juli* used its centered location to end forever.[56] The novelist tries to unmask these stories as nothing worthwhile. More than the story, the novelist wants to transport his hate and cynicism into the status quo as a normalized strategy for marking as nothing—for negating—the oppressive canon that only ensured the recycling of the failures of modernity. The novelist had nothing to do but fail. He had nothing left to do but leave.

This book mobilized a misunderstood constellation to unlock knowledge of a past that only fulfilled its prophecy in an unwanted future. West German punk's "no future" and its apocalyptic fantasies illuminate a series of crises, and its recurring and resolute attempts to stave off the future and bring down the present were ultimately no match for societal modernization. This book's diachronic reading of West Germany's recurrent crises through punk's recurrent failures narrates the temporal trajectory punk feared. Though seemingly enacting what Jacques Derrida calls an "anarchivic" drive[57]—an archive-destroying drive—punk's apocalyptic "no future" radiates even today in texts, photographs, sounds, and paintings. Examining the simultaneous emergence and retreat of German punk this book turned to the dialectical tensions at punk's core—witness the contemporaneous existence of such contradictory iterations of punk in the forms of FSK, S.Y.P.H., Fehlfarben, *Irre, Mode & Verweiflung,* and *Mai, Juni, Juli. Punk Rock and Germn Crisis* thereby sought to make unmistakable the manifold ways through adaptation of its given conditions punk repeatedly tested new means of socio-aesthetic resistance. Concurrently, the above chapters uncover the fantasies, failures, and crises of German history that punk experienced and encouraged; this investigation is as such a project wherein punk's scrambling of codes neither created a utopian epiphany nor a moment of terror and violence, but rather revealed inflections of a complex subcultural field fundamental for understanding the mainstream crises that girded 1980s' West Germany. The "lightning flashes"[58] of punk's brief half-lives created a legible archive of aftershocks of self-destructive gestures and anarchy, repeated avant-garde "explosés" that call into question the coming of the future whose possibility punk foreclosed. Envisioning themselves as the cure to cities burning with bore-dom, the disparate means with which punk resisted its present, when syn-ched with one another, make clear that, contrary to "no future," punk's logic is immanently invested in what came after punk. Why else would it declare "no future," if it was not preeminently concerned with the effects of its aftershocks? Thus what becomes clear by reading the detritus of West German punk is how it did not really want "no future," it resisted the future promised in 1977. The future punk did not want is a past of con-sent within a logic of unification and normalization in the wake of the sixties' and seventies' theoretical and violent insurrections. Dominated by crises of space and power, of production and reception, and of progressive postmodernism that could be mistaken for the continuation of resistance past or the growth pains of a new nation, punk's post-punk future after 1977 embraced those crises against the future legacy of violent insurrec-tion, of American occupation, and of aesthetic production. Punk's post-1977 future of West German crises of space and power, of production and reception, of social corruptibility played out in the preceding chapters. Through the lens of "no future" and failure, this book has looked back at thatf uture.

Notes

Introduction

Unless otherwise noted, all translations from the German originals are the author's own. Any references to "Germany" throughout are for "West Germany."

1. Einstürzende Neubauten, "Kollaps" *Kollaps* (ZickZack 65, October 1981).
2. See Heinz Strunk's *Fleisch ist mein Gemüse: eine Landjugend mit Musik* (Reinbek bei Hamburg: Rowohlt, 2004); Rocko Schamoni's *Dorfpunks* (Reinbek bei Hamburg: Rowohlt, 2004), or the filming of *Verschwende deine Jugend*, double CD (Brunswick: Universal, 2002) (in which the word "punk" is never mentioned) for popular simplifications of punk.
3. For more on the "Economic Miracle," its problems, and its origins, see Sabine von Dirke, *"All power to the imagination!": the West German Counterculture from the Student Movement to the Greens* (Lincoln: University of Nebraska Press, 1997) 9–66. For details on the origins, members, and actions of German domestic terrorism see Stefan Aust *Der Baader Meinhof Complex* (Hamburg: Hoffmann und Campe, 1985) or "Baader Meinhof.com" (http://www.baader-meinhof.com/).
4. See Jeremy Varon, *Bringing the War Home: the Weather Underground, the Red Army Faction, and the Revolutionary Violence in the Sixties and Seventies* (Berkeley: University of California Press, 2004); or Richard Langston, *Visions of Violence: German Avant-Gardes after Fascism* (Evanston, IL: Northwestern University Press, 2008).
5. The "German Autumn" is most canonically narrated in the omnibus film *Germany in Autumn*. Alf Brustellin et al. (Germany: Filmverlag der Autoren, 1978).
6. Though it continued to be active into the early 1990s, the RAF's "first generation" came to a definitive end with the deaths (by suicide or state assassination) in Stammheim prison of leaders Andreas Baader, Gudrun Ensslin, and Jan-Carl Raspe on October 18, 1977 (see Aust, *Der Baader*).
7. November 9 could be framed, alternately, vis-à-vis the year 1848, 1918, 1923, or 1938.
8. See for example, Tina Campt, *Other Germans: Black Germans and the Politics of Race, Gender, and Memory in the Third Reich* (Ann Arbor: University of Michigan Press, 2005); or Deniz Göktürk, David Gramling, and Anton Kaes, eds. *Germany in Transit: Nation and Migration, 1955–2005* (Berkeley: University of California Press, 2007).

9. Peter Glaser, personal interviews with author (2006 and 2009). Hereafter cited as *Interview.* Thomas Meinecke and Michaela Melián, personal interviews with author (2006 and 2009). Hereafter cited as *Interview.*
10. Langston, *Visions of Violence* 3 .
11. Here I bracket out the rise of queer rights and subsequent new waves of feminist interventions into the political in the eighties whose normalizing force in mainstream society functions in fundamentally different ways from the legacy of 1968 (witness Joska Fischer, Peter Sloterdijk, or Horst Mahler).
12. Theodor Adorno, "On Popular Music" in *On Record: Rock, Pop, and the Written Word,* ed. Simon Frith and Andrew Goodwin (New York: Pantheon Books, 1990) 302–303.
13. The existentialist youth are another part of this field of postwar youth subcultures, who, von Dirke argues, shared with punk an important outlook. "The youth of both decades," she writes, "saw 'No Future' written on the horizon" (*"All power to the imagination!"* 21). See also Uta G. Poiger *Jazz, Rock, and Rebels: Cold War Politics and American Culture in a Divided Germany* (Berkeley: University of California Press, 2000).
14. See for example Poiger, *Jazz, Rock, and Rebels*; von Dirke, *"All power to the imagination!"*; Richard Langston, "Roll Over Beethoven! Chuck Berry! Mick Jagger! 1960s Rock, the Myth of Progress, and the Burden of National Identity in West Germany," in *Sound Matters,* ed. Nora M. Alter and Lutz Koepnick (New York: Berghahn, 2004); or Diedrich Diederichsen, *Sexbeat: 1972 bis heute* (Cologne: Kiepenheuer & Witsch, 1985).
15. Poiger, *Jazz, Rock, and Rebels,* 1–2. Poiger's work seeks to rectify the theretofore trend of overlooking resistive youth cultures of the fifties and the ways in which such groups such as the Halbstarken have been erroneously cast as apolitical.
16. Lawrence Grossberg, "Another Boring Day in Paradise: Rock and Roll and the Empowerment of Everyday Life" *Popular Music,* vol. 4, Performers and Audiences (1984), 239.
17. von Dirke, *"All power to the imagination!"* 21–37 and 49–60.
18. Langston, "Roll over Beethoven," 184. For more on the *Schlager* and the establishment of German national identity see Mark Terkessidis, "Die Eingeborenen von Schizonesien: der Schlager als deutscheste aller Popmusik," in Mark Terkessidis and Tom Holert, eds., *Mainstream der Minderheiten: Pop in der Kontrollgesellschaft.* (Berlin: Edition ID-Archiv, 1996).
19. Langston," Rollo verB eethoven."
20. Theodor Adorno, *Dissonanzen: Einleitung in die Musiksoziologie* in *Gesammelte Werke,* vol 14, ed. Rolf Tiedemann (Darmstadt, Germany: Wissenschaftliche Buchgesellschaft, 1998).
21. Langston, "Roll over Beethoven" 185.
22. See Arne Koch and Sei Harris, "The Sound of Yourself Listening: Faust and the Politics of the Unpolitical" *Popular Music and Society* 32.5 (December 2009): 579–594. See also Timothy Brown, "Music as Weapon? *Ton Steine Scherben* and the Politics of Rock in Cold War Berlin," *German Studies Review* 31.1 (2009): 1–22.
23. Big rock shows such as the "Internationale Essener Songtage" music festival or the "Love and Peace Open Air Festival" are but two examples of this.
24. Langston, "Roll over Beethoven," 189.

25. Simon Reynolds, *Rip It Up and Start Again: Postpunk 1978–1984* (New York: Penguin Books, 2006) x. This epicenter can be contested, but this book is not invested in an argument over *the* epicenter of West German punk. What is undeniable is, as detailed in what follows, that Düsseldorf was a crucial location for West German punk subcultures. For more on Iggy Pop in Berlin see Reynolds, *Rip It Up,* xxi.

26. Richard Merritt, "Divided Airwaves: The Electronic Media and Political Community in Postwar Berlin" *International Political Science Review / Revue internationale de science politique* 7.4 (1986): 370.

27. While the above binary brackets out the French sector of West Germany, this zone was not particularly central during punk's fleeting existence, and was perhaps more dominated by American culture than French. This is historically evident by the stationing of 750,000 American troops by 1951 in the state of Rhineland-Palatinate, originally part of the French occupation zone (Poiger, *Jazz, Rock, and Rebels* 34).

28. Peter Glaser, *Interview.* Thomas Meinecke and Michaela Melián, *Interview.* For more on the "Neue deutsche Welle" (German New Wave) and underground cassette exchange see Frank Apunkt Schneider, *Als die Welt noch unterging: von Punk zu NDW.* (Mainz: Ventil, 2007).

29. For more on British subcultures, see for example: John Clarke et al., "Subcultures, Cultures and Class: A theoretical Overview" in Stuart Hall and Tony Jefferson, eds., *Resistance through Rituals* (London: Hutchinson, 1976); Dick Hebdige's *Subculture: The Meaning of Style* (London: Methune, 1979); or Jon Savage's *England's Dreaming: Anarchy, Sex Pistols, Punk Rock and Beyond* (New York: St. Martin's Griffen, 2002).

30. Glaser states that "in Düsseldorf the Ratinger Hof was the most important meeting point. The Ratinger Straße [street] where the bar was [...] and above all: the Art Academy was nearby. There were always a lot of punks, musicians, and artists together. That was basically totally normal. The art scene with the most important galleries later moved to Cologne, but the end of the 70s /beginning of the 80s it was all in Düsseldorf together" (personal email from 18.2.10). For more on this see the contributions reflecting on punk and the year 1977 in *Zurück Zum Beton: Die Anfänge Von Punk Und New Wave in Deutschland 1977-'82: Kunsthalle Düsseldorf, 7. Juli–15. September 2002,* ed. Ulrike Groos and Peter Gorschlüter (Cologne: König, 2002), or consider that Düsseldorf was the chosen location for this punk retrospective. For British punk's "year zero" see Reynolds *Rip It Up,* xx.

31. Peter Hein, "Alles ganz Einfach," in *Züruck zum Beton,* ed. Groos and Gorschlüter, 131.

32. Peter Hein, liner notes, *Verschwende deine Jugend.*

33. Thomas Meinecke, qtd. in Diedrich Diederichsen, "Freiwillige Selbstkontrolle," *Sounds* 5 (1982): 34.

34. Tony Bennett, "The Politics of 'the Popular' and Popular Culture" in *Rethinking Popular Culture: Contemporary Perspectives in Cultural Studies,* ed. Chandra Mukerji and Michael Schudson (Berkeley: University of California Press, 1991) 15.

35. The severely stratified German school system, with its working-class and professional-class tracts, would appear to contradict Baacke's contention.

36. More problematically, this sociological vein of cultural studies continues to be considered more "legitimate" by German researchers. See *Cultural Hacking: Kunst des strategischen handelns*, ed. Thomas Düllo (Vienna: Springer, 2005).
37. See Hein's *Protestkultur und Jugend: ästhetische Opposition in der Bundesrepublik Deutschland*, ed. Peter Ulrich Hein and Maria Eva Jahn (Münster: Lit, 1984), particularly pages iii, 27, and 57–60. Hein reinforces this position in *Künstliche Paradiese der Jugend: zur Geschichte und Gegenwart ästhetischer Subkultur* (Münster: Lit, 1984).
38. The crucial point behind *Widerspenstige Kulturen* is its decisive move to a non-*Kulturwissenschaft* (cultural sciences) platform that does not seek totalizing markers for society in the tradition of the Frankfurt School. See Karl Hörning and Rainer Winter, *Widerspenstige Kulturen: Cultural Studies als Herausforderung* (Frankfurt am Main: Suhrkamp, 1999) 7–12.
39. See Thomas Lau, *Die heiligen Narren. Punk 1976–1986* (Berlin: de Gruyter, 1992) 123 and 134–135. In an afterword to *Schocker: Stile und Moden der Subkultur* (the German-language version of Hebdige's *Subculture*), Olaph-Dante Marx drafts a very quick story of West German subcultures since the fifties via music, drugs, and styles. In Marx's essay all post-'45 youth groups are destined to fail, and working class and subculture are equated by referencing Schwendter—Marx, "Endstation Irgendwo: Ein Flug durch die Zeit," in Diedrich Diederichsen, Dick Hebdige, and Olaph-Dante Marx, *Schocker: Stile und Moden der Subkultur* (Reinbek bei Hamburg: Rowohlt, 1983).156. In *Mainstream der Minderheiten: Pop in der Kontrollgesellschaft* (Berlin: Edition ID-Archiv, 1996), Mark Terkessidis and Tom Holert briefly look back at subcultures of the 1980s in order to work out the problems of 1990s subcultures in which they see a constant battle over representation in the popular as a potential site of social resistance within a cycle of dissidence and co-option.
40. For more on West German punk and terrorism, see Cyrus Shahan, "The Sounds of Terror: Punk, Post-Punk and the RAF after 1977," *Popular Music and Society* 34.3 (July 2011): 369–386.
41. Originally published in the *Göttinger Nachrichten* April 25, 1977: 10–12. The obituary can also be found in Brückner's *Die Mescalero-Affäre*. For more on the "Buback Obituary" see von Dirke's *"All Power to the Imagination!"* 96–103. Here the citations are from "Dokumentation des 'Buback-Nachrufs' von 1977" (http://netzwerk- regenbogen.de/mescalero_doku.html).
42. Klaus Theweleit argues this point extensively in *Ghosts: Drei leicht inkorrekte Vorträge* (Frankfurt am Main: Stroemfeld/Roter Stern, 1998).

1   Punk Poetics

1. Walter Benjamin, *Arcades Project,* trans. Howard Eiland and Kevin McLaughlin (Cambridge, MA: Belknap, 1999) N1,1.
2. For such fantasies see Bommi Baumann, *Wie alles anfing, How it all Began: The Personal Account of a West German Urban Guerrilla* (Vancouver: Pulp Press, 1977); Margit Schiller, *Remembering the Armed Struggle: Life in Baader-Meinhof* (London: Zidane, 2008). For a more analytical appraisal, see Jeremy Varon, *Bringing the War Home: The Weather Underground, the Red Army*

Faction, and the Revolutionary Violence in the Sixties and Seventies (Berkeley: California University Press, 2004); or Hans Kundnani, *Utopia or Auschwitz: Germany's 1968 Generation and the Holocaust* (New York: Columbia University Press, 2009)

3. For this critique of postmodernity, see Jürgen Habermas, *The Philosophical Discourse of Modernity* (Cambridge, MA: MIT Press, 1987); Fredric Jameson, *The Cultural Turn: Selected Writings on the Postmodern, 1983–1998* (London: Verso, 1998); Jean Baudrillard *Simulacra and Simulation* (Ann Arbor: University of Michigan Press, 1994); and Hal Foster, *The Anti-aesthetic: Essays on Postmodern Culture* (Port Townsend, WA: Bay Press, 1983).

4. See Jürgen Habermas, "Modernity: An Unfinished Project," in *Habermas and the Unfinished Project of Modernity: Critical Essays on The Philosophical Discourse of Modernity*, ed. Maurizio Passerin d'Entrèves and Seyla Benhabib (Cambridge, MA: MIT Press, 1997) 54.

5. Norbert Bolz reads chaos as a natural facet of the ritual repetition of social cycles that ultimately serve in the "winning of a collective border." As part of the stabilizing force of chaos, Bolz names student protests and the "Greens," whose chaos is negated and turned socially supportive when they are accepted into mainstream politics and place "Ordnungsgrenzen" (organizing borders) upon themselves. Norbert Bolz, *Chaos und Simulation* (Munich: Fink, 1992) 15. Here Bolz is citing, fittingly, Carl Schmitt.

6. While not explicitly Christian in their projects, social transformation in the seventies and eighties was repeatedly bound up with Lutheran and Protestant churches (more broadly: the Evangelical Church of West Germany). Consider Gudrun Ensslin's father, a pastor, as well as the Kirchentag of 1987 in the Gethsemanekirche in Berlin's Prenzlauer Berg.

7. In a letter to Benjamin, Max Horkheimer speaks of the Last Judgment and incompleteness. Horkheimer writes: "Perhaps, with regard to incompleteness, there is a difference between the positive and the negative, so that only the injustice, the horror, the sufferings of the past are irreparable" (qtd. in Benjamin, *AP* N8,1). It is the irreparable suffering of the past that punk sought to prolong in the present through its indictment of what it saw as the incompleteness of 1968 and the RAF.

8. Under-theorizing punk and punk literature becomes all the more problematic in light of punk's renaissance in Germany, evidenced by the 2004 publication of Rocko Schamoni's *Dorfpunks* (Reinbek bei Hamburg, Rowohlt, 2004); Heinz Strunk's *Fleisch ist mein Gemüse: eine Landjugend mit Musik* (Reinbek bei Hamburg: Rowohlt, 2004); or the filming of Teipel's *Verschwende deine Jugend*, Benjamin Quabeck (Munich: Constantin Film, 2004).

9. There also exists a quotient of literary production from American and British punk subcultures. In the United States this has been a fusion of musician and author, in the persons of Henry Rollins (Black Flag, Rollins Band) who has published several prose and short texts, sometimes coauthored with Ian MacKaye (Fugazi). Punk literature from the United Kingdom is signified perhaps most popularly by Irvine Welsh, but also by Stewart Home, Ben Richards, and Alan Warner.

10. Bettina Clausen and Karsten Singelmann, "Avantgarde heute?" in *Gegenwartsliteratur Seit 1968. Hansers Sozialgeschichte der Deutschen Literatur*

vom 16. Jahrhundert bis zur Gegenwart, ed. Klaus Briegleb and Sigrid Weigel, vol. 12 (Munich: Carl Hanser, 1992) 464.

11. Dave Laing, *One Chord Wonders: Power and Meaning in Punk Rock* (Philadelphia, PA: Open University Press, 1985) xiii. For more on British DIY see Dick Hebdige's *Subculture: The Meaning of Style* (London: Methune, 1979) 106–112. For West German DIY see Teipel's *Verschwende*, 55ff.

12. This avant-garde lineage comes from the various art schools around Düsseldorf, such as the Düsseldorfer Kunstakademie (where Joseph Beuys was an instructor) or the Kunsthochschule für Medien in Cologne.

13. Blixa Bargeld, *Stimme frisst Feuer* (Berlin: Merve, 1988) 106 (cited in *Kursbuch* 68).

14. See Alexander Kluge, *Die Patriotin* (Frankfurt am Main: Zweitausendeins, 1980).

15. Richard Langston, *Visions of Violence: German Avant-Gardes after Fascism* (Evanston, IL: Northwestern University Press, 2008) 26. See also 42–50.

16. Songs sung by the bands Mittagspause, Fehlfarben, and DAF, respectively.

17. Mittagspause, "Testbild," *Verschwende deine Jugend*, rec. 1979 (Brunswick: Universal, 2002).

18. Volker Hage, *Collagen in der deutschen Literatur: zur Praxis und Theorie eines Schreibverfahrens* (Frankfurt am Main: Peter Lang, 1984) 76–78.

19. See Richard Langston's "Roll Over Beethoven! Chuck Berry! Mick Jagger! 1960s Rock, the Myth of Progress, and the Burden of National Identity in West Germany," in *Sound Matters*, ed. Nora M. Alter and Lutz Koepnick (New York: Berghahn, 2004): 183–196; Uta Poiger's *Jazz, Rock, and Rebels: Cold War Politics and American Culture in a Divided Germany* (Berkeley: University of California Press, 2000) 10, 89–91, 110, 138, 184–187, and 193–205; and Sabine von Dirke's *"All Power to the Imagination!": The West German Counterculture from the Student Movement to the Greens* (Lincoln: University of Nebraska Press, 1997) 10.

20. Such a melee was a common occurrence at punk shows. See Teipel 281–300 and 304–317; or Meinecke and Melian, personal interview with author, 2006 and 2009. Hereafter cited as *Interview*.

21. Bargeld, *Stimme frißt Feuer*,9 5.

22. For more on xenophobia and Turkish emigrants in West Germany, see *Germany in Transit: Nation and Migration, 1955–2005*, ed. Deniz Göktürk, David Gramling, and Anton Kaes (Berkeley: University of California Press, 2007). For cinematic representation of this condition, see for example Rainer Werner Fassbinder's *Ali: Fear Eats the Soul* (Germany: Filmverlag der Autoren, 1974).

23. Thomas Meinecke and Michaela Melián, *Interview* (2009). Peter Glaser, personal interview with author, 2009. Hereafter cited as *Interview*

24. Bargeld, *Stimme frißt Feuer*, 110.

25. *Verschwende deine Jugend*, CD-inlay, Double CD (Brunswick: Universal, 2002) n.p.

26. Christian Jäger, "Wörterflucht oder: die kategoriale Not der Literaturwissenschaft angesichts der Literatur der achtziger Jahre" *Internationales Jahrbuch für Germanistik* 1 (1995): 93.

27. Ann Goldstein, organizer. *Martin Kippenberger: The Problem Perspective* (Los Angeles: Museum of Contemporary Art; Cambridge, MA: MIT Press, 2008) 63. See also introductory note 30.
28. *Problem Perspective*, 6. See Benjamin: "That things are 'status quo' *is* the catastrophe" (*AP* N9a,1).
29. *Problem Perspective*, 46–49. Goldstein is quoting Martin Prinzhorn.
30. Doris Krystof. *Martin Kippenberger: Einer von Euch, unter Euch, mit Euch* (Ostfildern, Germany: Hatje Cantz, 2006) 29.
31. Diedrich Diederichsen, "The Poor Man's Sports Car Descending a Staircase: Kippenberger as Sculptor" *Problem Perspective*, 130.
32. Also the case for the New Wave band Andreas Dorau & Die Marinas. See Ulrike Groos and Peter Gorschlüter *Zurück Zum Beton: Die Anfänge Von Punk Und New Wave in Deutschland 1977–'82: Kunsthalle Düsseldorf, 7. Juli –15. September 2002.* (Cologne: König, 2002) 71.
33. See also Dokoupil's cover art for the first Wirtschaftswunder-single (*Zurück zum Beton*, 86). This is addressed further in chapter four.
34. See Ulrich Krempel, "Die Wirklichkeit der Bilder" in *Jörg Immendorf: Cafe Deutschland / Adlerhälfte*, ed. Jürgen Harten and Ulrich Krempel (Düsseldorf, Germany: Kunsthalle Düsseldorf, 1982) 36–38.
35. *"Ostrich / ungewollt / Alles Tot / Tiefschlag / Ramsch / Langweil / Schmier / Arschtritt / Blödsinn / Abschaum / Sonderangebot / No Fun"* (Peter Glaser, "Geschichte wird Gemacht," in Groos and Gorschlüter, *Zurück zum Beton*, 124).
36. Martin Büsser, *If the Kids are United: von Punk zu Hardcore und Zurück* (Mainz: Ventil, 2000) 152. The legacy of such fanzines can certainly be tied to flyers made by students and more mainstream literary forms such as Rolf Dieter Brinkmann's collages in *Schnitte* (Hamburg: Rowohlt, 1988). For more on Brinkmann and sixties' avant-garde collages, see Langston, *Visions of Violence*.
37. Joachim Lottmann, "Ich wollte der neue Böll werden" *Der Tagesspiegel* May 6, 2003. See also Simon Reynolds, *Rip It Up and Start Again: Postpunk 1978–1984* (New York: Penguin Books, 2006) xxvii.
38. Alfred Hilsberg, "Die Revolution ist vorbei—wir haben gesiegt!" *Sounds 2*, 1978.
39. This account comes from Peter Glaser's text "Geschichte wird Gemacht," 124. Other volumes of *brauchbar/unbrauchbar* arrived wet, ripped into pieces, or previously wet and frozen together.
40. Peter Glaser, personal email from Feb 18, 2010.
41. Paul Michael Lützler, "Einleitung: Von der Spätmoderne zur Postmoderne. Die deutschsprachige Literatur der achtziger Jahre" *German Quarterly* 63.3 (1990): 350.
42. This condition continues, evidenced by research overwhelmingly oriented toward the success of authors of 1990s' pop literature such as Christian Kracht and Benjamin von Stuckrad-Barre. Moritz Baßler's *Der deutsche Pop-Roman* (Hamburg: C. H. Beck, 2002) and Johannes Ullmaier's *Von Acid nach Adlon und zurück: eine Reise durch die deutschsprachige Popliteratur*, ed. Johannes Ullmaier, Frieder Butzmann, and Sibylle Berg (Mainz: Ventil, 2001) are problematic because they are upheld as interventions into contemporary literature

including the eighties (or so Ullmaier's title) but they simply collapse the eighties with the nineties. Baßler's *Der deutsche Pop-Roman* does not represent an investigation into punk, or 1980s' literature, but is rather a meek gesture toward the eighties with an over-riding analysis under the vague umbrella of 1990s' "pop-literature." Likewise, Ullmaier's *Von Acid nach Adlon und zurück* briefly discusses Rianald Goetz and Thomas Meinecke, two 1980s' authors, but focuses on their post-1990 production vis-à-vis "pop-literature."

43. Hubert Winkels's *Einschnitte: zur Literatur der 80er Jahre* (Cologne: Kiepenheuer & Witsch, 1988) stands alone as a non-pop oriented monograph analyzing 1980s' literature. While Winkels's incisions into this literary corpus do not focus on punk, they use similar analysis-driving keywords that this book uses for analysis of punk and its use of representation: Dadaist verve, subculture, avant-garde, mobile adaptation, and ready-mades (Winkels, *Einschnitte*, 132, 217, 206, and 226).

2 Psycho Punk and the Legacies of State Emergency

1. Theodor W. Adorno, *Minima Moralia*, (1970), in *Gesammelte Schriften*, volume 4, ed. Rolf Teidemann (Darmstadt, Germany: Wissenschaftliche Buchgesellschaft, 1998) 26.
2. Harry Rag, "S.Y.P.H. 'eine kleine Biographie'" *S.Y.P.H.* http://www.syph.de/alt/olds.htm.
3. Jürgen Teipel, *Verschwende deine Jugend: Ein Doku-Roman über den deutschen Punk und New Wave* (Frankfurt am Main: Suhrkamp, 2001) 189. All remaining quotes in this and the following paragraphs pertaining to the story about the S.Y.P.H.'s album are from Teipel, *Verschwende*, 189–191.
4. For details on the Schleyer kidnapping or Christian Klar's and the RAF's actions around 1978 see Stefan Aust's *The Baader-Meinhof Group: The Inside Story of a Phenomenon*, trans. Anthea Bell (London: Bodley Head, 1987) particularly section five, "Forty-four Days in Autumn," 412–542.
5. For more see Richard Langston, *Visions of Violence: German Avant-Gardes after Fascism* (Evanston, IL: Northwestern University Press, 2008) 163–194.
6. For more on Jahnke's editing and other band members' fears see Teipel *Verschwende*, 189 and martinf, "S.Y.P.H.—Die Gevelsberg-Tapes (ergänzt)" (http://brotbeutel.blogspot.com/2006/06/syph-die-gevelsberg-tapes-ergnzt.html).
7. "klammheimlich" saw life first as "Die Düsseldorfer Leere" (a fanzine, 1979), by Ralf Dörper. Dörper then later recorded the song with Harry Rag in a fleeting composition of S.Y.P.H.
8. See for example Manfred Brauneck's *Autorenlexikon deutschsprachiger Literatur des 20. Jahrhunderts* (Reinbek bei Hamburg: Rowohlt, 1984) that begins Goetz's literary career in 1983 when he received the Literaturpreis des Deutschen Literaturfonds (236). Herman Kunisch and Dietz-Rüdiger Moser's *Neues Handbuch der deutschen Literatur seit 1945* (Munich: Nymphenburger, 1990) mentions his work for *Der Spiegel*, but focuses on his post-1983 publications in *Spex* (227). Thomas Wegmann has recently published an article "Stigma und Skandal, oder 'The Making of' Rainald Goetz" that addresses these two early texts. Wegmann's focus, however, is on the literary/public

personae of the author. *Mediale Erregungen? Autonomie und Aufmerksamkeit im Literatur- und Kulturwettbewerb der Gegenwart,* ed. Markus Joch et al. (Tübingen: Niemeyer, 2009).

9. "We just want to amuse ourselves, it is Carnival after all, and here is this nutcase dripping with blood," the reaction continues in Rainald Goetz, *Irre* (Frankfurt: Suhrkamp, 1983) 20. A video of the performance is currently online at YouTube: http://www.youtube.com/watch?v=_BEjgp9MAEY.

10. See for example Johannes Strasser "Über eine Neue Lust an der Raserei," *L'80* 44 (1987): 9–23; Petra Waschescio and Thomas Noetzel "Die Ohnmacht der Rebellion. Anmerkungen zu Heiner Müller und Rainald Goetz," *L'80* 44 (1987): 27–40; or Walter Delabar "Goetz, Sie reden ein wirres Zeug: Rainald Goetz und sein Wahnsinns-Ritt in die Literaturszene," *Juni* 4 (1990): 68–78.

11. See Goetz, *Irre*, 53 and 80 for the patient Adolf Straßmaier's cures of Hadol and Neurocil (182–184), for Schneemann smearing himself with feces, and (15) for Herr S. ripping off his fingernails.

12. Michel Foucault, *Madness and Civilization: A History of Insanity in the Age of Reason* (New York: Vintage Books, 1988) 33.

13. Gilles Deleuze and Félix Guattari, *Anti-Oedipus: Capitalism and Schizophrenia* (Minneapolis: University of Minnesota Press, 1983) 339.

14. This is another instance of reality intruding into *Irre.* Just like Goetz's Klagenfurt performance, this story was pirated from real events in which Goetz was involved, as documented in Rainald Goetz's 1993 montage-text *Kronos* (Frankfurt am Main: Suhrkamp, 1993) 51.

15. Rainald Goetz, "Im Dickicht des Lebendigen" *Der Spiegel* 43 (October 19, 1981): 235.

16. See Goetz, *Irre*, 40–42 and 122–124.

17. For a discussion of discourse of normalization and German literature, including Rainald Goetz's literary production from the 1990s, see Jürgen Link *Versuch über den Normalismus: Wie Normalität produziert wird* (Opladen, Germany: Westdeutscher, 1997) 15–26 and 67–74.

18. The literary instance of this back-and-forth in reproduced in Goetz, *Irre* too. As the narrative degenerates in the final third Raspe has his own invective: "I would so like to quietly and peacefully explain everything in order. That is why I have to constantly interrupt myself" (269).

19. Raspe's actions represent a struggle to break free from an organized and stabilized state, Julia Bertschik writes, "With instability and identity-transformation [...] 'that poses a problem for the modern "I", because they create fear and evoke an identity crisis.'" "Theatralität und Irrsinn: Darstellungsformen 'Multipler' Persönlichkeitskonzepte in der Gegenwartsliteratur: Zu Texten von Heiner Kipphardt, Unica Zürn, Rainald Goetz und Thomas Hettche" *Wirkendes Wort* 47.3 (1997): 398–423; 417.

20. The answer to this question comes five years later in Rainald Goetz's second novel *Kontrolliert*: "Everything is not a unity, rather exponentially everything" (Frankfurt am Main: Suhrkamp, 1986) 252.

21. Goetz, "Im Dichtigkeit des Lebendigen," 234–235.

22. In another over-critique of (male) student's fetishization of theory and exclusion of women from their discussions, Raspe remarks that "next to Wolfgang

had sat unnoticed for the whole evening his girlfriend, a woman, beautiful, quiet and jealous" (155).

23. Michel Foucault, *Discipline and Punish: The Birth of the Prison* (New York: Vintage Books, 1995) 26–27.

24. While other doctors recognize, privately, that electroshock is not a valid therapy, their inaction against it, as Raspe indicts his own observance-turned-assistance, indicts them all as "Täter" (contravener) (95).

25. This was the case with Fottner. This is also evident when Goetz's *Irre* juxtaposes the patient Bernd's voluntary "heroin-withdrawal program" and the patient Adolf Straßmair's regimen of psychotropic cures of Haldol and Neurocil (53 and 80). The drug-addict's Bernd's voluntary withdrawal program subverts the asylum's goal of the "voluntary taking of medications" (85). While the doctors keep Straßmair subdued via a rollercoaster of Haldol and Neurocil, Bernd refuses all medication. The doctors have no means with which to control him. Drugs provide motion and stillness, a cessation of time moving forward, a speed that continuously dismantles and creates movements and challenge strict demarcation of controlled spaces. Drugs are, in part, crucial for Raspe's chaotic misuse of the power that medical knowledge provides.

26. See R. D. Laing and A. Esterson, *Sanity, Madness and the Family* (Harmondsworth: Penguin, 1970).

27. Lainga ndE asterson, *Sanity, Madness and the Family*, 13.

28. Gilles Deleuze and Félix Guattari, *A Thousand Plateaus: Capitalism and Schizophrenia* (Minneapolis: University of Minnesota Press, 1987) 216–217.

29. *MM* 263.

30. Deleuze and Guattari, *Anti-Oedipus*, 15.

31. Indeed, the text narrates its own counter-surveillance of the police station across the street (297).

3   Post-Punk Poaching, Subversive Consumerism, and Reading for Anti-Racism

1. Peter Glaser, "Geschichte wird gemacht," in *Zurück Zum Beton: Die Anfänge Von Punk Und New Wave in Deutschland 1977-'82: Kunsthalle Düsseldorf, 7. Juli–15. September 2002*, ed. Ulrike Groos and Peter Gorschlüter (Cologne: König, 2002) 127.

2. "Is there Rock after Punk?" *On Record: Rock, Pop, and the Written Word*, ed. Simon Frith and Andrew Goodwin (New York: Pantheon Books, 1990) 114.

3. The band took their name from the West German self-censorship institution: F. S. K. Wiesbadener Selbstzensuranstalt (Wiesbaden self-censorship institution). The band's name can be (and has been) translated as either "voluntary self-control" or "voluntary self-censorship." To preserve the duality of control and censorship in both English and German and in the namesake institution, I use "censorship" exclusively. At its inception, FSK was Justin Hoffmann, Thomas Meinecke, Michaela Melián, and Wilfried Petzi.

4. Thomas Meinecke, liner notes, *Verschwende deine Jugend*. Double CD (Brunswick: Universal, 2002) n.p.

5. Thomas Meinecke and Michaela Melián, personal interview with author, March 27, 2007. Hereafter cited as *Interview*.

6. Alexander Kluge, "Authentizität," in *In Gefahr und größter Not bringt der Mittelweg den Tod* (Berlin: Vorwerk 8, 2002) 147–148.

7. Thomas Meinecke, *Mode & Verzweiflung* (Frankfurt am Main: Suhrkamp, 1998) 36. Hereafter cited in text as *MV*.

8. Lawrence Grossberg, *We Gotta Get out of This Place: Popular Conservatism and Postmodern Culture* (New York: Routledge, 1992) 246. Hereafter cited as *We Gotta*.

9. Negt and Kluge, *PS* 3, see also *PS* 12–18. In their monumental work *Geschichte und Eigensinn*, Negt and Kluge downplay the subversiveness available. They argue that a "circulation system" controls the number of variable representations. There is thus an "oscillation" that gives only the appearance (*Schein*) of transformative work and counterproducts. Oskar Negt and Alexander Kluge, *Geschichte und Eigensinn* vol. 2 *Der Unterschätzte Mensch* (Frankfurt am Main: Zweitausendeins, 2001) 222–229). Hereafter cited in text as *GE*.

10. Unless otherwise noted, all emphasis in Kluge and Negt and Kluge texts is in original.

11. See Negt and Kluge, *PS*, 96–129, 149–159. See also Kluge's *In Gefahr und größter Not bringt der Mittelweg den Tod*, 66–69 and 143–148.

12. The tension between Negt and Kluge and Fiske could also be cast as positions within the camp of modernism (Negt and Kluge) and postmodernism (Fiske). Negt and Kluge seek to rethink history to create subversive agency within modernity, whereas Fiske's unorthodox consumer finds agency in a postmodern pastiche of meaning on the television screen (See Negt and Kluge, *PS*, 12–18; John Fiske, *Television Culture* (London: Methuen, 1987) 224–264.

13. The title *Original Gasman Band* was a typographical error on a news report on FSK that was to have carried the title "One of the Most Original German Bands." It instead carried the title "One of the Most Original Gasman Bands." The misprinted mistake pleased FSK so much that they kept what the media had unintentionally produced (Meinecke and Melián, *Interview*).

14. A simplification that Klaus Theweleit also identifies as a failure of the 1960s and 1970s (see *Ghosts: Drei leicht inkorrekte Vorträge* (Frankfurt am Main: Stroemfeld/Roter Stern, 1998).

15. Kluge, *In Gefahr und größter Not*, 139.

16. Kluge, *In Gefahr und größter Not*, 147. See also Adorno, *ND*, 156–163, 172–174, and 220–233.

17. Walter Fuchs, "Armin Edgar Schaible & Martin Haerle: eine schwierge Beziehung" (http://www.haukestruebing.com/frameset.php?/erinnerungen/armin_edgar_schaible.htm). See also Willett, particularly pages 86–98, where Willett discusses the musical seesaw between jazz and "'hillbilly' or 'cowboy'" music for the GIs. Ralph Willett, *The Americanization of Germany, 1945–1949* (London: Routledge, 1989) 91.

18. FSK expanded this network beyond the song by recording the album *American Sector* in Leeds, England. They added another source of cultural input to somehow complete their American Sector of West Germany.

19. Kluge, *In Gefahr und größter Not*, 86.

20. Kluge, *In Gefahr und größter Not*, 147–148.

21. See also Kluge, *In Gefahr und größter Not*, 92.
22. In the song "Frau mit Stiel" (Woman with steel/style), FSK sings that "if you look carefully, then you can sense a breath of revolution."
23. FSK found such gaps in sensational media clichés. Their song "Ein Kind für Helmut" (A child for Helmut), from the album *Stürmer*, resignifies then-chancellor Helmut Kohl's complaint that Germans were dying out as Adolf Hitler's call for Germany babies whereby "Babies for Hitler" becomes "Babies for Kohl." Furthermore, the song uses Americanisms such as "come on, let's make love" [*Liebe machen*] on the *Stürmer* album to parlay their American solution to make love with the legacies of fascist propaganda.
24. Kluge, *In Gefahr und größter Not*, 142.
25. "Mit der Kirche ums Dorf" translates to "with the church around the village." It is a figure of speech akin to the English-language "to take the long way around," that is, to take a detour, to make things more complicated than normal. Thomas Meinecke, *Mit Der Kirche Ums Dorf* (Frankfurt am Main: Suhrkamp, 1986) hereafter cited parenthetically in text as *MdK*
26. For an extensive discussion on the importance of mourning history in Negt and Kluge's works see Richard Langston, *Visions of Violence: German Avant-Gardes after Fascism* (Evanston, IL: Northwestern University Press, 2008) 42–50.
27. Langston, *Visions of Violence*, 61.
28. Alexander Kluge, *Die Patriotin* (Frankfurt am Main: Zweitausendeins, 1980) 254 and 294.
29. Negt and Kluge, *PS*, 152. Of course, FSK did not pioneer this in the Federal Republic. Also synchronous with the moment of punk's birth, the omnibus film *Germany in Autumn* could be read as the first attempt to hack into and misuse mainstream hysteria. Just as the vignettes in the film, the images in Meinecke, *Mit der Kirche* fragment the text.
30. From the song "Kleiner Polizist" (Little cop) from the album *Stürmer*.
31. For more on the importation of blackness—particularly in the person of musical performers—into West Germany and mainstream racism in response, see Kira Thurman, "Black Venus, White Bayreuth: Race, Sexuality, and the Depoliticization of Wagner in Postwar West Germany" *German Studies Review* 35.3 (2012): 607–626, specifically 608 and 614.
32. Meinecke and Melián, *Interview*.
33. The German word "Neger" can be translated either as *nigger* or *negro*. Using the word in German is slippery because the pejorative connotations of nigger versus negro cannot be separated out. Nor can the mainstream assumptions in the United States of the connotation nigger versus negro be justly applied here.
34. Schneider identifies this as punk's unique critique. See "My Future in the SS," or the discussion in chapter four on Lottmann and Schneider's instances of punk's rejection of inadequate reckoning with Germany's fascist past in contemporary sociopolitical thought.
35. For more on the abject and affect, see Julia Kristeva, *The Powers of Horror: An Essay on Abjection* (New York: Columbia University Press, 1982).
36. See Kluge, *In Gefahr und größter Not*, 78.
37. But that American brutality and racism seeps into German popular culture through media does not indicate something new in Germany. Americanized

popular media did not import racism into Germany; Germans always had their own instances of racism. See Tina Campt, *Other Germans: Black Germans and the Politics of Race, Gender, and Memory in the Third Reich* (Ann Arbor: University of Michigan Press, 2005).

38. The "Atomium" is a monument of an iron crystal built by André Waterkeyn for the 1958 Brussels World's Fair.

39. This is also the case for Joachim Lottmann's novel *Mai, Juni, Juli: Ein Roman* (Cologne: Kiepenheuer & Witsch, 1987), discussed in the next chapter.

40. Meinecke spoke directly to this collective experience and potential in an interview in *die tageszeitung* in October 1997. Meinecke spoke of the attempt "to formulate the German as political by using an American detour." Thomas Meinecke, "Originalität ist ein Ablenkungsmanöver" *die tageszeitung* October 15, 1997.

41. Andreas Huyssen, "The Politics of Identification," in *After the Great Divide: Modernism, Mass Culture, Postmodernism* (Bloomington: Indiana University Press, 1986) 94.

42. This indictment of literary and aesthetic trends—here critiquing the "new realism" of the late 1960s and early 1970s—as well as the parallel interest in multimedia art conjoins Meinecke with pre-punk Rolf-Dieter Brinkman and both Meinecke and Brinkmann with the target of the next chapter, on the political failure of literary aesthetics.

43. Miriam Hansen, "Introduction" in Negt, Oskar and Alexander Kluge, *Public Sphere and Experience: Toward an Analysis of the Bourgeois and Proletarian Public Sphere*, trans. Peter Labanyi, Jamie Owen Daniel, and Assenka Oksiloff (Minneapolis: University of Minnesota Press, 1993) xv.

4 After Punk: Cynicism and Social Corruptibility

1. Fehlfarben, "das sind geschichten" *Monarchie und Alltag* (Cologne: EMI, 1980).

2. Though beyond the scope of this monograph (not only by dint of temporal constraints), FSK's ever more resolute transnational musical fusion and Meinecke's own prolific literary production both testify to this. See for example FSK's album *Sound of Music* (1993), recorded in Richmond, Virginia with David Lowrey; *First Take, Then Shake* (2004), recorded with Detroit techno-producer Anthony "Shake" Shakir; or Thomas Meinecke's novels *Pale Blue*, trans. Daniel Bowles (Las Vegas, NV: AmazonCrossing, 2012), orig. *Hellblau* (Frankfurt am Main: Suhrkamp, 2001); *Tomboy*, trans. Daniel Bowles (Las Vegas: AmazonCrossing, 2011), orig. (Frankfurt am Main: Suhrkamp, 1998); *Musik* (Frankfurt am Main: Suhrkamp, 2007).

3. Frank Apunkt Schneider, "Musik gegen Musik. Vorüberlegungen zur Wiederveröffentlichung von 'Stürmer,'" CD-booklet to FSK's *Stürmer* (Cologne: a-musik, A36V [2011]) 1.

4. Schneider, "Musik gegen Musik," 1.

5. Joachim Lottmann, "Ceterum censeo Catharginem delendam esse…" *Spex* 59 (October 1985): 27

6. I am indebted to my former colleague Anthony Hunter for this insight into Cato the Elder.

7. Joachim Lottmann, "Der politische Fernsehapparat" *Spex* 69 (August 1986): 55.

8. See Herbert Marcuse, *One-Dimensional Man* (Boston: Beacon Press, 1966) 8–17.

9. Joachim Lottmann, "Voilá, un Punk" *Die Zeit* April 4, 1986.

10. Ostentatious because Lottmann was friends with both Meinecke and Melián and well-versed in the theory at work in the band's songs and fanzine *Mode & Verzweiflung* (Thomas Meinecke and Michaela Melián, personal interview with author, 2007, 2009. Hereafter cited as *Interview*.).

11. Joachim Lottmann, "Ist Japan besser?" *Die Zeit* August 29, 1986.

12. Jürgen Habermas, "Modernity: An Unfinished Project," in *Habermas and the Unfinished Project of Modernity: Critical Essays on The Philosophical Discourse of Modernity*, ed. Maurizio Passerin d'Entrèves and Seyla Benhabib (Cambridge, MA: MIT Press, 1997). See also Jürgen Habermas's *The Philosophical Discourse of Modernity* (Cambridge, MA: MIT Press, 1987).

13. Schneider uses the phrase "church of Habermas" while addressing the "anti-values" that underwrote FSK's fanzine *Mode & Verzweiflung*. See Schneider, "Musik gegen Musik," 2.

14. Habermas, "Modernity: An Unfinished Project," 41.

15. See Helge Malchow, "Nachwort" in Joachim Lottmann, *Mai, Juni, Juli: Ein Roman* (Cologne: Kiepenheuer & Witsch, 1987) 250.

16. Peter Glaser, "Aufbruch in die Achtziger," *Monarchie und Alltag*, CD-Booklet (London: EMI, 2000).

17. Glaser, "Aufbruch in die Achtziger."

18. See for example, Thomas Friedrich, "Lall-Laute" *Ultimo* 6 (March 1987); n.a. *Salzburger Impuls* 2.4 (April 1987); or ABL, "Lottmanns Leben" *Statblatt* (Osnabrück) 102 (July 1987).

19. Friedrich, "Lall-Laute."

20. Peter Sloterdijk, *Kritik der zynischen Vernunft* (Frankfurt am Main: Suhrkamp, 1983) 17. Hereafter cited as *Kritik*.

21. Peter Sloterdijk, *Zorn und Zeit* (Frankfurt am Main: Suhrkamp, 2006) 70 and 103. See also 352–356.

22. Sloterdijk, *Kritik*, 27–28.

23. Lawrence Grossberg, *We Gotta Get out of This Place: Popular Conservatism and Postmodern Culture* (New York: Routledge, 1992) 222. Hereafter cited as *We Gotta*.

24. See Lawrence Grossberg, "Is there Rock after Punk?" in *On Record: Rock, Pop, and the Written Word*, ed. Simon Frith and Andrew Goodwin, (New York: Pantheon Books, 1990), or "Rock Postmodernity and Authenticity" in *We Gotta*.

25. Grossberg, *We Gotta*, 232.

26. Lottmann, *Mai, Juni, Juli*, 24. Hereafter cited parenthetically in text as *MJJ*.

27. Grossberg, *We Gotta*, 224.

28. Glaser, "Aufbruch in die Achtziger."

29. Hubert Winkels, *Einschnitte: zur Literatur der 80er Jahre* (Cologne: Kiepenheuer & Witsch, 1988) 132.

30. BettinaW ündrich, *Szene Hamburg* 14.3 (May 1987).

31. The "Neuen Wilden" or "Jungen Wilden" (new wilds or young wilds) were young artists, in Cologne, Berlin and Düsseldorf who rejected established artistic style in favor of a fluid style. The Neuen Wilden rejected programmatic and explanatory theories, of, for example, the Futurists or Expressionists, and instead changed their style as they saw fit. For connection between *Rawums* and the "young wilds," see Peter Glaser, ed., *Rawums: Texte Zum Thema* (Cologne: Kiepenheuer & Witsch, 1984). For the review dismissing Lottman, *Mai, Juni, Juli* and Glaser, *Rawums*, see *Salzburg Impuls* 2.4 (April 1987).

32. Glaser, "Explosé" in *Rawums*, 15.

33. See "Ich wollte der neue Böll werden" in Lottman, *Der Tagesspiegel* May 6, 2003.

34. Judith Ryan has argued that Süskind's *Das Parfum* is "the ultimate exemplification of the particular postmodern process" of recycling. See "The Problem of Pastiche: Patrick Süskind's Das Parfum," *German Quarterly* 63.3 (1990): 396–403.

35. Matei Cálinescu, *Five Faces of Modernity: Modernism, Avant-Garde, Decadence, Kitsch, Postmodernism* (Durham, NC: Duke University Press, 1987) 252.

36. Hans Magnus Enzensberger declared the death of socially relevant literature in "Gemeinplätze, die Neueste Literatur betreffend," *Kursbuch* 15 (1968): 187–197. For more on the debate unleashed by *Kursbuch* 15 see for example Kieth Bullivant and Klaus Briegleb "Die Krise des Erzählens—'1968' und dannach" in *Gegenwartsliteratur Seit 1968. Hansers Sozialgeschichte der Deutschen Literatur vom 16. Jahrhundert bis zur Gegenwart*, ed. Klaus Briegleb and Sigrid Weigel, vol. 12 (Munich: Carl Hanser, 1992) 302–339. Recall Glaser's punk explosé from *Rawums* that also rejected the literary sentiment of academics such as Hans Magnus Enzensberger: "academics build their own / mood of downfall, / they discuss yet again / 'The end of literature'" (*R* 15). The intertextuality of the text, of a failed novel, of 23 failed novels, harks back to the modernist moments of literary failure such as Thomas Mann's *Der Tod in Venedig*, 1912 (New York: Oxford University Press, 1973). or Franz Kafka's *In der Strafkolonie*, 1919, Frankfurt am Main: Suhrkamp, 2006.

37. Christian Jäger, "Wörterflucht oder: die kategoriale Not der Literaturwissenschaft angesichts der Literatur der achtziger Jahre," in *Internationales Jahrbuch für Germanistik* 1 (1995): 96.

38. The term "New Subjectivity" refers to, Richard McCormick writes, literature that "rejected rationalistic objectivity—a 'politics of the self' that gloried in personal expression and anarchistic spontaneity—and influenced West German literary and cinematic output of the 1970s" (see Richard McCormick, *Politics of the Self: Feminism and the Postmodern in West German Literature and Film* (Princeton, NJ: Princeton University Press, 1991) 8.

39. Edward Verrall Lucas, *Swollen-Headed William: Painful Stories and Funny Pictures* (London: Methune, 1914).

40. Theodor Adorno, "Kulturkritik und Gesellschaft," in *Gesammelte Schriften* 10.2, ed. Rolf Tiedemann (Darmstadt, Germany: Wissenschaftliche Buchgesellschaft, 1998) 13.

41. Dick Hebdige *Subculture: The Meaning of Style* (London: Methune, 1979) 19.

42. Diedrich Diederichsen, *1.500 Schallplatten: 1979–1989* (Cologne: Kiepenheuer & Witsch, 1989) 18.

43. For Leslie Fiedler's plea for a new kind of literature, see his talk "Cross the Border—Close the Gap," *Collected Essays*, vol. 2 (New York: Stein and Day, 1971) 461–485.

44. Rolf Dieter Brinkmann, "Angriff aufs Monopol: Ich hasse alte Dichter" in *Roman oder Leben: Postmoderne in der deutschen Literatur*, ed. Uwe Wittstock (Leipzig: Reclam, 1994) 65.

45. Brinkmann, "Angriff aufs Monopol" 66.

46. Rolf Dieter Brinkmann, *Keiner weiß mehr*, 1968 (Reinbeck bei Hamburg: Rowohlt, 1993) 132.

47. Eric L. Santner, "History Beyond the Pleasure Principle: Some Thoughts on the Representation of Trauma," in *Probing the Limits of Representation: Nazism and the "Final Solution,"* ed. Saul Friedländer (Cambridge, MA: Harvard University Press, 1992) 152–153.

48. Frank Apunkt Schneider, "'My Future in the SS'.Zur Identifikation mit den Täter_innen im deutschen (Post-) Punk" *We Are Ugly but We Have the Music. Eine ungewöhnliche Spurensuche in Sachen jüdischer Erfahrung und Subkultur. "Jüdische Identität und Subkultur,"* ed. Jonas Engelmann et al., vol. 1 (Mainz: Ventil, 2012) 155–156.

49. *Verschwende deine Jugend*, CD-booklet (Brunswick: Universal, 2002) 5.

50. Schneider, "My Future in the SS," 157.

51. Schneider, "My Future in the SS," 158.

52. See for example, Fredric Jameson, "Postmodernism and Consumer Society" in *The Anti-Aesthetic: Essays on Postmodern Culture*, ed. Hal Foster (Port Townsend, WA: Bay Press, 1983).

53. Dick Hebdige *Hiding in the Light: On Images and Things* (London: Routledge, 1988) 185.

54. Santner, "History Beyond the Pleasure Principle," 144.

55. Adorno, "Kulturkritik und Gesellschaft," (10.2), 30.

56. Theodor Adorno, "Was heißt Aufarbeitung der Vergangenheit?" *Gesammelte Schriften* 10.2, ed. Rolf Tiedemann (Darmstadt, Germany: Wissenschaftliche Buchgesellschaft, 1998) 566.

57. Jacques Derrida, *Archive Fever: A Freudian Impression* (Chicago: University of Chicago Press, 1996) 10.

58. Benjamin, *AP*, N1,1

BIBLIOGRAPHY

ABL. "Lottmanns Leben." *Statblatt* (Osnabrück) 102 (July 1987).

Adelson, Leslie A. *Making Bodies, Making History.* Lincoln: University of Nebraska Press, 1993.

Adorno, Theodor W. *Gesammelte Schriften.* Edited by Rolf Tiedemann. 20 Volumes. Darmstadt, Germany: Wissenschaftliche Buchgesellschaft, 1998.

Adorno, Theodor W. and J. M. Bernstein. *The Culture Industry: Selected Essays on Mass Culture.* London: Routledge, 1991.

Agamben, Gorgio. *Homo sacer: Soverign Power and Bare Life.* Translated by Daniel Heller-Roazen. Stanford, CA: Stanford University Press, 1998.

Ang, Ien. *Watching Dallas: Soap Opera and the Melodramatic.* London: Methuen, 1985.

Anz, Thomas. "Die traurige Wirklichkeit des Wahnsinns." *Frankfurter Allgemeine Zeitung* October 11, 1983.

Arnold, Heinz Ludwig and Jörgen Schäfer. *Pop-Literatur.* Vol. 10. Munich: Edition Text + Kritik, 2003.

Attali, Jacques. *Noise: The Political Economy of Music.* Minneapolis: University of Minnesota Press, 1985.

Aust, Stefan. *Der Baader Meinhof Komplex.* Hamburg: Hoffmann und Campe, 1985.

Aust, Stefan and Anthea Bell. *The Baader-Meinhof Group: The Inside Story of a Phenomenon.* London: Bodley Head, 1987.

Baacke, Dieter. *Jugend und Jugendkulturen: Darstellung und Deutungen.* Weinheim and Munich: Juventa, 1987.

———, ed. *Neue Wiedersprüche.* Weinheim and Munich: Juventa, 1985.

Bargeld, Blixa. *Stimme frißt Feuer.* Berlin: Merve, 1988.

Baßler, Moritz. *Der deutsche Pop-Roman.* Hamburg: C. H. Beck, 2002.

Baudrillard, Jean. *Simulacra and Simulation.* Ann Arbor: University of Michigan Press, 1994.

Baumann, Bommi. *Wie alles anfing, How it all Begän: The Personal Account of a West German Urban Guerrilla.* Vancouver: Pulp Press, 1977.

Baumgart, Reinhard and Uwe Wittstock, eds. *Roman oder Leben: Postmoderne in der deutschen Literatur.* Leipzig: Reclam, 1994.

Becker, Bettina T. "Women, Violence, Nation: Representations of Female Insurgency in Fiction and Public Discourse in the 1970s and 1980s." *Women in German Yearbook* 16 (2000): 207–220.

Benjamin, Walter. *Arcades Project.* Translated by Howard Eiland and Kevin McLaughlin. Cambridge, MA: Belknap, 1999.

Benjamin, Walter. *Gesammelte Schriften.* Edited by Rolf Tiedemann and Hermann Schweppenhuser. 7 Volumes. Frankfurt am Main: Suhrkamp, 1972.

Bennett, Andy and Kieth Kahn-Harris, eds. *After Subculture.* New York: Palgrave Macmillan, 2004.

Bennett, Herman L. "The Subject in the Plot: National Boundaries and the 'History' of the Black Atlantic." *African Studies Review* 43.1 (2000): 101–124.

Bennett, Tony. *Rock and Popular Music: Politics, Policies, Institutions, Culture.* London: Routledge, 1993.

———. "The Politics of 'the Popular' and Popular Culture." *Rethinking Popular Culture: Contemporary Perspectives in Cultural Studies.* Edited by Chandra Mukerji and Michael Schudson. Berkeley: University of California Press, 1991.

Berman, Russell A. "Du Bois and Germany: Race, Nation, and Culture between the United States and Germany." *The German Quarterly* 70.2 (1997): 123–135.

Bernhard, Thomas. *Der Italiener.* Munich: W. Heyne, 1978.

Bertschik, Julia. "Theatralität und Irrsinn: Darstellungsformen 'Multipler' Persönlichkeitskonzepte in der Gegenwartsliteratur: Zu Texten von Heiner Kipphardt, Unica Zurn, Rainald Goetz und Thomas Hettche." *Wirkendes Wort* 47.3 (1997): 398–423.

Bloch, Ernst. *Aesthetics and Politics.* London: Verso, 1980.

"Blut Performance." *Die Lust am Erzählen: 25 Jahre Ingeborg-Bachmann-Preis: 1983.* http://bachmannpreis.orf.at/index25.htm.

Bolz, Norbert W. *Chaos und Simulation.* Munich: Fink, 1992.

———. *Stop Making Sense!* Würzburg: Königshausen & Neumann, 1989.

Braidotti, Rosi. "Organs without Bodies." *Differences* 1.1 (1989): 147–161.

Brauneck, Manfred. *Autorenlexikon deutschsprachiger Literatur des 20. Jahrhunderts.* Reinbek bei Hamburg: Rowohlt, 1984.

Breger, Claudia. "Pop-Identitäten 2001: Thomas Meineckes Hellblau und Christian Krachts 1979." *Gegenwartsliteratur* 2 (2003): 197–225.

Briegleb, Klaus and Sigrid Weigel. *Gegenwartsliteratur Seit 1968. Hansers Sozialgeschichte der Deutschen Literatur vom 16. Jahrhundert bis zur Gegenwart.* Edited by Klaus Briegleb and Sigrid Weigel. Vol. 12. Munich: Carl Hanser, 1992.

Brinkmann, Rolf Dieter. *Keiner weiß mehr.* 1968. Reinbeck bei Hamburg: Rowohlt, 1993.

———. *Westwärts 1 & 2.* Reinbek bei Hamburg: Rowohlt, 1975.

Brinkmann, Rolf Dieter and Ralf-Rainer Rygulla. *Acid. Neue Amerikanische Szene.* Darmstadt, Germany: März, 1969.

Brown, Timothy. "Music as Weapon? *Ton Steine Scherben* and the Politics of Rock in Cold War Berlin." *German Studies Review* 31.1 (2009): 1–22.

Brückner, Peter. *Die Mescalero-Affäre: Ein Lehrstück für Aufklärung und politische Kultur.* Hannover: n.p., (1977/78).

Brustellin, Alf et al. *Deutschland im Herbst* (*Germany in Autumn*). Germany: Filmverlag der Autoren, 1978.

Bürger, Peter. *Theory of the Avant-garde.* Minneapolis: University of Minnesota Press, 1984.

Bürgerliches Gesetzbuch. http://www.buergerliches-gesetzbuch.info/.

Büsser, Martin. *If the Kids are United: von Punk zu Hardcore und Zurück.* Mainz: Ventil, 2000.

Büsser, Martin. "Ich stehe auf Zerfall: Die Punk- und New-Wave-Rezeption in der deutschen Literatur." In *Text + Kritik*. Edited by Heinz Ludwig Arnold. Munich: Richard Boorberg, 2003.

Butler, Judith. *Bodies that Matter: On the Discursive Limits of "Sex."* New York: Routledge, 1993.

Cálinescu, Matei. *Five Faces of Modernity: Modernism, Avant-Garde, Decadence, Kitsch, Postmodernism*. Durham, NC: Duke University Press, 1987.

Campt, Tina. *Other Germans: Black Germans and the Politics of Race, Gender, and Memory in the Third Reich*. Ann Arbor: University of Michigan Press, 2005.

Clarke, David B., Marcus A. Doel, and Kate M. L. Housiaux, eds. *The Consumption Reader*. London: Routledge, 2003.

Clausen Bettina and Karsten Singelmann, "Avantgarde heute?" in *Gegenwartsliteratur Seit 1968. Hansers Sozialgeschichte der Deutschen Literatur vom 16. Jahrhundert bis zur Gegenwart*, edited by Klaus Briegleb and Sigrid Weigel. Vol. 12. Munich: Carl Hanser, 1992, 464.

Cohen, Robin. "Diasporas and the Nation-State: From Victims to Challengers." *International Affairs* 72.3 (1996): 507–520.

Creswell, Catherine J. "'Touch Me I'm Sick': Contagion as Critique in Punk and Performance Art." In *GenXegesis: Essays on "Alternative" Youth (Sub)Culture*. Edited by John M. Ulrich and Andrea L. Harris. Madison: University of Wisconsin Press, 2003.

Davies, Jude. "The Future of 'No Future': Punk Rock and Postmodern Theory." *Journal of Popular Culture* 29.4 (1996): 3–25.

de Certeau, Michel. *The Practice of Everyday Life*. Berkeley: University of California Press, 1984.

Delabar, Walter. "Goetz, Sie reden ein wirres Zeug: Rainald Goetz und sein Wahnsinns-Ritt in die Literaturszene." *Juni* 4 (1990): 68–78.

Deleuze, Gilles and Félix Guattari. *A Thousand Plateaus: Capitalism and Schizophrenia*. Minneapolis: University of Minnesota Press, 1987.

———. *Kafka: Toward a Minor Literature*. Minneapolis: University of Minnesota Press, 1986.

———. *Anti-Oedipus: Capitalism and Schizophrenia*. Minneapolis: University of Minnesota Press, 1983.

Derrida, Jacques. *Archive Fever: A Freudian Impression*. Chicago: University of Chicago Press, 1996.

Diederichsen, Diedrich. *1.500 Schallplatten: 1979–1989*. Cologne: Kiepenheuer & Witsch, 1989.

———. "Freiwillige Selbstkontrolle." *Sounds* 5 (1982): 33–34.

———. "The Poor Man's Sports Car Descending a Staircase: Kippenberger as Sculptor." *Problem Perspective*, 130.

———. *Sexbeat: 1972 Bis Heute*. Cologne: Kiepenheuer & Witsch, 1985.

Diederichsen, Diedrich, Dick Hebdige, and Olaph-Dante Marx. *Schocker: Stile und Moden der Subkultur*. Reinbek bei Hamburg: Rowohlt, 1983.

"Dokumentation des 'Buback-Nachrufs' von 1977." http://netzwerk- regenbogen. de/mescalero_doku.html.

Drügh, Heinz J. "Verhandlungen mit der Massenkultur-die neueste Literatur (-Wissenschaft) und die soziale Realität." *Internationales Archiv für Sozialgeschichte der deutschen Literatur* 26.2 (2001): 173–200.

Düllo, Thomas, ed. *Cultural Hacking: Kunst des strategischen handelns.* Vienna: Springer, 2005.

Einstürzende Neubauten. *Kalte Sterne.* EP. Hamburg: ZickZack 40, 1981.

———. *Kollaps.* LP. Hamburg: ZickZack 65, 1981.

Engel, Peter. "Ein Roman ohne Biß." *Frankfurter Allgemeine Zeitung* April 14, 1987.

Enzensberger, Hans Magnus. "Baukasten zu einer Theorie der Medien." *Kursbuch* 20 (1970): 159–186.

———. "Gemeinplätze, die Neueste Literatur betreffend." *Kursbuch* 15 (1968): 187–197.

Fassbinder, Rainer Werner. *Angst essen Seele auf. (Ali: Fear Eats the Soul).* Germany: Filmverlag der Autoren, 1974.

Fehlfarben. *Monarchie und Alltag.* Cologne: EMI, 1980.

Fiedler, Leslie. *Collected Essays.* Vol. 2. New York: Stein and Day, 1971.

Fiske, John. *Television Culture.* London: Methuen, 1987.

Fiske, John and John Hartley. *Reading Television.* London: Routledge, 2003.

Flud, Werner. "Naiv, Modisch und Brutal." *Frankfurter Allgemeine Zeitung* September 20, 1986.

Foster, Hal. *The Anti-aesthetic: Essays on Postmodern Culture.* Port Townsend, WA: Bay Press, 1983.

Foucault, Michel. *Society Must Be Defended: Lectures at the College De France, 1975–1976.* Edited by Mauro Bertani and Alessandro Fontana. New York: Picador, 2003.

———. *Discipline and Punish: The Birth of the Prison.* New York: Vintage Books, 1995.

———. *Madness and Civilization: A History of Insanity in the Age of Reason.* New York: Vintage Books, 1988.

———. *The History of Sexuality.* New York: Vintage Books, 1980.

———. *The Birth of the Clinic: An Archaeology of Medical Perception.* New York: Pantheon Books, 1973.

———. *The Archaeology of Knowledge.* New York: Pantheon Books, 1972.

Friedrich, Thomas. "Lall-Laute." *Ultimo* 6 (March 1987).

Frith, Simon and Andrew Goodwin, eds. *On Record: Rock, Pop, and the Written Word.* New York: Pantheon Books, 1990.

Fuchs, Walter. "Armin Edgar Schaible & Martin Haerle: eine schwierge Beziehung." http://www.haukestruebing.com/frameset.php?/erinnerungen/armin_edgar_schaible.htm.

Gansel, Carsten. "Zu Bildern jugendlicher Subkulturen in der zeitgenossischen problemorientierten deutschen Jugendliteratur." *Vortrage des Augsburger Germanistentags.*T übingen:N iemeyer,1 991.

Gemünden, Gerd. *Framed Visions: Popular Culture, Americanization, and the Contemporary German and Austrian Imagination.* Ann Arbor: University of Michigan Press, 1998.

Gendolla, Peter. "'Der übrige Körper ist für Verzierungungen bestimmt': über die Kunst der Einschreibung und den Sinn der Nachricht." In *Scönheit Und Schrecken.* Edited by Peter Gendolla and Carsten Zelle. Heidelberg: Winter, 1990.

George, Olakunle. "Modernity and the Promise of Reading." *Diacritics* 25.4 (1995): 71–88.

Gilroy, Paul. *The Black Atlantic: Modernity and Double Consciousness.* Cambridge, MA: Harvard University Press, 1993.

Glaser, Peter. "Aufbruch in die Achtziger." *Monarchie und Alltag.* CD-Booklet. London: EMI, 2000.

———, ed. *Rawums: Texte Zum Thema.* Cologne: Kiepenheuer & Witsch, 1984.

Goethe, Johann Wolfgang. *Götz von Berlichingen mit der eisernen Hand.* 1773. Stuttgart: Reclam, 2002. Goetz, Rainald Maria. "Der macht seinen Weg. Privilegen, Anpassung, Widerstand." *Kursbuch* 54 (1978): 31–43.

Goetz, Rainald. "Im Dichtigkeit des Lebendigen." *Der Spiegel* 43 (October 19, 1981): 232–239.

———. *Hirn.* Frankfurt am Main: Suhrkamp, 1986.

———. *Irre.* Frankfurt am Main: Suhrkamp, 1983.

———. *Kontrolliert.* Frankfurt am Main: Suhrkamp, 1986.

———. *Krieg.* Frankfurt am Main: Suhrkamp, 1986.

———. *Kronos.* Frankfurt am Main: Suhrkamp, 1993

Göktürk, Deniz, David Gramling, and Anton Kaes, eds. *Germany in Transit: Nation and Migration, 1955–2005.* Berkeley: University of California Press, 2007.

Goldstein, Ann, Organizer. *Martin Kippenberger: The Problem Perspective.* Los Angeles: Museum of Contemporary Art; Cambridge, MA: MIT Press, 2008.

Gramsci, Antonio. *Letters from Prison.* Edited by Frank Rosengarten. New York: Columbia University Press, 1994.

Grewal, Inderpal and Caren Kaplan. *Scattered Hegemonies: Postmodernity and Transnational Feminist Practices.* Minneapolis: University of Minnesota Press, 1994.

Griffith, D. W. *The Birth of a Nation.* 1915. New York: Kino Classics, 2011.

Groos, Ulrike and Peter Gorschlüter. *Zurück Zum Beton: Die Anfänge Von Punk Und New Wave in Deutschland 1977–'82: Kunsthalle Düsseldorf, 7. Juli–15. September 2002.* Cologne: König, 2002.

Grossberg, Lawrence. "Another Boring Day in Paradise: Rock and Roll and the Empowerment of Everyday Life." *Popular Music.* Vol. 4. Performers and Audiences. 1984.

———. "Putting the Pop Back into Postmodernism." In *Universal Abandon?: The Politics of Postmodernism.* Edited by Andrew Ross. Minneapolis: University of Minnesota Press, 1988.

———. *We Gotta Get out of This Place: Popular Conservatism and Postmodern Culture.* New York: Routledge, 1992.

Guattari, Félix. *Molecular Revolution: Psychiatry and Politics.* New York: Penguin, 1984.

Habermas, Jürgen. *The Philosophical Discourse of Modernity.* Cambridge, MA: MIT Press, 1987.

Hage, Volker. *Collagen in der deutschen Literatur: zur Praxis und Theorie eines Schreibverfahrens.* Frankfurt am Main: Peter Lang, 1984.

Hall, Stuart. "Notes on Deconstructing 'the Popular.'" In *People's History and Socialist Theory.* Edited by Raphael Samuel. Boston: Routledge and Keagen Paul, 1981.

Hall, Stuart and Tony Jefferson, eds. *Resistance through Rituals.* London: Hutchinson, 1976.

Hamsun, Knut. *Hunger*. 1890. New York: Knopf, 1920.

Hansen, Miriam. "Unstable Mixtures, Dilated Spheres: Negt and Kluge's *The Public Sphere and Experience*, Twenty Years Later." *Public Culture* 5.2 (1993): 179–212.

Harbers, Henk. "Gibt es eine 'postmoderne' deutsche Literatur? Überlegungen zur Nutzlichkeit eines Begriffs." *Literatur für Leser* 20.1 (1997): 52–69.

Harten, Jürgen and Ulrich Krempel, eds. *Jörg Immendorf: Cafe Deutschland /Adlerhälfte*. Düsseldorf, Germany: Kunsthalle Düsseldorf, 1982.

Hayles, N. Katherine. *Chaos Bound: Orderly Disorder in Contemporary Literature and Science*. Ithaca, NY: Cornell University Press, 1990.

Hebdige, Dick. *Hiding in the Light: On Images and Things*. London: Routledge, 1988.

————. *Subculture: The Meaning of Style*. London: Methune, 1979.

Hecken, Thomas. *Avantgarde und Terrorismus: Rhetorik der Intensität und Programme der Revolte von den Futuristen bis zur RAF*. Bielefeld: Transcript, 2006.

Hein, Peter Ulrich. *Die Brücke ins Geisterreich: künstlerische Avantgarde zwischen Kulturkritik und Faschismus*. Reinbek bei Hamburg: Rowohlt, 1992.

————. *Künstliche Paradiese der Jugend: zur Geschichte und Gegenwart ästhetischer Subkultur*. Münster: Lit, 1984.

Hein, Peter Ulrich and Maria Eva Jahn. *Protestkultur und Jugend: ästhetische Opposition in der Bundesrepublik Deutschland*. Münster: Lit, 1984.

Hell, Julia. "Soft Porn, Kitsch, and Post-Fascist Bodies: The East German Novel of Arrival." *South Atlantic Quarterly* 94.3 (1995): 747–772.

Hilsberg, Alfred. "Die Revolution ist vorbei—wir haben gesiegt!" *Sounds* 2. 1978.

Holub, Robert C. "Confrontations with Postmodernism." *Monatshefte für Deutschen Unterricht, Deutsche Sprache und Literatur* 84.2 (1992): 229–236.

Horkheimer, Max and Theodor W. Adorno. *Dialektik Der Aufklärung*. Frankfurt am Main: S. Fischer, 1969.

Hörning, Karl H. and Rainer Winter, eds. *Widerspenstige Kulturen: Cultural Studies als Herausforderung*. Frankfurt am Main: Suhrkamp, 1999.

Huffman, Richard. *Baader-Meinhof.com: The Baader-Meinhof Gang and the Invention of Modern Terror*. http://www.baader-meinhof.com/.

Hussey, Andrew. "Requiem pour un con: Subversive Pop and the Society of the Spectacle." *Cercles* 3 (2001): 49–59.

Hutcheon, Linda. *A Poetics of Postmodernism: History, Theory, Fiction*. New York: Routledge, 1988.

Huyssen, Andreas. *Twilight Memories: Marking Time in a Culture of Amnesia*. New York: Routledge, 1995.

————. *After the Great Divide: Modernism, Mass Culture, Postmodernism*. Bloomington: Indiana University Press, 1986.

Jäger, Christian. "Die 'härteste Band von Allen': Terrorismus in der gegenwartigen Literatur und Populär-Kultur." *Jahrbuch Literatur und Politik* 1 (2006): 117–127.

————. "Wörterflucht oder: die kategoriale Not der Literaturwissenschaft angesichts der Literatur der achtziger Jahre." *Internationales Jahrbuch für Germanistik* 1 (1995): 85–100.

Jäger, Christian. "Die Geburt der 68er aus dem Geist der 80er. Zur Konjunktur eines subkulturellen Diskurses." *Houellebecq & Co. Die Rückkehr der großen Erzählungen und die neue Weltordnung* Berlin: n.p., January 18, 2003.

Jameson, Fredric. *The Cultural Turn: Selected Writings on the Postmodern, 1983–1998*. London: Verso, 1998.

Kafka, Franz. *In der Strafkolonie*. 1919. Frankfurt am Main: Suhrkamp, 2006.

Kaiser, Alfons. "'an fürsorglicher Hand': Die Rezeption Uwe Johnsons bei Rainald Goetz." *Internationales Uwe Johnson Forum* 4 (1996): 181–189.

Kippenberger, Martin and Albert Oehlen. *No problem / No Problème*. Stuttgart, Germany: Edition Patricia Schwarz and Galerie Kubinski, 1986.

Kluge, Alexander. *In Gefahr und größter Not bringt der Mittelweg den Tod*. Berlin: Vorwerk 8, 2002.

———. *Die Patriotin*. Frankfurt am Main: Zweitausendeins, 1980.

Koch, Arne and Sei Harris. "The Sound of Yourself Listening: Faust and the Politics of the Unpolitical." *Popular Music and Society* 32.5 (December 2009): 579–594.

Koepnick, Lutz. "Reframing the Past: Heritage Cinema and Holocaust in the 1990s." *New German Critique* 87 (Autumn, 2002): 47–82.

Kristeva, Julia. *The Powers of Horror: An Essay on Abjection*. New York: Columbia University Press, 1982.

Krystof, Doris. *Martin Kippenberger: Einer von Euch, unter Euch, mit Euch*. Ostfildern, Germany: Hatje Cantz, 2006.

Kühn, Rainer. "Bürgerliche Kunst und antipolitische Politik: Der 'Subjektkultkarrierist' Rainald Goetz." In *Neue Generation—Neues Erzählen: deutsche Prosa-Literatur der achtziger Jahre*. Edited by Walter Delabar. Opladen, Germany: Westdeutscher, 1993.

Kundnani, Hans. *Utopia or Auschwitz: Germany's 1968 Generation and the Holocaust*. New York: Columbia University Press, 2009.

Kunisch, Hermann and Dietz-Rüdiger Moser. *Neues Handbuch der deutschen Literatur seit 1945*. Munich: Nymphenburger, 1990.

Kyora, Sabine. "Postmoderne Stile: Überlegungen zur deutschsprachigen Gegenwartsliteratur." *Zeitschrift für deutsche Philologie* 122.2 (2003): 287–302.

Laing, Dave. *One Chord Wonders: Power and Meaning in Punk Rock*. Philadelphia, PA: Open University Press, 1985.

Laing, R. D. and A. Esterson. *Sanity, Madness and the Family*. Harmondsworth: Penguin, 1970.

Langston, Richard. "Roll Over Beethoven! Chuck Berry! Mick Jagger! 1960s Rock, the Myth of Progress, and the Burden of National Identity in West Germany." In *Sound Matters*. Edited by Nora M. Alter and Lutz Koepnick. New York: Berghahn, 2004.

———. *Visions of Violence: German Avant-Gardes after Fascism*. Evanston, IL: Northwestern University Press, 2008.

Lau, Thomas. *Die heiligen Narren. Punk 1976–1986*. Berlin: de Gruyter, 1992.

Link, Jürgen. *Versuch über den Normalismus: Wie Normalität produziert wird*. Opladen, Germany: Westdeutscher, 1997.

Loos, Adolf. "Ornament und Verbrechen." In *Schriften*. Wien: 1962.

Lottmann, Joachim. "Ceterum censeo Catharginem delendam esse…" *Spex* 59 (October 1985): 27.

Lottmann, Joachim. "Der politische Fernsehapparat." *Spex* 69 (August 1986): 55.

———. *Mai, Juni, Juli: Ein Roman.* Cologne: Kiepenheuer & Witsch, 1987.

———. "Ich wollte der neue Böll werden." *Der Tagesspiegel.* May 6, 2003.

———. "Ist Japan besser?" *Die Zeit.* August 29, 1986.

———. "Realitätsgehalt: Ausreichend." *Spex* 11 (1986).

———. "Voilá, un Punk." *Die Zeit.* April 4, 1986.

Lucas, Edward Verrall. *Swollen-Headed William; Painful Stories and Funny Pictures after the German.* London: Methuen, 1915.

Lützler, Paul Michael. "Einleitung: Von der Spätmoderne zur Postmoderne. Die deutschsprachige Literatur der achtziger Jahre." *German Quarterly* 63.3 (1990): 350–358.

Mann, Thomas. *Der Tod in Venedig.* 1912. New York: Oxford University Press, 1973.

Marcus, Greil. *Lipstick Traces: A Secret History of the Twentieth Century.* Cambridge, MA: Harvard University Press, 1989.

Marcuse, Herbert. *An Essay on Liberation.* Boston: Beacon Press, 1969.

———. *One Dimensional Man.* Boston: Beacon Press, 1966.

Matejovski, Dirk. "Goetz/Meinecke. Wortgemetzel." *Apart* 8 (1987): 30.

martinf. "S.Y.P.H.—Die Gevelsberg-Tapes (ergänzt)." http://brotbeutel.blogspot. com/2006/06/syph-die-gevelsberg-tapes-ergnzt.html.

McCormick, Richard. *Gender and Sexuality in Weimar Modernity: Film, Literature, and "New Objectivity."* New York: Palgrave Macmillan, 2001.

———. *Politics of the Self: Feminism and the Postmodern in West German Literature and Film.* Princeton, NJ: Princeton University Press, 1991.

———. "Re-Presenting the Student Movement: Helke Sander's the Subjective Factor." In *Gender and German Cinema: Feminist Interventions.* Edited by Sandra Frieden and Richard McCormick. Providence, RI: Berg, 1993.

McLuhan, Marshall and Quentin Fiore. *War and Peace in the Global Village.* Corte Madera, CA: Gingko Press, 1968.

McLuhan, Marshall, Quentin Fiore, and Jerome Agel. *The Medium is the Massage: An Inventory of Effects.* Corte Madera, CA: Gingko Press, 2001.

McLuhan, Marshall and W. Terrence Gordon. *Understanding Media: The Extensions of Man.* Corte Madera, CA: Gingko Press, 2003.

Mecky, Gabrijela. "Ein Ich in der Genderkrise: Zum Tomboy in Thomas Meineckes *Tomboy.*" *Germanic Review* 76.3 (2001): 195–214.

Meinecke, Thomas. *Hellblau.* Frankfurt am Main: Suhrkamp, 2001.

———. *Mode & Verzweiflung.* Frankfurt am Main: Suhrkamp, 1998.

———. *Mit Der Kirche Ums Dorf.* Frankfurt am Main: Suhrkamp, 1986.

———. *Musik.* Frankfurt am Main: Suhrkamp, 2007.

———. "Originalität ist ein Ablenkungsmanöver." *die tageszeitung.* October 15, 1997.

———. *Pale Blue.* Translated by Daniel Bowles. Las Vegas, NV: AmazonCrossing, 2012.

———. *Tomboy.* Frankfurt am Main: Suhrkamp, 1998,

———. *Tomboy.* Translated by Daniel Bowles. Las Vegas, NV: AmazonCrossing, 2011.

Mercer, Kobena. "'1968': Periodizing Postmodern Politics and Identity." In *Cultural Studies.* Edited by Lawrence Grossberg, Cary Nelson, and Paula A. Treichler. New York: Routledge, 1992.

Merritt, Richard. "Divided Airwaves: The Electronic Media and Political Community in Postwar Berlin." *International Political Science Review / Revue internationale de science politique* 7.4 (1986): 369–399.

Müller, Wolfgang, e d. *Geniale Dilletanten*. Berlin: Merve, 1982.

Murphy, Richard. *Theorizing the Avant-Garde: Modernism, Expressionism, and the Problem of Postmodernity*. Cambridge: Cambridge University Press, 1989.

Nagele, Rainer. "Modernism and Postmodernism: The Margins of Articulation." *Studies in Twentieth Century Literature* 5.1 (1980): 5–25.

n.a. *Salzburger Impuls* 2.4 (April 1987).

Negt, Oskar and Alexander Kluge. *Geschichte und Eigensinn*. Vol. 2. *Der Unterschätzte Mensch*. Frankfurt am Main: Zweitausendeins, 2001.

———. *Public Sphere and Experience: Toward an Analysis of the Bourgeois and Proletarian Public Sphere*. Translated by Peter Labanyi, Jamie Owen Daniel, and Assenka Oksiloff. Minneapolis: University of Minnesota Press, 1993.

Nehring, Neil. *Flowers in the Dustbin: Culture, Anarchy, and Postwar England*. Ann Arbor: University of Michigan Press, 1993.

Nelson, Cary and Lawrence Grossberg. *Marxism and the Interpretation of Culture*. Urbana: University of Illinois Press, 1988.

Oberschelp, Jürgen. "Raserei: über Rainald Goetz, Hass und Literatur." *Merkur* 41.2 (1987): 170–174.

Pantenburg, Volker and Nils Plath. *Anführen—Vorführen—Aufführen: Texte zum Zitieren*. Bielefeld: Aisthesis, 2002.

Passerin d'Entrèves, Maurizio and Seyla Benhabib, eds. *Habermas and the Unfinished Project of Modernity: Critical Essays on The Philosophical Discourse of Modernity*. Cambridge, MA: MIT Press, 1997.

Patterson, Tiffany Ruby and Robin D. G. Kelley. "Unfinished Migrations: Reflections on the African Diaspora and the Making of the Modern World." *African Studies Review* 43.1 (2000): 11–45.

Poiger, Uta G. *Jazz, Rock, and Rebels: Cold War Politics and American Culture in a Divided Germany*. Berkeley: University of California Press, 2000.

Quabeck, Benjamin. *Verschwende deine Jugend*. Munich: Constantin Film, 2004.

Rag, Harry. "S.Y.P.H. 'eine kleine Biographie.'" *S.Y.P.H.* http://www.syph.de/alt/olds.htm.

Reynolds, Simon. *Rip It Up and Start Again: Postpunk 1978–1984*. New York: Penguin Books, 2006.

Ryan, Judith. "The Problem of Pastiche: Patrick Süskind's *Das Parfum*." *German Quarterly* 63.3 (1990): 396–403.

Santner, Eric L. "History Beyond the Pleasure Principle: Some Thoughts on the Representation of Trauma." In *Probing the Limits of Representation: Nazism and the "Final Solution."* Edited by Saul Friedländer. Cambridge, MA: Harvard University Press, 1992.

Savage, Jon. *England's Dreaming: Anarchy, Sex Pistols, Punk Rock and Beyond*. New York: St. Martin's Griffen, 2002.

Scarry, Elaine. *The Body in Pain: The Making and Unmaking of the World*. New York: Oxford University Press, 1985.

Schamoni, Rocko. *Dorfpunks*. Reinbeck bei Hamburg: Rowohlt, 2004.

Schiller, Margit. *Remembering the Armed Struggle: Life in Baader-Meinhof*. London: Zidane, 2008.

Schneider, Frank Apunkt. *Als die Welt noch unterging: von Punk zu NDW.* Mainz: Ventil, 2007.

Schneider, Frank Apunkt. "Musik gegen Musik." Vorüberlegungen zur Wiederveröffentlichung von 'Stürmer.'" CD- booklet to FSK *Stürmer.* Cologne: a-musik, A36V (2011): 1–8.

———. "'My Future in the SS.' Zur Identifikation mit den Täter_innen im deutschen (Post-) Punk." In *We Are Ugly but We Have the Music. Eine ungewöhnliche Spurensuche in Sachen jüdischer Erfahrung und Subkultur. "Jüdische Identität und Subkultur.*" Edited by Jonas Engelmann et al. Vol. 1. Mainz: Ventil, 2012.

Schultz-Gerstein, Christian. "Der rasende Mitläufer: über Rainald Goetz und seinen Roman *Irre.*" In *Rasende Mitläufer.* Edited by Christian Schultz-Gerstein. Berlin: Ed. Tiamat, 1987.

Schumacher, Eckhard. *Gerade, Eben, Jetzt: Schreibweisen der Gegenwart.* Frankfurt am Main: Suhrkamp, 2003.

———. "Klagenfurt, Schnitte," *Anführen—Vorführen—Aufführen: Texte zum Zitieren.* Bielefeld: Aisthesis Verlag, 2002.

Schwendter, Rolf. *Theorie der Subkultur.* Cologne: Kiepenheuer & Witsch, 1971.

Shahan, Cyrus. "The Sounds of Terror: Punk, Post-Punk and the RAF after 1977." *Popular Music and Society* 34.3 (July 2011): 369–386.

Simpson, Patricia Anne. "Germany and its Discontents: Die Skeptiker's Punk Corrective." *Journal of Popular Culture* 34.3 (2000): 129–140.

Sloterdijk, Peter. *Kritik der zynischen Vernunft.* Frankfurt am Main: Suhrkamp, 1983.

———. *Zorn und Zeit.* Frankfurt am Main: Suhrkamp, 2006.

Spencer-Steigner, Steven. "Do-it-Yourself Punk Rock and Hardcore: A Conflux of Culture and Politics." *Thresholds: Viewing Culture* 8 (1994): 59–63.

Strasser, Johannes. "Über eine Neue Lust an der Raserei." *L'80* 44 (1987): 9–23.

Strunk, Heinz. *Fleisch Ist Mein Gemüse: eine Landjugend mit Musik.* Reinbeck bei Hamburg: Rowohlt, 2004.

Svich, Caridad. "'Back to the Bawdy: Shockheaded Peter's Punk Archaeology of the Music Hall'." *Contemporary Theatre Review* 14.1 (2004): 39–49.

Teipel, Jürgen. *Verschwende deine Jugend: Ein Doku-Roman über den deutschen Punk und New Wave.* Frankfurt am Main: Suhrkamp, 2001.

Terkessidis, Mark and Tom Holert, eds. *Mainstream der Minderheiten: Pop in der Kontrollgesellschaft.* Berlin: Edition ID-Archiv, 1996.

Theweleit, Klaus. *Ghosts: Drei leicht inkorrekte Vorträge.* Frankfurt am Main: Stroemfeld/Roter Stern, 1998.

Thiessen, Rudi. *Urbane Sprachen: Proust, Poe, Punks, Baudelaire und der Park: vier Studien über Blasiertheit und Intelligenz: eine Theorie der Moderne.* Berlin: Vorwerk 8, 1997.

Thurman, Kira. "Black Venus, White Bayreuth: Race, Sexuality, and the Depoliticization of Wagner in Postwar West Germany." *German Studies Review* 35.3 (2012): 607–626.

Ullmaier, Johannes, Frieder Butzmann, and Sibylle Berg. *Von Acid nach Adlon und Zurück: eine Reise durch die deutschsprachige Popliteratur.* Mainz: Ventil, 2001.

Varon, Jeremy. *Bringing the War Home: The Weather Underground, the Red Army Faction, and Revolutionary Violence in the Sixties and Seventies.* Berkeley: University of California Press, 2004.

Venturelli, Aldo. "Avantgarde und Postmoderne: Beobachtungen zur Krise des Expressionismus." *Recherches Germaniques* 22 (1992): 103–121.

Verschwende deine Jugend. Double CD. Brunswick: Universal, 2002.

von Dirke, Sabine. *"All Power to the Imagination!": The West German Counterculture from the Student Movement to the Greens.* Lincoln: University of Nebraska Press, 1997.

Ward, James J. "'this is Germany! it's 1933!': Appropriations and Constructions of 'Fascism' in New York Punk/Hardcore in the 1980s." *Journal of Popular Culture* 30.3 (1996): 155–184.

Waschescio, Petra and Thomas Noetzel. "Die Ohnmacht der Rebellion. Anmerkungen zu Heiner Müller und Rainald Goetz." *L'80* 44 (1987): 27–40.

Wegmann, Thomas. "Stigma und Skandal, oder 'The Making of' Rainald Goetz." In *Mediale Erregungen? Autonomie und Aufmerksamkeit im Literatur- und Kulturwettbewerb der Gegenwart.* Edited by Markus Joch, et al. Tübingen: Niemeyer, 2009.

Werber, Niels. "Intensitaten des Politischen: Gestalten souveräner und normalistischer Macht bei Rainald Goetz." *Weimarer-Beiträge* 46.1 (2000): 105–120.

Wicke, Peter. "Rock Music: A Musical-Aesthetic Study." *Popular Music* 2 (1982): 219–243.

———. "Sentimentality and High Pathos: Popular Music in Fascist Germany." *Popular Music* 5 (1985): 149–158

Wildner, Siegrun. "'Flower-Power, Punk und Rebellion': 1968 im Spiegelbild der Literatur." *Seminar* 35.4 (1999): 323–341.

Willett, Ralph. *The Americanization of Germany, 1945–1949.* London: Routledge, 1989.

Winkels, Hubert. *Einschnitte: zur Literatur der 80er Jahre.* Cologne: Kiepenheuer & Witsch, 1988.

———. "Orschaden: zu Rainald Goetz und Texten." *LiteraturMagazin* (1987): 68–84.

Wittstock, Uwe. "Der Terror und seine Dichter: Bodo Morshauser, Michael Wildenhain, Rainald Goetz." *Neue-Rundschau* 101.3 (1990): 65–78.

Wittstock, Uwe. *Roman oder Leben: Postmoderne in der deutschen Literatur.* Leipzig: Reclam, 1994.

Wogenstein, Sebastian. "Topographie des Dazwischen: Vladimir Vertlibs *Das besondere Gedächtnis der Rosa Masur*, Maxim Billers *Esra* und Thomas Meineckes *Hellblau*." *Gegenwartsliteratur* 3 (2004): 71–96.

Wündrich, Bettina. *Szene Hamburg* 14.3 (May 1987).

Zimmer, Dieter E. "Wie, bitteschön, geht das Leben?" *Die Zeit* October 14, 1983.

Žižek, Slavoj. *Violence: Six Sideways Reflections.* N ewY ork:P icador,2 008.

Index

Page numbers in italics refer to figures.

Fassbinder, Rainer Werner, 8
Fehlfarben, 86, 123, 132, 136
  Monarchie und Alltag (Monarchy
    and daily life), 86, 132
  "too late," 85, 95, 120
  see also "no future"; production; progress
Fiedler, Leslie, 118, 150
Fiske, John, 90
  see also Kluge, Alexander; production
Foucualt, Michel, 54, 61, 68–78, 81, 84
  see also boundaries, blurring; "no
    future"; progress
Frankfurt School, 2, 25, 86
  see also Adorno, Theodor; Benjamin,
    Walter; Habermas, Jürgen

Gemünden, Gerd, 94–5
  see also production; United States of
    America
geography, 12, 159n. 30
  see also music, radio
"German Autumn," *see* fascism;
    Kluge, Alexander; production;
    progress; terrorism; United States
    of America
German Expressionism, 31–2, 44
  see also schizophrenia; time;
    violence
Gilroy, Paul, 101–2, 104, 109
Glaser, Peter, 82–5, 116, 136
  aesthetic "explosé," 27–31, 51, 54,
    58–60, 82, 101, 154
  see also aesthetics, and violence
"Grand Coalition," 9
  see also progress;
    Vergangenheitsbewältigung
Grass, Günter, 63, 118, 132, 137
Grossberg, Lawrence, 8, 87–9, 134–5
Guattari, Félix, 71, 81, 84

Habermas, Jürgen, 4
  and the avant-garde, 30, 135, 143
  and modernity, 25, 129–30, 152
  and progress, 33, 126–30, 133–8, 142

Hage, Volker, 34–5, 96
Halbstarken, 7–8, 10, 11
  see also United States of America
Hall, Stuart, 14, 159n. 29
Hamburger Abschaum, 21, 46–7, 50,
    123
  see also fanzines; mainstream media;
    production
Hamsun, Knut, 132, 137–8, 148, 151
Hansen, Miriam, 99–100, 118–20
  see also Kluge, Alexander;
    production
Hayles, N. Katherine, 37, 45
Hebdige, Dick, 11–15, 38, 149, 153
  semiotic guerilla warfare, 38–9
  see also Birmingham Center for
    Contemporary Cultural Studies
hegemony, 10, 90–9, 128–9, 153
  and affirmation, 75, 85, 144
  see also Adorno, Theodor; music;
    "no future"; production
Hein, Peter, 12–13, 35, 73, 85, 131–2
  see also Fehlfarben
Hein, Peter Ulrich, 15
Hilsberg, Alfred, 12, 49
hippies, 7, 9, 13, 39, 43, 73–83, 152–4
  see also student movements
history, 4, 14, 25, 36, 110–16, 150,
    167n. 9, 167n. 12,
  and catastrophe, 24–34, 40, 54,
    62–5, 134, 163n. 28
  and progress, 98–9, 113, 132
  see also "no future"; progress; time;
    Vergangenheitsbewältigung
"Holocaust" (TV show), 114–16
  see also history; mainstream media;
    time; *Vergangenheitsbewältigung*
Horkheimer, Max, 54, 79, 115, 161n. 7
  see also progress

Immendorf, Jörg, 31, 45
  see also progress
Institute for Social Research, *see*
    Frankfurt School

Printed in Great Britain
by Amazon

10331524R00122